Jaci Burton is a *New York Times* bestselling author who lives in Oklahoma with her husband and dogs. She has three grown children, who are all scattered around the country having lives of their own. A lover of sports, Jaci can often tell what season it is by what sport is being played. She watches entirely too much television, including an unhealthy amount of reality TV. When she isn't on deadline, Jaci can be found at her local casino, trying to become a millionaire (so far, no luck). She's a total romantic and loves a story with a happily ever after, which you'll find in all her books.

Find the latest news on Jaci's books at www.jaciburton.com, and connect with her online at www.facebook.com/AuthorJaciBurton or via Twitter @jaciburton.

Praise for Jaci Burton:

'A wild ride' Lora Leigh, No. 1 *New York Times* bestselling author

'It's the perfect combination of heat and romance that makes this series a must-read' *Heroes and Heartbreakers*

'Plenty of emotion and conflict in a memorable relationship-driven story' *USA Today*

'Strong characters, an exhilarating plot, and scorching sex . . . You'll be drawn so fully into her characters' world that you won't want to return to your own' *Romantic Times*

'A beautiful romance that is smooth as silk . . . leaves us begging for more' *Joyfully Reviewed*

'A strong plot, complex characters, sexy athletes, and non-stop passion make this book a must-read' *Fresh Fiction*

'Hot, hot, hot! . . . Romance at its best! Highly recommended!' *Coffee Table Reviews*

'Ms Burton has a way of writing intense scenes that are both sensual and raw . . . Plenty of romance, sexy men, hot steamy loving and humor' *Smexy Books*

'A wonderf   nporary   The Romance I

'Spy the name Jaci Burton on the spine of a novel, and you're guaranteed not just a sexy, get-the-body-humming read, but also one that melds the sensual with the all-important building of intimacy and relational dynamics between partners' *Romance: B(u)y the Book*

'The characters are incredible. They are human and complex and real and perfect' *Night Owl Reviews*

'One of the strongest sports romance series available' *Dear Author*

'As usual, Jaci Burton delivers flawed but endearing characters, a strong romance and an engaging plot all wrapped up in one sexy package' *Romance Novel News*

By Jaci Burton

Hope Series
Hope Smoulders (e-novella)
Hope Flames
Hope Ignites
Hope Burns
Love After All
Make Me Stay
Don't Let Go
Love Me Again

Play-by-Play Series
The Perfect Play
Changing The Game
Taking A Shot
Playing To Win
Thrown By A Curve
One Sweet Ride
Holiday Games (e-novella)
Melting The Ice
Straddling The Line
Holiday On Ice (e-novella)
Quarterback Draw
All Wound Up
Unexpected Rush
Rules Of Contact
The Final Score

Love Me Again

Jaci BURTON

HEADLINE
ETERNAL

Published by arrangement with Berkley,
a member of Penguin Group (USA) LLC.
A Penguin Random House Company.

First published in Great Britain in 2017
by HEADLINE ETERNAL
An imprint of HEADLINE PUBLISHING GROUP

1

Cataloguing in Publication Data is available from the British Library

ISBN 978 1 4722 4799 5

Offset in 11.7/12.29 pt Times LT Std by Jouve (UK)

Printed and bound in Great Britain by CPI Group (UK) Ltd, Croydon, CR0 4YY

Headline's policy is to use papers that are natural, renewable and recyclable
products and made from wood grown in well-managed forests and other
controlled sources. The logging and manufacturing processes are expected
to conform to the environmental regulations of the country of origin.

HEADLINE PUBLISHING GROUP
An Hachette UK Company
Carmelite House
50 Victoria Embankment
London EC4Y 0DZ

www.headlineeternal.com
www.headline.co.uk
www.hachette.co.uk

For Michelle and Kaylynn

Acknowledgments

To my editor, Kate Seaver, and my agent, Kimberly Whalen. Thank you for everything you do for me. I could not do this without you.

Thanks to Matt and Julie, and Lincoln, for the dog inspiration.

Chapter 1

LORETTA SIMMONS JUMPED at the sound of a loud crash next door.

What was that? It was only six thirty. She'd come in to The Open Mind bookstore extra early this morning to unload inventory before her store opened, expecting quiet.

This was not quiet.

Maybe it was nothing. A rodent or something, since the building had been closed for years.

Another loud banging sound made her pause.

Okay, something was up. She hoped no one was breaking in next door. Maybe she should peek out the front window.

She left the storeroom and glanced quickly at her daughter, Hazel, who was sitting on one of the sofas in the reading section. Hazel obviously hadn't heard a thing, since she had her headphones on and was watching a movie.

Loretta made her way to the front, cautiously pulling at the blinds. There was a truck parked out front, but since it was still dark outside she couldn't make out the lettering on it. It appeared to be a work vehicle—and what burglar would park in plain sight?

Deciding to step outside, she opened the front door and walked across the porch so she could get a better look.

At the same time, a tall, imposing figure walked out the front door of the building.

Oh, crap.

Deacon Fox. She instantly made the connection to the truck parked out front.

It was a Fox/McCormack Construction truck, which could only mean one thing. The building next door must be undergoing renovation, and Deacon Fox was in charge of that renovation.

A cloud of dust followed him. He had on worn jeans, with a tool belt strapped to his hip. He was sweaty and had dirt smudges on his face and a handful of debris slung over his shoulder. She'd never seen a man look hotter.

Though why she'd notice his hotness was beyond her. She shouldn't notice that. About Deacon. Or any man, for that matter. Male hotness was not at the top of her radar right now.

He'd spotted her, so after he slung the pile of wood into the oversized trash bin that was parked in the street, he walked over to her.

"Loretta."

"Deacon. I see you're working on the Harden building."

"Yeah."

"Who bought it?"

He shrugged. "Some investor. I guess they're leasing out all three floors. My job is to gut it and renovate it for office space."

Office space would be good. Potential customers for her bookstore. "I see. Kind of noisy over there this morning."

"Yeah."

He obviously wasn't in the mood for conversation. But she was curious.

"So, is that noise thing going to take long?"

He nodded. "A while. It'll get worse before it gets better."

She heaved a sigh. "That's not good for my customers."

"Sorry. I have the permits to do the job, so your customers will have to get used to a little dust and noise."

She had been afraid he was going to say that. The last thing she needed for her fledgling business was inconvenient parking and the upheaval of reconstruction going on next door. "Fine. I'll put up apology signs."

"Yeah, you do that."

The tension between them was palpable, and had been ever since she'd moved back to Hope last year. Which was entirely her fault, of course, since she'd dumped Deacon in high school and had married someone else. Still, that had been years ago. Surely he was over it—over her—by now, right? So maybe she could do something to start easing the tension between them.

"How about coffee? I have some freshly made in the shop."

"I've already had coffee. I gotta get back to work."

His tone with her was short. Clipped. No warmth in his voice. They used to be so close. She remembered his smile. He had a devastating smile, and she'd seen him use it on her friends since she'd returned to Hope. But not with her. Never with her.

"Okay. I guess I'll . . . see you later?"

"Yeah. See ya, Loretta."

He walked back inside, and she felt a twinge in her middle. She knew guilt and maybe a hard stab of remorse caused that twinge. She and Deacon had made so many plans for the future together. And she'd blown up all those plans the day she'd told him she didn't love him anymore.

That had been a lie. She had always loved him. Part of her always would. But she'd chosen a different life, and that life hadn't included Deacon in it.

Okay, maybe she hadn't exactly been the one to choose that life. She'd been pushed, cajoled, and needled by her parents until she'd been convinced that Deacon wasn't the right choice. Going to college in Texas had been the right choice. Following Tom Simmons to Texas had been the right choice. Marrying Tom had been the right choice.

Or so she'd thought.

In the end, she'd made all the wrong choices.

"Hey, Mom?"

She turned at the sound of her daughter's voice, the one amazing thing she'd done in the past twelve years. At nine years old, Hazel was the bright spot in her life. She smiled at her daughter.

"What's up?"

Hazel peered around her at the structure next door. "What's going on over there?"

"Someone bought the old building, so now they're gutting it—taking out everything inside and putting all new stuff in."

Hazel nodded. "Ooh. Can I watch?"

Her daughter was always curious, and anything that had to do with dirt or a mess was her jam. After Hazel had been cooped up in a super-sterile condo in Dallas for so long, Loretta was inclined to let her experience all the dirt she wanted to.

"It's dusty and noisy, so don't get too close. It could be dangerous."

"I know. But I wanna hang out here and watch. Is that okay?"

"Yes, but don't go inside that building, and stay on this part of the porch."

"I will."

Loretta remained with Hazel for a few minutes, watching as her daughter found a spot on the top step and sat. Other than the netbook she used for watching movies and playing video games, Hazel had no toys with her. Today she wore capri jeans, a short-sleeved T-shirt, and her favorite baseball cap. Her entire wardrobe had changed since they'd moved from Dallas. Tom had always expected his daughter to dress appropriately. And by *appropriately* he had meant pinks and purples and dresses and sweaters.

Hazel had hated that she'd never been given the freedom to choose her own clothes.

After the divorce, Loretta had told Hazel she could wear whatever she wanted to. She'd rebelled against her father's rules and chosen jeans, T-shirts, and baseball caps, her long blond hair pulled up into a ponytail and wound through the hole in the back of the cap. And she always wore her favorite pair of black Chucks tennis shoes. With no socks.

Whatever. As long as her daughter was happy, then Loretta was happy. Loretta's parents disapproved, of course, which also made Loretta smile. So maybe Loretta was experiencing her own bit of rebellion, even if it was a bit passive-aggressive.

She might have eked out a bit of independence with the divorce, but she hadn't yet gotten to the part where she would tell her parents to go to hell. They might have pushed her into making life changes as a teenager, but she'd been the one who'd ultimately made the choices, and she had no one to blame but herself.

After taking one last look at Hazel, who seemed content to watch the goings-on at the building next door, she sighed and headed back inside the bookstore to start her day. And to start making those apology posters for her customers.

Maybe she should consider making one of those apology posters for Deacon. Though she doubted that would be enough to make up for what she'd done to him.

She could never make enough apologies to Deacon for what she'd done.

DEACON FOX WORKED with his crew ripping out the cabinets that lined the wall of the first floor of the building they were going to renovate. It wasn't even eight in the morning yet and he was already drenched in sweat. This old building had seen better days, the place was piled high with years' worth of junk, and this project was going to be a nightmare.

He looked around and grinned as dust motes filled the air, a rain of gray obliterating the summer sun trying to come in through the open front door.

Yeah, it was a mess. Just the way he liked it.

He hauled a piece of demolished cabinet out to the

Dumpster. On his way back, he spotted a little girl sitting on the front step of Loretta's bookstore. She looked up at him but didn't say anything, so he didn't say anything back. He noticed on his next several trips out to haul discarded debris that she was still there . . . watching.

He knew that was Loretta's daughter. She was cute, with her ponytail sticking out of her baseball cap. And she seemed to be interested in what he was doing. He wanted to go talk to her, but he wasn't about to. It was best he keep his distance from Loretta and her kid.

When he dropped another load in the Dumpster, the little girl smiled at him.

What could he do? Whatever he felt about Loretta, he wasn't going to take it out on her kid. So he smiled back, then went back inside and picked up more crap to drag outside.

He and his partner, Reid McCormack, had discussed whether or not to bid on this job. Deacon had known it was next door to Loretta's bookstore. Reid had told him he'd understand if Deacon wanted to pass on this one.

But it was going to be a decent-sized job. The building had three floors and was similar to the renovation Reid had done on the building Loretta now occupied. It wasn't an historical building like that one, but it was a large project, and Deacon wasn't going to let his past with Loretta make them pass up an opportunity for a moneymaking job.

Reid said he'd take it, but by the time they'd bid on and gotten the job, Reid was working on designing a new building for one of the town's large medical practices. That project would tie him up for a while, which meant Deacon was going to have to take the reins on this one.

He was fine with it. What he and Loretta had was in the past, and he sure as hell could handle working next door to her for the next few months.

They lived in the same town now, and they shared many of the same friends. It stood to reason they were going to occupy the same orbit every now and then. He might as well get used to seeing her.

Except seeing her dragged in all the old memories, opening that door to the past.

The past had been golden. They'd been young and in love, and they'd made plans together. And unlike some things in his past, his life with Loretta wasn't clouded. It was vivid. Every moment they shared together was like it had been yesterday.

The way her hair used to curl at the ends. The way her lips used to tilt when she smiled.

Her laugh.

Her perfectly painted pink toenails.

The sound of her breathing when they . . .

Shit.

He forced the past away and stared out at the sunlight, at those dust motes slowly falling to the ground, every one of them holding memories. He shoved them aside.

Yeah, every time he saw Loretta now it hurt just a little damn bit.

His only option was to keep that door firmly closed, because he'd hurt enough over her already.

As for the job and the close proximity? He'd just suck it up and deal with it.

He could handle it.

Chapter 2

LORETTA LAID THE grocery bags down on the old, scarred wooden table in the kitchen at their house. Hazel trailed in behind her and put another sack down.

"What's for dinner, Mama?"

"Fried chicken, macaroni and cheese, and Brussels sprouts."

Hazel scrunched her nose. "Bleh. I hate Brussels sprouts. Can we have broccoli instead?"

It was hard to argue with a kid who liked broccoli. "Broccoli it is. Go wash your hands and you can help me."

"Okay."

Hazel wandered off, so Loretta unpacked the groceries and put them away, then sifted through the day's mail. Bills and junk. She checked her e-mail and discovered one from her lawyer.

Nothing unexpected. Her ex requested Hazel's appearance at a fund-raiser for his political campaign during the third week in June. Which didn't fall at all on his normal visitation schedule. In fact, Tom hadn't seen Hazel in the past two months. Because it wasn't about him wanting to see his daughter—it was about making Hazel available at a time and venue that suited Tom.

Loretta would never keep Hazel from her father. And even though she knew he'd only spend the briefest amount of time with her during that visit, she e-mailed her attorney and told him she'd make sure Hazel was there. Since school was out for the summer, it was an ideal time for Hazel to make the trip. Even if she wouldn't spend as much time with her father while she was there that Loretta would like her to.

Tom was a cold man. It hadn't started out that way, but it sure had been that way for the last five years of their marriage. Tom was all about building his political career. One would think he'd want to show himself as a family man, at least outwardly. Instead, he liked to pretend his daughter didn't exist.

Probably because the new family he was setting up for himself was so much better suited for his future in politics. Better political connections. More money. And with his new wife, Melissa, already pregnant, the visibility factor of a smiling, socially appropriate pregnant woman would be well accepted by the voters in his congressional race.

Loretta ignored the pang in the vicinity of her heart. The way Tom treated Hazel, as if she was a political pawn to be dressed up and paraded around only at certain times that benefited him . . .

No. She wasn't going to go there. Instead, she called Hazel into the kitchen, and the two of them set about making dinner.

At nine, there were some things Hazel couldn't do in the kitchen yet. Not that you could tell her that. Her daughter had an independent streak the size of Oklahoma, and Loretta didn't want to discourage her, so she very cautiously watched while her daughter learned the fine art of frying chicken. Something every Southern girl—and boy—should know how to do.

They even cut up the broccoli together, and if there was one thing Hazel liked to do, it was wield a knife. She knew how to be careful, because Loretta had told her that if she treated handling a knife with anything but seriousness, her days cooking with her mama were over.

Hazel had taken that instruction to heart, and she was always focused and methodical as she sliced.

Before long, dinner was ready, which was good, because frying chicken made Loretta hungry.

They ate at the dining room table, a ritual from their former life—the one rule of Tom's that Loretta had whole-heartedly agreed with. No cell phones and no television. This way, they could talk to Hazel and find out about her day. It had been the one time her daughter had had her father's undivided attention. Loretta had enjoyed those times, and she intended to continue them with Hazel.

"I heard from your dad today. He wants you to come to Texas this month."

"Really?"

Seeing Hazel's eyes light up caused a mixture of joy and pain in Loretta's heart.

"Yes."

"I wonder if we'll go camping."

And there went the tight squeeze in her stomach. "Actually, he's doing some fun things for his political campaign."

"Oh. That doesn't sound fun."

"But you'll still get to see him. Won't that be nice?"

She poked the broccoli around on the plate. "Sure. I guess so."

"I'll talk to him and see if he can squeeze in some fun things for you two to do together."

Hazel shrugged. "He'll just say he's busy with his politics stuff, like always."

One thing she gave her daughter credit for was that she knew her father, and knew him well. She never gave up hope that maybe one day he might want to see her just to spend time with her and have some fun, but she knew it was typically to drag her around for campaign stops.

Smart girl. Loretta didn't want to give her false hope.

But she'd still call Tom tonight, as much as she did not want to speak to her ex.

So after dinner, when Hazel was outside kicking around the soccer ball, Loretta took out her cell phone and tapped Tom's number.

He answered on the third ring.

"Hello, Loretta."

"Tom. I heard from my attorney today that you want Hazel for a week this month."

"Yes. I have important campaign stops in Houston and Austin."

"It might be nice if you visited your daughter according to the terms of our divorce decree."

He paused before answering. "I'm very busy."

She rolled her eyes and swallowed the retort that hovered on her tongue. "I know you are. But she misses you and wants to do something fun with you. Maybe you could carve out some time that week for something that doesn't have to do with your political career? Even if it's just to take her out for ice cream?"

"I'll have my assistant check my schedule. Otherwise, I'll e-mail you the specifics of when we'll be there to pick her up."

Uh-huh. "We" being either his personal assistant or a hired nanny. Tom would never take time out of his "busy schedule" to come fetch his daughter himself.

"Great. You do that."

She hung up, then threw her phone across the table.

Waste of time. She knew the entire week would be filled with political appearances and Hazel would come home Sunday night grouchy and once again disappointed in her father.

Loretta made a note in her calendar to do something fun with Hazel after she got back from that week with her dad.

Tom might be a shitty parent, but Loretta wasn't. And she'd do everything in her power to make sure her daughter was happy.

Chapter 3

DEACON AND HIS crew had spent three days doing demo on the old building. That was two days longer than he had expected it to take. But there was more crap in there than he'd realized, and hauling it out had been a bitch. Which meant they were already behind—and this project was still in its infancy.

But now that they had the old place cleared out and swept from top to bottom, they could really start working. The first thing they had to do was put up a few temporary support beams on the main floor, because load-bearing walls were coming down and those upper structures needed support.

So he was outside measuring and sawing when he caught sight of Loretta's daughter. She was standing just on the edge of the bookstore property, studying him. He lifted the saw and took off his safety glasses.

"Hey," he said.

"Hi. I'm Hazel Simmons. I'm nine. My mom owns this bookstore. She told me you're Deacon Fox and you're going to be working on this building for a while."

He was surprised Loretta had told Hazel anything about

him other than to stay away from him. "Nice to meet you, Hazel. Do you like to read?"

She nodded. "I read a lot. But that's not all I do. I'm really smart."

He resisted the urge to grin. "Is that right?"

"Yes. My last report card I got all A's."

"That's great. What's your favorite subject?"

She shrugged and stepped onto the porch. "Math. Science is pretty fun, too, I guess. Hey, what are you doing with that thing?"

"This is a table saw. I'm cutting wood with it."

"What are you gonna do with it?"

"I'm going to use several pieces just like this to hold the beams in the ceiling steady. Then I'm going to take a wall down."

Her eyes widened. "Really? Can I watch you do that?"

"I don't know. You'd have to ask your mom."

She nodded. "She'll probably say no and that it's dangerous."

"She's probably right. It's not a place for kids."

"I like to build things. And I like to draw. I'm good at sports, too. Oh, and I'm getting a dog this week."

He loved kids' minds, the way they could contain multiple topics at once.

"You are, huh? What kind of a dog?"

"Don't know yet. We're going to the shelter to pick one out. Mama told me I could have any dog I wanted."

"Well, aren't you lucky?"

Hazel grinned, and her smile reminded him of Loretta's. "Yeah. I am."

"Have you thought of names for your dog yet?"

Hazel shook her head. "I have to see him or her first. Then I'll know."

"You're very smart."

Hazel laughed. "I already told you that."

Just then Loretta came out of the bookstore, looked around, and saw them. She walked over.

"Hazel, what did I tell you?"

"About what?"

"You know what I'm talking about. You're supposed to stay on the porch."

Hazel looked down at her feet. "I am on the porch."

Loretta rolled her eyes. "Don't get smart with me. Go on inside the bookstore."

"Did you know that Deacon is taking a wall down, and he's going to use that wood to—"

Hazel looked at Deacon.

"Brace the beams in the ceiling."

"Yeah, that. Do you think I can watch him do that, Mama?"

"Not on your life. It's too dangerous."

Hazel turned to Deacon. "I told you she'd say that."

Deacon's lips curved. "Yup. You did."

"Okay, well, I gotta go. See ya later, Deacon."

"See you, Hazel."

After Hazel disappeared inside the bookstore, Loretta turned to him. "Please don't encourage my daughter."

"Encourage her to do what? Be smart? Be curious about learning new things? She came over here and started asking me questions, Loretta. What was I supposed to do? Tell her to get lost?"

"I . . ."

He waited, but he knew she didn't have a position here.

"She's a great kid."

Loretta sighed. "Thank you. I know she is."

"And I told her it was too dangerous to be inside the building when the wall came down. But if she's interested, she can watch it from outside the window here. Maybe you could let her? It's actually kind of cool."

Loretta looked over at the window on the porch, then back at Deacon. "She's bored here, but I don't want to leave her with a sitter."

"She said she likes reading."

"She does. But she needs more activity."

"I could put her to work. She looks tough. I'll bet she could wield a hammer."

"Funny. And she probably could. But no."

"Okay."

He waited for her to leave. Instead, she hung out on the porch with him.

"What time are you taking that wall down?"

"It'll take a couple of hours to measure all the wood, cut it, then brace the wall. So probably not until after lunch."

"Okay."

He knew what she was asking. "I could come get Hazel and let her know when we're ready to bring it down. If you're okay with her watching."

She waved her hand. "No. You're busy."

"Not that busy that I can't walk a few steps across the porch and into your store, Loretta."

"If you're sure it's no trouble."

"It's no trouble. I'll come get her."

"All right. Thanks."

"Sure."

She lingered a few more seconds, then said, "I guess I'll let you get back to work now."

"Okay."

She turned and wandered off and he stared at the spot where she'd just stood.

He'd hated every second of their exchange. It had been stilted and uncomfortable and not at all like their conversations when they'd been together all those years ago. Back then, they'd found anything and everything to talk about.

But that was the past, and this was now.

And now sucked.

"That was awkward."

He turned to see Reid McCormack standing on the porch steps. He hadn't even seen Reid drive up.

"When did you get here?"

"About five minutes ago. I parked in the back. Walked in through the rear door. Saw you talking to Loretta out front, so I didn't want to interrupt you. I came out the side door to get something out of my truck. I couldn't help but hear the tail end of that conversation."

"Yeah. It was awkward, all right."

"You two are like strangers. And from what you've told me about your prior relationship with Loretta, which admittedly isn't a whole lot—you aren't strangers."

"No. But there's a lot of history between us."

"Some of it was good, though, right?"

"A lot of the history between Loretta and me was good—until it wasn't. And then it was really bad. It's the really bad part that presents itself when we have conversations now."

"I'm sorry, man. Maybe we shouldn't have taken this job."

"Hey, I'm fine."

Reid arched a brow. "Are you?"

"Yeah, I am. I'll be even more fine if we talk work, and not my past with Loretta. So let's go inside and I'll show you what's going on."

"Sure."

They went over the details of the demo, and Deacon walked Reid through all three floors. They discussed the schedule and manpower as well as the materials Deacon had ordered.

"Sounds like you have it all under control," Reid said as they made their way down to the main floor. "I don't see anything that might pose a problem."

"Yeah, no ancient elevators like you had in the building next door."

Reid laughed. "Thank God for that. And we already know plumbing, electrical, and HVAC will all need to be replaced here, which was included in the bid, so we shouldn't find any surprises."

"Hopefully. How's your project going?"

"Good. Working out final design specs with the group. Doctors are on-the-spot decision makers when it comes to medicine. Get a group of them together to decide on a building, though? That takes forever."

Deacon laughed. "I imagine a lot of that has to do with X-ray departments and lab departments and exam rooms and outpatient surgery and whatnot."

"Yeah. A lot of that. But I should have final approval

from them by the end of the week, then we'll be able to get started."

"Good."

They talked over a few other projects they had in the works, then Reid headed next door, where the main company office was located on the third floor. Deacon also had an office there, but he didn't use it all that often. Mainly because he was used to running an office out of his truck. He was on the go from job site to job site all the time, so he had a laptop and a netbook that contained all the job information and blueprints. What else did he need?

He and Reid argued about that all the time. Reid repeatedly reminded him that their company occupied a large portion of the third floor of the old mercantile building, and when they had gone into business together, Reid had set up a great office for him.

Unfortunately, Loretta had leased the entire first floor of the building around the same time. Seeing her every day hadn't been on his list of fun things to do, though occasionally Deacon did have to attend meetings with Reid and new clients at their offices.

So far he'd managed to avoid Loretta.

It didn't look like he was going to have a lot of success in the avoidance department now that he was working on the building next door.

LORETTA WAS ON her knees stocking shelves in the nonfiction section when she heard her name called.

It was busy this summer—something she was grateful for. She'd had to hire two new employees, Kendra and Camila, which gave her a great amount of joy. She knew that Kendra was up front at the register, but it wasn't her voice that had called out, so she got up and headed toward the front of the store, smiling when she saw Chelsea Palmer.

Chelsea was having a whirlwind summer so far. She'd gotten married, found out she was pregnant—not in that order—and was currently in baby-planning mode.

"Oh, hey, Chelsea."

"Hey, yourself. I hope I didn't interrupt you."

"You didn't. I was stocking."

"I came by to grab some books since I'm not teaching summer session."

"Great. What can I help you with?"

Chelsea rubbed her belly, which was starting to show with a slight baby bump. "I want to browse the childbirth and parenting sections. I've already been to the library, and Jillian helped me out there. But I want to buy some books I can make notes in."

"Sure. Let's go take a look."

They browsed the childbirth section first. Loretta made some recommendations. She pulled one book out and handed it to Chelsea. "This one was my bible during pregnancy. I read it cover to cover and made notes."

Chelsea scanned the back cover copy, then flipped through the table of contents before nodding. "I can see why. It looks very no-nonsense. A lot of books are filled with fluff about pregnancy. I need the real deal."

"This one is the real deal. With pictures."

"Awesome."

"Now let's move down to the parenting section."

Again, Loretta made some recommendations, sticking to infancy for now. Chelsea selected two books, and Loretta carried them to the counter and told Kendra to put them on hold, while Chelsea made her way to the comfy chairs at the back of the store.

"Would you like some tea?" Loretta asked.

"That sounds really good. Though wine sounds better. I miss wine."

Loretta laughed. "I imagine you do." She poured two glasses of tea and handed one to Chelsea, then took a seat in the chair next to her friend.

Chelsea sipped the tea. "My OB allows me a couple of glasses of wine per week, so it's not like I feel all that deprived. But sometimes after a particularly stressful day I just want to stop in at Bash's bar and down several glasses."

"You'll be able to do that after the baby comes."

"I know." Chelsea rubbed her belly. "And she's worth waiting for."

Loretta raised a brow. "She? You know the sex already?"

Chelsea grinned. "Not yet, since it's still a little early. I'm just hoping it's a girl. Bash is sure it's a boy, but I think secretly he's hoping it's a girl, too."

"So you plan to find out?"

"Yes. We thought about waiting, but I want the nursery decorated to the hilt. If it's a girl, Bash expects pink glitter everywhere, but honestly, my plan is to be more understated than that. Though right now I'm torturing him with thoughts of pink glitter."

Loretta's lips curved. "Of course you are. Not-so-secretly, I hope it's a girl, too. I can tell you that having a daughter is one of the best things ever."

Chelsea looked over at Hazel, who currently sat on the other side of the room reading a book. She sighed. "I can't wait. But honestly, I'm so happy about this baby I don't care what sex it is. I don't even care if it's a giraffe."

Loretta laughed. "I don't think it's going to be a giraffe."

"I don't think so, either. I can't wait to find out at next month's OB appointment."

"We're all excited for the big reveal." Loretta smiled.

"I'll be sure to let everyone know. I wish I could find out before book club so I could let everyone know at once, but since book club is next week, it's a little early."

"Too bad. We could celebrate with pink or blue cupcakes. That Megan would of course make for us."

Chelsea laughed. "Yes. Oh, and speaking of book club, there's a new teacher at Hope High. I met her the other day when I stopped in to have lunch with Jane."

"Really?"

"Yes. Her name is Josie Barnes. She just moved to Hope about a month ago. She's teaching summer session English, and she'll be on full-time in the fall."

"That's great."

"Jane invited her to lunch with us, and it was a blast. She's great, very fun and down-to-earth. I think she's a little lonely, though. She doesn't know anyone in town. I told her I'd introduce her to . . . well, you know. Everyone. And she loves to read, so I invited her to book club next week."

"Of course. She's more than welcome."

"She's very anxious to meet people. I'm sure it's lonely being new in town and knowing no one."

"I'm sure it is. Even growing up here in Hope, after being gone for so long, it's been hard to get reestablished. People move around. Friendships change. Some of my old friends from high school have moved away, and others have . . . Well, let's just say coming back has been hard. A lot like starting over for me."

Chelsea reached over and grasped her hand to give it a squeeze. "You've had a lot of upheaval in your life since . . ." She looked over and saw that Hazel had put in her earbuds and was watching a movie on her netbook. "Since the divorce. But you have all of us now. We're your friends, and you can always count on us."

Loretta felt a warm twinge in her heart. "Thank you. That does mean a lot to me."

"How's Hazel doing, by the way? Since the divorce and the move and everything?"

"Hazel? She's doing great. That kid can roll with the punches better than anyone I know."

"Awesome. Then how are you doing? Since the divorce and the move and everything."

Loretta took in a deep breath and looked around to see that she had a couple of customers browsing the bookshelves, two checking out, but Kendra had them handled. So she leaned back into the chair and took a deep breath.

"Honestly? It's been really hard. I feel like the weight of the world is on my shoulders. I'm trying to carve out a good life for Hazel here, but I don't know if I'm getting it right, or all wrong."

"She seems happy, Loretta. I'd say you're getting it right."

"I hope so. She does seem happier now, and I do know she was unhappy in Dallas. So was I. But I'm hoping I'm not just projecting my own feelings onto her. She was miserable living in that condo, though, and she talked all the time about wanting to live on a farm or a ranch. She wanted animals and space to run. That's one of the main reasons I moved back here, because I knew I could buy property that would give her what she needed, plus we'd be near both sets of her grandparents. Tom might not have time for her, but his parents do love her. So do mine."

"That's important."

"Yes."

"So quit second-guessing yourself. Kids are resilient. More than you think. I really do know this, because I spend a lot of time with them during the school year. And even when they reach high school, they can still bounce back from traumas that would level us adults. So cut yourself some slack."

"I guess so." She looked over at Hazel, who was humming one of the tunes from her favorite movie. "She does seem a lot happier now."

"She has you and you love her. That's really all she needs." Loretta smiled at Chelsea. "Thank you for that."

Chelsea stood. "Hey, we all need a boost now and then. Besides, it's the truth. Now I need to get out of your way so you can get some work done. I think I'll go next door and annoy Deacon for a while. I saw him sweating outside a little while ago."

"Yes, you should do that."

"How are the two of you doing with him working in such close proximity?"

"We're being . . . polite to each other, I guess is the best way to describe it."

Chelsea wrinkled her nose. "That's boring. You should go pick a fight with him or something. That would be way more entertaining."

Loretta laughed. "I don't think that would be a good idea."

"Why not?"

"Because I'm the reason we're not speaking to each other. That'd be like pouring salt in the wound. And what we had was in the past. He's over me."

Chelsea waved her hand back and forth. "I don't think so. I've seen the way he looks at you. Trust me, whatever the two of you had? It's definitely not in the past."

After Chelsea left, Loretta didn't have much time to mull over what she'd said about Deacon. The store got busy, so she helped customers find the books they were searching for, then she got back to stocking.

Later that afternoon, Deacon stopped in looking dusty and dirty and utterly magnificent, which she tried not to notice. She utterly failed at not noticing.

"We're ready to take that wall down if you want to bring Hazel outside."

"Oh. Sure. Thanks for letting me know."

She rounded up Hazel, who was so thrilled to be able to watch a wall come down that she was practically vibrating.

"It's probably not going to be very exciting," she told her.

"Yes it will, Mama. Are you gonna watch?"

"Sure." But only to make sure Hazel stayed on the porch and didn't wander inside. Not because she was at all interested in watching Deacon work.

They had already removed most of the drywall along that very long main wall, but there were several large posts and a balcony of sorts that Deacon and his crew had tied rope to. She noticed smaller posts had been wedged or nailed to a main beam, which lay across the top of the ceiling.

Pulling down the wall took a crew of three men tugging and pulling on those ropes. Loretta found herself watching only Deacon, her gaze transfixed on his bulging biceps and forearm muscles as they heaved on the ropes until, suddenly, the entire balcony and the massive wall came toppling down in a cloud of dust.

Hazel turned to her and grinned. "That was awesome."

Loretta didn't know how awesome watching a wall come down had been, but watching Deacon's muscles at work? That had been a sight to behold.

"Come on, Hazel," she said, putting her arm around her daughter's shoulders. "Let's get back to the bookstore."

She needed to focus on work, not on Deacon's hot body.

Chapter 4

IT HAD BEEN a long, hot day, and Deacon wanted nothing more than to cool off in his friend Bash's air-conditioned bar and end the day with an icy cold beer.

Bash's Chihuahua, Lou, greeted him as he walked through the door. He bent and petted her, then Lou scurried off, so Deacon wandered up to the bar.

Bash took a look at him and reached behind the bar for a cold bottle and opened it, then slid it across the bar. "Hot day?"

"Brutal for June. This summer is going to kill me."

"That's because you're old and out of shape."

Deacon took a few deep pulls from the bottle, letting the cold brew slide down his throat and quench his thirst. He put the bottle down and grinned at Bash. "Yeah, you'd like to be as out of shape as me, old man."

Bash laid his palms on the bar. "We're the same age."

"You're old and sedentary. And you're married and expecting a baby."

"And I still kick your ass at our weekly basketball games, so don't give me that Old and Married bullshit."

Deacon grinned. He loved to give Bash a hard time about the marriage and children thing. He took another swallow of his beer. "Bought a minivan yet?"

Bash laughed. "Not yet. But I do have my eye on a nice Jeep."

"That'll do."

After a while they were joined by Carter Richards and Brady Conners, who'd just gotten off work at Carter's auto shop. Bash gave both of them beers.

"Damn, it's hot already," Brady said. "I think I sweated out about ten pounds in the paint bay this afternoon."

Deacon nodded. "I feel ya. If it's like this in June, what's August going to be like?"

"Boiling," Carter said.

"You should probably have steak and loaded baked potatoes to replenish your reserves."

Deacon nodded at Bash. "We should."

"I can't tonight," Carter said. "Molly and I have plans, so I just stopped in for one beer."

Deacon turned to Brady. "How about you?"

"I'm game. Megan is working late at the bakery. She's doing some kind of special cake for a business event first thing in the morning. It was a last-minute request, so she told me she wouldn't be home until later."

"Then I guess it's just you and me for steaks."

Just then, their friend Zach Powers showed up.

"Did I hear 'steak'?"

Deacon turned to him. "What, do you have steak radar or something?"

"Yeah. So are we having steak or not?"

"We're having steak."

Bash took out his order form. "Tell me how you want 'em."

It had been great ever since Bash expanded the No Hope At All bar to include a restaurant, because it meant whenever Deacon got hungry while having beers, he could order food there. After they put in their steak orders, the guys took their drinks and moved to one of the tables.

"How's the auto shop business?" Deacon asked.

"Busy," Carter said. "In both mechanical and paint. And with Brady set to open his own shop, it's going to get busier."

"Hey, I'm training the new guy. He's good."

"Yeah, but he's not you."

"But he's good. I told you I wouldn't leave until I found a replacement. And you like Andy."

Carter smiled. "Yeah, Andy's really good. But he's still not you."

"So you settled on a place, Brady? Is it the one Reid mentioned a couple of months ago?"

Brady nodded. "Yeah. The one out on the highway near town. It's a good location with great visibility. And I won't have to build new. The concrete is already in place. We'll just have to add some walls for offices, and all the plumbing, HVAC, and electrical."

"That's a good call. So who's going to do the job for you?"

"I was hoping you and Reid would."

He was hoping Brady would ask. "I'm sure we can manage that. Why don't you give the office a call tomorrow and set up an appointment with us?"

"Will do. Thanks."

They ate dinner, then hung out awhile longer to talk sports and work. After they said their good-byes, Deacon made his way home to his town house. He parked out front and made a short right to stop at the complex mailbox to use his key and pick up the mail. Then he headed up the stairs to his town house, opened the door, and breathed a sigh of relief at the arctic feel of his place.

He had preset his thermostat to start cooling the place down at five p.m. so that it would be icy cold by the time he got home. He laid his keys and the mail on the table by the front door, then headed upstairs toward his bedroom.

First thing on the agenda was to shower off the dirt and sweat of the day. So he stripped down and turned the shower on lukewarm, then stepped inside, closed his eyes, and let the water rain down over his head.

Damn, that felt good. He let all the grunge slide off of

him as he stood there under the spray. He could stay here
for hours, but he grabbed the soap and washed, rinsed, and
turned the water off. He got out, then grabbed a towel and
dried himself. He went to the bedroom and grabbed a pair
of shorts, slid those on, then went downstairs and headed
for the fridge, grabbing a bottle of beer. He retrieved the
mail he'd left by the table at the front door and took that and
his beer and stretched out on his sofa, putting his feet up on
the coffee table.

Nothing much in today's mail but a couple of bills and
some junk, so he went through his e-mail, answered a couple
of pressing ones, then made a note in his calendar about
Brady's shop so he'd remember to talk to Reid about it and
follow up with Brady.

He finished his beer and finally felt like his body was
cooled down. If this weather kept up he was going to feel
boiled from the inside out by the end of summer. Maybe
they'd get lucky and would get a good, cleansing rainstorm
to cool things off.

He picked up the remote and turned on the TV, then
scrolled through the channels and found a baseball game.

At the commercial, he got up and fixed himself a glass
of ice water, then went back to the sofa and waited for the
return of the game.

He thought about the day. It had been productive, and
they were back on track. It felt good to finally have the main
wall down. Which reminded him of Hazel. She'd been
delighted to watch its destruction. Cute kid. Of course she'd
be cute, with Loretta as her mother. She looked a lot like
Loretta—same face shape, same smile. She was going to
be beautiful like Loretta when she grew up.

His thoughts wandered to Loretta, to the way she'd
looked today in her jeans and sleeveless silk top. The jeans
had molded to her body and every time the wind had blown,
the top had pressed against her breasts. That top she'd had
on had been blue. It had always been his favorite color on
her. Not that it mattered what color she wore, since she
looked good in everything. But the blue brought out the

unusual amber color of her eyes. Her eyes had been the first thing he'd noticed about her when they'd been in geometry class together in high school. She'd sat right across from him, and he'd constantly gotten in trouble that first week because he couldn't stop staring at her.

And then when Mr. Walker had told him if he didn't start paying attention he could move his desk out into the hall, Loretta had smiled at him and told him to keep his eyes on the blackboard and not on her.

God, she had an amazing smile. But he figured his dad would kick his ass if he got kicked out of geometry the first week of school, so he'd done his best to focus on the class and not on Loretta until the bell rang. Then he'd talked to her and asked her if she'd like to have lunch with him that day.

She'd said yes.

His lips curved as he remembered what that had been like. That first yes. That first lunch date. The first of many things they'd shared together.

It had been perfect back then, like a lot of teenage romances. He thought they'd had a future together. Maybe a forever together.

Until Loretta had blown them apart.

He picked up his water and took a long swallow, deciding that particular walk down memory lane hadn't done him any favors.

Time to focus on the game on television, and not on the past.

Chapter 5

LORETTA WAS NOT looking forward to this task. But a promise was a promise, so as she stood outside the shelter, she knew she was going to have to follow through.

"What do you think, Mama?" Hazel asked as she tugged on Loretta's hand. "Maybe a mastiff?"

Loretta cast a horrified look down at her daughter. "You're joking, right? Those things are the size of horses."

Hazel giggled. "They're not that big."

Loretta opened the door of the Hope Animal Shelter and waited for Hazel to walk in. "How about a Yorkie? Or maybe a Chihuahua like Chelsea has?"

Hazel grimaced. "No. I don't want a small dog."

Of course she didn't. Nothing with Hazel was ever simple.

But she'd made a promise to her daughter, and she intended to keep it. And maybe somewhere along the way, Hazel would fall madly in love with a tiny dog.

After all, tiny dogs were cute. Cuddly. Adorable.

All little girls loved small dogs. A miniature dog? Loretta could totally handle that.

They went to the front desk and filled out paperwork, then waited for one of the volunteers to take them back to the cages.

"Maybe a Labrador?" Hazel asked.

"Those are big dogs, Hazel."

"But they're so sweet. And easy to train."

The problem with her daughter was that she'd done her research. She knew all about dogs. All about the different breeds and their temperaments, potential health risks, and behavioral problems. All Loretta knew was sizes.

She wasn't going to win no matter what she said.

Loretta had told Hazel when they moved to Hope and bought the ranch that she could have any dog she wanted. They had plenty of space, so it didn't really matter if Hazel got a big dog. Except for the manageability issue, of course.

Chelsea often brought Lou into the bookstore. She was so cute and petite and so well behaved. Loretta wouldn't mind a Chihuahua.

And she'd met Megan's dog, Roxie, who was small and adorable and utterly manageable.

Since they occupied the same building, Reid's dog, Not My Dog, was always wandering around. Hazel loved that dog.

Everyone had a dog. And now it was time for Hazel to have one of her own. It was past time, actually.

The volunteer came out and called their name, so they got up and headed back toward the cages. The first thing Loretta heard was a lot of barking. A lot of very loud barking. No doubt from the very large dogs.

She sighed.

Hazel walked ahead with the volunteer, so Loretta stayed a step behind while the gentleman, whose name was Terence, told her about all the dogs.

There were quite a few of them at the shelter, which broke Loretta's heart. Some were strays that had been picked up; others had been dropped off by people who couldn't—or wouldn't—care for them any longer.

Every dog needed a home and someone to love them.

Loretta quickened her step to listen to what Terence was telling Hazel.

"The smaller dogs tend to get adopted faster," Terence said. "Everyone loves tiny dogs."

Loretta certainly did. And there certainly were some cute ones, from Shih Tzus to poodles to a few small terriers to mixed breeds of all types. But Hazel hadn't stopped at any of their cages.

She did stop at a cage that housed a cute black Lab.

"This is Casey. He's two years old, but he's already spoken for," Terence said.

"Oh, okay," Hazel said, then smiled at the dog. "Hey, Casey, I'm glad you've found a forever home."

Loretta's heart squeezed.

They kept walking, and then Hazel noticed a dog in one of the cages. She stopped. So did Loretta's heart.

Oh, God, no. Not *that* one.

Terence was talking about the dog, and Hazel listened to him, but her focus stayed on that dog. Hazel was grinning.

Loretta's legs started shaking.

And then Terence opened the cage and the beast lumbered out. Hazel dropped to her knees and wrapped her arms around the thing. The thing licked her, and Loretta saw the light of love shine in Hazel's eyes.

Right then, Loretta knew it was over.

Oh, crap.

Chapter 6

DEACON WAS ON his knees working on the wiring on the first floor when something nudged his butt. He figured it was one of the guys trying to get his attention.

"Not now." He swiped the sweat from his eyes and focused on fitting the wiring into the connection box when he felt another nudge, this time between his legs.

"What the fuck?" He jumped up, ready to do battle with whoever had just grabbed him by the balls.

Only it wasn't a person. It was a dog. A damn big one, too. And in his work space.

The dog came over and licked his entire hand, his tail whipping back and forth and causing a breeze in the room. He was black-and-white with short, sleek hair and was, Deacon had to admit, beautiful. But huge.

"Okay, dude." He checked to make sure it was a dude, and it was. "You're obviously lost."

"He's not lost. He's mine."

He looked up to see Hazel standing in the doorway. "This is your dog?"

"Yup. Got him a couple of days ago."

"He's bigger than you."

"Is not. He's the perfect size."

"Come on, dog," Deacon said. "Back outside for you."

Fortunately, the dog followed him, practically knocking Hazel over when he greeted her on the porch. Then he licked her entire face, which only made her laugh.

Hazel giggled. "Isn't he great?"

"Yeah. Great. Did you name him yet?"

She nodded. "His name is Otis. He's a Great Dane and he's almost a year old. So he's like still a puppy. Oh, and he knows how to sit, don't you, Otis? Otis, sit."

The dog wagged his tail and licked Hazel's hand, but didn't sit.

Deacon gave the dog a critical eye. "I think your dog needs some training."

"I'm gonna train him. I was doing that on the porch but he slipped out of the leash and ran off."

"You have experience training dogs?"

"No. This is my first dog ever. Mama and I went to the animal shelter and I got to pick him out."

"So you decided on a horse?"

She laughed again. "He's not a horse, Deacon."

He loved the sound of Hazel's laughter, which was filled with pure, unfiltered joy. There was nothing like a happy kid. "He looks like a pony."

"Mama already told me I can't ride him. Not that I would. She told me I have to be responsible for him. I have to get up in the morning and let him out, and when we're here I have to watch him, take him for walks, and train him not to eat my shoes."

Deacon arched a brow. "He ate your shoes?"

"Only one of them. We got him some toys so he'll have stuff to chew on. Oh, and he likes to fetch tennis balls. But we can't do that here cuz of the street."

"Where's his leash?"

"It's over here." She ran over to the bookstore's porch and brought back the flimsiest leash Deacon had ever seen.

"That kind of leash will never work on a dog Otis's size. You'll need a stronger one."

"I will?"

"Yes. And how are you training him?"

"By telling him stuff. He did sit that one time when I told him to. And I push on his rump while I tell him to sit."

She looked proud of herself when she told him that. "I've been looking up stuff on YouTube."

Kids and technology. At least she was trying. "Here, let me show you a few tricks."

He didn't have dog treats in his truck, but he did have some chicken breast that he'd brought along for lunch. He went to the cooler, pulled out a hunk of the chicken, then took Otis's leash and brought him out to the sidewalk.

There, he showed Hazel how to hold a tiny hunk of chicken up high, then back the dog up enough to force him to sit while using the command. When Otis sat, he let him nibble on a small piece of the chicken. They worked on it several times until Otis did it instinctively. Of course, he expected a small piece of chicken every time, but eventually he'd associate the sit command with a treat. Until he'd do it with just the command.

"But you have to do it every time in the same way. A dog learns by routine," Deacon explained to her.

Hazel nodded. "Got it."

"Hazel. What are you doing?"

Deacon looked up to see Loretta standing on the front step of the bookstore.

Hazel turned around and smiled at her. "Deacon's teaching me how to train Otis. Look, Mama."

Hazel broke off a small piece of the chicken and held it up high. "Otis. Sit."

The dog sat and Hazel let him nibble on the chicken. "Good boy."

Loretta walked down the steps. "Deacon has work to do, Hazel. He doesn't have time to play with you and Otis."

"We're not playing, Mama. We're working. He already

knows how to sit because Deacon helped me." Hazel turned
to Deacon. "Can you help me train Otis some more?"

"Actually, I have to get back to work now, Hazel."

"You have to stop bothering Deacon," Loretta said.

"She's not a bother, Loretta."

"See? I'm not a bother, Mama. Maybe you can come over
for dinner tonight and we can work some more with Otis.
Can Deacon come over for dinner, Mama?"

Loretta looked horrified at the thought. Deacon tried to
hide his amusement behind a cough.

"Oh. Uh, I don't know if that's a good idea, honey."

Hazel's smile disappeared. "But why not? We were doing
really good together."

Deacon hated to see the disappointment on Hazel's face.
"I'd love to come over tonight, Hazel."

And there was that bright smile again. "Awesome."

"Hazel, go take Otis inside and let him have a drink of
water. I'm sure he's been working hard."

"Okay. See you later, Deacon."

"See you, Hazel."

After she walked inside with the dog, Loretta turned to
him. "It's not good to make promises like that to Hazel. I
don't want her to be disappointed."

"First, I never make promises I don't intend to keep. You
don't have to make me dinner. I'll come to your place and
give Hazel a few light training tricks for her dog. Then I'll
leave."

Loretta stared at him, and he wondered what was going
on in her head. Likely things he didn't want to know about.

"Fine. We'll be home about six."

"Okay. I'll see you sometime after that."

She turned to head back inside.

"Loretta?"

She stopped. "Yes?"

"I don't know where you live."

"Oh." She gave him her address, and he put it in his
phone.

"See you tonight, Loretta."

She gave him a look, then nodded. "Right. See you tonight, Deacon."

When she disappeared inside, Deacon headed back up the stairs and into the building, wondering what the hell he'd just done. He didn't want to see Loretta any more than she wanted to see him.

So why had he offered to come to her place tonight?

He knew why.

For Hazel. And only for Hazel.

Chapter 7

LORETTA HAD NO idea what she was doing making homemade biscuits and stew for dinner. Or why she was making such a large pot of it. It wasn't like she was actually going to invite Deacon to stay, because she wasn't.

Otis sat at her feet. Or rather, on her foot, which was a crushingly painful experience.

"Off my foot, Otis." She looked down at the dog, which wasn't a very far distance, since his giant head nestled against her waist.

The dog ignored her, instead looking at the pot of stew like it was the best thing ever.

"Not a chance, buddy. And please remove your enormous foot from my foot."

She finally had to nudge his head gently with her hip. Only then did he move. Actually, he lumbered not-too-gracefully to the door, barking in his Oh My God That Is So Loud dog voice.

It was too early for Hazel to be home, so that meant someone else had pulled into the drive.

As watchdogs went, he was pretty good, so she had no

complaints there. About the only complaint she didn't have about the dog so far. She turned the heat down on the stew to a simmer and went to the door just as the doorbell rang, which made Otis bark even louder. If that was even possible.

She opened the door, and Otis launched himself at Deacon, head butting Deacon right in the crotch.

Loretta winced, but Deacon had put his hands in front of his more tender parts and staved off the attack. At least it was a loving attack. Otis's bark might sound fierce, but so far he loved everyone he saw.

"Hey, there, Otis. Obviously we need to work on the stay command."

"Yes, please do that. And come in."

Deacon walked in, Otis trying to entangle himself in Deacon's feet.

"Where's Hazel?"

"She went home with a friend from her soccer team. She should be back soon."

"Okay. You want me to wait outside until she gets here?"

Loretta frowned. "No. Why would I make you do that?"

"Because it's obvious you didn't want me here in the first place."

She headed toward the kitchen. "I didn't want to inconvenience you. I didn't say I didn't want you here. Would you like some iced tea or a beer?"

"Iced tea will be fine. Thanks." He followed her into the kitchen. She grabbed a glass and put ice in it, then poured from the pitcher of sweet tea she'd made earlier. She handed the glass to him, and he took a couple of swallows.

"It's good."

"Of course it's good. A Southern girl never forgets how to make sweet tea. Though I have to admit it's been a while. Tom didn't care for anything with sugar in it. He was very careful about his diet and wouldn't allow it in the house."

"Well, he was no fun, was he?"

"You have no idea."

"He probably didn't even let you have popcorn and Sno-Caps when you went to the movies, did he?"

She was surprised he remembered her favorite movie snacks. "No. And we rarely went to the movies."

She realized that had been a very sharp answer, and she didn't want to talk about her ex-husband, especially with Deacon. "So how are things coming along with the renovation?"

"Fine. Going along according to schedule. I didn't know you'd bought a farm, Loretta."

"Yes. I bought a farm."

"Big undertaking for one person. How many acres do you have here?"

"Five."

"That's a lot."

"Yes, it is. Hazel and I hated living in the condo. She always talked about having space to run around, and she wanted animals. Lots of animals." Loretta looked down at Otis. "He's a start. I know she'll want more dogs. And cats. She wants chickens and goats and horses, too. Maybe a cow or two."

"So, a real farm, then."

"Yes, a real farm."

"Are you sure you can handle that?"

"Honestly? I don't know. But we're going to give it all we've got. Hazel loves animals. Now I can finally give her the chance to realize her dream of having a farm, all this space, and the animals she's always wanted to take care of. She wants to be a veterinarian."

"She does? That's not surprising. The kid seems to really like the dog. And seems determined to train him right. That's a good start."

"Thank you for offering to help her. I never had pets, so I'm not the ideal person to assist. I know she's been watching videos."

His lips curved. "She told me that. I can give her some pointers on how to train Otis."

"You would know best. I remember all the dogs your dad had at his farm. Let's see, it was Smiley, Red, um, Peanut, and . . ." She held up her hand when he would have helped her. "Don't tell me, it'll come to me."

She finally raised her gaze to his and smiled. "Stripe."

He smiled, and her heart squeezed.

"You remembered them all."

"Of course I did. I loved all those dogs. They were the only exposure to animals I had."

"If I recall correctly, your parents would complain that you'd come home from my dad's house with dog hair all over your clothes."

She laughed. "Yes. One of the many things they disliked about you."

"Yeah."

He went quiet, and Loretta realized the last thing he needed from her was a reminder of how much her parents had disapproved of him.

"So, tell me about your place. How about you give me a tour while we wait for Hazel?"

She nodded. "I can do that."

She needed to keep things between them neutral. Dredging up the past would only hurt him, and she'd already done plenty of that.

She showed him around the house. "It's four bedrooms. More space than we need, really, but we were so cramped in that two-bedroom condo that when I saw this place I felt like for the first time in years I could actually . . ."

She paused.

"Breathe?" he finished for her.

"Yes. Plus, it has the acreage I wanted, and the house is in decent enough shape."

He wandered into her kitchen and turned on the sink, wincing at the sound. "Decent? Plumbing is ancient. Did you have an inspection done?"

"I did. I know it needs work. I plan to hire someone to get to that."

He nodded, then followed her into the living area.

He stopped in the living room, taking in the built-in bookshelves that were crammed solid with books. "What? Not enough books in the bookstore for you?"

She lifted her chin. "There could never be enough books. And I like to read."

"You always did. I don't think I can ever recall you being without a book in your hand, in your backpack, or in your purse."

"Oh, and you didn't? We were always at the library together." One of her best memories of their time together.

He looked at her and didn't say anything. She realized he didn't intend for this to be a romantic walk down memory lane.

"Anyway, this is the living room," she said, hoping to get back on neutral ground.

"Big living room. Hazel will be able to have a lot of friends over."

"That's the idea. We couldn't do that in Dallas. Plus, Tom didn't like kid noise, so Hazel was never allowed to have sleepovers."

"Tom's an asshole."

Her lips tilted upward. She wasn't going to argue that point. She moved him through the hallway toward her office, where she had even more bookshelves filled with books, plus a desk and her laptop.

"This is a nice setup."

"Thanks. I keep all my financials for the bookstore here so I can work at home more and Hazel doesn't have to spend as much time at the bookstore. The carpet's totaled, but underneath is original hardwood, so I intend to rip it up and refinish the wood."

He arched a brow. "By yourself?"

She shrugged. "Eventually."

He gave her a dubious look, but she moved on, out of the office and down the hall, opening the door into Hazel's room. Her gaze zeroed in on Hazel's dog, who had a guilty expression and one of Hazel's favorite books in his mouth. A book that was now in shreds.

"Dammit, Otis." She marched over and retrieved the soggy literary mess, then stretched out her arm and pointed to the doorway. "Out."

Otis apparently understood that word, as well as the fact

that he was in deep trouble, because he hung his head low as he walked past her.

"Does he have chew toys?" Deacon asked.

"About fifteen of them. But he loves anything and everything in this room."

"This room needs to be off-limits until he learns what's his—and what's not his."

"You can take that up with Hazel." She dropped the now-useless book in the trash.

Deacon took a long look around. "Her room is cute, and not at all girlie."

"Hazel isn't girlie at all." Loretta smiled. "She doesn't like pink or purple. We decorated this room together. She picked the yellow paint for the walls, and I suggested the white shelves for her sports trophies and the bookshelf for her vast collection of animal books."

Loretta watched Deacon tilt his head to the side as he pondered Hazel's window.

"Yes, it's off-kilter," Loretta said.

Deacon went over and tried to open it. It wouldn't budge.

"This window needs to be replaced. First hard rain you get you're going to have water in here. You already have water damage here, so the casing and windowsill need replacing, too."

"I know. It's a priority. I just have to find . . . people."

He turned to her. "I'm people."

She frowned. "What?"

"I'm a contractor, Loretta. I can do that for you."

"No."

"Why not?"

"Because . . . no."

"It's important this gets done, and you want it done right. It would only take me a couple of hours."

That was an awful idea, for so many reasons. "Don't you have enough work to do?"

"More than I know what to do with, but it's no problem

for me to do it after hours. It doesn't sit right with me that Hazel has this leaky, ill-fitting window."

She stared at him for a minute. Like . . . a full minute, unsure of how to respond. On the one hand, it would save her from searching for a reputable contractor. On the other hand . . . Deacon.

Finally, she said, "I'd of course pay you."

"Hell yes, you'll pay me."

That made her feel somewhat better. And she had intended to get the window fixed. She just hadn't gotten to it yet. Along with several other things on the property that needed repairing or replacing. The bookstore had been a priority, and the window hadn't leaked—yet, though she knew she was pushing her luck there.

"Fine. And thank you."

"Not a problem." He wandered out of the room and down the hall. She followed after him.

"That's just my bedroom."

He stopped. "What? You have whips and chains, or maybe some kind of sex swing, and you don't want me to see them?"

Her eyes widened as she imagined a sex swing in there. And all the things she could do in one. With the right person. Parts of her that had been untouched for so long suddenly came flaring to life as she imagined Deacon and her . . .

Oh, no, Loretta. We are not going there.

"Uh, no. Nothing sexual is happening in my bedroom."

His lips curved. "Too bad for you."

But he walked past her without going in her room. "Nice house. Let's see the outside."

She had no idea why she didn't want him going in her bedroom. She'd made the bed this morning and the room was picked up. Maybe it was because the last time they'd been in a bedroom together . . .

And there went that sudden flare of heat again. She and Deacon had been a lifetime ago. And like she'd told him, there was nothing going on in her bedroom these days other than sleeping. Still, the thought of his big body in her bedroom—with her in it with him . . .

Whew. She was conjuring up images in her head she had no business thinking about. Especially about a man who hated her.

Forcing those hot thoughts aside, she led Deacon outside and showed him the grounds, Otis alternately walking between them and stepping on her feet, causing her to wince. "We have a big barn and several paddocks. And a chicken coop."

She showed him the chicken coop first. He went inside the fenced-in area and checked out the coop. When Otis went to follow him, Deacon held his hand out and said, "Stay." Otis followed him, and Deacon gave the command with his hand over and over again until Otis finally stayed behind.

Okay, that worked. At least for now.

Deacon came out of the coop area and patted Otis on the head. "Good boy." He turned to Loretta. "This is in decent enough shape. You could probably clean it up some and get some chickens right away. Nothing like fresh eggs."

She was glad to hear that. She remembered having fresh eggs at his parents' house, and they'd been great. "That's good to know."

"Chickens aren't a lot of work, so I think you can handle that to start with."

"Thanks."

He walked ahead, and she hurried to catch up as he made his way to the barn, opened the large double doors, and headed inside. He flipped on the light and wandered around inside. She had no idea what he was doing, but she stayed right with him as he made his inspection.

"You have some loose boards that need to be replaced," he said. "I'd like to climb up and check the roof outside, because I can see daylight from in here, and that's not good. You want the inside of your barn to stay nice and dry."

"You don't need to do that."

He turned to her. "I want to."

"Fine. There's a ladder over there that's probably tall enough."

He grabbed the ladder and took it outside, and she held her breath while he easily climbed up and walked around on the roof as if it was no big deal. When he came down, he put the ladder back inside.

"Roof has a few shingles that need replacing as well. Windows in the barn are shot. You need better insulation in there."

She made a mental list of those items. "Okay."

"I also noticed you have inadequate fencing around some of your fields. If you intend to put goats or eventually cattle in any of those pastures and paddocks, that'll need to be replaced, because one good, strong windstorm and those fences will come down."

Another thing to add to her list. "Got it. No goats or cows until the fences are replaced."

"Do you have the funds to make all these repairs and replacements?"

She nodded. "Yes. I got a good settlement from my divorce that allowed me to buy this property and put money aside for repairs."

"Good. We can get started making the repairs if you want to."

She stared at him. "Deacon. You don't have to do this."

"I know. But someone has to, and I'm the best."

She didn't understand why he was even offering. "But you don't like me."

He frowned, clearly uncomfortable with her statement. "I don't dislike you, Loretta. What went down between us is in the past. Besides, this is for Hazel."

She couldn't deny the tiny stab of pain his words caused. But he'd offered, and she wanted this property to be in working order for Hazel. "Thank you. I'll take you up on your offer to fix the property."

"Okay."

A car pulled up, and Hazel hopped out, then came running toward them. At the same time, Otis took off running at Hazel.

"That dog runs like a big dork," Deacon said.

Loretta laughed. "Yes, he does. And he sure has fallen in love with Hazel in a hurry."

"That's a good thing. A girl needs a special pal like a dog." He looked over at Loretta. "And maybe some chickens and a couple of goats."

Her lips curved. "I'll get on that."

She watched Hazel drop to her knees and wrap both arms around Otis, who knocked Hazel to the ground with great exuberance. Deacon walked over and, with a few commands, got Otis to sit, then showed Hazel the stay command.

"Did you see Otis stay, Mama?" Hazel asked.

"I did."

"What else has he learned, Deacon?" Hazel asked.

"Nothing yet. I was waiting for you, so your mom showed me around the ranch."

"It's great, isn't it?"

"It's pretty cool."

"I'll finish dinner while you two work with Otis. Deacon, Hazel and I would very much like it if you'd stay for dinner."

Hazel took Deacon's hand. "You're having dinner with us. Right, Deacon?"

Deacon looked down at Hazel, then over at Loretta before nodding. "Sure, I'd like that. Thanks."

Loretta nodded. "I need to go inside to check on the stew. I'll let you know when dinner is ready."

"Okay, Mama. See ya. Come on, Otis, let's learn some stuff."

And just like that, her daughter was fully absorbed in her dog. Loretta headed toward the house, but she turned to watch Hazel, who laughed at Otis, then at something Deacon said.

Yeah, her kid was in love with her dog, and maybe a little bit enamored with Deacon, too.

Loretta couldn't blame her for that.

Chapter 8

DEACON TOOK HAZEL—and Otis—through some basic training. He explained to Hazel that when you trained a dog, you didn't want to overwhelm them. It was best to teach them only a couple of things, and then, once they grasped those, move on to new tasks.

Fortunately, Otis was a smart dog, so he had pretty much mastered sit and stay by the time Loretta called them in for dinner.

"That's good enough for today," he told Hazel as they walked toward the house. "And you need to keep him out of your room. He ate one of your books."

Hazel scrunched her nose. "He did?"

"Yeah."

"Uh-oh. Was Mama mad?"

"She didn't seem too mad, but if he keeps eating things he shouldn't, she'll probably start getting mad about it, don't you think?"

"Probably."

"It's best to limit his areas until he understands what's

his stuff and what's your stuff and your mom's stuff. Outside and maybe living room for now."

Hazel nodded. "Okay. And maybe after he's like totally trained he could sleep in my room?"

"After he's trained. You also need to play with him a lot, run off his excess energy, and use his toys for fetching and tug-of-war and things like that. When he plays with his toys, praise him."

"Got it. I'm hungry. Are you hungry? You wanna come wash your hands with me?"

He loved how a kid's mind worked. He knew Hazel had been listening, but then her mind could immediately switch gears to food.

He had Hazel give Otis the sit and stay commands in the living room so they could test him, then they went into her bathroom and washed their hands. When they came out, Otis was still patiently sitting in the middle of the living room.

"He did it," Hazel said, giving Deacon a happy smile.

"Yup. You can release him now and give him a treat."

While she did, Deacon went into the kitchen. "Smells good in here."

"It's the biscuits. How did Otis do?"

"Very well. I'll let Hazel tell you about it."

"I can't wait."

"What can I do to help you?"

She turned to look at him. "Um, you can carry the biscuits to the table, because the stew's ready to eat."

Since Loretta had already set the table, he guessed there wasn't much else he could do to assist.

"Me and Deacon already washed our hands, Mama," Hazel said as she took a seat at the long bench at the table.

"That's good."

Otis propped his head on the kitchen table, obviously waiting for his bowl.

"Oh, I don't think so," Loretta said.

Deacon got up and called the dog into the living room, then told him to sit and stay. Otis didn't seem too happy about that idea, because he didn't stay the first time. In fact, it took Deacon several tries and the liver treats he'd brought along, but eventually Otis stayed, and Deacon made his way back to the table.

"Thank you," Loretta said.

"He really likes the smell of our food," Hazel said.

"I'm sure he does," Deacon said. "But a dog doesn't belong at the kitchen table at dinnertime. You'll have to work very hard with him on that, Hazel."

She nodded. "Okay, I will."

She was a good kid, and she didn't mind being told what to do. Obviously a product of her upbringing. Or at least of Loretta's influence.

"Thank you for inviting me to dinner," Deacon said as he laid the napkin in his lap.

"It's the least I could do, since you're helping us to train Otis. And since you're going to repair so many things around this place."

Hazel turned wide eyes to Deacon. "You're gonna fix some stuff around here?"

"Yes, I am."

"That's so cool. My bedroom window leaks air and sounds like ghosts whistling at night. It's kinda scary."

Deacon's lips curved. "I promise to take care of that."

Dinner was good, and Deacon had to admit, it felt kind of nice to eat a home-cooked meal. He ate at his mom's house once a week, but this was different. He liked Hazel, and though he would have never expected he would be sitting across the table sharing a meal with Loretta, it wasn't as uncomfortable as he'd thought it might be.

Loretta engaged Hazel in conversation about Otis, and Hazel was definitely a talker, so there were never any uncomfortable silences. Hazel talked to him, and Loretta did, too. It was obvious Loretta was trying her best to make Deacon feel welcome.

"How long is your job at the old Harden building supposed to last, Deacon?" Loretta asked.

"Three months. That should give us plenty of time to

finish putting up the new walls, add in all the HVAC, electrical, and plumbing, and then put in new flooring and paint."

"I'm looking forward to you being finished."

He laid his spoon down. "Trying to get rid of me already?"

"Your noise, yes."

"It hasn't been all that bad since we finished demo, has it?"

"Okay, not that bad."

"Mama, I'm finished eating," Hazel said. "Can I go practice with Otis now?"

"Yes, you may. Take your bowl and plate to the sink. And work with Otis outside."

Hazel nodded. "I will. Thanks for coming over tonight, Deacon. Will you be by tomorrow?"

"I don't know. But I'll see you when I'm at work, right?"

"For. Sure." She giggled and wandered off to rinse her plate and bowl, then loaded them in the dishwasher before she ran out the door with Otis.

"She's a great kid, Loretta."

"Thanks. I think so, too."

"Does Tom have visitation?"

"He does. Not that he uses it."

"I'm sorry to hear that. I can't imagine having a kid and not wanting to see her."

"He's running for Congress, and that's occupying a lot of his time. That, and his new, pregnant wife."

It took a few seconds to let what she'd said soak in. "Whoa. What?"

She waved her hand and got up from the table. "Nothing you want to hear about."

He carried his dishes to the sink. "I wanna hear about it."

She shook her head. "I made that bed, Deacon. Unfortunately, Hazel is the one paying for my mistake."

She had turned on the water to rinse the dishes, and it was obvious this was a tender topic. So he let it drop—for now—and asked her where the storage containers were so he could dump the rest of the stew from the pot in it.

"Would you like to take some home with you?" she asked. "I made plenty."

"I'm sure you want to freeze that for you and Hazel."

"Like I said, I made plenty for all of us. Grab those two containers down there, along with the matching red lids."

He did, then poured equal amounts in both and put them in the freezer. Then he nudged her out of the way so he could wash the pot.

"That is totally unnecessary," she said.

"Yeah, well, I'm washing it, so don't argue with me about it."

"Fine."

She bagged a couple of the biscuits and set those on the counter, then she wiped up the kitchen table while he finished up the pot and laid it in the rack to dry.

"See? Done already," he said.

"I put those biscuits aside for you to take home. And you can take one of the containers of stew."

"Thanks. I appreciate it. The only home cooking I get is once a week at Mom's."

She turned and leaned against the kitchen counter. "How's your mom doing?"

"Good. She's still working at the energy company in Tulsa, with no plans to retire anytime soon."

"Is she still living in Tulsa?"

He nodded. "She really likes it there. She and Phil are doing great. They'll celebrate their fifteenth wedding anniversary this year."

"Wow. I can't believe it's been fifteen years for them."

"Yeah."

"She always did like the city. That was the problem between your parents before the divorce. Your dad was a farm guy, and she was a city girl."

"Yup. They were much happier after they split. Too bad my dad didn't live long enough to get to enjoy retirement on the farm."

She laid her hand on his arm. "I'm so sorry, Deacon."

"Yeah, me, too. But for as long as he lived, he was happy, so that counts for something, I guess."

"It should. Happiness definitely makes a difference."

"So they say. I think I'll see how Hazel's doing with Otis before I go."

"Sure. I'll go with you."

As they walked outside, he realized both of them had shit they didn't want to talk about. Even though it had been a lot of years since his dad had died, he still missed him, still wished they'd had more years together.

Hazel was outside with Otis, who was sitting about twenty feet in front of her while Hazel slowly backed away from him.

He had to give the kid credit. Most kids liked the idea of having a dog and training it—in theory. The actual practice of it was something else.

Deacon held Loretta back. "Let's watch."

Hazel seemed determined, even when Otis bounded off toward her. She walked him back to the spot and told him to sit. When he did, she gave him the stay command and walked away again. And then again. And again. She never seemed to get tired or distracted, and when Otis finally stayed for a good thirty seconds, she called him to her and praised him.

"She's good with him."

"I told you, she loves animals." Loretta called out Hazel's name, and she came running over with a huge smile on her face.

"Did you see Otis? He did good."

Loretta nodded and smiled at her. "You both did good. Now if only we could keep him from chewing up things in the house."

"Yeah, he's gonna have to work on that part."

Deacon laughed. "Keep him out of your room. That'll probably help some."

"Probably."

"Time for you to take a shower and get ready for bed," Loretta said.

"Okay. See ya, Deacon. Come on, Otis."

"Bye, Hazel."

After Hazel and Otis ran off, Deacon turned to Loretta. "I should get going."

She walked with him into the house, reaching into the freezer for the leftover stew. She put it in a grocery bag, along with the biscuits. "Thanks again for helping Hazel with Otis."

"No problem. I'll make up a list of the things that need to be fixed around here and come up with an estimate for you."

They headed outside to where his truck was parked. "Are you sure the extra work isn't going to be a burden?" Loretta asked.

He put the grocery bag on the passenger seat, then turned to her. "Not at all."

"Thank you, Deacon. It means a lot to me, and to Hazel, that you're willing to help us."

When Loretta lifted her gaze to his, he was lost in the depths of those amber eyes. And suddenly it was like all those years had evaporated and they were behind the bleachers again. He remembered the first time he had pulled her into his arms, the first time he'd kissed her. She'd been fifteen and he'd been sixteen.

She'd been soft and pliant, and she had leaned against him, her fingers clutching his shirt like she was going to fall if she wasn't holding on to him.

Damn, that had been a good feeling.

He could still remember how she had tasted. Like bubblegum and soft lips, all tentative but eager at the same time. They'd both been a little awkward, but it had been so good. Really damn good.

"So I'll see you tomorrow, then?"

He shook himself out of that memory and nodded. "Yeah. Tomorrow."

He slid into his truck, angry with himself for going back there, for letting himself remember the sweetness of her taste. He put the truck in reverse and got the hell out of there, putting himself firmly in the now.

Now was where he belonged, and as he drove home he dredged up memories of betrayal, of hurt, of how she'd broken him when she'd told him she didn't love him anymore. That bitterness tasted sour on his tongue, obliterating those sweet memories in an instant.

Yeah, that's where he belonged—in the real world. And that's where he intended to stay.

LOVE ME AGAIN

Chapter 9

———————

LORETTA LOVED SETTING up the bookstore for book club night with her friends. The bookstore closed at six, and everyone came around six thirty. Over the past few days she had read tonight's discussion book—the new Julie James romance.

She'd loved it and couldn't wait to talk about it. It had been an incredibly hectic day, and she was more than ready for some girl time.

After she closed the store, she made fresh coffee and iced tea, then set up plates and napkins around the table and comfortable chairs in the back of the bookstore.

When she heard the first knock, she headed to the front, and she smiled when she saw Chelsea Palmer and Jane Gardner, along with someone she didn't recognize.

"Hi, you two. And I see you brought a guest."

Their guest was a beautiful young woman with short raven hair and the most stunning blue eyes Loretta had ever seen.

"We did," Chelsea said as they stepped inside. "Loretta Simmons, this is Josephine Barnes, but everyone calls her Josie. She's the new teacher at Hope High I told you about."

"Oh, right." Loretta shook her hand. "It's so nice to meet you, Josie."

Josie offered up a genuine smile. "It's wonderful to meet you, too, Loretta. I've been meaning to make my way over here, but teaching summer school and moving into my house has kept me busy."

She started to lead them to the back of the store. "You bought a house?"

Josie nodded. "I did. It's a cute one-story ranch with a huge yard, and I fell madly in love with it. Recently renovated, too, so I didn't have to do a thing other than move my furniture in."

"And only a block from my house," Chelsea said. "So we're neighbors, and Josie won't feel like she's all alone here."

"That's wonderful," Loretta said. "Where did you move from?"

"Atlanta, Georgia."

Loretta grinned. "Ah, so big city to small town. Do you have family here?"

"Not in Hope, no. I grew up in Oklahoma, in the southern part of the state."

"So you have family nearby?"

Josie nodded. "A few hours away. This is like coming home to me. It's nice to be back in the state."

"Well, then," Loretta said. "Welcome home, Josie."

Josie grinned. "Thank you."

There was another knock on the door. "Excuse me."

"We'll head to the back and make ourselves at home," Jane said.

Loretta nodded, and went to the door to let in Megan and Sam.

"We stopped and picked up the pizza," Sam said.

"Thanks, Sam," Loretta said.

"And I brought dessert," Megan said.

"Of course you did." Loretta smiled. Since Megan owned the bakery and coffee shop in town, she always brought dessert. And it was always incredibly fattening and absolutely delicious.

Loretta saw Des and Emma driving up, so she stayed at the front of the store. "You two go on back. I'll wait here for Emma and Des."

She opened the door for them. "Where are the babies?"

"Martha has Ben," Des said. "Logan had to make a run into the next town over to look at some cattle."

"And Luke has Michael," Emma said.

"Aww, I thought you'd bring them."

"Mommies are taking the night off tonight," Des said with a grin.

"Oh, and Molly and Carter have some biz meeting or another tonight, so Molly won't be able to make it," Emma said.

"Okay."

It was hard to believe looking at both of them that they'd just had babies two months ago. They both looked trim and gorgeous.

It had taken Loretta a full year to get her figure back after she'd given birth to Hazel. She didn't know how Des and Emma had done it.

Magic genes, she supposed. She remembered Tom being unhappy that her figure hadn't returned right away. One of the many things he'd been unhappy about.

Whatever. That was in the past, and as far as she was concerned, that's where Tom and his opinions could stay.

Jillian Reynolds, who ran the Hope library, pulled up just as she was about to lock the door, so she waited. Loretta smiled at Jillian's boundless energy, at the way her hair bounced as she hurried up the stairs and onto the porch.

Jillian grinned as Loretta opened the door. "Am I late?"

"No such thing as late. You're right on time."

"Perfect. This is my favorite event, you know."

"You'd think being surrounded by books all day, you'd want to get away from them."

Jillian arched a brow. "Hello, pot; meet kettle. Do *you* want to get away from them?"

Loretta laughed. "Never."

"Exactly how I feel," Jillian said.

"Go on back. I'll just lock up."

She relocked the front door and headed to the back, where everyone was sipping tea and some of them had poured the wine Megan had brought. It looked like Chelsea and Jane had introduced Josie to everyone, because she was chatting away and didn't seem shy, which was good, because as Loretta had learned with this group, you just had to dive right in.

"Wine?" Sam asked.

Loretta nodded.

"Where's Hazel?" Chelsea asked.

"She's at home with a sitter. Working on training her new pup. And by *pup*, I mean *pony*."

"I've seen him," Megan said. "He's adorable. I stopped by to pet him and talk to Hazel when she was outside with him the other day. Otis, right?"

"Yes. He's a Great Dane."

Emma's eyes widened. "Oh, that's a beautiful breed. Very good with children, and easy to train. Have you brought him by the vet clinic yet?"

Loretta nodded. "One of the first things we did. We got him at the shelter, so he's neutered and up-to-date on his shots, but I wanted the doc at your clinic to check him over. He's also microchipped."

"Good," Emma said. "I can't wait to see him."

"You'll have to bring Hazel and Otis by the library for pet day next week, Loretta," Jillian said. "We read stories about animals."

"I'll be sure to do that."

"I can't wait to do that with Michael when he's older," Emma said.

"Are you still on maternity leave, Emma?" Josie asked.

Emma nodded. "One more month with my precious bundle. I'm planning to enjoy every moment of it."

"Except for tonight," Des said. "Because occasionally we need a night off."

"How about you, Des?" Jane asked. "How long are you taking off from the movie business?"

"I don't have anything coming up for a few more months, so I plan to enjoy idyllic mommyhood for a while yet." Des smiled. "And the sleepless nights to go with it."

"It's a lot of work caring for a baby," Jane said. "I can't believe I'm going to start over again. What was I thinking?"

Loretta cast a wide-eyed look at Jane. "Jane. Are you pregnant?"

"Well, not yet. Not that I'm aware of. Maybe. I threw up this morning. But it could have been the two donuts I had, along with a bowl of oatmeal." She looked up from her glass of iced tea.

"Did you take a test?" Emma asked. "I still have some extras at my place. We didn't use them all up for Chelsea's pregnancy test bonanza."

Chelsea cracked a half smile. "Yeah, I only peed on six of them."

Jane shook her head. "I'm going to wait. We've only been trying for like six weeks. It couldn't happen that fast. I mean, the last time I was pregnant was . . . nine years ago? Ugh. What was I thinking?"

"That you wanted a baby with Will because you love him?" Megan said.

"Right. I do want a baby. But I have a twelve-year-old and a nine-year-old. They're almost perfect ages. I don't need to start over again. I'm insane. I have a job I love."

Chelsea rubbed her stomach, where her tiny baby bump was just starting to show. "And you wanted to be pregnant at the same time as me."

"There's that, too. Still, a stupid idea."

Loretta laughed. "Would you like us to go get you some pregnancy tests?"

"No. I'd like some pizza. And whatever Megan brought in the way of baked goods. I'm hungry. And let's talk books, not babies. I'm going to live in denial for a bit."

Chelsea nodded. "Let's do some denial, then. And hand over that pizza."

They ate and drank, and Loretta kicked back and relaxed

while they discussed the book at length. It was all positive vibes, because the book, of course, had been amazing. It was a great night. She had a glass of wine, and they all listened to Des and Emma talk about their babies while Chelsea detailed her pregnancy so far and Megan and Sam talked about setting up homes with their new loves.

It was nice to be in the company of these women. Not that long ago, she'd felt so isolated, only throwing dinner parties for Tom's friends. Not her friends—his. She'd been unbearably lonely.

And now she was making friends of her own choosing, and so was Hazel.

She had no idea why she'd waited so long to make these changes, to grow a backbone and divorce her husband. Now that she had, she was much happier.

"This is an amazing bookstore," Josie said later in the evening while everyone was up stretching and moving around.

"Thank you. How are you adjusting to life in Hope?"

"It's new and different and exciting. I love teaching at the high school, even though it's just summer school. I'm actually looking forward to the fall, when the regular school session begins and I can settle in. In the meantime, there's the house and getting all my things in place."

Loretta smiled. "I imagine that's a big enough task to keep you busy throughout the summer."

"A lot. I had a condo in Atlanta, and I sold most of my furniture, so I bought everything new for this house. It's been so much fun to just . . . start over. New location, new house, new furnishings. It's like a brand-new me, which I desperately needed."

Loretta wondered what brought about all these changes in Josie's life, but she didn't know her well enough to pry. "I hope it all makes you happy."

"Oh, it will. I know it will. And I have amazing book-shelves in my living room that are begging to be filled. I already have some of my books that I shipped from Atlanta, but I'm anxious to buy some new ones. I'm going to stop in after school one day next week and browse your shelves."

"I'd love that."

"Thank you, Loretta." Josie looked around the bookstore. "I spent so much of my time as a child in libraries and bookstores. This feels a lot like home to me, too."

"I'm happy to hear you say that. I feel much the same way. You'll have to get to know Jillian Reynolds better. She runs the town library. She's here tonight, and I know she'll be happy to show you around the library."

"I'd like that, too. You can never have too many books, you know."

Loretta laughed. "Amen to that."

After Josie wandered off, Loretta went up to the front to organize her paperwork. She picked up an envelope she hadn't seen earlier, then realized it had a Fox/McCormack Construction label on it. Deacon must have left it with Camila.

As she walked back to the group, she opened up the envelope and pulled out a sheet of paper. There was a note attached.

Loretta: Here's the bid for the work at your farm. Talk soon. D.

Short and to the point, but she supposed Deacon was busy and didn't have time to write her a long note. She smiled at his barely legible scrawl, then remembered the notes he used to write to her and pass her in between classes. Those had been short, too, but he'd write her sweet notes about how pretty her hair looked that day, or how much he liked her sweater.

He'd always been so thoughtful, had always noticed things most guys wouldn't.

If only she'd been smarter back then, more courageous.

"Is that from Deacon?" Sam asked, coming up next to her.

She looked up. "Yes. He's going to do some work out at my farm. Repairs and things."

"Really?" Chelsea said. "And how's that going to work out for you?"

Loretta frowned. "Not sure what you mean."

"I thought the two of you weren't on speaking terms."

"Oh, we're speaking. He was over for dinner the other night."

"Really?" Jillian smiled. "That's so interesting."

"Not really. Hazel asked him for dinner. He's helping her train Otis."

"And how did that go?" Des asked.

"It went well. Otis learned to sit and stay."

"Hmm. Very interesting," Jane said.

Loretta wasn't sure what was so interesting about all of this, but she suddenly found all sets of eyes on her.

"Who's Deacon?" Josie asked. "Or am I not supposed to ask?"

"Deacon was my high school boyfriend. We broke up, and I went off to college in Texas and married someone else. Deacon owns a construction company, and he's working on a renovation project next door, so we've kind of run into each other a lot recently. My daughter, Hazel, who's nine, really likes him. Oh, and Otis is Hazel's new dog."

"So . . . let me see if I've got this straight," Josie said. "You and Deacon are exes. Your daughter likes him and you don't?"

"Oh, I don't dislike him at all. It's more the other way around."

Josie nodded. "Oh. You broke his heart?"

"You could say that. Only with a lot more complications."

"Ouch."

"Yes."

"But now Deacon came over for dinner. Which means maybe the ice is thawing around you two?" Chelsea arched a brow.

"I don't know. Maybe. He's still pretty frozen."

"But you're hot, Loretta," Sam said. "And if anyone can thaw him out, it's you."

Loretta laughed. "I think I've got enough on my plate right now without having to think about thawing out a hot man."

"Aha. You still think he's hot," Chelsea said.

"I didn't say that. Did I say that?"

"You totally said that." Jillian nodded.

"Oh. Well, hell."

Everyone laughed.

"Seriously, though, Loretta. What do you think about Deacon right now? And about the chances between the two of you?" Jane asked.

"I . . ." She thought about it. If she was honest with herself, she'd been thinking about Deacon a lot lately, and not in the hired hand or dog trainer kind of way. A natural thing, she supposed—since she'd been seeing more of him lately, it made sense he'd be on her mind.

But she had burned him so badly in the past, and she wasn't sure there was any coming back from that.

"I don't know. I hurt him."

"Men can be very forgiving," Emma said. "So give him a chance and maybe see what happens. If anyone is deserving of love and happiness, Loretta, it's you."

She'd tried for love and happiness, and it hadn't worked out so well. As far as Deacon, she'd settle for friendship. If she could get that with him, she'd be happy.

Though giving herself that honesty kick again, she knew she wanted more. And she wasn't deserving of that. Not with him.

"Thank you. I'll leave the door open and we'll see."

"Sometimes second chances can be the best thing that could ever happen, if we only allow ourselves the opportunity to experience them. But you have to leave your heart open."

Loretta looked at Josie. "Thank you. I'll definitely consider it."

Fortunately, the conversation switched to another topic and off of Loretta and Deacon, which gave Loretta a considerable amount of relief, because the focus on her and Deacon had made her profoundly uncomfortable. Not only because she honestly didn't know where she stood with him but also because she knew the reason she and Deacon were at a standstill was her fault.

And maybe it was time to do something about that instead of standing back and letting fate run its course.

She was entitled to happiness. She'd made a mistake and screwed things up when she'd married Tom. She'd let herself be swayed by other people's opinions, she'd let them make decisions for her, and when she'd decided to divorce Tom, she'd told herself that wasn't going to happen again.

She felt unsettled around Deacon. Guilty and ashamed of the way she'd treated him. But she also didn't want to open that can . . .

No, it was more than a can—it was a Pandora's Box of the past between them, and opening it might lead to something painfully explosive. So she'd avoided bringing it up, which was likely cowardice on her part. It was best to just let things happen naturally. Which meant nothing was happening.

So maybe it was time to make something happen.

Stop being a coward, Loretta. This is the new you, remember?

Right. And the new her was taking charge of her life.

Time to take charge.

Chapter 10

DEACON PULLED UP to Loretta's house in his work truck and unloaded his gear.

Otis was the first to greet him, bounding toward him until Deacon gave him a stern look and a firm sit command.

Otis sat immediately. Deacon smiled. Hazel had obviously been working with him over the past couple of days, because without constant reinforcement, those commands would be lost in a young dog.

Hazel came running around from the side of the house and grinned when she saw him. "Oh, hi, Deacon. Did he sit for you?"

"He did. You've been practicing with him."

"I have."

"I haven't seen you at the bookstore the past couple of days."

"I was at my Grandma and Grandpa Simmons's house. They like to see me."

His lips curved. "I'll bet they do. Did you bring Otis with you?"

She nodded. "I showed them how Otis can do sit and stay. They said he's really smart."

"He is. Let me tell your mom that I'm here. I'm gonna do some work around your house first, then I'll work on Otis's training with you some more."

She slid her small hand in his and led him toward the house. "Let's go."

He hadn't been around many kids in his life, but he had to admit there was something about Hazel that captured him. Maybe it was her outgoing nature, her natural exuberance, or the way she laughed. Or maybe it was because there was so much of Loretta in her. But the kid just got to him.

She pushed the front door open. "Mama, Deacon's here."

Loretta was nowhere to be found. "Maybe I should wait outside."

"Nah. I'll go get her." Hazel disappeared, leaving him standing in the foyer with Otis, who licked his hand.

Deacon ran his hand over the dog's head and rubbed his ears. Otis sat—on his right foot. Deacon looked down at him.

"Off."

No reaction, so Deacon nudged his foot and Otis moved.

"Good boy." He petted him again.

"Sorry," Loretta said as she came down the hall. "I was folding laundry."

"No need to be sorry about that. If it's not too inconvenient I can go ahead and get started on the plumbing."

"Since I'm the one who's inconveniencing you, you can work on whatever you'd like. Hazel and I will stay out of your way."

Hazel looked over at Loretta. "But I wanna help him, Mama."

"No, you'd just be in his way."

"Actually," Deacon said, "I could use your help, Hazel."

Her eyes brightened. "Really?"

"Yeah. Come on over."

He laid out his tools and let Hazel help him unload the items from under the kitchen sink. Loretta brought over some boxes, and she loaded things in there.

After he turned on the water, Deacon took out his flashlight and crawled under the sink to look things over.

Hazel crawled in there with him.

"Whatcha lookin' for?"

"Rust." He pointed to a dark orange spot. "See this spot here?"

"Yeah."

"That's rust."

Hazel wrinkled her nose. "And that's bad, right?"

"Yes, that's bad. And there's a lot of it."

"So what happens when there's rust?"

"It can corrode—or eat—through the pipes, and cause water leaks."

"Oh. That can be really bad."

"You got it."

"So whatcha gonna do about it, Deacon?"

"We're going to replace all these old pipes with newer, stronger ones. Ones that won't leak."

"Okay. Let's do that."

Hazel was a surprisingly adept pupil. She learned to identify wrenches and PVC pipe, and she was good at handing him tools. She didn't get bored easily, or get offended when he needed her to move out of his way, either. All in all, a perfect assistant.

While they worked, they also drilled Otis on his sit and stay commands. And when they took a break, Deacon taught Otis the down command, which he took to right away. Good thing the dog liked treats. So Otis lay on the kitchen floor while Deacon and Hazel worked. It took a couple of hours to replace the kitchen pipes, and he had brought a new faucet, so he installed that, too.

"This is amazing," Loretta said, smiling as Deacon wiped his hands after he'd washed them.

"I helped, Mama."

"You did?" Loretta looked at Hazel, then at Deacon, who nodded.

"She's a good apprentice. I might hire her."

Loretta laughed. "Well, she's a little young to work in construction, but I'm not at all surprised. She loves doing anything dirty or greasy."

"It was very greasy," Hazel said with a wide grin.

Loretta leaned down to rub a spot of grease on Hazel's cheek. "You need a shower before dinner."

"Okay."

Hazel disappeared down the hall. Otis stayed in the kitchen where he'd been told to until Deacon took mercy on him and called the dog outside with him while he packed up his truck.

Loretta followed him. "Thank you again for doing this."

"Not a problem. This weekend I can start working on the barn."

"And you'll send me an invoice, right?"

He closed the truck door and turned to face her. "Yeah."

"I'm making grilled chicken and salad for dinner. Would you like to stay?"

"Loretta, you don't have to feed me every time I come over."

"But you're here during dinner. How could I not invite you? You haven't eaten yet, have you?"

"No. But that doesn't mean—"

"Good. Then you'll stay for dinner, right?"

He didn't know what to say to that, and he wasn't sure whether she was inviting him because she wanted him here or because she felt some sense of obligation. Still, he was hungry.

"Sure."

"Great."

They stood and stared at each other, and it was almost like Loretta wanted to say something to him, so he waited.

"Uh, I cleaned out the chicken coop."

"Did you?" He didn't think the chicken coop was what had been on her mind.

"Yes. Would you like to see it?"

"Sure."

He followed her down the gravel path toward the back of the house, where the coop was located.

She'd done a good job. All the weeds and old hay had been removed. She'd thoroughly washed out the house where the hens would be located, and it looked brand-new. He walked inside and looked around, checking the wires and fence to make sure there were no holes. It was solid.

"Ready for some chickens now," he said as he closed the gate.

She smiled. "Yes, it is, as Hazel has mentioned no less than fifteen times today alone."

"I'm sure she's anxious."

"I actually am, too. I'm looking forward to fresh eggs, so we'll probably pick up some chickens in a couple of weeks."

"Why not right away?"

"Hazel's going to see her father. I'll wait until she comes back. She'll want to be here to help me pick them up."

"Oh. Yeah, she would. Well, let me know when you get them. I'll come over for breakfast."

She looked surprised, then smiled. "Really?"

For a fraction of a second, he enjoyed seeing that look of utter joy on her face. "I was kidding, Loretta."

"Oh. Sure. Of course you were." She headed back to the house. He followed, and he could have sworn he saw disappointment on her face.

Man, he didn't know how to act around her. It was like they were two strangers, which was odd as hell, because he'd known Loretta better than he'd ever known anyone. They'd told each other everything, had trusted each other with all their dreams and all their disappointments.

At least that's what he'd thought until that day . . .

"Hey, where did you two go?" Hazel asked, brushing her damp hair away from her face.

"I showed Deacon the chicken coop."

"Ohhh, that's right. Did you know we're gonna get some chickens, Deacon?"

"I heard all about that. Are you excited about a rooster waking you up at dawn every morning?"

Hazel nodded. "The more animals you get, the more chores you gotta do."

Nothing fazed this kid. He admired her more every time he saw her.

"Hazel, come wash the lettuce," Loretta said.

"Okay, Mama."

"Anything I can do?" Deacon asked.

"You know how to slice some fat chicken breasts for grilling?"

"I'm pretty sure I can handle it." He washed his hands, then followed Loretta's instructions. If there was one thing he'd learned from his mom, it was that when you were in someone else's kitchen, you did it their way.

"Where's the grill?" he asked.

"Out back."

He grilled the chicken while Loretta and Hazel fixed the salad. He had to admit grilled chicken was one of his favorite meals, so he had no complaints about staying, other than feeling a little odd that she'd asked him to—again. He wished he could get over this uncertain feeling where Loretta was concerned, but that's where they were. He could have left things alone, but he was the one who'd offered to train the dog and work on her place, so he'd have to get used to being around her.

When the chicken was done he brought it inside.

"I'm so hungry," Hazel said.

"Me, too."

"Good thing I bought plenty of chicken, then," Loretta said. "And Hazel and I made a monstrous salad. Mainly because she's finally old enough to chop things, so she likes using the knife."

"And I'm good at it, plus I'm very careful because Mama said if I'm not I can't use it anymore. I sliced the tomatoes and the cucumbers."

Deacon peered into the salad bowl. "They look magnificent."

Hazel beamed a smile. "Thanks."

"Let's eat," Loretta said. "Otis, out."

Deacon was impressed that Otis listened to Loretta's

command. The dog made his way into the living room, circled a few times, then lay down.

Deacon looked over at Loretta. "Been practicing that one?"

"Repeatedly."

"Seems to be working."

"Only sometimes. I think he only did it tonight because he wanted to impress you."

Deacon laughed. "I don't think he's trying to impress me. I think he's trying to impress *you*."

"Uh-huh. We'll see. He could stop eating my shoes. That would impress me."

Hazel filled her plate with salad, then looked over at Deacon. "He chewed the heel off of one of Mama's bestest fancy shoes. The Loo-boo-tuns."

Deacon had no idea what those were, but from the grimace on Loretta's face, he wasn't about to ask. Instead, he concentrated on the food in front of him, which looked fantastic. In addition to the chicken and the salad, they also had green beans and a fruit salad. All together it looked like a feast.

"Sorry I didn't make any potatoes," Loretta said.

"I actually prefer more fruits and vegetables with my protein."

"That's what Mama says, too," Hazel said. "Though I do like French fries. And tater tots."

"Well, who doesn't? But they're better for you in small doses."

"Now you sound just like Mama. Anyways, I like broccoli. And salad. And I really like fruit."

"Me, too." Deacon spooned some fruit salad into his bowl. "What's your favorite fruit?"

"Watermelon. What's yours?"

"Blueberries. So don't eat them all."

Hazel giggled.

Deacon looked over at Loretta, who was smiling at him. His stomach tightened, and he focused instead on his food.

"This is really good, Loretta."

"Thank you. The chicken is great. Thanks for grilling it."

"You're welcome."

After dinner, he helped her clean up, then hung out with Hazel and Otis until Hazel yawned and stretched out on the sofa. He watched TV with her for a few seconds, then stood.

"I need to go. I'll see you soon, Hazel."

She yawned again. "Okay. See ya, Deacon."

Deacon went into the kitchen. Loretta was at the table working on some papers.

"I'm heading out."

She stood. "Okay. I'll walk you out."

As they made their way outside, Deacon noticed that Hazel was already asleep on the sofa and Otis was lying on the floor at her feet.

"That was fast," he said. "I just said good night to her."

Loretta nodded. "She plays hard all day, and she crashes fast."

He opened his truck door. "Thanks for dinner—again."

"Thanks for fixing my kitchen plumbing. The new faucet is great. I really appreciate it."

"Like I mentioned earlier, I'll come out this weekend to fix Hazel's window and work on the barn if that's okay."

"Hey, it's not my timetable, it's yours, so whatever works for you."

"Okay, I'll text you and we'll work something out."

"Sounds good."

He lingered, though he didn't know why.

"Deacon?"

"Yeah."

"Do you think at some point we should talk?"

He frowned. "About?"

"You know . . . the past. What happened between us."

And things between them had been going so well. "I don't think dredging that up is a good idea, Loretta."

He had his truck door between them. She stepped around it so she was standing right in front of him. "I disagree. You're working next door to me, and now you're fixing things around here and helping Hazel with her dog. It might be time for us to have a talk about what happened. What I did and why I did it."

He really did not want to talk about this. "I know why you did it. Because you fell in love with someone else."

She looked down at the ground, then raised her gaze to his. "That's not exactly what happened."

He frowned. "What exactly did happen, then?"

She looked toward the open front door. "How about we talk about it this weekend when you're here? I don't want to get into it with Hazel just inside."

Oh, great. Now she'd opened up the past and then shut it down just as fast. "Sure. Whatever you want."

She laid her hand on his arm. "I don't want to hurt you by dredging it up. I just think it would be good for both of us to clear the air."

"You mean good for you. You feel the need to get some guilt off your chest by explaining things that can't be explained."

He saw the hurt in her eyes, and he wasn't going to take responsibility for that, because he hadn't put it there.

"I deserved that. Maybe that's why we need to talk it out. Because I know I hurt you. And maybe I can't explain it in a way that you'll find forgivable. But I'd like to try."

Well, shit. "Okay. We'll talk."

Her hand still lingered on his forearm. She gave it a squeeze. "Thank you. So I'll see you this weekend."

"Sure. See you, Loretta."

He climbed into his truck and wished like hell she'd go into the house. Instead, she stood outside, the wind blowing strands of her hair across her face. He wanted to sit there and stare at her, because she was still so goddamn beautiful she made him forget to breathe.

Instead, he backed his truck down the driveway and got the hell out of there. He needed to get home, grab a beer, and find some goddamn sanity.

At home he went straight for the fridge, grabbed a beer, and set it down on the coffee table in front of the TV. He pulled off his work boots and popped open the can, taking several long swallows.

He grabbed the remote and found a baseball game, trying to let the sound drown out his thoughts.

He made it a half inning before Loretta invaded his head.

He'd been doing just fine since she got back in town. He'd been cool and calm and had kept her at an emotional distance. Sure, her kid was cute. He could get emotionally attached to Hazel and her dog, because Hazel wasn't part of his past.

Hazel had never hurt him. And the dog was pretty damn adorable. He could compartmentalize Hazel and the dog as if they weren't related to Loretta. Detaching himself emotionally from Loretta had been fairly easy.

Until tonight. Until she'd brought up wanting to talk about the past. He knew damn well if they actually started talking to each other—really talking to each other—he'd have to emotionally engage with her.

He wasn't sure he could do that.

Because there was a part of him that was still in love with Loretta, and always had been. And he was afraid if she started talking to him, he might listen. And if he listened, he might just find a way to forgive her.

And that would be really damn dangerous to his heart.

Chapter 11

LORETTA HAD RUSHED home after she closed the bookstore at noon. She cleaned the house from top to bottom, which was ridiculous since Deacon probably wouldn't pay the slightest bit of attention to the state of the house. But she had all this nervous energy and she needed to do something with it, so cleaning was as good a place to expend it as anywhere else.

She intended for the two of them to talk. Indoors, at the table or on the sofa, like two adults. Or so she hoped. She had stopped at the liquor store and bought beer and wine, then at the grocery store to pick up some food fixings. She whipped up some salsa and guacamole and put those in the fridge to chill, and now that she knew Deacon ate on the healthy side, she marinated some flank steaks to grill, which would go nicely with an almond and strawberry salad for dinner.

Now if she could just get her jittery stomach to calm down, maybe she could get through tonight. She needed something to occupy her time. Fortunately, the vegetable garden needed major weeding and some rich, fertile soil, which she'd had delivered the other day, so hopefully that might keep her mind off of Deacon. She changed clothes and headed out back to get started on that task.

When she heard Deacon pull up, she walked around to the front of the house. He was just getting out of his truck. Her heart did a little flutter at the sight of him. He was wearing worn dark jeans and a navy T-shirt. It looked like he'd already been at work today, because he also wore a thin layer of dust on his clothes.

"Did you work at the building this morning?"

He nodded. "I put in a few hours over there to stay on schedule. You look like you've been doing some work yourself."

"Vegetable garden. Otis has been helping, and not in a good way."

She looked down at Otis's nose, which was covered in a splotch of dirt.

Deacon rubbed Otis's ears. "He didn't go with Hazel?"

"No. Tom is on the road for his campaign, so taking Otis along wasn't an option, unfortunately. Hazel already misses him terribly. She FaceTimed with him early this morning."

Deacon laughed. "I'm sure Otis enjoyed that."

"He licked my phone screen, then tried to run off with the phone. So fun."

"Yeah, I'll bet." He ran his fingers over the dog's head. "You're probably tired. Are you sure you're up for this today?"

His lips curved in that way that made her insides clench. The first time she'd laid eyes on him, he'd dropped that hot grin on her. It was a sexy, confident smile, and even as a boy, he'd looked like a man.

He was even more a man now.

"I think I can handle a little hard work, Loretta."

She'd bet he could handle more than that, which sent her thoughts off in a wayward direction.

"Of course you can."

He carried his tools out to the barn. Loretta followed with the keys so she could unlock the barn doors.

"Ladder's inside."

"I have my own, but thanks."

She nodded. "Is there anything I can do to help?"

"No, I'm good."

"Okay. I'll be behind the house working on the garden if you need anything."

"You got it."

She went back to work, pulling weeds from the beds. Every time she pulled a weed, Otis grabbed it in his mouth and ran off with it. She figured he thought it was some kind of game of catch, though he didn't eat the weeds, just discarded them around the yard and came back for the next one. As long as it amused him and kept him out of trouble, it suited her just fine.

Eventually Otis got bored with fetching weeds and decided to take a nap under one of the tall, shady oak trees. She continued to work, and when she finally had pulled all the weeds from the garden, she smoothed the dirt with her rake, making sure it was level.

Then she went into the shed to grab the shovel and started scooping up piles of the very foul-smelling manure and whatever it was that the garden store had told her would make excellent ground soil and fertilizer for her garden.

Wow. This stuff stank. She would definitely need a shower before dinner tonight. And if she'd been smart, she would have waited until she had the beds cleaned out first and then had them dump this stuff directly into them. Instead, she had to load it one painfully smelly shovelful at a time.

Sometimes you are not smart, Loretta.

Probably more often than *sometimes*. And it was a hot day, too, which meant the craptastic odor wafted up all too often. It even got the attention of Otis, who had awakened from his nap and had come over to take a sniff. He started to step into it.

"Out," she said.

His paw lingered just at the entrance to the garden. He looked up at her, and she gave him a stern look.

"Out," she said again.

He took a step back. Whether that was because of her command or Otis deciding maybe he didn't want to roll around in the stink, she wasn't sure.

"Need a hand with that?"

She turned around and saw Deacon standing there.

"Oh, I've totally got this handled."

"Do you? It looks like a big load of dirt, and I'm pretty good with a shovel."

In her new and improved life she was a total feminist. She could do everything for herself and for her daughter, and she needed no man in her life. But this dirt stunk like shit and she wasn't stupid. The faster she got it done, the better. "I surrender. I'd love some help. There's another shovel in the shed over there."

He disappeared for a minute and came back with the bigger, heavier shovel, the one she'd bought thinking she could shovel like a boss, only to discover she could barely lift the damn thing. She figured once she'd built up some muscle she'd be able to use that one.

Deacon dug the shovel into a mound of dirt and lifted it up as if it were a speck of lint, his biceps bulging with the effort.

She ogled while he threw the dirt into the bed, then effortlessly lifted another large pile of dirt and tossed it in, and then another, sweat pouring down his arms. He didn't seem bothered at all.

Loretta, on the other hand, was definitely bothered.

"Sorry it smells so bad."

His lips lifted. "Shit makes stuff grow."

She laughed. "I suppose it does."

She found herself watching Deacon instead of doing work. How could she not? Sweat glistening on his skin, muscles rippling . . .

The man was a distraction. She moved to the other end of the bed to shovel, trying her best to keep her attention on the vegetable bed and not on Deacon.

Within a half hour they had all the dirt shoveled into the bed. Deacon grabbed the rake and smoothed it out for her.

"Do you have stuff to plant in there?"

She nodded. "I have seedlings in the kitchen and on the back porch that I've been growing in pots."

"Let's get them planted. You're already well behind on planting season."

"I know. But they're growing like gangbusters in the pots, which is why I needed to get this bed finished."

Deacon helped her grab the pots and trays and carry them to the bed.

"Tell me what you've got here and where you want everything planted."

They got everything into the ground in no time at all. Planting, at least, was the easy part. She watered everything with the hose and laid the hose down.

"Thanks so much for helping me with this. I'm afraid it might have taken me the entire weekend—or maybe a couple of weekends—to get all that dirt shoveled in without your assistance."

"I think you could have handled it. But now it's done."

"Yes. And now I've taken up time you were going to be working on the barn."

His lips curved. "Barn's not going anywhere. But those vegetables needed planting."

"You're right. They did. How are things coming along at the barn?"

"Good. I replaced the shingles on the roof, since that was the top priority. Windows will be next, but those can wait. Today I want to replace the window in Hazel's room. Since you said she was going to be off visiting her dad, I figured now would be a good time to work in her room."

"Oh, thanks. Would you like to do that now?"

"Doesn't matter. I can—"

"Dammit, Otis."

Loretta turned and ran off after the dog, who had torn across the property with a length of unattached garden hose in his mouth. She chased after him, but once he got a head of steam going, he was fast.

Deacon just stood there, not helping at all.

"Head him off," she hollered.

Deacon shook his head. "If you stop chasing him, he'll stop running away with your hose."

She skidded to a stop. Sure enough, Otis stopped running and dropped the hose. Deacon walked over and grabbed the end of the hose. Otis picked up the other end.

"Otis, sit," Deacon commanded.

Otis sat.

"Otis, stay."

The dog didn't move, so Deacon walked over toward him and grabbed the other end of the hose. When he had it wound up, he gave Otis a treat from his pocket.

Loretta came over. "I can't believe you're giving him a treat after he ran off with the hose."

"He doesn't realize he did anything bad. All he did was find something he thought would be fun to play with. And you encouraged it by chasing him around the yard. Plus, he did sit and stay, so that's what he's being rewarded for."

She sighed. "Fine." She took the wound-up hose and put it in the shed, then closed the door.

Deacon had walked over toward the shed, Otis right on his heels.

She would not comment on how well behaved Otis was whenever Deacon was around.

"Would you like to come inside and work on Hazel's window now?"

"Sure."

Loretta glared at Otis. "You can stay outside. Play with something that might actually be one of your toys for a change."

Otis cocked his head to the side and gave her a dog smile, as if to say, "Everything outside is my toy."

She shook her head. She wiped her feet on the back door mat. Deacon had pulled some supplies from his truck, so she waited for him, and they went inside.

"I'm not sure how much of a mess Hazel's room is," she said.

"I'll have to move some stuff around to clear space to take that window out anyway, so don't worry about it."

"Okay. I'm going to go take a shower. I'll be back shortly."

"Fine."

Deacon headed into Hazel's room and turned on the light. She'd done a good job cleaning her room, so Loretta had nothing to worry about. There was a chair and a small stand next to her window, so he moved those out of the way.

A book fell onto the floor, so he picked it up. He was about to lay it on her nightstand when he happened to glance at the open page where Hazel had handwritten a list. It must be her diary or journal or something.

Fun Things to Do with Daddy Someday

His stomach clenched. He shouldn't read this, but he couldn't help himself.

Picnic at the lake
Popcorn and movies
Camping
Learn to fish

Hadn't Hazel already done these things with her dad? Apparently not, because the date on the page was recent. What kind of father was Tom, anyway?

It wasn't his business, and he knew it, but at least she was with her father this week, so maybe they were off doing some of those fun things right now.

He hoped so. He laid down tarp and took the old window out, carting it to his truck. On his way back down the hall with the new window, he heard singing coming from the closed door to Loretta's room. His brain blew up with visuals of a naked Loretta dancing and singing in her bedroom, her arms extended as she twirled around her bed, then lay down on it to stretch out her body and . . .

Bad idea, Fox. Don't go there.

Loretta was someone else he had no business thinking about. Business with her was all he had going, and he was determined to remember that. Still, he couldn't help but smile as he remembered her chasing after Otis, her ponytail swaying back and forth as she stopped and started while trying to corner the dog.

She'd always been athletic, had always had a lithe body he had never tired of running his hands over.

Great. Now he was getting hard thinking about Loretta, and that was the last thing that should be happening. He needed to keep his mind firmly on work and not on a naked Loretta.

Damn, it had been a long time since he'd seen her naked. It had been after his high school graduation. There'd been a huge party out at the McCormack ranch, since Reid McCormack had graduated the same year. Deacon and Loretta had snuck off to somewhere private and had gotten busy in one of the barns. He could still remember sliding the straps of her sundress down her arms, the silken feel of her skin as he pressed his lips to her neck, the way she had moved on top of him, the way she had looked with the sliver of moonlight streaming over her from the hayloft window . . .

"So, how's it going in here?"

He jerked his attention back to the here and now to see Loretta leaning against the doorway. She had put a goddamn sundress on, and the past mixed with the present in a very uncomfortable way.

He cleared his throat. "Moving along fine. I should have this window in shortly."

"Great. So, I don't know about you, but I'm hungry. I was going to grill a flank steak for dinner and serve it with a strawberry salad. I also made some killer salsa and guacamole. And of course there's beer. You interested?"

He was interested, all right, but not in food. Not when her hair was damp and wavy and he wanted to lick the droplet of water that was sliding down her collarbone, headed for that valley between her breasts. "Uh, sure. Thanks."

"Great. I'll get things started."

When she disappeared, he exhaled.

God, he was in so much trouble. Because keeping his
hands off Loretta was getting harder and harder every time
he was around her. And the last thing he wanted was to
start up something he already knew was destined to end
badly.

He'd been down that road with her once before. He didn't
intend to travel there again.

Chapter 12

WHILE DEACON FINISHED up in Hazel's room, Loretta dried her hair, then grilled the flank steak and made the strawberry and almond salad. She saw Deacon pass by with his tools and head out the front door, so she assumed he was wrapping up. When he came back in, he headed into the hall bathroom, and when he came out, he made his way into the kitchen.

"All done?"

"Yeah. That new window is secure now. No air or water leaks. I also put in a new frame, because the one surrounding the window was shot. The paint around the frame has to dry. I'll come back Monday to rehang the drapes."

"That's not necessary. I can handle that part."

"I don't mind taking care of it."

"Okay. Thanks so much, Deacon. I know Hazel will be thrilled."

"Not a big deal."

"Ready to eat? And how about that beer?"

"Yes to both."

Loretta brought out beer and a pitcher of sangria she'd

made earlier. Deacon helped her take all the food to the table.

"This is really nice of you, Loretta, but I'm beginning to feel like you think you need to feed me every time I'm here."

She laughed. "No. It's just a total coincidence that I'm hungry every time you're here."

"That makes me feel a little better."

"Good. Then let's eat—without guilt."

She had sliced the flank steak into thin portions, making it easy to layer it onto the plate or even add it to the salad, depending upon preference. It was a nice, lean meal, and the guac and salsa were a spicy bonus.

Deacon took a large bite of the steak and salad, followed by a long swallow of beer.

"So tell me, did you fix this healthy food for me, or for yourself?"

"I fix what I like to eat. I try to fix healthy food for Hazel. Tom was a big fan of burgers or fatty steaks at every meal, and I'm trying to change her diet."

He nodded. "I like a cheeseburger and a good juicy steak, but you know what they say."

"I have a weakness for those, too, but yeah, everything in moderation. I want my daughter growing up making decent choices. Or at least knowing what a vegetable is."

He laughed. "That's really all you can do. And this is great food, Loretta. Thanks."

"You're welcome. I'm looking forward to having fresh vegetables to add to the table."

"You're off to a strong start. You've already got a few tomatoes growing."

"Having a nice sunny spot on the back porch helped, but they really needed to get into the ground. Hazel wanted me to wait until she got back so she could help me plant them, but I just couldn't wait any longer to start the garden."

"Hopefully she's having some fun with her dad."

Loretta let out a snort.

"So . . . she's not having fun?"

"I doubt it. He doesn't see her on his regular visitation

schedule. He only asked for her because he wanted her to come with him on a campaign run. He's using her for photo ops."

"Ouch. I'm sorry."

"So am I. Hazel loves her dad and wants nothing more than to spend time with him. Real time, not him parading her around campaign stops. I keep hoping he'll change, that he'll realize what a treasure of a daughter he has before it's too late."

Deacon laid down his fork. "And?"

She shook her head. "It hasn't happened yet, and I'm giving up hope that it will. His new wife is pregnant, and she's from a political family, so his head is already into building the new dynasty, but he knows the optics mean he can't ignore Hazel. He has to periodically show her off to prove he's a good father. But I already know he won't spend a second of non-camera time with her while she's there. When they're not in front of the camera, she'll be with the nanny, and she'll come home disappointed as usual."

Deacon grimaced. "What a dick. I'm sorry he's not a better father."

She scooped a chip into the guacamole. "So am I. Hazel deserves better."

"She's an awesome kid, Loretta. You've done an amazing job raising her."

She lifted her gaze to Deacon. "Thank you. At least she's happier here than she was in Dallas. More relaxed. And God knows she's having a lot more fun."

"I'm glad to hear that." He resumed eating, and Loretta felt bad for burdening him with her woes about Tom.

"Was it rough on her? On you?"

She frowned. "Was what rough?"

"The marriage."

Her stomach twinged as the question bordered on very dangerous territory. "You don't want to hear about that, Deacon."

He took a swallow of beer and laid the bottle on the table. "I asked, didn't I?"

He had, but she wondered why. "In the beginning, it was fine. I had this dream of what I thought it could be, that I had made a decent match. And Tom was a good enough guy to start out. I admit I wasn't madly, passionately in love with him. Not like—"

She stopped herself before she admitted something she shouldn't, something that would hurt him.

"Not like what?"

"Not like I felt I should have been. My parents pushed the relationship, and so did his. I guess I fell in line. When he asked me to marry him, I said yes because it seemed only natural, part of the plan."

His gaze showed interest, not condemnation. God knew he had the right to condemn her for the choices she had made.

"But not your plan."

She let out a short laugh. "I'm not sure I ever got to be part of the plan. It was more of a whirlwind. I wanted to get my degree, and that's where my head was. We got married midway through college, and after that we lived in an apartment on campus until after graduation. Tom went to law school, and I taught school for a couple of years until Hazel was born. After that I took some time off to care for her. When he got his law degree, we moved to Dallas, and he went to work at one of the big firms and started moving up the ladder pretty quickly. I wanted to go back to teaching, but he wanted me to be there for him for all his important social events. He was going places in a hurry, and he needed constant reassurance and a wife who intended to stand by him."

"So you had to give up your career for his."

"I didn't see it at the time because I was trying to be supportive, but yes. I had Hazel, and she was such a joy to be around. The last few years, though, were tough. Tom was running for city council and working nonstop. He was barely at home. I tried to talk to him about spending time with Hazel, at least, and he told me his career was the most important thing in his life and Hazel and I were just going to have to understand that."

"What the hell? She's a child. How was she supposed to understand the lack of her dad's presence in her life?"

"Exactly. But Tom is all about Tom and his needs and wants. No one else matters. It took me a long time to figure it out, but once I came to the conclusion that no amount of reasoning with him was going to change who he was, I got out. And he had already chosen wife number two anyway. Someone with better political connections. So Hazel and I leaving him didn't hurt him any, other than the family money he had to part with in the settlement."

"I hope you gouged him in the divorce. The Simmons family has plenty of money."

She shrugged. "I don't care about him or his money. I made sure there was money put aside for Hazel for her future and for college, and enough to set us up here with a decent house and land. I wanted to start my own business, because I'd given years of my life to seeing to his needs. And of course he pays child support until Hazel is eighteen. I made sure Hazel was provided for no matter what. Other than that, I just wanted out."

"I'm sorry it was such a shit show for you."

"Which was my fault and no one else's. I'm just sorry Hazel is paying for it. She's such an amazing kid."

"Other than having an ass for a father, I don't think she's suffering, because she has a great mom."

She blinked back tears. "You have to stop doing that, Deacon."

"Stop what?"

"Telling me how great I am. You know what I did to you. What I did to us. You should hate me."

He pushed his plate to the side and picked up his beer. He studied her, and she waited for the condemnation. God knows she deserved it—had prepared herself for whatever wrath he was going to rain down on her.

"For a long time after you broke up with me, I did hate you. I was hurt, and then I was pissed. What we had together was really good, and I couldn't understand how your feelings could turn on a dime like that."

She started to say something, but held it back. Nothing she could say could explain what she'd done. And it was Deacon's time to talk.

"But you can't hold on to shit like that. It'll eat you alive. I let go of that anger a long time ago, Loretta. You need to let go of it, too."

She was surprised that he wasn't yelling at her and, in fact, was telling her to let go of any negative feelings she might have over her marriage to Tom. "I'm not angry."

"No, but you're dwelling on it."

She had dwelled on it for a lot of years. And she couldn't believe he hadn't taken this opportunity to really let her have it for what she'd done to him. "I don't think you just let go of something monumental that happened in your past—erase it as if it didn't happen."

"I didn't say I erased it. I know it happened. Every time I look at you I remember. Every time I'm around you I'm reminded of what you and I had together. Of what might have been. But if I let bitterness enter the equation, it'll choke me until I can't breathe. And what good will that do me? I can't change what happened. Neither can you. We were both kids back then. Kids don't always make the best choices. You did what you thought was right at the time. Maybe if we'd stayed together it would have been great. And maybe we wouldn't have ended up staying together. Who the hell knows, Loretta? I don't. Do you?"

She stared at him, shocked by this philosophical, almost Zen-like being he had become. "I guess not. I had always pictured you as being so profoundly pissed at me. It was one of the things that gave me pause before I moved back here."

His lips curved. "You expected me and my posse to hunt you down as soon as you came back to town so I could hit you with twelve years of suppressed anger and resentment?"

"Okay, when you put it like that it sounds kind of ridiculous. But I didn't know how you felt. The last thing I remember was you being really angry."

He dragged his fingers through his hair. "I *was* really angry. When I was nineteen. That was a long time ago. And when you came back to town? I'll freely admit I wasn't all that happy to see you. Out of sight, out of mind and all that, ya know? I'd made peace with the decision you'd made. Years had passed. I was over you. And then you came back. I can't say I was all that thrilled to see you again."

"I understand that." Though Deacon had never truly left her mind. She'd thought about him a lot after the divorce, especially when she'd made the decision to return to Hope. She knew it wasn't going to be a happy reunion between them, and maybe she had expected him to hunt her down and yell at her.

That hadn't happened, of course, and she'd felt ridiculous for even thinking it would.

"I just wanted you to know how sorry I am for the callous way I treated you."

He shrugged. "Like I said, it's in the past, and I'm over it."

Somehow she didn't think those wounds were as healed as he wanted her to believe. Leaving him had hurt her. Thinking about how she'd done it still hurt her. She remembered the look on his face when she'd told him it was over, that she didn't love him anymore. The pain and confusion in his eyes was something she'd never forget. And walking away from him was the hardest thing she'd ever done.

That first year at college in Texas, all she'd thought about was Deacon. She'd developed a relationship with Tom, but a part of her was still threaded to Deacon. She was homesick and miserable and her heart ached for the boy she'd loved and hurt. How could she explain to him that she had broken up with him out of a sense of duty? That made her seem so weak.

Seem? Ha. She *had* been weak back then. A docile, obedient daughter who'd done what she was told. Who'd become a docile, obedient wife. At least for a time.

"I've changed."

He looked up from his plate. "Into what?"

"A different person than I was before."

"I liked who you were before just fine."

She shook her head. "Back then I let other people make

decisions for me. I'm not making excuses for what I did to you, Deacon, or laying the blame on anyone but myself. But I didn't have the strength—or maybe it's the backbone—back then to stand up for what I wanted. It took a lot of years for me to find that inner strength, to learn to say no to being manipulated into doing things that aren't good for me or for my daughter."

He nodded. "Glad you were able to do that. It'll help Hazel become a strong woman someday."

She smiled. "Hazel was born with an inner strength. I don't think that'll ever change. She's very self-assured and knows exactly what she wants—and what she doesn't want. I don't think anyone will be able to deter her."

"I can see that about her. She got you to bring Otis home, didn't she?"

She looked over to where Otis was asleep on the living room floor, then smiled. "Yes, she did."

"I don't think you'll ever have to worry about Hazel."

She dragged in a deep breath, then let it out. "I think there will be a million times when I'll worry about Hazel. Like this week while she's with her dad."

"Nothing you can do about her relationship with him. You'll just have to let her work that out on her own."

"I know. It just makes me sad for her."

"All you can do is be there for her and let her know that you love her. She'll eventually grow up and realize her dad is a dick."

The thought of it filled her with an aching sadness. "Yes, she will."

He stood and grabbed his plate and his empty bottle of beer. "You can't fix everything, Loretta. Sometimes you just have to let things happen."

She got up and followed him into the kitchen, allowing his words to soak in. Was that what she'd been trying to do? Fix the past, and maybe the present, too?

If so, Deacon was right. She needed to stop it. It was counterproductive.

They did the dishes together in companionable silence. She was thinking about their dinner conversation. Maybe he was, too. She wondered if he was upset that she'd brought up the past. A lot of guys buried it and never wanted it dug up again.

She'd brought it up, but they hadn't really talked about it in depth. It had been more like circling around the topic without hitting it head-on. They'd ended up talking more about her marriage than their past. And maybe that had been Deacon's way of avoiding such a touchy topic between them.

One of the things she'd worked on as part of building her strength and self-esteem was not shying away from uncomfortable subjects. Maybe tonight wasn't the night to push Deacon any further on the past, but at some point, they'd have to talk it over further. Because he might say he'd put it aside, but she knew better.

The past wasn't dead and buried between them just yet.

"Another beer?" she asked after she put away the last pot.

"Sure."

She pulled a beer out of the fridge, then poured herself a refill of sangria.

"Let's sit out back," she said. "Otis can run off some energy that way."

They stepped outside. There wasn't much out here yet, but she had ideas for it. Right now it was just a slab of cement, a few chairs and a table. But the landscape back here just called for something better.

She settled in and watched as Otis grabbed on to one of the thick rope toys they'd bought for him. He shook his head back and forth, growling with ferocious fervor, occasionally bonking himself on the head with the rope as he let go of it.

She laughed.

"He's entertaining, isn't he?" Deacon said.

"Never a dull moment with that dog."

Deacon looked around. "This is a great backyard. Tall trees, lots of shade, and a good view of your land. You can see the chicken coop and the garden from here."

"Yes, it was one of the selling points for me. I'm going to put in border flowers around the perimeter as soon as I build . . . *something* here, besides this plain old cement slab."

"What you need is a deck," Deacon said.

"You think so? I was just thinking about expanding the concrete."

Deacon stood, beer in hand, and wandered the edge of her small patio. "Nah. You have such a nice view. You need a deck to increase your sight line. Great place to host barbecues, and you have the space for it." He walked it out, extending the space by about twenty feet. "You could take it this far and not have to dig up any of your foliage—and still have plenty of space for stairs leading down the side to the vegetable garden."

She thought about it, how a deck would look filled with patio furniture and a nice new grill instead of the second-hand charcoaler she'd picked up in the interim. She could put a couple of cushioned chaises on a deck, along with a table, a few more chairs, and some pretty throw pillows. She could really make it an entertaining space for herself and her friends.

"I like that idea. What would it take to make that happen?"

He arched a brow. "You want me to build a deck for you?"

"Of course, you're plenty busy enough. It would be your company, if you have the time and you don't feel this job is too small or not worth your time."

"It's not too small."

"Then you could do up a design and a bid for it, right?"

"Reid could draw up a design. I'd want to bring him out here to look over the space. Then we'd give you a bid."

She nodded. "Okay, why don't you do that."

"I'll take care of it."

"Thanks." She could already see it in her mind. Pretty, finished, and colorful. She wanted to furniture shop right now. "How long would it take to build?"

He thought about it for a minute. "About four weeks."

"Not too bad at all." She looked around, envisioning how

it would all look, then shifted her attention to Deacon. "Is this how you drum up new business? You visit people's houses and dream up additions, then make us lust after them until we fork over all our money to make it happen?"

He laughed. "Yeah, that's me. Forcing the fine people of Hope to renovate against their will."

"I thought so."

Otis reappeared from the back of the property, dragging a large tree limb. He dropped it at Deacon's feet.

Deacon looked at Otis. "Dude. That is not a fetching stick. Try again."

Otis cocked his head to the side, his tongue lolling to the side of his mouth, his tail wagging rapidly. He stared at the tree branch, then at Deacon.

"Nope." Deacon motioned with his hand toward the woods. "Go find a smaller stick."

Otis ran off.

"Do you think he has any idea what you just said?"

"Doubtful. But to him, it's a game."

"I just hope he doesn't come back with an entire tree this time."

Deacon laughed, then got up. "Maybe I better go wander in that direction to see what he's up to."

She stood. "I'll go with you."

"You sure you're up for a walk in the woods? It's getting dark."

"I've got a flashlight."

He nodded. "They draw bugs, but it's good to carry one with you just in case. Got any bug repellent?"

"Yes."

"Get that, too. There'll be mosquitos and chiggers in the woods. Maybe ticks."

She nodded. "I'll be right back."

She dashed into the house and went into the kitchen. She had stored the flashlight in one of the bottom drawers, and she found the bug repellent under the sink.

"I only have lotion," she said as she pushed through the screen door.

He grimaced. "It's not girly stuff, is it?"

"What the hell does that mean?"

"I mean it's not perfumey."

"No. It's unscented."

"Good."

He took the bug repellent bottle and lotioned up his arms, then his neck.

"Your turn," he said, pouring some onto his hands. He crouched down to apply it to her exposed legs.

Well. This was unexpected. He rubbed it in along her calves and ankles. She tried not to be affected by the feel of his hands smoothing along her legs, but this was the first time he'd touched her in years, and she was definitely affected.

"Hold out your arms."

She did, and she felt the cool lotion on her shoulders. She was grateful she'd chosen a repellent that didn't have an unpleasant scent, and even more thrilled that Deacon decided he'd rub the repellent into her arms as well.

She could hear him breathing; could feel the warmth of his breath against her neck as he stepped behind her to apply the repellent onto her shoulders. She shuddered as he moved to the other arm.

"Lift your hair."

She had a ponytail holder on her wrist, so she grabbed it and wound her hair up into a messy half ponytail, half bun high on top of her head.

"How do women learn to do that so fast?" he asked, his voice going low and gruff as he massaged some of the lotion into her neck.

"Years of experience."

"It's cute."

She liked that he thought anything about her was cute. "Thanks."

"Let's go figure out what Otis is doing in the woods."

"Okay."

He held the flashlight and led the way as they walked toward the woods. She'd explored a bit back here when she first looked at the place, but since then hadn't bothered. She knew it was deeply wooded with thick trees and bushes. She had wandered in far enough before she purchased the property to realize two things: One, she wouldn't have to mow it, and two, one of these days she'd have to clear it out—but not right away.

"Be careful."

She looked down where Deacon was pointing to see two fallen limbs crisscrossed over each other. Because of the denseness of the trees in here and how fast they were losing daylight, it was getting hard to see. If Deacon hadn't pointed them out she probably would have tripped over them.

About twenty feet farther, there was a fallen tree trunk. "Someone needs to come in here with a Bobcat and clear this land."

"Yeah, it's on my list for someday. Just not right away."

They climbed over the trunk. Deacon took her hand to assist her, but didn't let go of it as they moved deeper into the woodland.

"Dammit."

"What's wrong?" she asked.

He pushed his way past several thin, low-hanging branches. "Should have brought my machete. You need a path in here, at least."

"It's easier to see in the daylight."

"Won't help you much if you need to go hunting for your dog. Or a missing goat or chicken. Or something that comes onto your land at night that you need to shoot."

She stopped, and since he was holding her hand, he stopped as well. "Uh, something I need to shoot?"

"Yeah. Like a possum or a skunk or something coming after your chickens."

"I am not going to shoot an unarmed critter."

He laughed. "City girl."

"I know how to use firearms. I am not a city girl."

"Is that right?"

"Yes. But I'm not keeping guns in the house. Not with Hazel around."

Deacon went quiet for a few seconds, then said, "She should learn to handle firearms safely."

Loretta opened her mouth to object, but Deacon held up his hand. "You're not living in the big city anymore, Loretta, and Hazel's going to be around other kids whose parents might have shotguns and rifles and handguns just lying around. Education about them is much better than ignorance."

"You're right about that. I'll have to teach her to shoot. And all about gun safety."

Something else to add to her list of things to educate her daughter about. Living on a farm in a small town was often a lot different than living in a condo in the city. And she needed to remember that.

Loretta heard barking. "He's up this way."

Deacon took her hand again and led the way. It was pitch-dark now, and thickening clouds obscured the moon, making it even harder for them to maneuver their way through the heavy bushes and brambles. Deacon still hadn't turned the flashlight on. No doubt to keep the bugs away.

"Can't we just whistle for him?"

"We could, but I'd like to know what he's barking at."

They finally made their way through the woods. "We've hit the fence line," Deacon said.

There was Otis, head tilted back, barking at a cat that was sitting on the other side of the fence. Otis was jumping up and down trying to get at the cat, who sat completely calm as he observed Otis.

"That cat is mocking Otis," Loretta said.

"Of course he is. He knows damn well Otis isn't going to jump that fence or he'd have already done it. So he knows he's safe. Now he's just egging him on."

Loretta sighed. "Well, at least Otis is getting plenty of exercise."

Deacon let out a short whistle, and Otis whipped his head around in attention.

"Let's go home, boy."

And just like that, the dog was at Deacon's side, as if the two of them had some kind of psychic bond.

They wound their way back through the woods and to

the house, where Otis completely emptied his water bowl in about ten seconds, then went over to Loretta and drooled all over her shoes.

Deacon shook his head and went to get the water hose so he could refill the water bowl.

"You have him on a flea and tick medication, right?"

She nodded. "One of the first things I did when we got him, because of the woods on the property."

Otis had already started drinking again as soon as Deacon began to refill the bowl.

"Worked up a thirst on your hunt tonight, didn't you?" Deacon asked, then leaned over to scratch Otis's ears.

"Another beer?" she asked.

"No, I'm good. But I could use something cold to drink."

"Let's go inside where it's cooler. Come on, Otis."

Otis followed them as they went inside. He went right to the cold tiles in the kitchen, turned in a circle, dropped to his stomach and laid his head on his paws, and went right to sleep.

Loretta moved around him to get to the refrigerator and poured two glasses of iced tea.

"Will this keep you awake?" she asked as she handed one to him.

"Not much keeps me awake after a hard day of work."

"I'm sorry. If you're tired—"

He laughed. "Loretta, it's barely dark outside. I don't go to bed at nine o'clock."

"Okay. I didn't want to keep you if there was someplace you needed to be. Or if you were tired, or if you had, like . . . a date or something."

He gave her a look she could only fathom as direct and interested. "No date. No place else I need to be. You trying to get rid of me?"

"No. It's actually kind of lonely here without Hazel's constant noise. Maybe I'm trying to keep you here awhile longer to stave off that incessant quiet."

"Then I'll stay awhile longer."

She had to admit she was grateful for that. While she

loved the remoteness of the farm, the past day or so without Hazel had made her realize just how remote it really was out here.

And then Otis started to snore.

"Not *too* quiet, though, is it?"

She laughed. "He doesn't sleep in my room."

"That's probably a good thing."

"You want to watch TV or something?" she asked.

"Sure."

They went into the living room and sat on the sofa. She grabbed the remote and handed it to him. He handed it back to her.

"You find something. I'll be good with whatever you choose."

That was unusual. Tom had always chosen the shows. It was only when he was late coming home or out of town that she got to watch what she wanted.

"You sure about that?"

"Yeah. Why wouldn't I be?"

She shrugged and randomly searched, deciding on a West Coast baseball game.

He looked over at her. "Oh, now you're just placating me."

She laughed. "I like baseball, and you know that."

"That's right. You do like baseball."

"I came to all your games. I played on the softball team."

"I remember. I went to your games, too."

Her lips lifted. "Yes, you did. You used to throw peanut shells at me through the dugout cage."

"Until your dad would yell at me that I was messing with your concentration. Your dad yelled at me about a lot of things."

"Which never bothered you."

"Not really. I was only interested in what you thought."

Her lips curved. "I liked the attention from you. You always showed up."

He smiled. "You were good at first base. I was better."

She had kicked off her tennis shoes. She flipped around on the sofa and pulled her feet up. "That's bullshit. I was much better—more limber, and therefore had a longer reach. You know damn well I was better."

Deacon liked seeing Loretta riled up instead of watching every word she said, as if one wrong word would send him into some kind of rage or make him leave.

"Think so?"

"I know so."

"Still have your glove?"

"They'll bury me in it."

He liked that answer. "I play in a summer league. Maybe you can put that arm where your mouth is."

She gaped at him. "I haven't played in years."

He shrugged. "Then maybe you're not as good as you thought."

"Screw that. I'm in. When's the next game?"

"We practice Sunday afternoons, which would be tomorrow if you can make it. Games are on Tuesday nights. Usually someone is out of town or can't make it because they're working late, so we always need bodies. They'd love to have you—if you're any good, of course."

"Oh, I'm still good. I might be rusty, but I'm still good. And I can make practice tomorrow."

He liked seeing that fire ignite within her. He didn't exactly know everything that had gone down in her marriage, but he'd bet Tom hadn't built up Loretta's self-esteem any. He'd also bet he hadn't played with her, either, hadn't explored Loretta's fun side. Deacon had always known Loretta as someone who enjoyed life to the fullest. Maybe she'd lost some of that over the years.

He intended to rectify that. Not only in mother, but in daughter, too. He settled in to watch the game on TV, satisfied he was off to a strong start by inviting her to join the softball league.

"Dammit, Deacon."

He pulled his attention away from the game. "What?"

"Well, now it's dark outside, and I want to go dig out my glove and warm up my arm."

He laughed. "I can come over before practice tomorrow and warm you up."

"Would you? I don't want to walk in there completely cold."

"Sure."

"Thanks. Remember when we'd play catch over at your dad's farm?"

"Yes. And you always told me I stood too far away and you couldn't throw that far."

She cocked her head to the side. "You have a faulty memory. It doesn't matter how far away you stand. I can throw the ball just fine."

"I guess we'll see tomorrow, won't we, champ?"

"I guess we will."

He could see her mind working as she tapped her fingers on her knees while she watched the game. Finally, she stood. "I need a glass of wine. You want something?"

"A water would be good, thanks."

"I'll be right back."

He watched her walk off, and he could tell by the way she moved she was riled up now. Good. He enjoyed seeing her a little edgy.

She came back with a full glass of wine in her hand.

"Sure it wouldn't have been better to bring the whole bottle and a straw?"

"Oh, aren't you the funny one?"

"Usually."

She took a long, deep swallow of wine, then another. Deacon felt the tension in her body as she sat next to him. Maybe something was on her mind and she needed the wine to get it out. He watched the game, figuring she'd either say it or not.

When she emptied the glass, she set it on the table, then shifted to face him. "You should kiss me now."

Not much shocked Deacon, but that had. "What?"

"Kiss me, Deacon. It's not like you don't know how."

"I know how, Loretta. I'm just trying to figure out why you'd ask me."

"Because there's this tension between us, and we should eliminate it."

He studied her, squinting a little so he could zero in on her features. "Are you drunk?"

"Of course not. Not yet, anyway."

His gaze scanned her empty glass. "That's why you poured the oversized glass. A courage drink."

"Maybe a little."

He stood, then took her by the hands and hauled her off the sofa. "Loretta, if you wanted me to kiss you, all you had to do was ask."

He slid his hand around her neck to cup her nape, drew her mouth to his, and paused.

Her gaze lifted, and he remembered what it was like to be drawn in by her sweet amber eyes.

"You sure you want this?"

She pressed her palms against his chest. "Oh yes."

Yeah. So did he.

He pressed his mouth against hers.

Chapter 13

LORETTA DIDN'T KNOW what possessed her to ask Deacon to kiss her. Some form of temporary insanity, probably. But right now his mouth was on hers, hard and insistent, and felt nothing like it had back in high school.

This was the way a man kissed a woman. This was the way a woman wanted to be kissed. It was a dizzying, toe-curling kind of kiss that let a woman know the man who kissed her knew exactly what he was doing, exactly what he wanted.

She knew what she wanted, too—a lot more of this. She grabbed his shirt and hauled him closer, rewarded with his groan. He snatched her hair in his fist and deepened the kiss, exploring her mouth with his tongue until she thought she might collapse from the overwhelming sensations. His work-hardened body pressed against hers, and his free hand drifted down her back to cup her butt, drawing her close to his erection.

Maybe it was the wine that made her feel light-headed, but she was more inclined to believe it was Deacon. He'd always had an effect on her, even as a boy.

Deacon wasn't a boy any longer. He was all man, and

she wanted him. And when he pulled his lips from hers, his mouth traveling down her throat, she let out a whimper.

Yes. She needed to get Deacon into her bedroom. Her nipples were tight points of need, and every part of her quivered.

"Deacon."

He responded with an "Mmmm" as he continued to kiss his way along her collarbone and shoulder.

"Let's move this to the bedroom," she said.

He stilled for a second, then lifted his head and stared at her. The desire in his eyes only served to drive hers higher.

He kissed her again, wrapping his arm around her, but this time, the kiss was gentler, as if his own internal storm had calmed. Hers, on the other hand, still raged out of control. And when he pulled his mouth from hers and took a step back, she knew they weren't headed toward her bedroom.

"Loretta, I think we need to take a step back."

She inhaled a deep breath. "Okay. I understand. You don't want this."

He moved into her and took her hand, pressing it against his hard cock. "I think you know better than that. I want this. I want you. But I don't think tonight is the right time."

She lifted her gaze to his, saw the dark passion flaring in his eyes. "Why not tonight?"

"Because I think a part of you is alone for the first time in a long time, and you don't want to be. And maybe I don't want to be just a bed warmer for you tonight."

She opened her mouth to object, then closed it. Was that what she was doing? She had to admit, with Hazel gone, and her all alone at the farm, the loneliness had hit her harder than she'd expected. Was she reaching out to Deacon—enticing him into her bed—for all the wrong reasons? "You might be right about that. At least partially."

"Secondly, I just don't think I'm ready yet."

She wondered what he wasn't ready for. Ready to forgive her? To open up old wounds? Or to start up something with her that might end badly again? They'd already covered some deep topics tonight, and she was suddenly too tired to delve any further.

She nodded. "That's fair. I'll walk you out."

Otis had gotten up and wandered toward her, so he went outside with them. Deacon walked beside her, but he didn't hold her hand or touch her in any way. She had to admit that left her feeling cold and a bit out of sorts.

But when he got to his truck, he turned to her. "I can come by tomorrow at noon and we can throw the ball around a bit before softball practice."

At least he wasn't pushing her away. "That sounds good. And thanks again for the work you did and for helping me out today."

"Anytime." He started to get in the truck, then stopped, turned and came toward her, drew her against him, and kissed her—a long, deep kiss that fired her up all over again. When he let her go, he said, "You know, it's taking all the willpower I have to walk away from you tonight."

That, at least, made her feel a lot better. "I'm not the one who stopped."

His expression was filled with regret, with passion. "Yeah, I know. I'll remember that when I have to take a cold shower because my dick's hard and I can't sleep."

Her lips curved. "Good night, Deacon."

"Night, Loretta."

She watched him drive away, then sighed once he was out of sight.

Deacon had been right about one thing—she *was* lonely. But had that been the catalyst for the kiss? She didn't think so. She'd been lonely before and hadn't once asked some guy to make out with her. No, this had come from something else—a need she had for Deacon.

She didn't quite know what to do about that.

Otis did his business, then came back to sit at her side. She rubbed his head.

"Ready to go to bed, buddy?"

He looked up at her with total adoration in his eyes.

"Yeah, I miss Hazel, too. Come on, doofus. You can sleep in my room tonight. But don't eat my shoes."

She held the door open for Otis, then walked inside and shut the door.

Chapter 14

LORETTA WAS THRILLED to discover she hadn't lost her prowess at first base.

Not all of it, anyway. After all, she wasn't seventeen anymore, and she couldn't do a split reaching for a ball. But she could still field and throw, and she could still hit. After she'd worked the kinks out at Sunday's practice, she'd gone into tonight's game with renewed confidence in her abilities. So far, she was two for three with a single, a double, and two runs batted in.

Right now she stood on second base and Zach Powers was up to bat. Deacon had scored on the double she'd just hit, so he was in the dugout, hollering and cheering for Zach to drive her home.

Her focus was on Jane, who was currently coaching third base. Jane would let her know whether to stay at second base on a hit or run for home. And when Zach singled to far right field, she took off. When she reached third base, Jane signaled for her to keep going.

She did, noticing the catcher crouching down to make a play at home plate. She dug in and ran for all she was worth, making a headfirst slide at the plate. She felt the tag, but heard the ump holler out, "Safe!"

Elated that she had scored, she leaped up and was surrounded by her teammates and friends.

"That was one hell of a hit," Reid said, patting her on the back as she made her way back to the dugout.

"And an even better run and slide into home," Sam said. "Though judging from your knees and arms, you're going to pay for that slide."

She looked over her skinned elbows and knees and grinned. "Totally worth it."

They ended up winning the game by six runs, and everyone decided to head over to Bash's bar for drinks and food to celebrate their victory. Deacon had picked her up after he got off work and brought her to the field, so he asked if she wanted to go to the bar to celebrate.

She definitely wanted to go.

"I haven't felt this good in a long time," she said as they got out of his truck and headed toward the door.

"Is that right?"

"Yes. A little exercise, some camaraderie. I'm really starting to feel part of Hope again."

He stopped. "You've been here awhile now, Loretta. Are you saying you haven't felt that before?"

She shrugged. "A lot of my friends from high school moved away. Some didn't take too kindly to my return. I've lost a lot of friendships. It's nice to have made new ones."

He frowned. "Why would people be upset about you coming back?"

She moved forward, so he came with her. "Let's just say not everyone is as friendly, as welcoming, or as forgiving as the new friends I've made."

Deacon had no idea what to make of what Loretta had said. But since she had walked inside the bar, he didn't get a chance to ask her.

He made a mental note to do that later.

Loretta looked around the bar. Jane and Will and Chelsea had already set up a big table for them. Jillian Reynolds walked in behind her. Her face was smudged with dirt from the ball field.

"Hey, Jillian," Loretta said. "You have dirt on your face."

Jillian gave her a crooked smile. "I do? I guess I should go wash that off. I'll be right back."

Jillian skirted to the restroom and Loretta headed to the table.

"I'm sorry you couldn't play with us tonight, Chelsea," Loretta said as she pulled up a chair.

"Oh, I never play. Sports are not my thing. But Bash plays when he has a night off, which he didn't tonight, unfortunately. Good thing you were there, though. I was just filling him in on how good you were."

"Thank you. I appreciate that."

Sam and Reid came in just as they got their drinks, followed by Emma and Luke and Des and Logan. Molly and Carter arrived shortly thereafter.

"Now it's a party," Sam said, lifting her glass of wine. "To Loretta, a great addition to the Blasters softball team."

"I'll drink to that," Emma said, "even if it is just iced tea."

"Between the nursing mothers and the pregnant women around here, there aren't too many of us drinking alcohol these days," Loretta said.

"Oh, we'll more than make up for what the rest of them aren't drinking," Molly said with a wink.

"Agreed. I'm single, not pregnant, and more than willing to have a drink or two," Jillian said.

Loretta noticed Jane was drinking a glass of water, but she'd heard no official announcement yet, so she wasn't about to ask. Instead, she decided to order an appetizer or two for the table in celebration.

"I'll be right back," she said, then got up and headed to the bar.

"What can I do for you, slugger?" Bash asked.

She laughed. "How about an order of some nachos and potato skins?"

"I'll have those right up for you."

"Great. Thanks, Bash." She turned and had started to push away from the bar when three women surrounded her.

"I cannot believe you had the nerve to come back here."

Loretta blinked, then sighed as she recognized them. Tanya Baker, Piper Swift, and Krista Friedman had been her three best friends in high school. They had been on the cheerleading squad together. They'd done everything together. They had been the fearsome foursome. Inseparable.

But now it was like they were mortal enemies, and for no other reason than Loretta had divorced Tom Simmons. And that, in their eyes, made Loretta a social pariah. This wasn't her first run-in with them since she'd returned to Hope. They'd made their feelings about her clear when she'd first opened the bookstore. She'd hoped it would be the last time she saw them.

Apparently not.

"If you'll excuse me, ladies." Loretta started to make her way around Tanya, but Tanya stepped in her path.

"If you think we're just going to allow you to have friends in this town, to laugh and have fun and have a business of your own as if you didn't totally break the code, then you are wrong."

The code? The code? She fought back a laugh. "Oh my God. That was in high school, Tanya. Twelve years ago."

"And it still holds true today. You stay true to your man. You fly the colors of fidelity and honor."

What a joke. If only they knew what a cheating bastard Tom had been. Of course, to women like this, that code only worked one way. Social status was everything, and sometimes sacrifices had to be made. Like sacrificing their own dignity and self-respect.

"Get out of my way."

Piper moved in and got in Loretta's face. "You will not succeed in this town. We will ruin you."

She knew better than to engage them, but frankly, they were pissing her off.

"You three should get a life. And maybe grow up in the process."

"Oh, we have lives," Krista said. "Rich, successful ones. So did you, once, until you threw it away by divorcing a fine man like Tom Simmons. What were you thinking, Loretta? And taking up with the likes of that group over there?"

Krista motioned her head over to the table where her friends were sitting.

She couldn't believe these women in front of her were once her friends. Maybe she'd been blind back then.

Okay, no *maybe* about it. There were a lot of things she'd been blind to all those years ago. But cold reality had hit her now. "Those people are my friends, and if you insult them, you insult me. Not that you have any understanding about what true friendship is like. Now get the hell out of my way before I knock you on your ass."

Piper huffed. "You wouldn't dare."

"Try me."

Josie had come up behind her. "What's going on here?"

"Mind your own business, shortcakes," Krista said.

Josie moved up to Loretta's side, and there was fury on her face. "What are you, twelve?" She looked over at Loretta. "Are these girls bothering you?"

Loretta noticed Josie's use of the term *girls*, instead of *women*. "They're definitely bothering me."

Piper looked over at Josie with disdain. "Sugar, go back to your table before someone hurts you."

"Oh, it's on. I'm not wearing earrings and I left my purse in the car, so I'll be happy to kick the shit out of all three of you right here."

"Is there a problem here?"

Deacon had shown up. So had the rest of her friends. All of them. The women as well as the men.

Krista sniffed. "Yes, there's a problem, all right. But you can have her."

Just as Loretta had suspected, as soon as they were outnumbered, their bravado evaporated. All three women pivoted and walked away.

"What the hell was that about?" Chelsea asked.

"Snobby bitches that I used to call my friends. But it's over now, especially since Josie threatened to beat them up."

"A little firecracker, aren't you?" Zach asked, grinning at Josie.

"I got into my share of scrapes when I was younger. And those women looked like a gust of wind wouldn't hold them up. I could have taken all three of them."

Deacon laughed. "You threatened to do just that."

Josie was obviously still pissed as she glared after the women who had walked back over to their table. "Loretta would have backed me up, wouldn't you, honey?"

"You bet."

Chelsea shot the group a vicious look as they headed back to the table. "Do we need to finish them off? Because I might be pregnant, but I think I could still take all three of them down."

Bash came over from around the bar and put his arm around Chelsea's shoulder. "Calm down and keep your heels on, tiger. I don't think we're going to have a girl brawl in the bar."

"We're not?" Zach asked. "Because I was about to lay money on our women. Those three looked like they wouldn't dare do anything to break a nail."

Loretta grinned. "Thanks for coming to my defense, all of you."

"Want me to ask them to leave?" Bash asked. "Because I don't have a problem booting their designer-clad asses out the door."

Loretta laughed. "No, I don't think that'll be necessary."

Frankly, Loretta was surprised they had even shown up in Bash's bar. Krista, Piper, and Tanya tended to congregate at the Hope Country Club, and she wouldn't have thought they would ever stray to a bar like this. She got the idea this had been an ambush.

And a failed one, at that.

Chelsea was still shooting visual daggers at the women. "Well now you have to tell us all about them, because I love gossip."

They took their seats, and Deacon sat next to her. "I'm going to want to talk to you about this later."

She nodded, and smiled when he laid his arm around the back of her chair, as if he half expected the three women to come at her from behind.

She felt protected by her crew, and she couldn't be happier about that.

She noticed the women had gotten up and walked out. Just as she'd surmised, they hadn't come to the No Hope At All bar to hang out. They'd come here specifically to confront her.

"Well, the air is so much more breathable now that cloyingly designer-perfumed group has left," Sam said with a wrinkle of her nose. "Who wants a drink refill?"

While Sam and Reid went to refill their drinks, Josie turned to Loretta. "So what is it with those women?"

Loretta grabbed her beer and leaned back in her chair. "We were best friends growing up and all through high school. We were cheerleaders together. We did everything together. But I guess their idea of friendship and mine don't exactly mesh. After I divorced my ex and moved back to Hope, they stopped in the bookstore to . . . express their extreme disappointment in my life choices."

Josie frowned. "What? Why?"

"Because they're all about social status. My ex is running for Congress. His family is well connected here in Hope."

"They're the country club type," Chelsea said.

"Oh." Jillian wrinkled her nose. "So money and status mean more than lifelong friendship."

She stared down at her bottle of beer. "I suppose so."

"Well, screw that," Molly said. "You don't need them when you have us. We may not be fancy money people, but we'll always have your back."

Emma nodded. "Absolutely. Consider us your lifelong friends now."

Sam held up her glass of wine. "Let's drink to true friendship, where we don't give a damn about money or social status or how fancy your shoes are."

Chelsea nodded. "This is true. I have fancy shoes, and you all love me anyway."

Loretta laughed. "I really like you people."

"Give us time, Loretta," Chelsea said. "You'll fall madly in love with us."

She glanced over at Deacon, who gave her an enigmatic look.

Loretta gave the entire table a grateful smile. "Oh, I have no doubt of that."

Chapter 15

THEY ATE THE appetizers Loretta had ordered, then ended up staying for dinner. She had a wonderful grilled chicken salad, which tasted so good when washed down with the iced tea she'd switched to for the meal. After the hard work of the game, she was hungry.

Deacon had a grilled chicken salad along with iced tea as well.

"Good?" she asked.

"Yeah. I was hungry."

"Me, too. Running bases works up an appetite. I'd forgotten how many calories I burn playing softball."

He grinned. "You'll be sore tomorrow."

"No doubt."

"Did you have fun tonight?"

She grinned. "I had a great time."

Everyone decided to leave after dinner since it was a work night for most of them. She hugged all of them for coming to her defense.

"You're all my heroes. Thank you. And thanks for letting me play on the team."

"You're one of us, now, Loretta," Sam said. "Though you were one of us before the softball game anyway."

Sam hugged Josie, too. "And you're one of us, too. Especially since you were ready to brawl. Here you are, all sweet and unassuming, and you were the first one threatening to kick the shit out of those women."

Josie laughed. "Well, no one threatens my friends."

"Obviously we need to keep an eye on you, Josie," Bash said, slinging an arm around her. "You're a good ally to have."

"And a good friend," Molly said. "So you might as well get used to all of us."

Josie looked taken aback, but she smiled anyway. "I really appreciate it. It's good to feel like one of the group."

Loretta pulled Josie aside. "Thanks again for having my back."

"You're welcome."

"Oh, and that book you ordered is in, if you want to stop by after school tomorrow."

"Thanks for letting me know. And I will."

Loretta and Deacon left the bar and got in Deacon's truck. He headed north toward her ranch.

"That was an eventful night."

She laughed. "I'll say."

"Did you enjoy the softball game?"

"Very much."

"So you're in as far as playing again?"

"I'd love to. And I know Hazel would enjoy coming along to watch once she gets back home."

"I'll bet she will."

When they got to her place, she opened the front door. Otis dashed outside and attacked them with love.

"Otis, down," she said, not that it did any good. She turned to Deacon. "Want to come inside for some iced tea or water?"

"Sure."

She was happy he didn't hesitate. He followed her inside, and she dropped her things at the front door, then headed into the kitchen to pour the iced tea. She turned, and Deacon was right behind her.

"Oh. I didn't know you were there."

"Sit."

He was frowning. And then she frowned. "I am not Otis."

"But you are limping. Sit so I can take a look at you."

She laughed. "I'm fine. I can do that later."

"Your elbows are scraped from that slide at home plate. I want to see your knees."

She cocked her head to the side. "Oooh, you want to see my knees? Is that some secret man code for 'I want to get you naked'?"

"No. If I want to get you naked, Loretta, you'll know it. Now sit."

Damn. She was hot and bothered and more than prepared to strip naked, as long as Deacon would be willing to do the same.

"Where's your first aid stuff?"

She lifted her gaze to his. "My what?"

"First aid stuff, Loretta."

"Oh. Under the hall bathroom sink."

"Okay. I'll be right back."

She watched him walk away, her focus on his butt. He'd always had a great behind. It was even better now. She'd loved to put her hands on him. She remembered grabbing handfuls of his butt when he was on top of her and—

"Okay, I think I've got everything I need," he said as he came out of the bathroom.

She watched him walk toward her.

Yeah, he definitely had everything *she* needed.

But he wasn't looking at her in the way she wanted him to. Dammit. She supposed she should get the fantasies of sex with Deacon out of her head. Or should she? Even watching him walk toward her was a turn-on. He moved like a predator stalking its prey.

Maybe she wanted to be the prey. Then again, maybe she was just reading things into his walk that weren't there.

But as he sauntered toward her, his hips swaying in a

dangerous fashion, she didn't think she was imagining the sexy. The man was just downright hot, no doubt about it.

And when he knelt down in front of her, she felt a little faint. Which was ridiculous, of course. This was Deacon, a man she'd known almost half her life. Nothing new here, right?

Except everything with him seemed new and different now, from the way they reacted around each other to the way he looked at her. And maybe the way she behaved around him, too, as if this was the first time . . .

"Ouch." She snapped her attention from fantasyland to downright pain.

"You bled. Your pants are stuck to the dried blood on your knees. This is going to hurt. I'm sorry."

He said the words calmly, as if he'd been the one to cause her knees to be scraped.

"It's okay."

He lifted his gaze to hers. "You ready?"

She was so ready—not for the first aid, but for him. She nodded. "Yes."

He gently raised her capri pants over her knees, taking his time pulling the fabric away from her skin.

This wasn't the first time she'd scraped her knees. She'd done it plenty in high school, so she knew the drill.

"Not so bad," he said as he looked her over, then wet a cloth and wiped the blood away.

It stung, but she held still and let Deacon wash off the blood and dirt. After he cleaned the wounds with soap, water, and hydrogen peroxide, he applied antibiotic ointment and bandaged them.

"These pants are toast, ya know."

She shrugged. "I'll get over it."

"Good. And you should slip out of them so they don't rub against these bandages. Here, let me help you up so you can take them off."

Now things were getting interesting. He held out his hand and helped her stand. Which she could do just fine, but hey, she wasn't going to give up the opportunity for touching.

"You do the top part," he said, "and I'll hold the bottom part out so they don't pull the bandages away, okay?"

"Works for me." She shrugged out of the pants, grateful she'd done laundry last night and had decent underwear on today. The pink silk ones, too. She hoped Deacon would notice.

She grabbed on to the waistband of her capris and tugged over her hips.

Deacon stilled.

"Something wrong?" she asked.

He cleared his throat. "Uh, no."

His voice had gone deeper. Her lips curved, because she caught him staring at her underwear.

Awesome.

She shimmied the pants down around her knees, then Deacon carefully drew them over the bandages and down around her ankles. She stepped out of them.

He looked up at her. "That's better."

Definitely better for her. "Thanks."

"Now sit again and we'll do your arms."

There were other parts of her she'd like him to "do," but she kept her thoughts to herself. For the moment, anyway.

He sat next to her on the bench. "You should probably pull your shirt off so we don't have to drag it over the wounds."

"Oh, sure, get me half naked while you're fully clothed." She drew her shirt off and set it aside.

Oh, yeah, buddy, matching pink satin demi bra. Ogle away.

And he did. Though he didn't look happy about it.

He leveled a most frustrated look at her. "Loretta, this isn't a game of Strip First Aid."

Her lips quivered into a half smile. "It's not? Because that sounds like all kinds of fun. We each take a piece of clothing off, and then take turns bandaging each other's . . . parts."

She took a quick glance at one of his parts, which was semierect.

Most definitely all kinds of fun.

"No."

She looked up at him. "Oh, come on. Where's your sense of adventure, Deacon?"

"I'm trying to help you out here."

"Yes, but you know, Deacon, there are other ways you could help me out."

He laid the clean washcloth in his lap, right over his erection. Too late—she'd already seen it.

"Loretta."

"Deacon." She made a point of giving him a look that told him in all raw honesty how she felt.

He dipped the washcloth in the water. "You're going to have to stop doing that."

"Stop doing what?"

He gently washed the scrapes on her elbows. "You know what. Looking at me like you want to eat me alive. Like you're hungry."

That was one way of putting it. "I want you, Deacon. I think I made that clear the other night."

He dragged in a breath, rinsed out the washcloth, and put the bowl on the kitchen table. He opened the bottle of hydrogen peroxide to clean her scrapes. "Stop it."

She let out a soft laugh. "I can't stop it." She tipped his chin with her fingers and lifted his face so he was looking at her, not at her elbows. "You don't really want me to stop, do you?"

"What I want is to bandage your elbows."

She took the bandages from his hands and laid those on the table, too. "You know what? My elbows are fine. I heal really fast."

She slid onto his lap and wrapped an arm around his shoulder. "What I'd really like is for you to kiss me."

"We've been over this."

"Yes, we have, but now I'm trying again and hoping you'll say yes." She teased her fingers into the silky softness of his hair.

The look he gave her was dark and dangerous, like a man

cocked and loaded with desire and just about near the edge of restraint.

Just where she wanted him.

"You know, Loretta, if you play with fire you just might get burned."

She shuddered as she drew in a breath. "Then burn it all down, Deacon, and take me with you."

When his mouth captured hers, it was like a strike of lightning. Hot, fast, and burning her up from the inside out.

Chapter 16

DEACON COULDN'T GET close enough to Loretta, couldn't breathe her in deeply enough, couldn't touch her skin enough to satisfy his need for her.

He'd tried like hell to stay away, to keep what was between them cordial and friendly and strictly hands-off.

Until she'd teased and flirted with him and asked him to kiss her—twice. And now she was in his lap in that wicked pink underwear, writhing against him and making his dick so hard he could bury himself inside of her right here on the kitchen table.

He had a lot of restraint, but she wasn't being coy about this at all, and he'd lost all his control when he'd had his head about an inch from Loretta's promised land. Her scent was the sweetest honey, and all he wanted to do was remove her underwear and spend the rest of the night making her cry out his name over and over again.

She whimpered against his mouth and wriggled against him and he swore if he didn't get inside of her tonight his balls would end up twisted together from the torment.

Because all he'd been doing lately was thinking about what it would be like to get Loretta naked.

Now she was halfway there, and there was no stopping him. He lifted her in his arms and carried her toward the bedroom. As they passed by a sleeping Otis, the dog's left ear twitched, but that was all the acknowledgment he gave them as they headed toward Loretta's bedroom.

Good. Because he was more than ready to shuck his clothes and the wisps of pink satin Loretta had on. Damn, that lingerie was driving him crazy.

He'd tried for so long not to imagine her underwear, or the softness of her skin, or the way she always smelled like strawberries, because doing so would only lead to walks down memory lane and trouble. He'd had enough trouble where Loretta was concerned, and if he was honest with himself right now, he shouldn't be taking her to bed.

But he wanted her, she wanted him, and he'd think about the repercussions of what they were doing later.

He deposited her on her bed, and she stretched out in the center of it, all long limbs and pink satin underwear.

His dick throbbed.

He tugged at his shirt and pulled it over his head, tossing it onto a bench at the end of the bed. "You know, when we were younger, we only did this what? Maybe a dozen times, despite the fact we were together all through high school."

She lifted up on her elbows, watching him intently. "Yes, and I remember all of them."

He kicked off his shoes and reached down to pull off his socks, then undid the buckle of his jeans. "Back then, there weren't a lot of places we could be alone. I always felt rushed with you."

Her gaze was hot as it traveled his body. He dropped his pants, then shrugged out of his underwear. He heard her sharp intake of breath, and oh, man, did that feel good.

"Yes, I remember that, too." She rose up on her knees and unhooked her bra, letting the straps slide down her arms. She took the bra and added it to his pile of clothes.

Damn, she was beautiful. More beautiful now than she'd been when she was a teenager. Her body had matured, was curvier than it had been back then. Her breasts were fuller, and he reached out to trace them with his fingertips, letting his fingers linger near her left breast to feel the mad thumping of her heart.

Yeah, he knew that feeling. This was intense—not really the first time for them, but for some reason it felt like the first time all over again.

He came over to the edge of the bed, and so did Loretta.

"But tonight we're alone, and I don't think Otis is going to interrupt us, so I intend to take all damn night long making love to you, Loretta. You okay with that?"

She wound her fingers in his hair. "Totally okay with that, Deacon. I have a box of condoms I bought on impulse the other day, so I think we're good."

He wrapped an arm around her. "Okay, but first I need to tell you that—"

She put her fingers up to his lips. "Deacon. I'm an adult now. I don't need romance. I know what this is, and what it isn't. We've been through that together already and, considering our history, I don't think we want to go there again. I know I don't. We're two consenting adults having sex. Nothing more. Okay?"

He nodded. He hadn't wanted to bring it up, but he also didn't want to mislead Loretta or in any way want her to think this was something other than just sex between them. "Okay."

She rubbed her breasts against his chest. "Good. Now that all the talking is out of the way, let's get to the fun stuff. Because I'm going to warn you, Deacon. It's been a really long time for me. There's been a severe drought. The well has been dry. Do you need me to spout any more euphemisms, or do you get the idea?"

"I more than get the idea." He pushed her down onto the bed, then gently pulled her legs to the edge. She might play all tough like nothing bothered or hurt her, but he'd slid to home plate before, and those kinds of scrapes stung, so he intended to be careful with her tonight.

Plus, it wasn't her knees or elbows he wanted to concentrate on. He leaned over her, feasting his eyes on the most beautiful woman he'd ever known, the one who'd captured his heart all those years ago.

Her dark hair was spread across the pillow like silken feathers, her eyes staring up at him with naked desire. He leaned in and brushed his lips across hers.

Like velvet. He pushed in farther, slipping his tongue in between her teeth. Her tongue met his and it was a slow tangle. He wanted to make sure he didn't hurry this along, because, oh, man, could he ever hurry this along.

But he wanted to touch Loretta's body, taste her, do all the things they'd never had the time for when they were younger.

Just . . . explore.

He smoothed his hand down her neck, pausing at her pulse, which was running fast. Yeah, so was his. Then he swept his fingers over her collarbone, her breasts, teasing the tips of her nipples with his fingertips. He pulled his mouth from hers so he could follow the map of his fingers, taking her nipple between his lips.

She was so soft there, until he flicked the nipple with his tongue. The bud hardened and she moaned, arching against him. His name floated on a whisper from her lips.

Everything between them when they had been teenagers had been a rush of getting at each other, needing to be together, grabbing the condom and barely taking their clothes off. There'd been dark spaces and a lot of heavy breathing. It had been damn good—for him. But it had been rushed because of circumstances and locations. He wasn't even sure he'd ever made her come. He'd been such a teenage boy back then, all about giving it to her, about being with her. He'd been so eager. Yeah, it had been good between them, but he wasn't certain she'd actually been getting off.

Tonight, he'd make sure she came. More than once.

He pulled her nipple from his mouth and gently blew on it, watching it pucker.

"Deacon."

"Yeah."

She didn't say anything else, so he wasn't sure if she was making a request or a plea. Either way, he was determined to slow it down tonight, to make sure this was all about Loretta's pleasure. He could wait for his.

He realized he enjoyed watching the way she moved under his hand, the way she writhed when he kissed her rib cage and moved his mouth lower. When he reached her underwear and tugged it with his teeth, she lifted up to watch him drag it down over one hip. He felt her body shudder when he pressed a kiss to the spot he had bared, breathing in the sultry scent of her.

He drew her panties down her legs and cast them aside, then parted her, draping her thighs over his shoulders.

This was where he hadn't been delicate with her before, where he'd paid her lip service in a hurry, in a perfunctory way. Now he owed her a nice slow ride to heaven.

He put his mouth on her sex and pressed his tongue against her, listening to her cry out as he tasted her.

Oh yeah. This was going to be good for him, too.

NIRVANA. HELL. HEAVEN. Torture. Sweet. Wicked. All those words mixed in Loretta's head as Deacon had his way with her body with his mouth and tongue.

She was certain she'd had great pleasure before. Deacon had been the one to give it to her. But not like this. Not this slow languorous ride to orgasm, where she felt like she had leisurely slid into the sweetest vat of her favorite gooey icing, only to have the perfect tongue lick every bit of it off of her.

She lifted up to watch Deacon, his head of thick hair buried between her legs as he gave her the most incredible pleasure she'd felt in far too long. It was delicious and decadent, and she rolled into a shockingly perfect climax that left her breathless. She panted through the waves of that bliss and lifted against him, unashamed in her quest for more. And oh, he gave it to her, taking her from one spiraling height to another. When she crested and cried out again, she let her body fall listlessly to the mattress.

Deacon's face loomed above her. She grinned and swept her fingers over his jaw. "You always were good at that. But now you're better."

He laughed. "Was I? I was just thinking that back when we were younger, we were always in such a hurry I might have made it all about me."

"Mmm. You have a faulty memory. It wasn't all about you."

His lips curved. "Good to know. How about a drink of water?"

"Sounds awesome. You're going to go get it, right? Because I think my bones have turned to liquid."

"Yeah, I'll go get it."

He left the room and she lay there, unable to move, feeling more satisfied than she'd felt in a very long time. And yet, she still wanted more. She couldn't remember ever being this insatiable.

She rolled over and laid her head on the pillow. No, she'd never been insatiable with her ex. She'd like to think she loved him, but it hadn't been a passionate kind of thing. More friendly, at least in the beginning. With Deacon, however . . .

Lord, they'd always had passion. As teenagers, they couldn't seem to keep their hands to themselves. Or their mouths, or any other part of their bodies. Getting alone time together had proved difficult, but they'd always found a way.

And now . . .

Wow. The man had learned a few new tricks, and she wasn't going to think about who he'd learned them with, because it was none of her business. She was just going to be grateful to be the recipient of all that skill.

She flipped over again onto her back and shoved the pillow against the headboard just in time to see Deacon walking back into her bedroom.

Now there was a sight. A naked man bearing two large

glasses of ice water. Though it wasn't the water she was staring at. It was the man—his amazing body and one rather prominent erection.

She smiled. "Thinking about me while you were in the kitchen?"

He handed her a glass, looked down at his cock, and grinned. "Let's just say you make some amazing noises when you come, and that was on my mind when I was fixing the ice water."

She took a couple of sips, then set her glass down and smiled. "I do, huh?"

"Yeah, you do." Deacon downed half his water in a couple of gulps, then set the glass on the nightstand. "I'd be happy to help you make those sounds again."

She climbed onto his lap and laid her hands on his chest. "Maybe I'd like to hear you make some sounds."

"I have no doubt you could do that. But tonight is about you."

"No, Deacon. Tonight is about us." She teased her fingers around his nipples and watched his breathing change, felt his cock grow harder underneath her.

If he thought she was just going to lie there and let him pleasure her all night, he was wrong. Because she would take so much pleasure in touching him as she was doing now, running her fingers over his broad chest and wide shoulders, letting her nails map a trail down his biceps and forearms, appreciating the incredible muscle that made up his body.

As a teen, he'd been strong and athletic. As a man, he was powerful, his body showing how hard he worked for a living.

She traced her fingertip over a two-inch scar on his forearm. "What happened here?"

"Sliced it with a saw blade."

She cringed. "Ouch."

"Yeah. That was when I was an apprentice, before I learned to be extra careful. Fortunately, it went into the meaty part of my arm, so I just ended up with stitches."

"Looks like you got quite a few stitches. Bet that hurt."

He shrugged. "I was fine."

Always a tough guy. "You could get a tattoo around it that says *Ouch*."

He cocked a half grin. "I don't think so."

Instead, he teased his fingers above her sex. "You could get a tattoo here that says *Tasty*. Or maybe *Lick Here*."

"Oh my God, Deacon." She laughed. "No."

He slipped his hand underneath her and teased her flesh with his fingers. "I could come up with a few more. How about *Sweet*? *Hot*? Or *Just About the Best Damn Thing Ever*?"

She shuddered at his words, trembling even more at the way he touched her, his fingers skimming over her body with an expertise that made her catch her breath. She leaned back, giving him access.

He'd always known her body better than anyone else. Not that there'd been anyone else other than her ex, but oh, Deacon had known how to get her hot and ready with his touch. And maybe the reason for that was the way she responded to him, the way she was in tune to his breathing and his sweetly coaxing words, because she was on the verge of another orgasm, undulating against his expert fingers.

And when she climaxed, she gave in to that sweet fall without hesitation as she quivered against the stroke of Deacon's questing fingers until she leaned forward, breathless and satiated.

He looked up at her with a satisfied smile on his face.

"That's not at all what I had planned," she said.

He quirked a brow. "It's not? Because I thought it went really well."

"I meant to pleasure you."

"I got a hell of a lot of pleasure out of it."

"You know what I mean." She took in a deep breath and let it out, trying to find her bearings after Deacon had tilted her world off its axis—again. "I meant to seduce you."

"Honey, you're doing one hell of a good job at that."

She reached over to the nightstand, opened the drawer,

and pulled out the box of condoms. "Let's see if I can do better."

He took the condom from her and unwrapped it, then spread it over his cock. "If you do much better than what you're already doing, Loretta, I could be in trouble."

She dug her nails into his chest. "Then let's start some trouble, Deacon."

He wrapped his arms around her, then flipped her over onto her back. "You are trouble."

He kissed her, his fingers diving into her hair to hold her head in place. There was something about the way he kissed that made her entire body go hot. He wasn't a demanding kisser, nor was he an impatient one. It was all about the way he moved his lips over hers, as if he had all the time in the world to pleasure her mouth, to tangle his tongue with hers, to tease and tempt her until she was writhing underneath him, her nipples hard points and her sex throbbing with need.

All because of his kiss. It had always been that way with him, a fast rush of incendiary desire, like a forest fire, an explosion of the most delicious heat. She had never been able to get enough of him.

Why on earth had she ever let this man go?

Because she'd been stupid. But she wasn't going to think about her lack of intelligence right now, because he had nudged her legs apart and pulled his mouth away, his gaze engaged with hers as he slowly entered her.

She reached up to run her hands along his shoulders, to feel the way his muscles contracted as he held himself above her.

"You feel good," he said as he seated himself within her. "I remember how this felt."

"Yes." She wrapped her legs around him and drew his head down for a kiss, needing that sensation of being fully joined with him. And this time, when he kissed her, she experienced the kind of emotion that pinged warning bells in her head.

Keep the emotion out of it. You can't go there. Not with Deacon.

She knew that. The logical side of her knew that. So instead, she concentrated on the delicious feel of his body moving over hers, the way his hands constantly snaked over her body as if he couldn't get enough of touching her. It was magical and sensual and brought her to new heights of awareness.

He rose up and smoothed his hands over her nipples, making her breath catch. There wasn't a part of her body he didn't touch while he continued to move in and out of her, occasionally taking her mouth in a breathtaking kiss. It was sensory overload in the best way, and as she climbed ever closer to orgasm, she was determined this time to take him with her.

She arched against him, rolling her hips at the same time. He groaned in response, deepening their kiss, sucking her tongue inside his mouth.

She came with a rush and a wild cry, and she grasped on to Deacon as a lifeline in this amazing maelstrom of sensations. He reached under her to grab her butt and lift her against him, and then he shuddered, the two of them rocking together in this wild ride.

When they both stilled, she was spent, and more than a little sweaty.

Deacon kissed her neck and mumbled something she couldn't quite decipher.

"What did you say?"

He lifted his head and she smiled. His hair was one hell of a mess.

"I said I need a shower now. And I sweated all over you."

She laughed. "I think I sweated all over you, too, so we both need a shower."

He hopped off the bed and then picked her up as well. They headed to the shower, and she turned the water on. She stepped in first, and Deacon followed. She ducked her head under the hot water, letting it rain over her, then moved out of the way so Deacon could do the same.

He poured some shampoo onto his hand. "Turn around."

She did and he rubbed the lather onto her hair, then massaged it in.

"Well, this is a first for us."

She had her eyes closed, but she smiled. "You know what? You're right. It wasn't like we had a lot of alone time to shower together. It was mostly fast sex and hurry-up-and get-dressed."

"Yeah. Rinse."

She rinsed, then applied conditioner and rinsed that off, too. She grabbed the liquid soap and put some on her hands, rubbing it onto Deacon's chest. "No time to linger. To play with each other." She dragged her palms down his chest, over his stomach, and circled his already hard cock.

"No. We never had time for this."

She saw the desire in his eyes. "Rinse."

He did, then he pushed her against the wall of the shower. "Plenty of time to play tonight."

He kissed her and swept his thumbs over her nipples. She gasped against his mouth.

"You wanna play, Loretta?" he asked.

"Yes."

His hand slipped between her legs, massaging the throbbing ache of desire that had built anew despite the number of orgasms he'd already given her tonight. With the warm water bearing down on them, it was like enjoying a waterfall, a sensual rain shower where she and Deacon played naked together.

"Too bad we don't have condoms in the shower or I'd already be inside of you."

She shuddered as he slipped a finger inside of her and rubbed her clit with the heel of his hand.

She reached for his cock and began to stroke it, needing him to feel the same pleasure she felt. "This will just have to do, then."

He let out a guttural groan, then increased his movements over her sex.

There was something so deliciously decadent about kissing and touching each other in the shower. His cock was hard and slippery wet, making it easy to stroke her hand over his steely erection. And what he was doing to her with his fingers and hand was criminally delicious, taking her ever closer to the edge.

When she burst, he went with her, both of them leaning against each other for support as they shuddered through their orgasms. Loretta held tight to Deacon while she rocked through an amazing climax that left her shaking and barely able to stand.

Deacon leaned his head against hers. "Good thing we're already in the shower, because you made me sweat again."

She laughed. "Ditto."

They did a quick rewash and rinse, then turned off the water and got out.

"Now we have to fix your bandages again," he said.

She looked down at her knees, where her wet bandages hung half off of her.

"You know, I'm feeling much better. And my wounds are very clean now."

He laughed. "Probably true."

She towel-dried her hair and combed it out while Deacon went to get dressed. Then she made her way to the bedroom and put on some clothes. Deacon had disappeared by then, so she went in search of him.

He wasn't in the kitchen, but the front door was open, so she stepped outside. He was standing out there wearing just his jeans and no shoes. The wind had picked up. It looked like a storm was blowing in.

God, the man looked magnificent standing there outlined against the cloud-filled night sky. His thick hair blew in the wind and his hands were on his hips as he surveyed the maelstrom of nature unfolding around him.

If she'd had her phone with her she probably would have snapped several shots of him.

She stepped up beside him. "Need some air?"

He turned, put his arm around her, and pulled her close. "Otis needed to go out."

"Oh."

"Storm's coming. There's lightning out to the southeast, and dark rain clouds are heading this direction."

"I noticed."

"I should head out. I've got an early day tomorrow. You probably do, too."

"I do." She was hoping he'd spend the night, something they'd never done together, but since he hadn't offered, she wouldn't ask him to.

He whistled, and Otis came running, a dark, lumbering shape emerging out of nowhere. He stopped in front of Deacon, who told him to sit. He did.

"Good boy. Come."

Otis followed them inside, then went and got a drink from his water bowl while Deacon found his shirt and put it on. He came over to Loretta, framed her face with his hands, and brushed his lips across hers. She breathed him in, her body responding naturally to the kiss.

Unfortunately, he pulled away when she wanted to lean in to him for more.

"I had a good time tonight," he said.

"Me, too."

"I'll see you tomorrow probably."

She nodded, already feeling the distance between them. "Sure."

She walked him outside. The lightning was getting closer. "Be careful driving home."

His lips curved as he climbed into his truck. "I will."

"Good night, Deacon."

"Night, Loretta."

She waited while he drove away, then she went inside, locked the door, and turned off the porch light.

Otis sat by her feet and cocked his head to the side.

She wasn't at all tired. She felt pent up and anxious, and she wished Deacon had stayed.

Then why didn't you ask him to?

Because it didn't seem like he wanted to stay, and she didn't want to face rejection from him.

Coward.

"Oh, shut up, inner voice."

Otis still stared at her, as if he wasn't sure whether she was talking to herself or to him.

"Not you, sweetheart. You're a good boy." She scratched his ears. "You want to sleep in my room tonight, don't you?"

His tail swept the living room floor.

"I'm glad someone loves me." She grinned and turned off the living room light, then headed down the hall, Otis right on her heels. Rain had already started to pelt the windows as she made her way into the bedroom. She loved the sound of rain.

Good. Maybe she'd be able to sleep tonight after all.

DEACON MADE HIS way into his house and threw his keys and wallet on the table. He shrugged out of his shoes, then headed to his bedroom to get out of his wet clothes. The rain had started to come down hard before he'd made it to the main road, and it hadn't let up since.

Good for Loretta's garden. It needed the rain.

He brushed his teeth, then got into bed, listening to the sound of the thunder, figuring it would lull him to sleep right away. It had been a long day, and a really long night.

But after about twenty minutes he found himself staring at the ceiling, wondering why the hell his body wasn't curved around a warm Loretta.

He'd hightailed it out of there in a hurry.

Why?

She'd seemed disappointed when he told her he had to leave, so she probably would have been okay with him staying the night. It had been him who'd wanted to leave.

He just wasn't ready for that level of commitment yet. Sex had come as a total surprise. Anything else would feel like they were having a relationship, and he'd gone down that road with Loretta once before and had gotten burned badly.

Different circumstances, yeah. But still, it wasn't like they were totally different people now.

Disgusted with himself for thinking at all, he got up and went to the kitchen and made himself a turkey sandwich, then turned on the TV and found an action movie to watch. He needed something to drown out the overworkings of his mind.

Unfortunately, this particular action movie had a romantic pairing, which inevitably led to a love scene. As he watched it, his thoughts drifted back to earlier, to being with Loretta.

They were totally different people now. Being with Loretta tonight had felt different. They weren't teenagers anymore.

But that was physical. It didn't mean circumstances wouldn't end up the same way. She was just getting out of a bad marriage. And he—

Well, he sure as hell didn't want to get involved with the woman who'd dumped him all those years ago.

Sex was one thing. Being stupid twice was something different.

He finished watching the movie and headed up to bed, realizing he'd figured out nothing other than he was going to be really damn tired tomorrow.

Chapter 17

LORETTA HAD BEEN crushed all day with customers, package arrivals, and phone calls. Great for business, but it frazzled her a bit. Fortunately, she had good organizational skills, so she had both Kendra and Camila tending checkout and phone calls while Loretta helped clients find what they needed. The new shipments were delivered to the back, and she'd deal with those after the store closed.

She was grateful for the crowds, and several women had brought their kids in with them, making her happy she'd set up an expansive children's book section. One of her first loves as a child had been reading, and between the library and the bookstore, her love of reading had been born. She hoped to foster that not only in Hazel but also in her clients' kids.

So far today, Otis had been on his best behavior, and he was a big hit with the kids, who loved playing with him in the store. Loretta, in turn, was grateful to have all the kids in the shop today to hang out and play with Otis so she didn't have to figure out what she was going to do to keep him occupied.

Kids and dogs—always a great combination. She missed Hazel, though, and was counting the number of days until she came home. She'd spoken to her this morning and she could tell her daughter wasn't happy. When she'd asked her what was wrong, Hazel had said nothing, but Loretta knew better. Once Hazel got home they'd sit down and have a long talk and Loretta would get the details about her week with her father, since Hazel wasn't opening up on the phone about it.

Loretta was working at the front desk when the door opened and Josie walked in. She smiled when she saw her.

"Hey, Josie. How was your day?"

"It went well. I'm acclimating to Hope High. Of course, I don't have the happiest of students, but that's what you get in summer session. No one wants to be there, teachers included."

Loretta laughed. "I'm sure that's true. But at least you're getting your feet wet that way and everything won't seem so foreign to you once the new school year starts in August."

"Yes. That's why I agreed to teach this summer. Plus, I'm getting to know some of the new teachers, and that's helpful, too. Starting over at a new school is always so daunting."

"Have you done it before?"

"Once. It's always hard."

"I'm sure it is. Have you got a few seconds to have an iced tea with me?"

"Of course."

Loretta left her assistants in charge at the front desk and with helping customers while she led Josie toward the back of the store, where she and her friends typically met for book club. She poured a couple of glasses of iced tea, then sat in one of the cushioned chairs. Josie took a seat as well. Loretta noticed Otis had curled up in a shady corner and was asleep. Good.

"Have you settled into your house yet?"

Josie nodded. "Just about. I'm still picking out furniture, so I'm not completely furnished yet, but I have a couch and a bed, and those are the most important things. The rest will come along."

Loretta laughed. "Yes, those are important. I assume you have kitchen appliances."

"Oh, yes. The house came with those. You should come over and see the place, maybe toss out some ideas, or at least help me choose a few things I'm debating on."

"I'd love to."

"Great. How about tonight?"

Loretta blinked, surprised by the immediate invitation. But she was game for it. "Tonight would be lovely. What time?"

"Say six thirty?"

"That sounds good. I might be a little late since I'll have to drop Otis off at the house first."

Josie waved her hand. "Oh, don't do that. I have a nice-sized yard. You should bring Otis with you."

"Okay, I'll do that. Thanks so much for the invitation. Is there anything else I can bring besides an oversized dog?"

"Honestly, I'm just happy to have the company. Being new in town means I don't know a lot of people."

"You know our group of people. And I'm kind of new all over again to Hope, so I know the feeling. We'll be newbies together, Josie."

Josie beamed a smile. "Thanks."

Loretta got up. "Let me get those books you ordered. I'll be right back."

As she walked away, Loretta felt an unexpected burst of positive energy surge through her, a happiness that made her smile.

It was good to make new friends. Hope was starting to feel like home again.

SWEAT DRIPPED DOWN Deacon's forehead and into his eyes. He swiped it away with the sleeve of his shirt and heaved the hammer above his head. Until the sweat poured again. Then it was lather, rinse, repeat.

Dammit. He'd be really happy once they got all the duct-work and the new air-conditioning system installed and running, because it was hotter than the fires of hell in this place today. Plus, he was working on the third floor, which made it even worse than hell—if that was possible.

He finally took a break and headed outside, grabbing the giant Thermos from his truck that he had loaded with ice water. He poured water into the oversized cup and guzzled it down in several swallows, then poured another and drank that one a little slower. At least there was a breeze outside, so he stood under the shade of the porch to let his body cool down.

He had about an hour's worth of work left, then he'd be done. The rest of the crew had already left for the day. He was putting in longer hours to make up for some of the delays they'd experienced over the past week. Material delivery had been late, and that had put them behind. Nothing unusual in his business, but it was always a pain in the ass. As the owner, you dealt with it, and sometimes that meant a longer day.

A longer day in the goddamn hotbox attic. He was tired and sweaty, and he wanted this day to be over.

He caught sight of Loretta coming out the front door, holding Otis by the leash. Deacon leaned against the porch post to watch as she balanced a bag and Otis's leash in one hand and used the keys in her other hand to lock the door.

She smiled at him as she turned.

"Oh, hi, Deacon. I didn't see you there." She walked across the porch toward him.

She looked pretty in her yellow and white sundress, which clung to her breasts and waist, then billowed out, stopping at her knees. She was wearing white flip-flops, and, hell, he even noticed her toes, which were painted a cute shade of pink. He was pretty sure that last night her toes had been painted purple. He wasn't sure why he remembered that. Maybe because she'd been naked and he'd noticed everything about her.

And she was the last person he wanted to see right now.

He was still confused about his feelings after their evening together. He knew he'd gotten too close to her, and he hadn't figured out what to do about that.

"Working late today?" she asked.

"Yeah."

"How come?"

"We're a little behind schedule, so I'm trying to get caught up."

She reached out and laid her hand on his forearm. "Sweaty work today, huh? And you have a cut on your arm."

He reacted to her touch, even though he tried not to. "Yeah, it's nothing."

He pulled his arm away. She noticed, and frowned. "Something wrong?"

"No. I'm just tired. And hot."

"I'm sorry. I'll bet you want nothing more than a nice shower and a cold drink."

"Soon as I'm done here."

"You know, I have dinner with Josie Barnes tonight, but after that I'm free. Do you want to come over later?"

He shook his head. "Only place I'm going tonight is home with takeout. Then I'm having a shower and a cold drink and bed."

She had definitely picked up on his mood. She gave him a short nod. "Okay. Well, I guess I'll see you later, then."

He knew he'd hurt her feelings, but in his current mood he wasn't fit company for anyone. And there was the matter of still not knowing how the hell he felt after last night. "I'll see you later, Loretta."

He watched her tug Otis by the leash and walk off. Even Otis gave him a dirty look.

Yeah, he'd acted shitty to Loretta. He felt shitty. Whatever. He turned and walked back inside, heading upstairs to hell.

Where he belonged.

Chapter 18

LORETTA WASN'T SURE what was on the menu tonight for dinner at Josie's place, but she stopped and bought two bottles of wine, one white and one red. She also stopped at Sam's flower shop for some help with a plant that she hoped would signal a welcome to Hope as well as a kind of house-warming gift. Sam put together a beautiful bonsai in a gorgeous antique lavender pot. Loretta loved it, and she hoped Josie would, too.

She stopped at home to drop off her things and to feed Otis and let him run for a bit. After she'd thrown the ball for him what seemed like a thousand times, he drank a gallon of water and she brought him inside. He'd been pretty good lately, but she still shut all the bedroom doors, gave him several of his chew toys and plenty of water, then told him to be good. Otis gave her a cocked head look, his tongue hanging out of his mouth. She hoped that was his signal of agreement.

She drove to Josie's house, which was located in the central part of Hope. It was near the high school, but also within walking distance of downtown. The neighborhood was filled with charming, well-maintained older homes. When she parked in the driveway, she smiled.

The house was a gray ranch frame with red shutters and a wide front porch. She could tell with a quick glance it had a large fenced backyard. She could see why Josie had chosen this place. It was stunning.

She gathered up her bag, headed up the steps to the front door, and rang the bell. Josie answered. She'd changed from her earlier outfit of black pants and a matching black short-sleeved silk blouse. Now she had on hip-hugger jeans with a wide brown leather belt, a bright red tank top, and a long silver chain.

She pushed open the screen door. "Come on in. I thought you were bringing Otis?"

"Oh, you know, he's fine at the farm. He has all his toys and food and water, and this way, I can sit back and relax and not have to worry about him eating parts of your house."

Josie laughed. "I wouldn't have worried about that, you know. I love animals."

But Loretta would have worried.

The inside of the house was magnificent, with curved archways, beautiful built-in shelves surrounding an amazing fireplace, and stunning wood floors. "This house is gorgeous, Josie."

Josie turned to her and smiled. "Thank you. I fell in love with it as soon as I saw it and knew I had to have it. I hadn't planned to buy right away. I was going to wait to settle in, but I was browsing online one day while I was here looking around, and the architecture was amazing. I just couldn't pass it up. Would you like some wine? I have Chianti, a chilled sauvignon blanc, and a pinot noir."

"I'd love the white. I also brought you a couple of bottles."

"Oh, that's so sweet of you. Thank you."

Loretta laid the box Sam had carefully packaged for her on the kitchen island. "And this is a housewarming gift for you."

Josie lifted her gaze to Loretta's. "Really? You didn't have to do that."

"I wanted you to feel welcome. Plus, you have a new house."

Josie opened the box, her eyes widening. "Oh, this is stunning. Did Sam make this?"

"She did."

"It's amazing. I love it so much." Josie came around the island and folded Loretta into her arms. "Thank you, Loretta."

Loretta experienced that warm friendship feeling again. "You're welcome."

"I know just where to put it, too. I have this idea for a table I want right under the living room window. This plant will look perfect on it."

"Now you have a reason to buy the table."

Josie laughed. "I do, don't I? Thanks for helping me make that decision. Now let's have a drink."

Josie poured the wine—the white for Loretta and the Chianti for herself.

"This kitchen is pretty awesome, too," Loretta said.

"Thanks. I was happy they modernized it. I'm all in for the retro look, but I didn't really want to cook in a 1950s kitchen."

Loretta laughed. "I don't blame you."

"Come on, we'll have a seat in the living room. It's a little warm today, so I grilled some salmon for dinner. We'll have salad with it. I cheated and bought bread at the store, since it's too hot to bake bread."

"That sounds amazing. And you bake your own bread?"

Josie sipped her wine and nodded. "Only in the cooler months. I'm not much for sweating in the house in the summer."

"I'm not, either. Then again, I'm not much of a baker."

"I love to bake. Mostly casseroles. And bread."

"You should get together with Megan Lee."

"She owns the bakery and coffee shop, right? I've yet to stop in."

"You have to. You two are meant to be friends."

Josie laughed. "I'll make a point of it, then."

Loretta took a sip of her wine. "This is excellent. And thank you for inviting me to dinner."

"You haven't tasted it yet."

"I'm sure it will be great. And I'm happy about the company."

"Me, too. It sucks being the new girl in town."

"So what made you decide on Hope?"

"Well, the job offer certainly helped," Josie said with a wry smile. "And being back in Oklahoma and near family is great."

"You said you have family in southern Oklahoma?"

"Yes. A few hours from here. But it's a very small town, and teaching positions there are hard to come by. When I saw this job opening, I jumped at the chance. I flew out here and interviewed and fell in love with Hope."

Loretta nodded. "It's a pretty great town. I missed small-town life when I was gone. Dallas is such a big city."

"So is Atlanta. I mean, there were great things about living there, but there's nothing like living in a welcoming community."

"Was that what drew you back? Small-town life?"

Josie stared at her wineglass. "That and the need to escape a hellish breakup."

There was some blunt honesty. "Oh. I'm really sorry."

"Thanks. So was I. I can't believe I was that stupid."

"You're preaching to the choir here, sister. I spent ten years being stupid. Only I married the guy."

Josie shook her head. "You'd think smart women wouldn't make dumb choices."

"I'm pretty sure it happens a lot. Then again, I don't know that we can accept all the blame. Sometimes men make promises in the beginning and turn out to be not who you thought they were at the end."

Josie nodded. "And sometimes they start out sweet and end up not so nice after a while."

Loretta frowned. "Did your ex hurt you?"

Josie sighed. "You know, sometimes it's just best to leave the past in the past." She lifted her gaze and smiled at Loretta. "I don't know about you, but I'm starving."

The one thing Loretta did know about was that sometimes the past was painful to talk about. And her friendship with Josie was new, so she'd give it some time. "I'm definitely hungry."

"Good. Let's eat."

Dinner was amazing. The salmon and salad tasted cool and refreshing, and the bread was perfect. They ate and chatted about Josie's job and Loretta's bookstore.

"I love that you get to do something you love," Josie said. "That must be a thrill for you."

"It really is. Coming home filled me with some trepidation, but so far it's been pretty good."

Josie buttered a slice of French bread. "Why trepidation?"

"Oh, you know. Things change when you're gone for a while. I found that out with my old friends, as you recall from the bar."

Josie nodded. "Bunch of hags. They can go screw themselves. You don't need friends like that."

Loretta laughed. "And this is why I'm glad you and I have become friends. Between the bookstore and Hazel and now the dog, I don't have a lot of time for a social life."

"I know how that is. I'm curious, though—when I drove by your bookstore the other day, I noticed you talking with the hot guy working on the building next door. Deacon, right? The one you have the past with?"

Loretta nodded. "Yes."

"And how's that going?"

"It's . . . complicated."

Josie stared at her for a few seconds, then said, "Hey, I get it. If you don't want to talk about it, feel free to tell me it's none of my business."

She hoped she hadn't offended Josie. The last thing she wanted was to lose a new friend. "Oh, no. That's not what

I meant at all. I meant it really is complicated. In fact, I could use an objective opinion."

"Oh. Okay. Well, then, hit me." Josie pushed her plate to the side and took a sip of her wine.

Though they weren't lifelong friends, there was something about Josie she really liked. Maybe it was her laid-back attitude. Maybe it was the fact that Josie had opened up to her some about her own past. Either way, she trusted her.

"We've been getting closer. He's spent time with Hazel, helping her to train Otis, and he's also been coming out to the farm to do some repairs."

"Convenient. So how do you feel about that?"

"I feel fine about him doing work on the farm. Hazel enjoys being around him, and he's good with Otis."

"But?"

"There's still chemistry between us."

"Like . . . lingering, Hey, I Think He's a Nice Guy kind of chemistry, or Oh, Hot Damn, It's Still Flaming Hot kind of chemistry?"

"Still flaming hot. So hot, in fact, that he and I had sex last night."

Josie's brows shot up. "Woo. Now that is hot. Good for you."

Loretta nodded. "I thought so. Hazel's in Texas with her dad this week, and it was nice for Deacon and me to spend some uninterrupted time together—something we didn't have much of when we were in high school."

"I'll bet. So you did the naked dance together all over your house all night long?"

Loretta laughed. "Something like that. Except he didn't spend the night."

"Did you want him to and he ran like hell? Or did you kick him out?"

"I definitely didn't kick him out. He left. And then today when I ran into him outside, he was . . . distant."

Josie took another swallow of wine, then sighed. "Men. I can't claim to understand the inner workings of their minds. But you did mention you were the one to stomp all over his feelings all those years ago, right?"

"Yes. I most certainly did that." Would she never be able to get past it? Not that she deserved to.

"So while the sex was fun and all, maybe he's not yet over the role you played as heartbreaker. And maybe he really liked hanging out with you last night and that caused him to take a giant step back. Because as much as we'd like to think guys don't have feelings, some of them actually do."

"You could be right about that." She leaned back in the chair and took a swallow of wine, contemplating what Josie had said. It made the most sense to her. They'd had a great time, and then he'd left. What guy would do that instead of staying for more fun and action? And then today he'd been moody and cranky and seemingly couldn't get away from her fast enough. Sure, some guys would go for sex and then distance, but she knew Deacon, and that wasn't like him at all.

So maybe he was backpedaling because he had felt something for her last night.

Which was both a good and a bad thing. And she definitely understood his reaction.

She looked over at Josie. "Thanks for your insight. I should probably give him some space, right?"

Josie shrugged. "It's not like I have a ton of experience dating nice guys. But I've had friends who have, those lucky bitches."

Loretta laughed.

"If it were me, and you think Deacon's worth it, then yes. I'd give him some space and let him come to you. Which I'm sure he will."

"That's some great advice, Josie. It seems to me you know men."

Josie let out a snort. "Honey, if I knew men at all I wouldn't have let the devil himself into my life. It's easy to be objective when you're not the one in the middle of the relationship."

"True. And I'm sorry someone hurt you. You certainly didn't deserve it."

"No, I didn't. But it's over and I've put it behind me. The only thing I'm interested in now is my career. And making new friends."

Loretta lifted her glass. "To a fresh start and new friends."

After dinner, they did the dishes and sat out on the front porch. Chelsea was out for a walk and ended up stopping by to sit with them.

"What's on the agenda tonight?" Chelsea asked.

"A great dinner," Loretta said, "followed by conversations about ex-boyfriends. Some good ones, some bad ones."

"Oooh, men," Chelsea said. "Other than shoes, they're my favorite topic."

"That's because you got one of the good ones," Loretta said.

Chelsea nodded. "True. But I dated plenty of bad ones. Like . . . years of bad ones."

"I'd say it was worth it to end up where you did," Josie said. "Married to the man of your dreams, expecting a baby, and living in a great house."

Chelsea rubbed her stomach. "It did turn out nearly perfectly, but honestly, Bash wasn't the man of my dreams. He wasn't even on my radar. Things just . . . happened."

"Isn't that the best way to fall in love?" Loretta asked.

Chelsea laughed. "Well, it wasn't in my grand plan, but it sure did work out well. I'm hoping the same will happen for both of you."

Josie shook her head. "I'm not looking to fall in love. I'd rather come down with a raging case of leprosy."

Loretta nodded. "Ditto."

Chelsea gave them both a knowing smile. "Trust me. It'll happen when you least expect it to. I know, because it landed on me like a ton of bricks."

"But you were looking for love at the time," Loretta said. "I'm not."

"Which doesn't mean love won't find you, honey," Chelsea said. "Just be open to it."

Was she open to it? She wasn't sure. The first time around had been an utter disaster. And she had Hazel to think about.

The last thing she wanted was to fail at love a second time and hurt her daughter in the process.

No. Playing around and having some fun was one thing. Falling in love?

That was off the table entirely.

Chapter 19

SATISFIED THAT THE duct system was in place and the air conditioning was finally going to be installed today, Deacon took what he thought was a well-deserved break for lunch. He ate his salad on the porch. After he finished, he made a few calls and was just about to go inside when he heard a commotion coming from Loretta's bookstore.

"I am so sorry, Janice. I don't know what got into him."

Loretta walked outside with Otis on a leash, followed by an older woman who didn't look happy.

"It's all right."

"It is not all right. You go on inside and Camila will fix you a nice glass of iced tea. I'm going to the flower shop right now to replace your bouquet."

Loretta caught sight of Deacon as she rounded the corner of her shop.

Loretta walked over to Deacon and thrust the leash at him. "Oh, good. Here, *you* deal with him."

"What did he do?"

"He ate Mrs. Harrison's bouquet of flowers. She set them on the counter to pay for her books, and he grabbed them.

Before I could stop him, he'd eaten the entire bouquet. I'm heading over to replace them. I'll be right back."

She shot a glare at Otis. "Very. Bad. Dog."

Otis hung his head and leaned into Deacon while Loretta stalked off.

Deacon resisted the urge to smile. Instead, he took a seat on the top step. He didn't even have to give the command for Otis to follow him. The dog had apparently grabbed a clue that he was in deep shit, since he was clinging to Deacon's side. He sat next to Deacon, who looked over at him and snorted as he realized the dog had pieces of daisies and other flower petals on his head and his nose. He swiped them away.

"Dude, what did you do?"

Otis just gave him a look that said, "Flowers are tasty."

"You know you made her really mad, right? You're gonna have to do better."

Otis responded by resting his head on Deacon's shoulder. Deacon shook his head.

"I'm not the one you need to impress. She's the one who buys your dog food and lets you sleep in the house at night. Eating a customer's flowers? Not cool, pal."

Otis raised a paw.

"Nope. Not playing with you right now. You're in the doghouse. Down, Otis."

With a heavy sigh, Otis slunk onto his belly and laid his head on his paws.

Otis had the sad, pitiful dog look down, but Deacon wasn't buying it, and sure as hell neither would Loretta. Deacon would have to figure something out that would bring her around, because she was downright pissed at the dog. She was probably pissed at him, too, since he'd been such a dick the day before. And when he saw her walking back up the street a short time later with an armful of flowers, he had an idea.

Otis lifted his head when he saw Loretta, his tail thumping back and forth.

She walked past him. "I'll be right back. And you," she said to Otis, "don't even look at me right now."

Otis whined.

"I told you, she's mad. We're both going to have to put some effort into making this up to her."

Otis looked at him and smiled a doggy smile. Deacon smiled back and scratched behind Otis's ears. Deacon was easy to impress. Loretta? Not so much.

A few minutes later Loretta came out with her client, who seemed placated and was smiling. And also had an armload of flowers and a bag of books.

"Thank you so much for being so understanding, Janice. I can assure you this will never happen again."

When the woman got in her car and left, Loretta heaved a frustrated sigh, then headed over to where Deacon and Otis were sitting on the porch steps. She stood on the sidewalk. "I'll take him now. Thanks for watching him."

"Looks to me like you replaced more than the one bouquet."

"I bought her extra flowers. And threw in three books for free. I was mortified."

"They were just flowers, Loretta."

"He ate her property." She glared at Otis. "Vandal."

Deacon snorted, and Loretta shot a scathing look at him. He raised his hands. "Okay, fine. He was very bad. I gave him a lecture."

"Oh, right. I'm sure that did a lot of good."

"Have you been using the sit and stay commands?"

She wrinkled her nose. "Well, we've had a lot of kids in the store, and they really love playing with him, so . . . I'm going to have to go with no to that."

"If you're not going to confine him to one area of the store or consistently make him stay, then you can't blame him for roaming freely. And when he screws up, then you have to accept partial responsibility for what he does."

She opened her mouth to object, then shut it again, folding her arms in front of her. She tapped her foot a few times, then finally nodded. "Fine," she said in a clipped tone. "May I have my dog now?"

"How about dinner tonight? You can leave the felon at home, and I'll take you out someplace nice to eat."

She looked like she might say no, but she finally answered. "Fine."

He resisted the urge to smile at her one-word answers. "Great. How about I pick you up about seven?"

"Fi— That would be great. Thank you for the invitation."

"You're welcome." He stood and walked down the steps, then handed her the leash. He gave Otis a firm look. "Behave."

Otis wagged his tail, then gazed lovingly up at Loretta.

It must have worked, because Loretta sighed. "Come on, doofus. We've got work to do."

Deacon grinned and headed back inside. He had work to do, too.

Chapter 20

IT HAD BEEN a crazy day. Between Otis eating her client's flowers and the bookstore being nonstop busy, Loretta was wiped out. What she really wanted to do was spend an hour in the tub with her favorite book and a glass of wine, then climb into a pair of shorts and watch television.

Unfortunately, she'd agreed to go out to dinner with Deacon tonight.

Not that going out was a bad thing, but she was tired and grumpy, and she probably wasn't going to be the best company tonight.

At least Otis had been on his best behavior since the "flower incident." He did his sit and stay like a champion and had been following her around the house ever since they'd arrived back home. On that front, at least, she had no complaints.

She took a shower and dried her hair, then tried to figure out what she was going to wear. Deacon had said a nice restaurant for dinner, so she pulled one of her favorite sundresses out of the closet. It was a colorful mix of blue, yellow, and red that always cheered her up. She could use some cheering up tonight. She ended up sliding into her bright yellow sandals and some silver jewelry, and by the time she finished up her makeup she felt better about the whole going-out thing.

She heard Otis bark near the front door, so she assumed it was Deacon.

When she opened the door, she was surprised to see Hazel standing there.

"Hey, honey. I thought you weren't coming home until Saturday."

Hazel shrugged. "Daddy said he had important things to do so he had to send me home."

Fighting back the rising ire over her ex-husband's total disregard for their daughter, she smiled and brought Hazel in for a hug. "I'm so happy to see you. I missed you so much."

"I missed you too, Mama."

The young au pair named Eunice, whom Tom had hired, stood at the doorstep. A black SUV sat in the driveway.

Eunice placed Hazel's bag just inside the door.

"Everything go okay, Eunice?"

The woman nodded. "Yes, ma'am. She ate very well, and slept well, too. Your daughter is a delight." Eunice looked down at Hazel. "We had fun, didn't we?"

Hazel managed a polite smile for Eunice. "Yeah. Thanks, Eunnie."

Tom might be useless, but at least he hired competent nannies. "Thank you so much, Eunice."

"You're very welcome."

After Eunice left, Loretta shut the door and followed Hazel, who stopped and dropped to the floor and loved all over Otis. Otis had been dancing around the door and around Hazel since Loretta had opened it. Now it was like Christmas, with both child and dog ecstatic.

At least Hazel's mood was improving quickly now that she was reunited with her dog.

Hazel tore her gaze away from her dog to look at Loretta. "How was Otis while I was gone?"

"He ate one of my clients' flowers."

Hazel giggled. "He did? Did you yell at him?"

"Yes."

"Awww." Hazel cradled Otis's face in her hands. "No flower eating, Otis."

Otis licked Hazel's face.

"Are you hungry, honey?" Loretta asked.

Hazel shook her head. "We had dinner on the plane."

"Okay."

While Hazel played with Otis on the floor, Loretta checked her phone, contemplating texting Deacon. But he should be on the way here, so she'd just tell him when he arrived. She looked over at Hazel. "Would you like to tell me about the trip?"

"I wanted to go camping, or maybe to the movies or to the zoo. Eunice took me to an amusement park one day, but only for a few hours, because I had to be with Daddy and Melissa for one of his campaign things." Hazel wrinkled her nose. "And I had to wear dresses."

Loretta wrinkled her nose, too. "I'm sorry, baby. I wish the trip had gone better for you."

Hazel sighed. "He never wants to do fun things like I want to do."

Loretta's heart ached for Hazel. She wished she could say no to Tom whenever he asked for Hazel for these campaign things, but he saw Hazel so little she couldn't.

When the doorbell rang, Hazel looked up. "Who's coming over?"

"Deacon. We were going out to dinner, but I'll tell him now that you're home we can't go."

Her eyes brightened immediately. "Deacon's here? I'll get the door."

Otis, of course, was already there, barking madly.

When Hazel opened the door, Deacon smiled broadly. "Hey, Hazel. I didn't expect to see you."

"I got home early."

"So I see. Welcome home, kid. We missed you around here." He pulled her in for a hug, and Loretta's heart tugged.

"Thanks. Did you know Otis ate one of Mama's clients' flowers?"

Deacon stepped in and shut the door behind him. "Yeah, I did. Did you know he got in a lot of trouble for that?"

"Yeah. What else did Otis do? Have you been here at the house working on stuff? Tell me everything."

Deacon glanced at Loretta, who gave him an apologetic look. "Sure. And I want you to tell me about your trip."

"Hazel, take your bags into your room first and unpack, and throw your dirty laundry into the hamper. Then you and Deacon can talk."

"Okay." She started, then stopped and turned around. "Don't go anywhere, Deacon. I'll be right back."

"Sure."

After she ran off with Otis right on her heels, Loretta turned to Deacon. "I'm really sorry about this. She just got dropped off about five minutes before you got here or I would have called you. Tom didn't even let me know they were bringing her back early, which is so typical of him."

He frowned. "Why the early drop-off?"

"Likely a change in Tom's plans that didn't require his daughter to make an appearance. He's always his first priority."

"I'm sorry to hear that."

"Well, I'm sorry about our dinner plans."

"Don't be. Your daughter always comes first."

And just like that, she wondered again why she had made the worst decision of her life all those years ago. "Thank you. You don't have to stay."

He frowned. "Why wouldn't I stay? I'm hungry. Let's get pizza."

"I like pizza." Hazel had come back in.

"You could not have unpacked yet."

"I'm a fast unpacker. And I like pizza."

"You told me you ate on the plane."

"I did. But I still like pizza."

Deacon laughed, then shot a smile at Loretta. "So we're having pizza?"

Loretta shook her head. "I guess we are."

* * *

DEACON ATE THE last slice of pizza, though he offered it to Hazel, who, despite saying she'd eaten on the plane, had gone pretty much slice for slice with him until the last one.

They sat at the kitchen table, and he got to hear all about Hazel's trip, which mostly consisted of campaign stops through the Dallas and Austin areas. At least the nanny had taken her to Six Flags, so she'd had a little fun while she was down there.

Deacon had always known Tom Simmons to be an ambitious sonofabitch with political aspirations, but to use his own daughter as a political tool was the lowest thing the man could ever do. The least he could have done was take off a couple of hours to watch a movie with her. Hell, he could have even taken media with him to show what a family man he was. But no, he couldn't even spare the time to do that.

The dick.

But now Deacon and Loretta and Hazel were all curled up on the sofa, laughing at the latest animated movie that Hazel had chosen. Deacon thought it was a great movie, and when Hazel fell asleep halfway through, he and Loretta wound up watching the rest of it.

At the end, he scooped Hazel up into his arms and carried her into the bedroom, then slipped out so Loretta could get her out of her clothes and into her pajamas. He went into the kitchen and grabbed a glass of ice water.

"She's really out," Loretta said a few minutes later when she resurfaced. "She didn't even wake up when I changed her clothes."

"Travel will do that to a kid."

"I guess so. Thanks for being so understanding about tonight. And for the pizza and movie night. It's one of her favorite things to do."

"Hey, it's one of *my* favorite things to do."

Loretta laughed. "Tonight turned out better than I expected it to."

Deacon arched a brow. "Oh, so you thought dinner alone

with me was going to be shit, but pizza and a movie was okay?"

"No, that's not what I meant. I had a rough day. You made it a good night despite all the roadblocks. And I appreciate it. Most guys would have bailed once Hazel showed up."

He leveled a look at her. "I'm not most guys, Loretta."

Her gaze never wavered. "No, you're not."

He laid his water glass on the kitchen counter and wrapped his arm around her waist, tugging her against him. She came willingly, and he had to admit, this had been what he'd thought about ever since he drove over here tonight. Touching her, feeling her body next to his, and putting his mouth on hers.

And when their lips met, it was a hot fusion of instantaneous passion, an explosion of need and want as Loretta's hands crept up and over his shoulders, her nails digging in.

Oh, hell yeah. He wanted a lot more than this, more tangling of tongues and her winding her sweet legs around his. But he also knew her daughter was asleep a short distance away, and before they got carried away he ended the kiss, enjoying the way her teeth bit down on her bottom lip and the passion-infused glaze of her eyes.

"So, next time," he said.

She breathed in and let it out. "Yes. Next time. Actually, since Hazel is home early, I know Tom's parents will want to spend some time with her. He rarely takes her on his assigned weekends, so they often ask to visit with her instead. I'll let them know she's home early, and I'll find out if she wants to go over there. They have that great pool, and she loves to swim."

He ran his fingertip over her shoulder, letting it slip under the material of her dress. Her breath caught. "Yeah, you do that. And then you let me know if you'll have some alone time this weekend."

"I'll definitely do that."

She walked him to the door.

He stopped and circled her wrist with his fingers.

"Loretta."

"Yes?"

"I'm sorry about yesterday. I was hot and in a bad mood and I took it out on you."

She frowned. "Yester— Oh. It's okay, Deacon. You're entitled to have a bad day."

"I know that. But it doesn't give me the right to take that bad day out on you. So I apologize for being a dick."

Her lips curved. "Apology accepted."

He pulled her into his arms again, this time for an all-too-brief kiss. Because if he let it linger, he might not walk away. He swept his thumb over her bottom lip and, with great regret, took a step back.

"See you later, Loretta."

"Good night, Deacon."

She lingered against the door while he got in his truck. Damn if she wasn't the most beautiful woman he'd ever laid eyes on.

And damn if it wasn't the hardest thing he'd ever done to drive away tonight.

Chapter 21

LORETTA DROPPED HAZEL off at her in-laws' on Friday night after she closed the bookstore, then went to deliver a few books to her parents. Her mom had wanted a book for herself and a couple for her dad, who had been ill this past week. Which meant the purpose of her stopover at her parents' was twofold, since she wanted to check in on her father. It wasn't like him to be sick.

She knocked twice, then turned the knob. As was typical, her mother had unlocked the door for her, so she opened it and walked inside. Her dad was in his favorite recliner watching television. He barely looked her way, just nodding when she came in.

Loretta went over and kissed her father on the cheek. "Hi, Dad. I hear you've been sick."

"My diabetes is acting up again, and those docs can't seem to get my meds right."

More likely it was her father's predilection for sweets coupled with stubbornness about sticking to a proper diet that was causing the problem, but she didn't intend to argue the point with him. "I'm sorry you're not feeling well."

He shrugged. "I'll be fine soon enough. Always am."

Her father was overweight, pigheaded as could be about his diet, and always thought he knew better than anyone in the medical profession. Loretta wanted to tell him to get off the recliner and go for a walk and start eating better, but she'd never argued with her father one day in her entire life. Today probably wasn't the day to start.

"Hi, honey."

She smiled as her mother entered the room. Her mother, on the other hand, still looked perky and youthful at fifty-five. She always wore a smile, which astounded Loretta, considering her mom had spent the majority of her adult life with the grumpiest man in the universe.

"Hi, Mom." Loretta straightened to give her mother a hug. "How was your day?"

"Oh, it was good. I went shopping with Lee and Peggy, then we had lunch. I stopped at the store to get a few things for dinner. Can you stay?"

"Unfortunately, I can't tonight, but thank you for the invitation. Some other time. I brought the books you asked for. I laid them on the bench by the door."

"Thank you."

"Did you get that new James Patterson I wanted?" her father asked.

"I did."

"And the history book?"

"Yes, Dad. I got that one, too."

"Not the World War II one, but the other one."

"Mom gave me the specific titles."

"I hope you didn't screw it up like the last time."

She looked over at her mother, who gave Loretta an apologetic smile. "I'm sure they're the right ones, Anthony."

Her father's only response was a grunt.

"Can you stay for a glass of iced tea?" her mother asked.

Loretta nodded. "I'd love to."

She followed her mother into the kitchen, realizing nothing had changed in here since she was a little girl. Same square white tile floors, same pale blue countertops, same oak cabinets.

"Have you ever thought about renovating in here?" she asked as her mother handed her a glass of tea.

Her mom took a seat next to her. "I thought about it, but your father says it's a waste of money. He said everything works, and making it pretty and modern is frivolous."

Her father *would* say that. "But what do *you* want, Mom?"

"I'm perfectly happy with the way things are."

She'd wager her mother would like a fancy new kitchen, one with an island and more space, but God forbid her mother ever contradict anything her father said. That's the way things had always been, and likely the way they always would be.

"And what are you doing this evening?" her mother asked.

"I . . . have a date."

Her mother's brows rose. "A date? So soon, Loretta? You're barely past your divorce."

"Tom and I have been divorced over a year, Mom."

"Yeah, and that was a big mistake," her father grumbled.

Loretta wasn't surprised that, despite the television blaring in the living room, her father was listening in on their conversation.

"It wasn't a mistake, Dad, and I told you why we got a divorce."

His father half turned in his chair. "No, *you* got a divorce. Tom didn't want one."

She rolled her eyes. "You know he cheated on me, right?"

Her dad gave a half-assed grunt, then shrugged. "He asked you to forgive him."

"He married her, Dad. He already had one foot out the door with the next wife. Come on, surely even you could see that."

Her father didn't have a response to that, so in typical fashion, he grunted again and resumed watching television. Loretta turned to her mother. "Why is it always my fault?"

Her mother patted her hand. "Your father sees things in black-and-white. People get married, they stay married, no matter what."

Frustration ate at her, making her stomach twinge. "Tom would have asked for the divorce eventually. At least this way I got a nice financial future for Hazel and a place for her and me to call home."

"Of course you did, honey. You did what you thought was best. We just feel that if maybe you had waited, you and Tom could have worked things out."

"That wasn't going to happen. Ever. My marriage to Tom was a mistake from the very beginning."

She waited, hoping for something, anything from her mother. She knew her father would never say it, but she always held out hope that someday her mother would apologize for pushing her into a relationship—into a marriage—that had been a mistake from the start.

Nothing. Her mother sipped her tea and talked about what she'd had for lunch earlier while she was out with her friends, while Loretta hid her disappointment. Again.

"So who's the guy you're goin' out with tonight?" her father finally asked.

Loretta could have made up a name, but she was just irritated enough to tell the truth. "Deacon Fox."

Her dad straightened in his recliner. "What? Why the hell are you going out with him again?"

"Because he asked me. And because we're seeing each other again."

"Oh, honey, do you really think that's a good idea?" her mother asked.

"I think it's a fine idea. I really like him. And he's somehow managed to forgive me for what I did all those years ago."

Her dad made his way into the kitchen and gripped one of the kitchen chairs. "You shouldn't be seeing him. Not after what he did to you."

Loretta shot a look of disbelief at her father. "What *he*

did? Don't you mean what I did? I'm the one who dumped him, Dad. I'm the one who broke his heart and left him for another guy. I'm the one who has had to ask for his forgiveness."

Her father's brows knit into an angry frown. "You don't owe him nothin'. You were kids. You changed your mind."

She stood. "No, you changed my mind. You and Mom both. You berated and cajoled me and told me what was best for me until I had no choice but to make that decision. It wasn't what I wanted—it was what you wanted."

Her mother stood and put her hands on Loretta's shoulders. "Loretta, we did what we thought was best for you at the time. How could we have known how it would turn out?"

"You couldn't. Neither could I. And some of the fault lies with me. I could have said no, and I could have stood firm. I didn't, and that's on me."

"Yeah, so don't go blaming us for your decision makin'," her father said. "But I still think Tom was the best choice for you. Look at where he is now. Some day you could have lived in the White House."

As if that ever mattered to her. "I just wanted to be loved. My daughter needed a father who would be there for her, who would love her unconditionally no matter what. Things like that are important to a child. But you would probably never understand that, would you, Dad?"

He advanced on her. "Don't you ever speak to me like that again."

Loretta had had enough years of being the dutiful daughter, of saying and doing all the right things, of taking the blame for everything that had happened. "Or you'll do what? Make me marry another man I don't love?"

Her mother got between her father and her. "Now, you two, don't fight."

She felt the trembling in her mother's body and knew it was time to back down. "No, Mom, we won't fight. I'm leaving."

She grabbed her purse and walked out the door, hating that she'd left things with her parents this way. But she realized that confrontation with her father had been a long time coming.

As she got into her car, she turned on the engine and let the air-conditioning cool down her anger some. The old Loretta would go back inside and apologize.

But she wasn't the old Loretta anymore, and sometimes with growth came pain. She respected her parents, but she wasn't going to continue to be a doormat any longer. Not to them. Not to anyone.

Maybe she was finally growing up after all.

Chapter 22

DEACON HAD BEEN looking forward to dinner and some alone time with Loretta. They hadn't run into each other in the past couple of days at work. He assumed she was spending time getting caught up with Hazel, and he'd been plenty busy putting walls up in the building, so he supposed they'd both been occupied doing other things.

Now he was anxious to see her.

He drove to the farm to find her pulling up at the same time he did.

"I'm sorry," she said. "I was running errands. I had to drop off Hazel at my in-laws', then I had to stop by my parents' house. Let me dash inside and change."

She looked flushed.

"Hey, no hurry," he said as he followed her inside. "I'm actually early. We have plenty of time."

"Okay, thanks. I won't be long."

She left the room, and he looked around. No Otis. Maybe he was with Hazel, which was a good thing. He knew how much Hazel loved that dog, and if Loretta's in-laws allowed her to have him with her, then Deacon was happy about that.

He went into the kitchen and fixed himself a glass of ice water. It was almost July, and the heat in June had been a ball-breaker. July was only going to be worse. He'd worked most of the day to get caught up on the schedule, and it had been hot as hell in that building. He downed the water in a few long swallows, then tucked the glass into the dishwasher. He stepped out the back door and took a turn around the corner.

He heard the clucking of the chickens right away and smiled. Hazel was probably thrilled about that.

Loretta's garden was doing well, though there were a few bare spots. It looked like it could use some water. He assumed Loretta was busy getting herself and Hazel out the door in the mornings, so she probably didn't always have time to water the plants. He grabbed the garden hose and sprinkled some water over her vegetables, then wound the hose back up, went inside, and washed his hands.

"I'm sorry I didn't mention it before, but you look amazing."

He had grabbed a paper towel to dry his hands, but turned at the sound of Loretta's voice.

He was wearing black pants and a white button-down shirt. He was average. Loretta, on the other hand, was the one who looked amazing. A black dress clung to her curves, and her red high heels made her legs look incredible. The dress showcased the swell of her breasts, and it was all he could do not to suggest another night in for pizza.

Pizza and sex—and not in that order.

But he'd asked her to go out to dinner, and that's what they were going to do. He walked over to her and nuzzled the side of her neck. "You look sexy. You smell even sexier."

She made a sound in the back of her throat that made his dick hard. "Thank you. Now step away before my dress falls off, because I'm hungry."

He laughed and took a step back. "We could have pizza again."

She spread her hands across his shirt, lifting her gaze to

his. "I do like pizza, but not tonight, buddy. Tonight we're going out. I'm having wine. I need to shake off this day."

"Sounds good. Let's go."

They took her car, but Loretta asked him to drive, which was fine with him.

"I noticed you got some chickens."

"Yes. I wanted to cheer up Hazel after that disappointing week with her father, so we got some hens and a rooster. She's ecstatic."

"I'll bet she is. Oh, and I watered your vegetable garden while you were changing clothes."

She looked over at him. "You did? Thank you. I meant to get to that today, but it was . . . let's just say it was that kind of day."

"You wanna tell me about it?"

"Maybe, once I have a glass of wine in my hand."

He wondered what had happened, but he didn't want to press her. He figured if she wanted to talk about it, she would.

They ended up at the French Hen. He'd wanted to take her someplace nice, since all their meals had either been ones she had cooked or of the take-out variety.

He got out of the car and came around to open her door and was rewarded with a nice peek at her gorgeous legs as she slid out.

"I don't believe I've ever eaten here," she said.

He took her hand. "Neither have I, but I looked it up online and it's been here since the eighties. It's gotten decent reviews, so I thought we'd give it a try."

They went inside and he gave his name to the woman at the front. They were seated right away. The decor was nice. Just enough of a dark ambience to be romantic, but not so dark like some restaurants where you needed a flashlight to read the menu. The restaurant had an authentic French feel, a little on the rustic side, but still elegant. They ended up seated at the back, somewhere private. He liked that. Their waitress brought them menus and a wine list. Deacon handed the wine list over to Loretta and let her choose.

"How do you feel about a sauvignon blanc?" she asked.

"I feel like I'll drink whatever you're in the mood for."

She smiled at that, and when the waitress came back they ordered a bottle, which was served nicely chilled and pretty fast.

"Appetizer?" he asked.

"That sounds good."

They ended up ordering the fried oysters along with their dinner. Deacon decided to have the duck breast, and Loretta chose the trout.

She leaned back and took several sips from her wineglass, and he noticed her sighing. The wine, at least, was good, so he hoped it would put her in a mellow mood.

"Bad day?"

"Work was busy. Hazel was looking forward to seeing her grandparents, and they her, so it was nice to be able to drop her off for the weekend there. And then I went by to see my parents to deliver some books and because my father hasn't been feeling well."

Deacon frowned. "Nothing serious, I hope."

She waved her hand. "He's okay. But then we got into an argument."

"I'm sorry. Do you want to talk about it?"

"Not really. They're not going to change, and I have, so we're at odds. No problems are going to be solved there."

He took her hand. "I'm good at listening, even if I can't fix your problems."

"Thank you. But trust me, you do not want to hear about this particular argument."

Which meant it was either about her ex or about him. "I'm pretty tough, Loretta, and if it's about me, it's not the first time I've heard it, so you aren't going to hurt my feelings."

She inhaled and let it out, then took another swallow of wine. "It's like they don't trust me to know my own mind or how I feel. Or what's best for Hazel and me. I made a decision—the right one—and they can't seem to understand that."

"Parents are always overprotective. It doesn't matter how old their kids get, they're always going to worry about you."

She nodded. "It goes beyond that, though. My father has always been . . . disapproving. No matter what I did, it wasn't good enough. I never made the right choices as far as he was concerned."

He pondered that while he took a swallow of wine. "Is that why you married Tom?"

She lifted her gaze to his, then didn't answer for a few minutes. Finally, she said, "I think partly it was. The other part was being the ever-dutiful daughter, something I'd been taught from an early age. They thought Tom was the right fit for me. I'd been taught they always knew best. So I did what they told me to do. I followed their instructions instead of . . ."

She trailed off.

"Instead of what?"

She stared at her glass. "It doesn't matter now. I can't change the past."

Finally, she looked at him. "And I honestly wouldn't change it. I would never change my past. It gave me Hazel."

"I don't blame you for that. She's pretty great."

"Or maybe I would if I could have walked a different road and still ended up with her. I don't know. It's so confusing. And it makes my heart hurt for her because I ended up giving her such a lousy father."

"Not your fault."

She laughed. "Entirely my fault."

Their waiter brought their appetizer, so Deacon waited to respond. Once the waiter left, he looked over at her. "You know, Loretta, at some point you're going to have to let it go."

She had been filling her plate with fried oysters. She lifted her gaze to his. "Let what go?"

"The guilt and the blame. Start looking toward your future and stop living in the past. Stop taking responsibility for all the mistakes. It's over and done now. You can't change it, so quit dwelling over it. And quit letting other people make you feel guilty for the choices you've made."

Loretta stared at Deacon, unable to form words to respond to what he'd just said. So many people had made her feel guilty and like a horrible person for the decisions she had made. He'd never said much to her all those years ago, but she knew she had hurt him. And now he was the one sitting across from her telling her to let it all go. Basically, to forgive herself and move forward.

She took a sip of wine and laid the glass on the table. "I would think you'd be the last person to tell me to put the past away."

"Why? I'm sitting here with you now, aren't I? I've let it go. Neither of us are the same people we were back then. We were kids, Loretta. Kids make dumb decisions all the time. God knows I did. If I felt bad over every asinine mistake I made in my teens and early twenties, I'd be consumed by guilt and wouldn't be able to climb out of bed every day. You have to start looking forward instead of backward."

"You're right, of course. And it's what I've been trying to do. But sometimes the past is hard to let go of, especially when people I'm close to keep reminding me of my mistakes."

"So don't let them. It's up to you to stand firm, to keep reminding them that the past is over and you're more interested in the now and in the future. You have to be strong, Loretta."

She was strong—when it came to Hazel. She'd fight to the death for her daughter's happiness. But for herself? Maybe she needed to work on that.

"I'll try."

He popped a fried oyster into his mouth and smiled as he chewed, then took a swallow of wine. "You don't sound convincing. Need me to toughen you up?"

That caused her lips to lift. "Oh, you think you can make me tough? How?"

"I don't know. Maybe we could practice by me hurling insults at you until you don't cry anymore."

"Hey, I'm not a crier. Never have been."

"Is that right?" He studied her. "If I recall correctly, we

went to see some romantic comedy when we were together in high school. It was some weird time travel crap where the girl was a young teen and suddenly she was thirty. You cried when the guy she loved went off to marry someone else."

Loretta's eyes widened. She couldn't believe Deacon remembered that movie. "Oh, that was *13 Going on 30*. I loved that movie."

"And you cried."

"Because Mark Ruffalo was going to marry someone else besides Jennifer Garner, who he had clearly been in love with since they were kids. Who he was still in love with, but she'd broken his heart. And when she's an adult she realizes she's in love with him. It was a movie about second chances. And in the end she made the right choice when she became a teenager again, so she could start over and do it all the right way."

"Uh-huh. Anyway, you cried."

She rolled her eyes. "Of course I cried. It was romantic and cheesy and heartbreaking and I loved it. And I was a teenager and madly in love with you and I—"

He looked at her. "Go ahead, say it."

"And I couldn't imagine not making the right choice. Which, of course, I didn't. Too bad I can't go back in time and fix my mistake. But that kind of thing only happens in the movies. In real life, you can't right the wrongs of your past."

"No, you can't. But that doesn't matter, because you're only looking forward now, remember?"

He made it sound so simple, when it was anything but. She was willing to try to lose the angst that seemed to constantly tie her up in knots, though. "True. And now I'm enjoying this appetizer. And the company. And this amazing wine."

"Good." He refilled her glass, and they finished off the oysters just in time for their dinner to arrive.

Now that she'd gotten past her awful day, Loretta relaxed into her meal and their date. She didn't quite understand why Deacon had been so forgiving, but she decided to stop questioning it and enjoy being with him. If he could get over their past, she supposed she should attempt to do the same.

It was time to start living in the moment and having fun. No reason to dwell on the past or worry about the future. Right now was pretty damn good.

So was dinner. She ate almost all of her trout, then asked Deacon for a bite of his duck, which melted in her mouth.

After dinner they shared a poached pear au chocolat. It was to die for.

"I'm so full I won't be able to walk to the car," she said as she laid her spoon on the plate. "I'll need a crane."

"You ate light and they were small portions. But we can take a walk if you'd like."

"I would like that. Thank you."

Deacon paid the bill, then they stepped outside. It was warm out, but not ridiculously hot, since the sun had gone down. In fact, a breeze had kicked in.

They strolled around the shopping center where the restaurant was located. It felt good to stretch her legs—and maybe her stomach.

"Thank you for dinner," she said. "It was lovely."

"It was. I wouldn't mind eating there again and trying a few other menu items."

"I'd be game for that as well."

Deacon led her to a bench in the center of the square. They sat and enjoyed the gentle breeze. She swung her legs back and forth and thought about how this day had gone from bad to good.

"Thank you for easing my mind about a lot of things."

"I didn't do anything."

"You've done more than you think. You've forgiven me, and you've taught me how to forgive myself. That's huge."

The wind was whipping up harder now, and her hair slapped her cheeks. He tucked a particularly annoying strand behind her ear. "I'm glad I could help. Maybe you could start being kinder to yourself."

"I'll work on it." She reached for his hand. "In the meantime, my goal is to live for today. Or, rather, tonight. So how about we make out on this bench?"

He laughed. "That's a good motto. Nothing like living in the present. And as far as your question . . ."

He surprised her by pulling her onto his lap. Then he kissed her, and as always, the minute their mouths were connected, there was fire between them. There always had been, and it had never been extinguished. If anything, the blaze had only grown hotter. She fell under a hazy spell of passion, and she wouldn't have it any other way.

She swept her hands over his shoulders, settling against his body so she could feel every part of him connected to her as his kiss grew bolder. His hand roamed over her back and cupped her butt.

Sure, she knew they were sitting right here on a bench in the middle of the shopping square, but it was mostly deserted, and frankly, she didn't care. She was focused on Deacon's mouth, the way his tongue flicked against hers, the low groan in the back of his throat as she shifted against the hard ridge of his erection.

Okay, maybe they needed to ratchet this down just a touch. At least until they got home.

She pulled her lips from his. "That was a good start, but maybe we should—"

A fat drop of water hit her cheek. Then another. And suddenly it was raining. Hard.

"Yeah, we should," Deacon said, sliding her off his lap.

He took her hand and they made a fast dash for the car, but both of them were soaked through by the time they made it there. Deacon opened her door and she slid inside. He came around to the driver's side and got in, then turned to her.

She was drenched. So was he. His hair had fallen over his forehead, rivulets of water dripping down his face. His clothes clung to his body. She wasn't faring much better. Her dress stuck to her like a second skin, and she was sitting in a pool of water.

Yuck.

It was thundering outside, and strikes of lightning lit up the sky.

"That was unexpected," he said.

"No kidding." She shivered.

Deacon reached around to the backseat and grabbed one of the rain jackets she kept back there and handed it to her. "This might help."

She slipped it over her head. "Thanks."

He drove them back to the ranch, but their progress was painstakingly slow. The storm intensified, and by the time he made it down the driveway to her house, it was raining even harder and he was dodging deep puddles of water. He pulled as close to the house as he could, but there was no denying they were going to get soaked again.

"You ready?" he asked.

She had already taken off her heels, figuring she could make a run for it barefoot. She nodded, and they dashed from the car to the house. Loretta already had the keys in her hand, so she opened the door and they stepped inside. She took off the jacket and dropped it to the floor, then laid her purse on the table.

Even though she'd had the rain jacket on, it was thin, and it was raining so hard she was soaked through.

Deacon was in even worse shape.

"You need to strip out of those clothes so I can dry them."

He started to unbutton his shirt. "You know, if you wanted to get me naked, Loretta, all you had to do was ask."

She laughed and turned her back to him. "Can you unzip me?"

He drew the zipper of her dress down. "It's usually not this easy."

"What?"

"Getting a woman out of her clothes."

"It's very easy when a woman is sopping wet and freezing her butt off. Laundry room is this way. There are towels."

She hurried into the laundry room, climbing out of her wet dress as she did.

"And the view just gets better and better," Deacon said behind her.

She smiled as she made her way into the room, letting the dress pool onto the floor at her feet. She stepped out of it, then shimmied out of her underwear.

"Can you undo my bra?" she asked.

"Those are magic words to a guy, ya know."

Deacon expertly undid the clasp, then removed his shirt, pants, and underwear while she grabbed towels from the shelf above the dryer. She handed him one, took one towel to vigorously dry her wet hair, and wrapped another one around her body. Then she scooped up all of their clothes.

"I assume all of these are washable?" she asked.

"Yup."

She tossed their clothes in the washing machine, added soap, and turned the machine on.

"How about some coffee?"

He nodded. "Sounds good."

They went into the kitchen, and she grabbed a couple of cups from the cabinet, then made coffee. She handed the first cup to Deacon. She had to admit that the sudden thunderstorm wasn't a bad thing. Ogling a sexy, chiseled man wearing nothing but a towel slung low on his hips was pretty much the highlight of her year.

Maybe of the past decade, actually.

She sipped her coffee and leaned against the kitchen counter, unable to pull her gaze from the way the towel balanced oh-so-precariously on Deacon's amazing hip bones. Maybe if he coughed the towel would fall off. Gee, that would be awful, wouldn't it?

"You're staring."

She put her attention on his face. "Yes."

"It's making me hard."

Her gaze traveled south, and she smiled. "So it is."

He put his cup on the table, then made his way over to her, taking her cup and setting it on the counter behind her. He settled his hands on the counter on either side of her, his skin brushing hers. "Warm now?"

"Very." She skimmed her fingertips down his chest and splayed her palms over his steely pecs. She lightly dug her nails into his smooth skin and delighted in his harsh intake of breath.

Yes, she was affected, too.

When she tilted her head back to look at him, she saw a firestorm of desire in his eyes.

He grasped a handful of her hair and held tight, then took her mouth in a kiss that seared her body in a ball of flaming sexual need.

Her towel fell from her body as she moved in closer to him. She reached down and tugged his towel away, needing to feel the heat of his body against hers. She wrapped her leg around his hip, his cock hard and heavy against her thigh as he rocked against her.

She whimpered in response and he pulled back, picked up a towel and laid it on the counter, then lifted her and sat her on it.

"I've thought a lot about you this past week," he said as he spread her legs and moved in between them. He framed her face with his hands, his thumb caressing her bottom lip. "About your mouth, how soft your lips are when I kiss you."

He brushed his lips across hers, giving her a light tease before drawing away. Then he teased his finger around one of her nipples. It puckered into a sharp point in response.

"About how soft your skin is—every part of you." He bent down and took a nipple into his mouth, sucking it gently until she felt the pull of need between her legs. Her breath caught as he teased each nipple, taking his time to bring her to delirious heights of pleasure before straightening.

He kissed her again, more passionately this time. It was a deep, soulful kiss meant to turn her world upside down. She was dizzy from pleasure, from desire, and this time, when he pulled away, she gripped his arms to keep her balance.

"And how sweet and tart you taste here."

He spread her legs and put his mouth on her sex. She leaned back and gave herself up to the fiery pleasure of his mouth and tongue, letting her head tilt back so she could soak in every sizzling, body-melting stroke.

She'd been wound up tight these past few days and she hadn't realized how much she needed the release that came all too fast for her. She cried out as she came, shuddering against him as wave after wave of euphoria crashed over her.

Deacon kissed his way up her thigh, her hip, and her belly, then took her mouth again in a blistering kiss that tasted of completion and renewed desire, ratcheting hers up to blistering levels. She wrapped her legs around him and pulled him closer, undulating her hips forward to brush against his rock-hard cock.

He lifted her off the counter and carried her to the bedroom, depositing her on the bed. He leaned over and grabbed a condom out of her nightstand drawer, put it on, then climbed onto the bed.

Loretta propped a couple of pillows against the headboard.

"Lean back," she said.

Deacon sat back against the pillows, then reached for her. "Come on."

She straddled his hips and slid down over his delicious erection, enjoying every inch of him as she seated herself on top of him. His cock twitched inside of her, and her body responded with quivers of its own.

Deacon ran his hands over her thighs, squeezing her flesh as she moved against him.

"You are so beautiful, Loretta." He reached out and circled her nipple, teasing the bud with the tip of his finger until it puckered, the sensation shooting directly to her sex, making her quiver and tighten around his cock.

His gaze held to hers. "Do you feel that?"

She nodded. "Yes. I feel everything. The way we're connected, the way you move inside of me. It's as electric as the lightning outside."

The storm grew in its intensity, both outside and within her, as thunder crashed all around them and the sky lit up as nature roared with all its fury. She felt that fury within as Deacon reared up and pulled her closer. She adjusted, wrapping her legs around him.

His mouth fused to hers and she tangled her fingers in his hair, holding on to him like a lifeline in this incredible sensation storm as he thrust into her while he kissed her with a driving passion that threatened to topple her every emotion until she couldn't think, couldn't see, could only feel their connection to the elements surrounding them.

It was wild, uncontrollable, and when he laid her on her back and drove into her, she splintered, falling apart with a broken cry. He was right there with her, kissing her, clutching her to him as he went right over the edge with her, both of them shuddering through the storm together.

She was panting, barely aware of her surroundings as she came to her senses again. Deacon's cheek was pressed to hers, her hair wet and plastered between them.

"I'm not sure," he said, "but I might have been struck by lightning."

Her lips curved. She swept her hand over his back, felt the perspiration there. "We need a shower."

"I'll say."

They got up and took a quick shower together. After she got out and dried off, she dressed, then threw their clothes in the dryer. The rain had let up enough for Deacon to dash out to his truck for a pair of jeans and a T-shirt while she fixed them something cold to drink.

"Storm's passed us by," he said after he came back inside and slipped on his clothes. "Still thundering and lightning out in the northwest, though, so we might get more rain tonight."

"You keep clean clothes in your truck?" she asked.

"Yeah. On the job site, it gets messy. And sometimes I'll have a client meeting right after work with no time to go home and change clothes. The last thing a client wants to see is a dust cloud of job-site dirt coming off my clothes." He turned around and held out his hands. "So I always keep a clean pair of jeans and a shirt in the truck."

"Oh. That makes sense."

She handed him a glass of ice water. "If you need to leave, I'll understand. But I'd like very much for you to stay tonight."

He laid the glass on the counter and drew her against him, then brushed his lips over hers. "I'd like to stay."

That made her smile. "Good."

"Besides, you're holding my clothes hostage."

She laughed. "And you need those for?"

He shrugged. "Nothing at all. But I would like to sleep with you tonight."

"Oh, we'll be sleeping?"

He finished off his water in three long gulps. "I like the direction of your thoughts, Loretta."

He scooped her up in his arms and carried her down the hall.

She looked up at him. "See? Now you got dressed in those clean clothes for no reason at all."

He grinned. "I have no problem taking them off for you."

She couldn't wait.

Chapter 23

SOMEHOW, DEACON HAD managed to arrange for time off and put a lake trip together in just a few days' time. It had all come about because Zach Powers had wrangled a cabin at the lake for the Fourth of July holiday. He'd invited Deacon to come along and told Deacon to bring whomever he wanted since the lake house was huge. And since Zach had invited all of his friends who wanted to come, and Deacon had heard there was going to be a big crowd, Deacon had invited Loretta and Hazel. He figured they would have a great time at the lake, and it would give him an opportunity to do some fun stuff with Hazel.

Loretta had balked at first, but he'd convinced her Hazel would have a blast. Jane and Will were coming and they were bringing their kids, Tabitha and Ryan, so he knew Hazel would have kids to hang out with. And they also had a dog. So did Brady and Megan, and Sam and Reid. Otis would have lots of company. It helped that Camila's boyfriend was on active duty with the National Guard that week, so she was free to handle the bookstore for a couple of days while Loretta enjoyed a minivacation.

Loretta had asked if she could invite Josie Barnes along, since she didn't know a lot of people in town yet. Deacon had called Zach, and Zach said he didn't care who came. He'd reiterated that the house had a lot of bedrooms and they'd make it work. So Josie was coming, too. It promised to be a fabulous house party with all of their friends.

Deacon had worked double time over the last couple of days to get caught up at the building, then this morning had met with the guys who'd take over for him while he was gone. He had a great crew, and they knew what they were doing. It had worked out perfectly with the Fourth of July holiday being on a Tuesday this year. They'd end up with four days on the lake. And since he'd be taking some weekend time and only one actual workday off, it wasn't a huge deal for him to be gone anyway, but he wanted to make sure everyone was on the same page. The walls were up and the flooring was in, so it was just a matter of getting the work orders in place and ensuring that stuff got done on time.

Now that his job stuff was settled, he packed up his truck. Loretta had said she'd take care of food, so all he had to do was make sure he had the necessary gear for the trip. He'd made a mental list of the activities he wanted to do with Hazel and threw in any supplies he would need on that front, along with clothes and blankets and outdoor gear. Then he drove over to Loretta's house. She already had several bags outside when he pulled up, so he loaded those into the back of his truck. Hazel came running out and threw her arms around him, giving him a gigantic hug.

His heart squeezed as he hugged her back.

"I'm so excited to be going to the lake, Deacon."

"Me, too. Do you have all your stuff packed?"

"Yup. I have my own flashlight. And Mama reminded me to pack bug spray. What are we gonna do at the lake?"

Otis was there as well, his tail whipping back and forth as he sought attention. Deacon made sure to pet him and give him lots of affection.

He followed Hazel into the house. "Lots of fun things. You ready to get dirty?"

Hazel laughed. "Yeah. Otis is coming along, too. That's okay, right?"

"Sure it is. You didn't think we were going to leave him at home, did you? He'll love it at the lake."

"Yeah, he will. I packed his bag, too, with his food, water bowl, leash, rope, and some other toys. Oh, and a blanket for him to sleep on."

"You did good." Deacon spied Loretta in the kitchen filling a large cooler, so he headed her way while Hazel turned and went down the hall to her room.

Loretta looked up as she saw him coming. "I'm just about finished here. Josie's driving out this way. I figured since there are so many of us plus Otis we'd take my car as well."

"That sounds like a plan. All the gear and coolers will fit in the back of my truck. And Otis can ride with me."

Loretta grinned. "I think you secretly adore that dog."

"Hey, no secret about it. What can I help you with?"

She handed him a few containers and directed him where to pack them in the two coolers. Then she told him where the soda and water were, so he loaded those in the truck as well. It took them about a half hour, and by then Josie had shown up.

"That's a pretty small bag, Josie," Loretta said as Josie walked in with something that looked no bigger than a backpack.

"I don't need much, and I know how to pack tight. Thanks for inviting me. I'm very excited about this. My only plan was to head downtown to watch the fireworks."

"Oh, there'll be fireworks at the lake," Deacon said.

She shot him a smile. "Then I'm excited all over again. Hi, Hazel."

"Hello, Miss Barnes," Hazel said.

"You can call me Josie."

Hazel grinned. "Okay, Josie. Mama told me you like dogs."

Josie crouched down and smoothed her hand over Otis's back, who then licked her face. "I love dogs. Hello, Otis. It's good to see you again."

"Okay, let's get this party started," Deacon said. "I think Otis should ride with me since he's so big."

"I want to ride with Deacon, Mama," Hazel said.

Loretta shot Deacon a wistful look. "I guess that's fine if it's okay with you, Deacon."

"It's great with me."

"Then Josie and I will take my car and we'll follow you." Deacon nodded. "Let's roll out."

Deacon headed out and onto the main road leading to the highway. He enjoyed listening to Hazel talk to him about games and sports and just about every topic. She even told him about Otis's toenails.

He grinned at that one.

Fortunately, it only took about an hour and a half to get to the lake exit, then another twenty minutes to find the cabin.

By then Hazel—and Otis—were more than ready to get out of the truck. Deacon parked, and they jumped out. Loretta and Josie met up with them.

"I'm going to take Hazel and Otis on a quick walk," Loretta said. "Let Otis release some of that pent-up energy he no doubt has."

"Why don't you let me do that?" Josie asked. "I could definitely stretch my legs."

"Yeah, Mama," Hazel said. "Let Josie take a walk with us."

Loretta looked at Josie. "Are you sure?"

"Of course. Come on, Hazel. Let's go explore."

"Thanks. Deacon and I will sort out arrangements in the house while you two are exploring."

"You got it." Josie and Hazel disappeared, leaving Loretta and Deacon alone by the truck.

Deacon looked around. There were a few parked vehicles, but no one outside. He took the opportunity while he had it and tugged Loretta against him for a kiss. She grasped his arms and held on, meeting his kiss with a passion that matched what he felt.

When he pulled away, she smiled. "I've missed you the past few days."

"Yes, it's been a busy week. Sorry."

She brushed her fingertip across his bottom lip. "Don't be. I just hope we can manage to carve out some alone time while we're here, though I don't know if that'll be possible with other people and Hazel and the dog and all."

"Trust me, I'll figure something out."

She lifted up and kissed him again. "I'm sure you will."

"Let's take some of this stuff inside and figure out who's staying where."

"It's really beautiful here. And this house—whoa."

"Yeah, 'whoa' for sure." The land was wooded, right on the lake, and the house was huge. Zach had said he rented a big cabin, but this was no cabin. It was a two-story mansion that sat right on the water. He couldn't wait to see inside.

Loretta couldn't believe this place. It certainly wasn't the "rustic" she'd pictured in her mind when Deacon had invited them along for this trip. Tom's family had money, and they'd lived in a big house after he'd graduated from law school, but this was larger than the house she'd had in Dallas. As they stepped into the foyer, they were greeted by an amazing amount of light, due to the floor-to-ceiling windows that showcased an incredible view of the back patio and the lake.

"Wow," she said. "That's a million-dollar view right there."

Deacon set their bags just inside the incredible living room. "Looks like everyone is out back by the pool."

She followed him as he made his way through the open, expansive door and out onto the covered patio. There was a kitchen outside, as well as the most beautiful infinity pool, which overlooked the lake. Brady and Megan sat poolside with Zach, who waved them over.

"Hey, you made it," Zach said. "Beer's in the fridge over there. There's a list on the kitchen counter with a map of the house. Everyone's names and room locations are on it. You should change into your swim stuff and get out here."

"Thanks, Zach," Deacon said.

Loretta looked over at Deacon. "I should find Hazel and Josie."

"Let's do that." Deacon nodded at Zach. "We'll be back. Don't drink all the beer."

"No guarantees," Brady hollered.

They stopped at the island to study the map of the house.

"We're close to each other," Deacon said. "Sadly, not in the same room."

She laughed. "That might be hard to work out, since I'm bunking with Josie and Hazel."

"Yeah. And I'm with Zach." He pulled her to the side of the kitchen and kissed her again, heating her body from head to toe just like he had out front. When he brushed his lips gently against hers to end the kiss, she sighed, filled with thoughts of being alone with him.

"We'll make time together."

She linked her fingers with his. "We are together. And right now that's good enough."

Just as they passed the front door, it opened, and Josie, Hazel, and Otis bounded in.

"We took Otis on a long walk, Mama, and he peed and pooped and fetched a stick. I threw it a whole bunch of times. We found the hose out front, so Josie gave him a big drink of water."

"That's great," Loretta said. "Let's take our stuff and get unpacked. Then you can put your swimsuit on."

Hazel's eyes widened and she looked around them. "Oh, there's a pool."

"Yes, there is."

Hazel took the map from her. "I'm good at reading maps. I can find our room, Mama. Oh, you're staying with us, Josie. And I can find your room, too, Deacon."

Deacon grinned. "Lead the way, Hazel."

Their rooms were both on the first floor, just across from each other. Convenient, but still not close enough. Loretta would love to be with Deacon, but she had Hazel to think about. So she waved to Deacon as he entered his room, then she followed a very excited Hazel into their room.

There were two queen beds and a bathroom. The room

was extremely spacious, which meant there'd be plenty of room for Otis. It was perfect.

"I hope you don't mind sharing a room with us," she said to Josie as they all unpacked.

"Are you kidding? This is great. And this room is huge. In college I shared a dorm room with two other girls and it was smaller than the bathroom in our room here."

Loretta laughed. "I remember college days. And you're right. This is perfect."

"Thank you so much for inviting me to come along," Josie said. "I haven't been to the lake since . . . forever. Maybe since I was around Hazel's age?"

Hazel turned around. "That's a really long time, Josie. You should go out and do fun things more often."

Loretta rolled her eyes. "Hazel."

Josie laughed. "Hazel's right. I should get out and have fun more often. It's on my list of things to do since my move here."

"Good idea. You should start by swimming in the pool."

Leave it to Hazel to be pushy. "Maybe she doesn't want to get in the pool, Hazel."

"Actually, I'd love to. Let me go get changed."

In the end, they all put on their swimsuits, cover-ups, and flip-flops. They stopped in the kitchen first to unpack the ice chests, since they had a huge refrigerator and freezer to store all the food and drinks in, then headed outside.

Sam and Reid had shown up as well and were already in the pool. Otis had already made friends with Sam's and Megan's dogs, Not My Dog and Roxie. The three of them barked and ran after each other.

That made her happy. Even Otis was going to be entertained during their stay here. She noticed one of Otis's bowls was out there, filled with water.

Deacon, no doubt. She smiled at the thought of him caring for the dog. Then again, of course he would.

"Come on over here, Loretta," Megan said. "The water and the view are amazing."

"Can I get in the pool, Mama?"

Hazel had had years of swimming lessons, so Loretta was confident in her abilities. "Yes. And no running."

Hazel rolled her eyes. "I know the rules, Mama."

Hazel walked to the deep end and leaped in. Loretta shook her head.

Her daughter had always loved water. Loretta had put her in swimming lessons from the time she was a toddler. She'd taken to it like a champion. At least Loretta didn't have to worry about her here at the lake this weekend. Hazel had always abided by the rules, because she knew she'd be land-locked if she didn't.

Deacon stood over by one of the covered areas having a beer and no doubt talking guy things with Reid and Brady. She tried not to ogle him, but he looked so fine shirtless, his board shorts slung low on his hips.

"If you don't stop shooting googly eyes at your hot boy-friend, you're going to trip and fall into the pool," Josie said.

Good thing she had her sunglasses on, because she went wide-eyed. "I was not googly-eyeing him."

Josie dragged her sunglasses down the bridge of her nose to shoot a direct look at Loretta. "Girlfriend. Please."

"Okay, so maybe I was. Can you blame me?"

"Absolutely not."

Loretta tore her gaze away from Deacon. She and Josie took a seat at the table next to the pool with Megan and Sam.

Sam poured them each a glass from the pitcher on the table. "Ice-cold margaritas. Made them myself. Isn't this place amazing?"

"Incredible."

"Chelsea's going to be so sad she missed this," Megan said, "but Bash has to work and she's not feeling well in this heat, so they had to pass on the weekend."

"I'm sorry to hear that. Who else is coming?"

"I think Jane and Will are coming with the kids," Sam said, "which should be fun for Hazel."

"Oh, right, Deacon mentioned they'd be here," Loretta said. "I know Hazel will enjoy hanging out with Tabitha."

Loretta took a sip of her margarita. "This is delicious."

"Thanks. Megan brought all kinds of baked goodies."

"I'm so thrilled to have some time off from the bakery," Megan said. "I've hired another person to help run the bakery, and she's not only an efficient manager, she's also an amazing baker. So I just decided to give her a chance to show off her stuff and I took a few days off."

"Good for you," Josie said. "Time off to recreate is so important."

Megan nodded. "I agree. Brady and I don't have nearly enough downtime."

"How's the progress on the new shop?" Loretta asked.

"Good. Reid and Deacon's company is going to do the work, so that's settled. Now that we have a timeline for the renovation, it's very exciting. Between that and building the new house, though, life is busy."

"I know all about that," Sam said.

"How is your house coming along, Sam?" Loretta said.

"Just finishing touches on paint and moldings and getting the appliances in. We should be able to move in within the next few weeks. Then I'm having everyone over for a housewarming party."

Loretta could feel the excitement vibrating through her friend. "I can't wait to see it."

"I'm hoping we can get Grammy Claire over there to see it as well."

"How's she doing?" Loretta asked.

Sam sighed. "She's having fewer good days. She doesn't recognize me as much as she used to. But then she'll have one day where all is as it used to be. I'm holding on to those moments like they're precious jewels."

Loretta reached across the table and squeezed Sam's hand. "That must be so hard for you."

"It is. But I'm taking it day by day and enjoying her brief moments of clarity while we still have them."

Loretta couldn't imagine what it must be like to lose someone you love so much to Alzheimer's disease. To know that someone you've loved and known your entire life, that

that person who held all your lifelong memories, was slipping away from you a little more every day. It had to hurt like hell. But Sam was strong, and she was handling it so well. Loretta wasn't certain she'd have the same inner strength.

Then again, she'd handled a rough marriage and a divorce. She'd moved her life and her daughter's life back to her hometown, and she'd started her own business. She'd bought a farm and she had started a vegetable garden. She'd weathered gossip and she'd made new friends. And Hazel seemed happier than she'd been in a long time, and that was her number one priority.

So maybe she was tougher than she gave herself credit for. As long as she lived life day by day and didn't look too far down the road into the future, she could handle this on her own.

She looked over at her daughter, who was happily swimming laps, and smiled.

Yes, it was going well. She was doing fine. And when Jane and Will showed up with their two kids, Ryan and Tabitha, and their retriever/Lab mix, Archie, it was a free-for-all of excited children and one more excited, barking dog.

Seemed as if even Otis was going to have all kinds of dog friends to play with for the next couple of days.

While Tabitha and Ryan dashed into the pool with Hazel, and Will headed over to grab a beer, Jane slid into one of the chairs.

"How's it going, Jane?" Megan asked.

Jane gave them all a serene smile. "Well, I'm officially pregnant."

Loretta jumped up and gave Jane a hug. So did everyone else.

"This is such exciting news," Loretta said as they all sat down again.

"Yeah, except for the fact you get no margaritas now," Sam said, pouring herself a refill.

"That just means more for us," Megan said with a grin.

Jane laughed. "Considering my level of nausea at the moment, the idea of alcohol repels me."

"Are you sure you wanted to come here?"

Jane looked over at Sam. "Oh, definitely. The kids are excited about this weekend. Will is, too, and I figure I can either hide in the house and nap or just sit in the shade or soak in the pool."

"But definitely no boat rides on the lake," Josie said.

"Ugh. No, no boat rides for me."

"I'm beyond thrilled for you," Sam said. "You must be so excited."

"Honestly, I am. A little freaked out about starting over again, since Ryan and Tabby are mostly self-sufficient now. But Will has assured me he's going to be there for me, and God, he's such a wonderful dad to them. I know he's so excited about having a new baby in the house. Tabitha is thrilled beyond belief to be a big sister."

Megan reached over and grasped Jane's hand. "You're a great mom. You're going to be fine. Plus, you have all of us."

"Thank you. And I'm so happy that Chelsea and I will both have babies so close in age."

"That'll definitely be fun," Loretta said.

After chatting awhile about babies and their jobs and personal lives, they all went inside and started prepping food for dinner. Tonight would be easy—burgers and hot dogs. Megan took the meat outside for the guys to start grilling. Loretta and Josie chopped up lettuce and vegetables for a huge salad, and they shucked corn cobs to put on the grill. Sam and Jane sliced strawberries and melon for a fruit salad. When Loretta and Josie were done preparing the salad and corn, they headed into the ridiculously oversized dining room to set the table for dinner.

"Who owns this place?" Josie asked.

Loretta shrugged. "I have no idea. I assume someone Zach knows."

"Huh." Josie spread out the utensils after Loretta laid the plates.

Loretta paused. "'Huh' what?"

"I don't know. I'm just wondering who knows someone who owns a place this . . ."

Josie didn't finish, so Loretta did. "Ostentatious?"

Josie laughed. "Yes."

"The condo I lived in in Dallas was over five thousand square feet."

Josie's brows shot up. "For a condo? Really?"

"Yes. If you look up *ostentatious* in the dictionary, there'll be a photo of my ex-husband next to the word. He was all about having the finer things. A doorman, a workout center, a business center, marble flooring, floor-to-ceiling windows, a security system, blah blah blah."

Josie wrinkled her nose. "Sounds very . . . sterile."

"It was. We weren't allowed to leave anything lying around, like toys or books, nothing that gave the appearance that someone actually lived there, just in case he wanted to bring a client home. We lived like houseguests in our own home."

Josie paused and gave her a sympathetic look. "No wonder you divorced the bastard."

She was quickly finding out that Josie said exactly what was on her mind. "Yes, well, it took me a while to summon up the courage to leave him, but eventually I did."

"Sometimes it takes a while to figure out how to get away from a bad situation. Which doesn't mean you lack courage, Loretta."

"Thanks for that. I'm working on that courage and independence thing every day."

They moved back into the kitchen. "Independence is a hard-fought battle. It doesn't happen overnight. There are so many factors and people who will try to keep us down, to make us think that we can't do it on our own."

Loretta tilted her head to the side and studied Josie. "You make it sound like you've fought your own battle for independence."

Josie shrugged. "Not the same one as you have, but I had to learn the hard way that trusting some people isn't always a smart thing to do, and the only person you can really rely on is yourself."

She was about to ask Josie to elaborate on that, but just then Sam and Megan came inside with plates filled with burgers. "These are done, and Jane's coming in with the corn."

"Perfect," Loretta said. "We have the table set. I'll go roust the kids out of the pool."

"Don't bother," Sam said. "Deacon and Will are taking care of that."

Which meant she didn't have to worry about her own daughter.

Having a guy around who actually handled things? Pretty awesome. And certainly new for her.

This weekend was going to be all kinds of fun.

Chapter 24

DEACON SAT BACK, completely stuffed after a huge dinner of burgers, hot dogs, vegetables, and fruit, not to mention the amazing cheesecake Megan had served. Now he was enjoying listening to his friends chat, mainly Reid and Zach as they argued about baseball teams. Occasionally Brady and Will would chime in as well. And then Josie had to add in her opinion, which got the women started on sports.

He smiled at that. Women could be just as opinionated about their favorite sports teams as men, sometimes even more ferociously. Loretta had been quiet for a while, but then she got into the middle of the fray, spouting off about her love for the St. Louis Rivers baseball team.

"They're my favorite, too," Josie said.

"Not the Atlanta team?" Sam asked.

Josie shook her head. "I've always loved the Rivers. I've been a fan since I was a kid. Don't forget I grew up in Oklahoma, and since we don't have a pro team, the Rivers were the team I chose to support."

"They're doing well this year," Brady said. "Should have

a shot at the play-offs if they keep playing the way they have been."

"I hope so."

"Unless Chicago kicks their butts, which they probably will." Zach grinned.

Josie shot him a glare. "Not gonna happen, buddy."

"We'll see who makes the postseason, won't we?"

Josie pointed her finger at his chest. "Yes, *I'll* see *you* crying come October."

Deacon laughed. "I have a feeling she's going to take you down, Zach."

Zach frowned. "Shouldn't you be on my side?"

"I dunno. I'm kind of afraid of her."

Josie looked over at Deacon and grinned. "I like you, Deacon."

"I like you, too, Josie."

"Well, I like New York," Hazel said.

Everyone turned to her, their mouths dropping open.

"That is not allowed," Reid said.

Hazel giggled. "Just kidding. I like the Rivers."

Then Hazel proceeded to get into an argument with Jane and Will's son, Ryan, who was a big fan of Kansas City. Deacon observed that argument with interest. Though Ryan was a few years older than Hazel, he was respectful. He teased her, but he wasn't mean. And Hazel was ferocious and stood up for herself and her team, like any red-blooded fan would. All in all, a decent argument that ended with both kids laughing.

After dinner, everyone cleared the table and did dishes, then headed outside for drinks by the pool. The kids went into the water again.

"Hazel's going to sleep soundly tonight," Loretta said.

Jane nodded. "That's the best part about swimming. It wears them out. Ryan and Tabby will be out cold as soon as their heads hit their pillows."

Loretta looked forward to a nice quiet night. Maybe she could sneak out and spend a few minutes of alone time with Deacon. There wasn't a huge crowd here, but the guys had tended to gravitate together, so it was possible he'd hang out with his friends tonight. Not that she'd blame him for that. He worked hard, and he'd spent a lot of his free time working on things at her ranch. He could use some downtime to catch up with the guys.

Jane wrangled her kids out of the pool around nine, and Loretta did the same with Hazel. Hazel grumbled about that, but Deacon came over to them.

"I thought we might go fishing early tomorrow morning."

Hazel's eyes lit up. "Really?"

"Yeah. But we'll have to get up really early, so you need to get some sleep."

"You got it."

"Can we go, too?" Tabitha asked.

"Sure you can."

"I definitely want to go fishing," Ryan said. "I'm great at it."

Tabitha nudged him. "You are not. You've never fished before."

Ryan shot his little sister an affronted look. "Have, too. With the Boy Scouts."

Tabitha raised her chin. "Well, I'll be better at it."

Jane rolled her eyes, then looked over at Deacon. "You don't have to take them if you don't want to."

Deacon laughed. "I'd love to take all of the kids."

"Now that that's all settled, it's time to head in for the night," Loretta said, shuffling Hazel off to the shower and to get ready for bed. She supervised her so she didn't waste time, but she could tell Hazel was exhausted from sun and pool time. Once she got into bed, Loretta read Hazel a chapter of the Nancy Drew book they were enjoying together. Then she left Hazel with a couple of her own storybooks to read. Hazel was yawning and barely saying a word, so she figured about fifteen minutes until she'd be asleep.

Otis had followed them into the bedroom. He'd had his share of fun playtimes today as well, so he curled up on his blanket on the floor at the foot of Hazel's bed.

Loretta kissed her daughter on the forehead. "Good night, pumpkin."

"Night, Mama."

She shut the door to the bedroom and went back outside. Everyone had gathered around one table, so she made her way there. She noticed Deacon had left an open seat next to him, so she took it.

"Thanks for inviting Hazel to go fishing tomorrow. I had no idea she was interested."

Deacon took a swallow of his beer. "I just threw it out there. Figured she could say no if she thought fishing was a disgusting idea."

Loretta laughed. "I think if it has anything to do with you, it'll be fun for her."

"I like doing things with her, too."

Loretta wanted to tell him how much it meant to her that he'd take time out of a free weekend to hang with Hazel, but she didn't want to make a fuss in front of everyone. She made a mental note to thank him later.

Instead, she stayed quiet and listened to Deacon and Reid talk about the various projects they had on their books. Of course, it didn't take long before Brady's building came up and he joined in their conversation as well. It turned out Deacon and Reid's business was much broader in scope than she had been aware of. They not only did renovations, but new builds as well, and after the renovation of the old building next door, Deacon and Reid would be in charge of construction on the new movie theater in town.

"We're all so excited about that," Megan said. "The current one is ancient. The screens are small, the seats are threadbare and uncomfortable, and we've been in need of a new movie theater for years."

"You'll like this one," Reid said. "It's state-of-the-art."

"Yeah. Even has cup holders and reclining seats."

Sam put her hand over her heart. "Don't tease us, Deacon."

"Not teasing. It's pretty fantastic. It'll be equipped with

the latest sound system, and you can 3-D yourself into ecstasy."

Loretta laughed. "Hazel will enjoy that."

"So will Tabby and Ryan," Jane said. "Will can take them to the 3-D movies. They make me nauseous."

"Babe, lately everything makes you nauseous," Will said, kissing her shoulder.

"This is true. But especially 3-D."

"Reid and I love 3-D movies," Sam said. "We'll take the kids or go with you."

"Done," Will said. "Always need help wrangling."

Josie had been inside, and she came out and pulled up a chair next to Loretta. "What did I miss?"

"New movie theater going in. And we were discussing 3-D movies."

"Oh, how exciting. I love movies."

"Let me guess," Zach said. "You like period films like that Jane Austen stuff."

Josie arched a brow. "Let me guess. You surmised that because I'm an English teacher? How very Neanderthal of you, Zach. Actually, I love action films. And kid movies. And horror. And I'll bet you enjoy sports movies, since you're the football coach."

Zach laughed. "You know I only said that to get a rise out of you. You take the bait way too easily, Josie."

Josie sighed, then turned to Deacon. "Does anyone like him?"

"No. We're only here with him because he knows people that own multimillion-dollar lake houses."

Zach took a long pull of his beer, then grinned at Deacon. "Bunch of users."

"Yeah, that's us." Deacon got up. "Who wants another beer?"

"I'll take one," Zach said.

Everyone else declined.

"I'm getting a cup of decaf," Loretta said. "Can I get anyone something from the kitchen?"

"If you find Chris Pratt in there, bring him back for me," Josie said.

Loretta smirked, then caught Zach's glare.

Interesting. Very interesting.

She had no more closed the French doors than Deacon had hauled her against him.

"Following me?" she asked.

"Yes."

"I need to check on Hazel first."

"Well, hurry up so I can kiss you before someone comes in."

She laughed. "Okay."

She went down the hall and into the bedroom. Just as she suspected, her daughter was sound asleep. She collected the books off the bed, then went back down the hall and into the kitchen. Deacon was still wearing his board shorts from earlier, but he'd added a tank top that showcased his broad shoulders and muscular arms.

She sighed in appreciation. The man had an amazing physique. She walked over and pressed her body against him. When he slid his hand into her hair and kissed her, she sighed. This was what she'd thought about ever since that brief kiss outside today. She craved his touch, the feel of his lips against hers, the way his heart pounded against her when they kissed, as if just being near her excited him. Knowing that turned her on.

Oh, who was she kidding? Everything about Deacon turned her on. And when his hand roamed her back, inching lower to cup her butt and draw her against his erection, she moaned against his mouth. She was damp with desire, and wanted nothing more than to be naked and feel him moving inside of her. The fact that they didn't have any alone time was so frustrating.

But then he took her hand and pulled her down the hall and into his room and shut the door. "Deacon, what are you doing?"

"I mentioned to Zach that I wanted some alone time with you. He knows not to come in."

She shouldn't, but oh, she wanted this. "Just a few minutes."

He pushed her against the door and framed her face with his hands. "Babe, I'm so hot for you right now, that's probably all it's going to take."

He pulled the straps of her sundress down her arms, then freed her breasts from her bikini top, cupping the globes in his hands. He flicked his tongue over each nipple until fiery desire shot through her nerve endings. Then he pushed the dress over her hips, taking her bikini bottoms with it, until she was naked.

He made quick work of his shirt and his board shorts, then slid his hand between her legs, coaxing a moan from her in response.

"I sure hope you thought to bring condoms with you this weekend," she said as she teased his shoulder with her teeth.

"Like I'd forget something as important as that when I know I'm going to be with you." He smoothed his hand over her sex, rubbing her clit until she was ready to explode.

"Deacon. I need you inside of me."

He walked away for a few seconds and grabbed a condom from his bag, then tore the wrapper, put it on, and pressed her back against the door. He cupped her butt in his hands, used his knee to spread her legs, and slid into her.

He filled her completely, grinding against her and taking her right where she needed to go. She was conscious of where they were, so she kept her responses low, focusing on Deacon, on the way he moved within her. She bit back the loud moan that hovered in the back of her throat in answer to him driving deep. Her body quivered and tightened around him.

She dug her nails into his shoulders and he groaned. The sound was like an aphrodisiac, spurring her on to the pinnacle of pleasure.

And when she felt the contractions of orgasm crashing through her, she bucked against him, clutching him as her lifeline. He grasped the back of her neck and took her mouth, breathing in her moans as she catapulted over the edge.

He went with her, pushing her back against the door as he thrust and shuddered against her. It was a wild ride as her climax roared through her body and Deacon's entire body shook with the force of his orgasm, prolonging her pleasure.

Spent, she fell lax, pinned against the door by Deacon, who pressed soft kisses along her jaw and neck.

"Everyone's going to know I had sex," she whispered.

He drew back and searched her face. "How? Are you planning to announce it to the group?"

She laughed while they disengaged and headed to the bathroom. Deacon flipped on the light.

"Well, no." She looked at herself in the mirror and straightened her wild hair. She had beard burn on her chin and cheeks. "And okay, maybe I just don't care."

"Good." He pulled her around to face him. "Because I sure don't. And surely people know we're together."

Together. Is that what they were now? She supposed they were. Sort of. She hadn't labeled it—hadn't wanted to label anything about Deacon and herself other than what was happening today.

"Is that okay with you, Loretta?"

She gave him a smile. "Perfectly okay." She lifted up and pressed a kiss to his lips. "I'm going to check on Hazel again."

He grinned down at her. "I don't think we were loud enough to wake her."

"I don't think an earthquake would wake her. But I'll check anyway."

"Okay. I'll see you outside."

She nodded and went to the bedroom door, opening it a crack to be sure the hallway was clear. It was, so she hurried across the hall and into her bedroom. Hazel hadn't even moved. Otis opened his eyes to check her out, then he dozed off again, so she went into the bathroom, washed her face and brushed her hair, then headed back outside.

Why was she being so ridiculous about her and Deacon?

What difference did it make if everyone knew they were together? They were a couple.

Yet the feeling caused a twinge of doubt in her stomach that wouldn't go away.

And that worried her all the way to the backyard.

Chapter 25

DEACON GOT UP before dawn and knocked on Loretta's door. She opened it, squinting at him.

"Morning."

She yawned. "Is it?"

He smiled. "Okay, not quite. But it's time to rouse Hazel."

She nodded. "Okay. I'll get her up now."

He went into the kitchen and started a pot of coffee. Will walked in, his dog, Archie, following along behind him.

"You're up early," he said.

Will nodded. "Jane said if you're taking the kids fishing, I have to go."

Deacon cracked a smile. "Sorry about that."

"Don't be. I haven't been in a while, so I'm looking forward to it. And Ryan and Tabitha are excited about it."

"I thought it might be something the kids would like." He poured a cup for Will and handed it to him, then another for himself.

Loretta came down the hall. "Good morning."

"Morning," Will said.

"You didn't have to get up."

"I thought I'd make some breakfast sandwiches for you to take along. Why don't you pour me a cup of coffee and I'll get started cooking."

He was about to tell her it wasn't necessary, but he knew she'd prepare something anyway, and it would be helpful to have something to eat. This way, they could stay longer and fish without the kids getting super hungry.

He poured her a cup of coffee.

Then Jane came in. "Oh, are you making breakfast sandwiches for them?"

"Yes."

Jane nodded. "I'll help."

"Thanks, Jane," Deacon said. "Will and I can start gathering supplies."

Deacon and Will packed up the poles, some lawn chairs, and other gear. Deacon grabbed his fishing cooler and shoved that into the back of his truck. Otis had gotten up, so he let him wander around for a bit, figuring Hazel would want to bring the dog with them. He went back inside to mention that to Loretta. She already had Otis's food bowl ready.

"I thought you might want to bring him along, so I'm going to feed him," she said.

"Archie will want to come along, too," Will said as he packed some things in Deacon's truck. "I'll make sure to feed him."

It figured Loretta would have thought ahead. She had amazing organizational skills.

While the dogs dove into their food bowls, Loretta disappeared down the hall, likely to make sure Hazel was getting ready. Jane already had Ryan up, so she left to check on Tabitha.

"Where are we going fishing?" Ryan asked.

"Just a few miles down the road," Deacon said. "There's a shady and quiet spot that not a lot of people know about."

"Does it have tons of fish?" Ryan asked.

Deacon laughed. "Well, I don't know about tons, but you have a pretty good shot at catching some."

Ryan smiled. "Great. I want to catch some fish." He

turned to Will. "Hey, Dad, if we catch some fish, can we cook them for dinner?"

"You bet we can. And hopefully we'll catch a bunch."

It took about a half hour to wrangle everyone, then they got into their trucks and Will followed him. They stopped at the shop to get fishing licenses and bait first, then drove to the spot at the lake where he wanted to fish. The sun hadn't risen yet, which meant it was still quiet when they took out their gear and made their way to the edge of the lake to set up.

"I've never fished before, Deacon," Hazel said as they got the poles out. "Will you help me?"

He looked down at her. "Yup."

"Do you think I'll catch a fish today?"

"I know you will."

Hazel was inquisitive and not at all afraid of the worms, so he showed her how to bait her hook. She asked a lot of questions, which was good, and before long he and Will had all the kids set up with their lines in the water.

He'd explained to them that too much loud noise would scare the fish, so Hazel and Tabitha whispered quietly to each other. Ryan stayed completely quiet and sat next to Will. The dogs had wandered around when they first got there, but Deacon put Otis on his leash, and now the dog was sleeping next to him.

Deacon opened his thermos and took a long swallow of coffee, enjoying the peaceful surroundings of predawn. He had a cute little girl sitting next to him, her tennis-shoed foot tapping up against his, and he wondered if, had things not changed between Loretta and him, this little girl might have been his.

He looked down at Hazel's ball cap with her little ponytail that poked through the hole in the cap and was suddenly struck in the heart with emotions he wasn't sure he could handle.

Hazel wasn't his. She'd never be his daughter. But damn if he didn't have strong protective feelings toward her.

She looked up at him, a worried frown on her face. "Nothing's happening, Deacon."

She looked so concerned his chest tightened. "It's okay. Sometimes it takes a while. You have to be patient."

She took in a deep breath, then let it out in an exaggerated sigh. "Okay. I'll try."

His lips curved. He realized patience in a nine-year-old wasn't an easy thing. Otis got up, stretched, leaned in to him to be petted, then went around and laid down next to Hazel. Archie had done the same thing, lying down next to Ryan.

Five minutes later from Tabitha: "Why aren't there any fish?"

Hazel answered before he could. "Tabby, you're just going to have to be patient."

Deacon's lips twitched.

A few minutes later he noticed the tug on Hazel's line.

"Hazel."

"Yeah?"

"Look at your line. You've got a bite."

Her eyes went wide. "What do I do now?"

He got up and showed her what steps to take; how to give the fish some line, but not too much. He made sure she was in control, letting her run the reel. She gritted her teeth and wound the reel, then gave it some slack.

"You're doing good," he told her. "He's on there, so don't pull too fast."

By then, everyone was behind her, spurring her on.

"You got this, Hazel," Ryan said. "Just bring him in."

She wound the line and hauled the catfish in, with some help from Deacon. It wasn't a big one, but Hazel was laughing with delight, and that's all that counted.

Will scooped it up in the net. They took a picture of Hazel holding it, and they bagged it and put it on ice in the cooler. Everyone was excited. She even got a high five from Ryan.

"Good one, Hazel," Ryan said.

Hazel grinned. "Thanks."

They stopped to eat their breakfast sandwiches. The kids all huddled in a group to talk about Hazel's fish.

"She did good," Will said.

Deacon looked over at her, animatedly using her hands

to talk about how she reeled in the fish. He laughed. "Yeah, she did."

"I'm glad you suggested fishing. I've been trying to find the time to take Ryan and Tabby, but work's been crazy. We've had a couple of guys leave, and we're taking on some new hires, so between training and double shifts, I barely have time to breathe."

Deacon took a sip of water and nodded. "And now you're adding another kid to the mix."

Will grinned. "Yeah, that'll be crazy, too."

"But you're happy about it, right?"

Will looked over at the kids, then back at Deacon. "Happier than I have a right to be. When I married Jane, she had Ryan and Tabitha and I thought that was it. And God, I love those kids as much as I love her. Adding another one to this family will only increase this windfall of insane happiness that is my life."

Deacon laughed. "Sappy sucker."

Will laughed, too. "I know. I'm pathetic."

"No, you're happy. It looks good on you."

"Thanks. And what about you and Loretta reconnecting after all this time? That had to be a surprise, huh?"

"More than a little."

Will crumpled up the tinfoil from his sandwich and tucked it into the cooler. "So is it getting serious between you two?"

Deacon shrugged. "I don't know. I think we're both a little wary considering how it all went down last time. So we're just taking it day by day."

"Probably a smart thing, especially since there's a kid involved."

"Yeah."

"My suggestion is to tread lightly. If you fall in love with her again, then that's great. If it's just fun and games between you two, keep in mind that Hazel's involved in this, too."

That gave him something to think about. "You're right about that. Thanks."

After they ate they went back to fishing. Will caught one,

and so did Ryan. Tabitha caught a couple of small ones, and Deacon caught a decent-sized catfish. All in all, a successful morning. By then the sun was well up and he could tell the kids were getting bored, so it was time to head back to the house.

Zach, Josie, Reid, Sam, Brady, and Megan had taken the boat out, so it was just Jane and Loretta at the house when they returned.

"We all caught catfish, Mama," Hazel said.

Loretta gave an appropriately excited response. "You did? That's amazing, Hazel. I'm so proud of you."

Hazel nodded and rocked back on the balls of her feet. "I caught a big one. Can we fix it for dinner?"

Loretta lifted her gaze to Deacon, who gave her a knowing smile. "Will and I will clean the fish."

Loretta laughed. "Then yes, we'll have fish for dinner."

"Awesome. Can we go in the pool now?"

"Yes, you can."

The kids all ran off. Jane took a peek at the cooler. "Ugh. I'm avoiding the whole fish thing until after they're cooked."

Loretta gave her a sympathetic look. "No worries. I'll take care of it."

Jane stood. "You're my savior. I'll go make sure the kids don't throw dirty socks or fishy-smelling clothes on our bed."

Jane and Will disappeared down the hall, giving Loretta a chance to talk to Deacon. "How did it go?"

"It went great. Hazel's a champion fisherwoman."

She laughed, then moved in against him for a kiss, wrinkling her nose as she stepped back. "You smell like raw fish."

He tugged her back against him. "What? That's not an aphrodisiac to you?"

She palmed his chest and pushed away. "No. Eau de catfish is not a turn-on."

"Then I guess I should go take a shower. Or maybe grab you and throw you in the pool."

She arched a brow. "That sounds fun. Jane and I have been lounging in the house enjoying the air-conditioning."

"Really? Why?"

She took a quick glance around Deacon toward the

hallway where Will and Jane had recently disappeared. "Mostly because Jane didn't feel good this morning. I think she's trying to put up a brave front, but she looked really pale."

"That makes sense. You're a good friend."

"I try to be. And she seems to be feeling better now. We watched a little television, and she took a nap. Then I made us something to eat, so I think that helped."

"I'm glad to hear that."

The kids all ran down the hall at the same time, with Will and Jane behind them.

"Ready to hit the pool, huh?" Deacon asked.

"Yup," Ryan said. "I'm gonna do a cannonball."

"Not if I get there first," Hazel said.

"Of course you are. Well, don't cannonball all the water out of the pool before I get there."

Ryan laughed on his way out the door. "Better hurry, Deacon."

Deacon looked over at Loretta. "I guess I should go change."

"I guess you should. I'll see you outside."

Loretta fixed herself a glass of iced tea, then wandered outside, where mayhem in the pool had already ensued. She imagined that the kids had to sit quietly while fishing, so now they had excess energy built up. Even Otis was excited, running around the edge of the pool barking at the kids, which then got Archie barking as well. Roxie and Not My Dog were outside, too, so then it was a free-for-all of barking dogs.

Fun.

It was a good thing they were used to noisy kids. She sat under the umbrella table with Jane.

"Feeling better?" she asked.

Jane nodded. "Much. Thanks for hanging back with me today. You didn't have to."

"I didn't mind. Sometimes the quiet is nice."

Jane's lips lifted as she stared out over the pool where all the kids were splashing each other and screaming. Will had joined in, so the battle was getting intense. "And rare."

"This is true."

Deacon came out. "Why aren't you two in the pool?"

"I think I'll pass on that," Jane said.

"Understood." He took Loretta's hand and stood her up, then scooped her into his arms. "You, on the other hand, don't get a pass."

Before she knew it, he had carried her to the water's edge and jumped in. She barely had time to hold her breath before they went under. She came up gasping, then pushed at him.

"You dumped me in the water."

He laughed. "You needed to get wet."

Hazel swam over and hung on to both of them. "Deacon got you, didn't he, Mama?"

She had no choice but to laugh about it. "Yes, he sure did."

"Come on and swim with us."

With a glare at Deacon, who leveled a smirk at her, she joined Hazel and the others. Before long they strung up the volleyball net and formed teams. Hazel decided she had to be on Deacon's team—traitor—and it was Hazel, Deacon, and Ryan against Will, Loretta, and Tabby.

Since Tabby was the weakest swimmer, they were in the shallow end of the pool, which suited Loretta just fine, since she could get off some zingers against the opposing team.

It didn't seem to help, though, because even in deep water Deacon managed to defend every one of her serves.

The bastard. And he laughed at her. Which only made her even more determined to take him down.

During a short break they took for Tabitha to use the bathroom, Will came over to her.

"Want me to swim over there and kick his ass?"

She laughed. "I might."

They played for another half hour until the boat returned. The kids were excited to see everyone, so they ended their volleyball game and greeted Zach, Josie, Megan, Brady, Reid, and Sam.

"How was the boat ride?" Loretta asked the women.

"It was exhilarating," Megan said. "We water-skied and tubed, and it was a blast."

Sam nodded. "Then we toured the lake and had a fabulous time. You have to go out on the lake, Loretta. It's fantastic."

"I agree," Josie said. "I haven't been out on the water in a long time. I had a great time."

"Hmm, maybe we'll get a chance to do that," Loretta said. "Are you all hungry?"

"Starving," Brady said.

"Let's fix lunch."

They put together turkey wraps with avocado for lunch. Megan and Jane made fruit salad, and Brady and Reid fixed up fresh salsa. They gathered around the dining room table and chatted about this morning's fishing adventure, as well as the trip around the lake.

"Can we go out on the boat, Deacon?" Hazel asked.

Deacon looked over at Loretta, who shrugged. "It's up to Deacon. And Zach, of course."

"I'd go out again this afternoon, if you all want to," Zach said.

"I'd love to go again, too, if you don't mind," Josie said.

"That's a yes, right?" Hazel asked.

"We want to go," Ryan said.

Will looked over at Jane, who shook her head. "You already know my answer, but if you want to take the kids, go ahead. I'm happy to sit in the shade by the pool."

"Great," Zach said. "We'll head out after lunch."

The kids had been going nonstop since before dawn, so both Loretta and Jane insisted they spend a few minutes taking some downtime to catch their breath before heading out. In the meantime, Loretta went and filled up a bag for the boat with towels and sunscreen, then went into the kitchen, where Josie was refilling the cooler with drinks.

"You're having fun?" Loretta asked.

"I'm having so much fun. I love being out on the water. And who wouldn't love this house? Isn't it amazing?"

"It is spectacular."

"The boat is the same way. Huge, with tons of fun equipment and lounging areas. You could live on that thing."

Loretta laughed. "I'm so glad you're having a good time."

Josie paused to give her a look. "You're having fun, too, though, right?"

"Absolutely."

Josie looked around, then leaned in. "And you've gotten some alone time with your hot guy?"

Loretta's lips tipped up. "A little."

"So you've gotten a little. That's better than none at all."

"So true."

"Are we ready here?" Deacon asked as he came into the kitchen.

Loretta stepped back. "I think so."

"I'll carry the cooler to the boat. The kids are squirming on the couch, and they might just self-combust if you don't release them from their imprisonment."

"I'll do that. They can help carry stuff."

She was worried about the boat accommodating them all. She needn't have worried. It was massive, with plenty of room for the number of people who climbed aboard. After Zach lectured the kids on the safety rules and made them repeat the rules back to him to make sure they'd been listening, they got the kids into their life vests and headed to the boat.

Otis followed.

"Not this time, buddy," Deacon said.

"Come on, Otis," Reid said. "You can come hang out with the other dogs."

Otis followed Reid, spied the other dogs, and took off in a run.

Zach started off slowly, then hit the throttle once they got out onto open water. Loretta was in heaven as she sat between Hazel and Deacon. The boat hardly bounced on the glassy water as they flew along the lake. Hazel giggled the entire time, her ponytail flying in the breeze.

Zach finally slowed, and they got out a couple of tubes and tied those to the stern.

Hazel stood next to her, practically vibrating with excitement. But Zach and Deacon went in the water first, making sure the tubes were secure. Once they gave the go-ahead, the kids got in the water.

It was a gloriously hot day. Loretta jumped in the water, too, and she and Josie swam while Deacon, Zach, and Will played with the kids.

Josie and Loretta swam over to the nearby beach and sat in the water, watching the guys play with the kids. The kids hung on the tubes while the guys dragged them around. Loretta smiled, listening to Hazel's squeals of laughter. She hadn't heard nearly enough of that over the past several years. It was a true delight hearing it now.

"She's happy," Josie said.

Loretta nodded. "Yes, she's having a wonderful summer. She's happy at the farm, she's made new friends, and she loves her dog."

"Wouldn't it be great if that's all it took to be happy?"

"Yes."

"Though I need to get a dog. Maybe a cat, too. And a rabbit."

Loretta looked over at her. "The secret to happiness?"

Josie laughed. "Maybe not. But it's a good start."

"Animal lover?"

"Absolutely. I lived in a town house in Atlanta, and I didn't get to have animals there. I'm going to have plenty at the house here."

"Hazel would be happy to take you to the animal shelter in Hope and help get you started."

Josie offered up a crooked smile. "I'll bet she would. I'd probably come home with way too many animals. I can't say no when I see them in their cages there."

"Then you need to take me with you. I'll make sure you start with only one."

"Done deal. In the meantime, all my friends have animals I can love on."

"This is true."

They swam back out to the tubes and climbed on. Eventually, they had all the kids piling on them, pushing them off, and then Zach suggested they take one of the tubes for a ride, so they took turns. Loretta held on to Hazel and went first.

It was exhilarating, with wind and water blowing on her face, the tube bouncing, and Hazel slamming against her. She was certain she'd be black and blue with bruises tomorrow. Also, she'd never had more fun than she'd had today. Hazel was screaming with laughter the entire time.

Will took Tabitha the next round, and it was even more fun watching them bounce over the water. Deacon went with Ryan, and she wasn't sure she'd ever seen Deacon laugh that much. It was kind of hard not to enjoy yourself when you had a kid in your arms and you were flying over the wake, tons of water splashing over you.

Then Josie went by herself, and Loretta could have sworn that Zach sped up the boat, because Josie bounced higher over the waves than any of the others had. When she flew off the tube, she tumbled over and over. But she was grinning when Zach pulled up alongside her, and she swam toward the boat.

"You totally did that on purpose."

Zach arched a brow as he reached for her hand to haul her back on board. "Did what on purpose?"

She shoved at him. "Now it's your turn."

"Oh, no. I'm the driver."

"Bull—" Josie looked around at the kids. "Puckey. I can drive the boat. You get on the tube."

"You can drive this boat?"

"Yes, I can. Go on, into the water with you. Trust me."

He gave her a dubious look, but then dove in and climbed onto the tube.

Loretta didn't know what to make of Josie's evil laugh, but Josie pushed the throttle forward and started slow, then picked up speed. And then she went a little faster, and even faster. Suddenly Zach was airborne, zooming over wakes just as Josie had been. And when he catapulted off the tube, she spun the boat around to go pick him up.

Loretta figured they were even. And when Zach swam up to the boat, Josie gave him a satisfied smirk.

"You did that on purpose."

She gave him an innocent look. "Did what on purpose?"

He shook his head, but gave her a smile.

Loretta noticed a definite spark between those two. She made a mental note to talk to Josie about it later, when they had time alone.

They enjoyed snacks and drinks on the boat, took a ride for a while, and did some water-skiing. Loretta begged off on that, but she watched the others. Deacon was very good at slalom skiing, expertly maneuvering his ski over the waves. He stayed up the entire time until he let go of the rope and dropped down in the water.

Will skied, and so did Ryan, who was very good at it and obviously had some experience.

Then Hazel wanted to try water-skiing, which gave Loretta some trepidation, but she figured her daughter had to learn sometime. Both Zach and Deacon gave her instructions on how to lean back and not forward, and how to let go of the rope when she fell.

"I promise not to go too fast with her, Loretta," Zach said.

"I totally trust you, Zach." Mostly.

Deacon sat at the back of the boat to watch her so he could signal Zach when she was down. Loretta decided to go back there to sit next to Deacon. That way she could keep an eye on her, too.

"She's going to be fine, ya know," Deacon said.

"Of course she will. Totally fine." Loretta wasn't sure if she was trying to convince Deacon or herself.

Deacon put his arm around her and squeezed. "Kids are better at this than adults. Trust me. I won't let anything bad happen to her."

She looked at him and realized she did trust him.

Hazel grinned and waved at them.

She went down immediately on her first try. Loretta didn't realize she'd been holding her breath the entire time until Hazel splashed into the water. Then she came up laughing, and Loretta exhaled.

"She's fine, see?" Deacon said.

Loretta nodded.

She went down again right away on her second try. And her third. She always came up smiling. But her daughter was nothing if not determined, and she got up the next time. Loretta stood in the boat and lifted up her arms, feeling triumphant. Hazel stayed up for a fair amount of time before falling. Then she got up again and went even longer.

"Let's pull her out," Zach said. "I don't want her to get too tired."

Deacon gave her the signal, and Hazel swam toward the boat.

Deacon grinned at Loretta. "She did good for her first time water-skiing."

"She did, didn't she?"

After Hazel climbed aboard, she came over to Loretta and gave her a tight squeeze. "I did it, Mama. Did you see me?"

"I did. You were so good."

"Did you see me, Deacon?"

"You skied like a champion."

Hazel grinned, then threw her arms around Deacon and hugged him. "Thanks, Deacon."

Loretta's chest tightened as she watched the bond forming between Deacon and her daughter.

After that, Tabby wanted to go, and since she'd skied before, she got up right away, though she wasn't quite as experienced as her older brother, who had skied like he'd been born to it.

"Everyone ready to head back?" Zach asked, making sure to address the adults, since it was obvious the kids would stay at this until dark.

Everyone agreed, so Zach drove the boat back to the house. The guys took the cooler inside, and Josie and Loretta followed to unpack everything and clean out the coolers.

Megan, Sam, and Jane were inside prepping dinner. Reid and Brady had already cleaned the fish, which was great, since Loretta was getting hungry, and she knew the kids would be, too. The kids had jumped in the pool for a swim while they fixed dinner, which was no surprise. All three of them were like fish. Loretta gave some thought to putting a pool in at the ranch. Hazel would enjoy that so much.

"I made mojitos," Sam said, handing her a drink.

"That sounds amazing. Mine's coming with me to sip while I take a shower."

She started down the hall.

"Hey."

She stopped and turned to see Deacon following her. "Hey."

"Did you have fun on the boat?"

Her lips lifted. "So much fun I might just squat in this house and never leave."

He laughed. "Hazel would enjoy that."

"She definitely would. Thanks for teaching her to water-ski today. She had such a good time."

"I could tell." He put his arm around her, then took a brief glance down the hall before brushing his lips against hers. "No alone time for us again."

"I know." She palmed his chest, letting her nails dig into his shirt. "Maybe later."

"Definitely later. These kids are all going to be tired by the time we get through fireworks."

He gave her another brief kiss, then rubbed his thumb across her lips. "At some point you and I need a weekend alone."

Just the thought of it made her entire body quiver. "We need to make that happen."

He took a step back, and she walked into her bedroom with a smile on her face.

Chapter 26

DEACON AND THE other guys took care of breading and frying the catfish for dinner while the women fixed some amazing side dishes. It was hot as hell outside, so they gathered up in the house and ate.

He ate a lot of fish. He had worked up an appetite being out on the water, and he wasn't about to apologize for filling his plate with the side dishes as well. He couldn't resist the coleslaw, potato salad, watermelon, spinach, and rolls.

And then Megan had made a blueberry and strawberry sponge cake topped with whipped cream that melted in his mouth.

"We should all live together," Sam said as she ate the last bite of her dessert. "I could get used to this food."

"I could get used to someone else cooking for me every day," Jane said. "Especially if there's dessert."

Will put his arm around her. "Glad to see you got your appetite back in time for dinner."

She leaned her head against his shoulder. "It was perfect timing. I would have hated to miss out on that cake."

"I like dessert," Ryan said.

"Me, too," Tabby said.

"At least the kids burn it all off," Loretta said. "I'm going to need a long walk before bed tonight. I'm so full."

After dinner, they cleaned up, then sat outside by the dock. It was just about sunset, which meant the lake community would be starting their fireworks show soon.

Fortunately, they had all brought some of their own fireworks for the kids, so as soon as it got dark enough, there were sparklers and snakes and a few sizzlers, which they set off near the water. Will had the hose at the ready, and they'd prepared a bucket of water to toss the used sparklers in. They left the dogs in the house with the TV sound turned up so they wouldn't be scared by all the loud noises.

Deacon loved watching Hazel's face light up as she dashed around the backyard with sparklers in both hands, waving them around. He enjoyed watching Loretta running around with her even more. She had a childlike enthusiasm about her that punched him right in the heart. And hearing her laugh with her daughter brought back memories to some of the Fourth of Julys they'd shared together.

When she collapsed in the chair next to him, he tucked a strand of her hair behind her ear. "Remember when we went to the lake on the Fourth that one summer?"

She looked at him for a few seconds, then nodded. "Oh, right. You and me and a bunch of our friends. We packed a cooler of food and drinks, swam all day, then sat on the bed of your truck and watched the fireworks. And then I ended up grounded because I got home late."

"I remember. We couldn't see each other for a week after that."

She nodded, then leaned over and brushed her shoulder against his. "It was worth it. Fun day."

His lips curved. "Yeah, it was."

He was glad she remembered the good parts of it. And now, as his gaze met hers, he wanted nothing more than to kiss her. But they were in a crowd of people, one of whom was her daughter, who sat right at her feet. But the way Loretta looked at him told him she wanted the same thing.

A little restraint was a good thing, right?

The first pop of fireworks across the lake distracted him from his need to put his lips against Loretta's. He settled in to watch the explosions of color and light. The kids all screamed and everyone yelled out as each firework seemed to get bigger and brighter.

"Oh, look at that one," Hazel said. "Did you see it, Mama?"

Loretta laid her hands over Hazel's shoulders. "I did. And look at that one, Hazel. All the colors."

Deacon sat back and enjoyed the show, both in the sky and on the ground. Hazel stomped her feet and squealed, then she and Tabitha held hands and giggled together as they watched.

Looked like Hazel had made a new best friend. He was happy for that. Hazel and Tabitha got up and went to the edge of the dock, letting their legs dangle as they sat together, their heads tilted back as they watched the rest of the show.

"I'll bet they'll be friends forever after this weekend," he said to Loretta.

Loretta nodded. "I sure hope so."

The fireworks ended with a finale of multiple, colorful explosions, then all went quiet.

They had the kids burn off some excess energy by letting them play outside with the dogs for a while before sending them inside to get ready for bed. Deacon, Zach, Will, and Brady cleaned up outside while everyone else went in.

"Hell of a party here," Deacon said to Zach as they put away all the lawn furniture and secured the boat. "We sure had a good time."

Zach grinned. "Yeah, it was fun, wasn't it? I'm glad my friends decided to spend the holiday in the Hamptons with their family."

Deacon arched a brow. "You must know some interesting people."

He shrugged. "Yeah, I know a few."

Zach was an enigmatic guy. He didn't reveal a lot about

himself other than that he loved teaching and coaching the high school football team. He was a great guy and Deacon had grown to like him a lot, but he didn't know a lot about his background. He knew he'd moved here to Hope a couple of years ago from Detroit, that he was an ex–football player who'd suffered a career-ending injury. Zach didn't talk much about his football career. Maybe he was just a guy who liked to look forward, not back.

Deacon knew all about the looking-forward thing. Mostly. Maybe he hadn't completely shut the door on the past. But everything in his past with Loretta hadn't been bad, so why would he want to shut that away?

"Anyway, thanks for inviting me. I had a great time."

Zach grinned. "Anytime. I'm all about gathering my friends together and having some fun."

They finished up in the backyard, then everyone headed inside. Josie was in the kitchen unloading the dishwasher, and Zach went to help her. Loretta came down the hall, so Deacon met her in the living room.

"Did you get Hazel settled in?"

Loretta nodded. "She's still a little hyped up from all the fireworks excitement, so I left her reading. I'm sure once she settles down, she'll fall right to sleep. It's been a hectic day, and I know she's tired."

He ran his hands down her arms. "Do you need to be in there with her?"

"Oh, no. If I stayed in there with her she'd want to talk all night, and then she'd never go to sleep. It's best if I give her some quiet time."

"Then how about a walk?"

She looked down the hall. "I don't know."

"I'll keep an eye on her for you," Josie said.

Loretta looked around Deacon to Josie. "Are you sure?"

"Of course. I'm not going anywhere but the sofa right now."

"Thanks, Josie. I won't be gone long."

Josie offered up a knowing smile. "Take your time."

"Yeah," Zach said. "Take your time. We've got this."

Deacon gave a nod to Zach, and they headed out the front door. As soon as he closed the door, he took Loretta's hand and they started up the path. It was hot and muggy outside, and Deacon could already feel his shirt clinging to him. There were probably already a billion mosquitos ready to dive-bomb them, but they'd put on repellent earlier before the fireworks, so hopefully that would protect them. All he wanted was a few minutes of alone time with Loretta before the end of the night.

"Did you have a good time?" he asked as they crested the hill.

She looked over at him and gave him a warm smile. "I had such a great time. Thank you for bringing Hazel and me. She had a blast. She's going to be so wiped out she'll probably need to go to bed early for the rest of the week."

"It's good for her to get out and try new things, have a little fun. Before you know it, school will be starting."

Loretta nodded. "Just a little over a month. That reminds me, I need to make a mental note to get some cute notebooks into the bookstore. I think the schoolkids would really like that."

"See? A little walk to clear your head and you're already thinking of work things."

She let out a quiet laugh. "Sorry. I didn't mean to let work intrude on our minivacation."

He stopped and turned to face her. "Hey, it's okay. That's your livelihood, and it's important to you. Don't ever apologize for making that a priority in your life."

She tilted her head to the side. "You've been so nice to me. Why?"

He frowned. "What?"

"Ever since we got past that initial period of being uncomfortable around each other. You've been nice to me. Forgiving. I don't know, Deacon. I just don't feel like I deserve the way you treat me."

"So you want me to be mean to you?"

She let out a short laugh. "I don't know. Maybe that's what I'm used to. Or maybe that's how I feel you should act around me. I was terrible to you, Deacon. I dumped you. I just don't understand how you could even speak to me, let alone want to be around me after all that happened between us in the past."

He placed his hands on her shoulders. "Are you the same person you were all those years ago? God, Loretta, you were barely eighteen then. We were just teenagers trying to make the best decisions we could. You had all those forces bombarding you. Me, your parents, Tom, his parents. Everyone was telling you what was best for your future. You made what you thought was the right choice. I didn't always make the best decisions at that time, either."

She'd been looking down at the ground, but she lifted her head, and he saw the misery reflected in her eyes. "But you didn't hurt anyone in the process."

"How do you know what I did or didn't do? You were gone. I made some tough choices, hurt some people in relationships. It happens. You feel shitty about it and you hopefully mend fences. Sometimes you don't, and you have regrets about it. You've got to stop beating yourself up over what happened between us. If I'm okay about it, shouldn't you be okay about it, too?"

She heaved in a deep breath. "I . . . guess."

He folded her against him. "Stop bringing it up, Loretta. It's over. It's in the past. It's done."

She laid her head against his shoulder. "Okay. I'll try."

He took a step back. "Try really hard."

"It's just that you're so . . . nice."

His lips curved. "I'm not always nice."

They started walking again. It finally started to cool off some, though for July, that meant it was probably ninety degrees instead of ninety-five. But the sun wasn't beating down on them, and that meant he wasn't sweating, so it would do.

"When were you not nice?"

His gaze snapped to Loretta. "What?"

"You. Not nice. When?"

"I don't know. Lots of times. Why?"

She shrugged. "It would make me feel better if you gave me an example."

He blinked. "Seriously?"

"Yes."

"You would make me tell you an awful story about myself to make you feel better about yourself?"

She gave him a half smile. "Yes."

He sighed. "Fine." He couldn't believe she was asking him to do this. But she'd been upset, and if this was what it took to make her happy again, he'd do it. God knows he'd been no Boy Scout. He'd made amends with the people he could, though some didn't want that. He understood why.

"Okay, fine."

"Oh, good. Make it a really bad one."

He laughed. "Loretta."

"Sorry. I'm feeling particularly lousy tonight."

He thought back to his youth, and one woman popped into his head. "After you left, I didn't date anyone until about six months later. Then it was random dates here and there, no attachments. I just wasn't ready for anything long-term after what I'd gone through with . . . after you . . . well, you know."

"This is not making me feel better, Deacon."

"Sorry. Anyway, I finally started dating this girl, Wendy. She was a waitress at the diner. Really sweet girl, working part-time while she went to the community college to start building credits for an art degree. She was pretty talented, too. She used to draw on my napkin when I'd stop in to eat on my lunch breaks."

"She sounds really nice."

"She was nice. Pretty, too. Kind of shy and quiet, but I liked her. As much as I could like anyone at that point. But it was clear after a while that she was way more into having a relationship than I was. I felt . . . suffocated. So I just . . . broke it off. Suddenly and brutally. I told her it was obvious that she liked me more than I liked her and that I wasn't interested in her that way."

Loretta frowned at him. "Ouch."

"Yeah. I hurt her and I knew it, but I was so into my own pain that I didn't realize how badly I'd broken her heart."

They'd made their way to the lake's edge. Loretta turned to him and grasped his arm. "Oh, Deacon."

"Yeah. Wendy didn't have a mean bone in her body, and I tore her apart without even thinking of how it affected her. And then I walked away without a backward glance. So the next time you want to kick yourself about how you dumped me, think about that. You're not the only one who's hurt someone, Loretta."

"Did you ever see her again? Ever talk to her?"

"I stayed away from the diner for a while after we broke up, figuring it'd be best if we didn't run into each other. She ended up quitting her job there to go to school full-time in Kansas. I ran into her at a club one night a couple of years later. She had a new boyfriend and a new job, and she was fine. But I apologized for hurting her and told her she had every right to hate me until the end of time."

"What did she say?"

"She said she did hate me for a while, but she moved on. And she forgave me, because that's the kind of person Wendy is. And then she hugged me and introduced me to her boyfriend, who already knew who I was, because Wendy had told him about me."

Loretta's brows rose. "Uh-oh. Did he want to punch you in the face?"

Deacon laughed. "Nah. Wendy explained that I'd apologized, and the guy was fine with it. He was a really nice guy, too. I heard they ended up getting married. They both live in Kansas now and have a two-year-old little boy."

Loretta sighed. "A happy ending. I like that."

"Yeah, me, too. I wasn't the right guy for her. I'm glad she found the right one."

They took a seat at the edge of the dock. Loretta leaned against him. "Even in this story where you were the bad guy, you ended up looking decent."

"Trust me, I wasn't decent. I hurt her. I made her cry.

And at the time, I didn't care. Plus, she wasn't the only woman I hurt. There were others."

She tilted her head back and looked up at him. "Care to tell me about them?"

"Not really. Looking back on all of them, I feel bad about every woman I hurt. But in the long run, it made me realize that you can't mess with people's feelings. It made me more honest."

"That's a good thing."

"I guess it is. We all have to grow up and evolve. We have to learn from the mistakes we made in our youth so we don't keep repeating them."

Loretta thought about what Deacon had said. God knew she'd made plenty of mistakes when she was younger. Deacon. Tom. The choices she'd made. She really hoped she'd evolved enough to not make the same mistakes again.

But here she was, reliving her past with Deacon. Though maybe it wasn't the past she was reliving with him.

She didn't know. A part of her was still so confused where Deacon was concerned, which was why she was still keeping her heart closed. She knew what she felt for him deepened every day. How could it not? He was still the same guy she'd fallen in love with all those years ago, only he was so much more than that now. Back then it had been fun and sexy and playful. And while those things remained, there was more of a thoughtfulness and depth to him that hadn't been there in high school.

It was like with every step he'd taken through life, he'd learned something about himself and applied it to becoming a better person.

Had she done the same thing?

Thunder rumbled off in the distance, and the clouds flittered with lightning.

"We should head back," he said.

She nodded, and took his hands when he held them out for her. He pulled her up and wrapped his arm around her.

"I'm sorry we didn't get much time alone together these past couple of days."

She rubbed her fingertip along the side of his jaw. "It's not necessary for us to be alone. I'm happy enough that we were together."

"Maybe we could have a date night sometime next week or next weekend."

"Hazel will be with her grandparents next weekend, so I'm sure we can arrange something."

He leaned in and kissed her, and they made their way back to the house. When they walked inside, Zach, Josie, Megan, and Brady were in the living room watching a movie, so Loretta and Deacon grabbed something cold to drink and settled in with them.

The movie was, of course, *Independence Day.* There was nothing better to wrap up the Fourth of July than watching people kill off Earth-invading aliens.

When the movie ended, the discussion turned to the best way to handle an alien invasion.

"You have to have the technology, but I think biological warfare is the key," Zach said.

Josie turned to him. "Which could also destroy human life."

"Oh, like the aliens aren't already intent on doing that? I'm just gonna say that our scientists will come up with an idea that will kill the aliens and protect the humans."

"Yeah," Deacon said. "Then we'll be able to pump it into the atmosphere and knock them all out."

"And you know the aliens all have a weakness," Brady said. "So once we figure out what that is, the humans will go after them, both barrels blazing."

Deacon nodded. "Alien-killing silver bullets. Only more like some kind of thermonuclear blasters."

Loretta turned to Josie and Megan and shook her head.

Megan shrugged. "Video games."

Deacon vehemently defending his point of view on alien-fighting weaponry was a side to him she'd never seen before. She sat back and enjoyed hearing him argue with Zach and Brady, trying to imagine him sitting in front of his television, at war with some imaginary world.

No wonder Hazel loved him. He could work his ass off all day long as an adult, then immediately enter a make-believe world. She'd never been able to do that. She could barely figure out how to use the controllers without having her characters walk into walls over and over again. It must be nice to be able to seamlessly make that transition from real world to pretend world. Although she did find her escape in books and their make-believe worlds. That was her love, her escape and her way to relax. Maybe it was similar.

And maybe someday she'd try video games again. Maybe Deacon could show her how.

She obviously had a lot to learn about this adulting thing. And maybe it didn't always have to be so serious.

Chapter 27

IT WAS ALMOST a week after the holiday before Deacon could make it out to Loretta's farm to work on the fence. The job site had been busy as hell, and he'd put in a lot of overtime hours. He'd called Loretta and let her know he wouldn't be able to make it until Friday, but she'd told him there was no hurry and his job had to come first.

He appreciated that she understood, but he wanted to finish the projects at her place.

They'd seen each other at their softball game on Tuesday night, and that had been fun. Hazel had come along, and he discovered she loved coaching them from the bleachers. But Loretta had paperwork to do after the game, so they hadn't hung out after.

So after work on Friday, he loaded up his truck with supplies and headed out to Loretta's house. When he parked in the driveway, he was surprised not to see Otis or Hazel already outside, or coming out to greet him like they typically did.

He got out of the truck and went to the front door to ring the bell. He heard Otis's deep bark announcing his arrival.

Maybe Loretta was keeping him inside because of the heat. When Loretta answered, the dog was right there at the door, his tail whipping back and forth.

"Hey," Loretta said. "Come on inside. It's blistering hot today."

It sure as hell was. The temps were only getting hotter, hovering right at the century mark. Deacon was damn glad they had the air-conditioning installed in the building they were working on, or it would be an oven in there.

He told Otis to sit, and when he did, he scratched him behind the ears, then followed Loretta into the kitchen.

"Where's Hazel?" he asked.

"Asleep on the sofa. She hasn't been feeling good the past couple of days."

Deacon frowned. "I'm sorry to hear that. What's going on with her?"

"I'm not sure. She's had a low-grade fever, and she's complaining of stomach pains."

"Huh." Since he didn't have kids, he had no idea what that could be. "Something going around?"

"Not that I know of. I've talked to the parents of some of her friends, and they're all fine. I'm hoping it's just a bug and it'll go away. But it's unusual for her to get sick. She's usually really healthy."

Now Deacon was worried. He wandered over to the living room, where Otis had taken up a spot lying on the floor in front of Hazel.

Good dog.

Deacon took a peek over the back of the sofa. Hazel was curled up, sound asleep, her cheeks tinged with pink. He brushed his hand over her forehead.

Yeah, it was warm.

Damn.

He wandered back into the kitchen, where Loretta had fixed him a tall glass of ice water. He picked it up and took several swallows, then set it down on the island. "Thanks. Did she eat anything unusual?"

Loretta shook her head. "She and I have eaten all the same things, and I'm fine. Though, honestly, she hasn't been eating much. She says she's not hungry."

"You worried?"

"Not yet. Kids pick up things all the time, especially viruses. Typically, they run their course, and then Hazel bounces back fast. But I'm keeping a watchful eye on her."

"You know best."

"Obviously she's not going to her grandparents' this weekend. Sorry about that."

He reached out and took her hand. "Don't be sorry. Hazel always comes first."

She sighed, then smiled at him. "You are so understanding. Don't you ever get mad?"

"You should see me on the job site. I get mad plenty. But about this? Never."

"Thanks."

"Mama, I don't feel so good."

Deacon looked over toward the living room. Hazel was sitting up, and she looked pale.

Loretta slipped off the bar stool and went over to the sofa. "What's wrong?"

"I feel sick."

"Let's go."

They disappeared down the hall and into Hazel's bathroom, shutting the door.

Otis wandered down the hall, staring at the closed door. He whimpered there, scratching at the door.

"Otis."

The dog came to him, so Deacon decided to distract him.

"Let's go outside and play. You can follow me while I work on some fence."

Otis wagged his tail and stopped whimpering, so Deacon figured getting Otis out of the house while Loretta tended to Hazel might be a good thing.

They walked out the front door. Deacon let Otis into his truck, and he drove off, heading down the property to work on the fence.

Maybe they both needed some distraction so they wouldn't worry about Hazel.

LORETTA DIDN'T KNOW what time it was when she finally got Hazel settled in bed, but it was dark outside. It had been a long bout of sickness, her poor baby girl. And she had totally forgotten about Deacon, who had probably gone home by now. She felt bad about it, but there was nothing she could have done. Hazel needed her. She hoped he understood.

She started down the hall, then realized she smelled something wonderful in her kitchen. She frowned, and when she turned the corner, she saw Deacon in there, cooking, Otis looking up adoringly at him.

"What are you doing?"

"I figured you might be hungry. I know I'm hungry." He paused. "How's Hazel?"

"Asleep, finally. But sick."

He rested a hip against the kitchen counter, and she saw concern cross his features. "How sick?"

"I don't think you want me to be graphic, especially while you're cooking."

"I have an iron stomach, Loretta. Go ahead."

"She threw up several times. But I think she's done now. I hope she's done now."

"I hope so, too. Poor baby."

"She's sleeping and seems calmer, so I'm hoping she's settled in for the night."

"I made chicken soup. I know it's hot outside, but I thought soup would be helpful for whenever Hazel's up for it. And for us."

"I am kind of hungry. But first, I need a shower, if you don't mind waiting."

"I don't mind at all."

She nodded. "Thanks. It won't take me long. I'll be right back."

She hurried into her bathroom and turned the water on,

stripped out of her clothes, and got into the shower, letting the water stream down over her. She took the fastest shower on record, but at least she felt clean after. She combed out her hair, put on fresh clothes, then went back into the kitchen.

"That was quick," Deacon said as he reached into one of her cabinets for bowls.

"I told you I wouldn't be long. Let me help you."

"No. You sit. I'll do this."

This was new, having a man deal with dinner. Admittedly, she enjoyed watching him spoon the soup into the bowl and present it to her, then slice the bread he'd made. Granted, it wasn't homemade bread, but it smelled wonderful, and she was suddenly starving. Frozen bread, thawed and heated in the oven, would do quite nicely. He took a seat next to her at the island, and they started to eat.

"Fence is fixed," he said after a few minutes.

"Oh, thank you. And thanks for staying. You didn't have to."

"I had work to do, and I was worried about Hazel. I wouldn't have left even if I didn't have things to do here."

Her heart was filled to bursting with the feelings she didn't want to have for Deacon. But they were there, and eventually she was going to have to face them.

But not tonight. Tonight she'd had enough to deal with. So she could live in denial a little longer.

"Thank you for being here."

"You're welcome. Oh, and I watered your vegetables. They're looking good. I also put some fencing and some cages around the tomato plants, since they were starting to look heavy."

"Thank you for that as well."

"No big deal. I thought the fencing would help keep Otis out. I saw his footprints in there."

She swallowed some soup, then laid her spoon down. "Yes. He thinks they smell good. He already jerked up one of the plants and was running around with it in his mouth the other day."

Deacon slanted a glare at Otis. "Dude. You did that? Not cool."

Otis gave him a wild thump of his tail from his spot in the living room.

"At least it was only one plant. I think after I yelled at him and even Hazel yelled at him, he's convinced the tomato plants are not good things after all. He might ignore me, but he doesn't like having Hazel unhappy with him."

"That's good."

They finished eating, and when Loretta went to do the dishes, Deacon insisted she go sit on the sofa and let him clean up. She argued.

"You had a rough day. I'll do this, and you go relax. We'll watch something on television together after I'm done in here."

He looked determined, and she was too tired to argue, so she finally went into the living room, grabbed a blanket off the back of the sofa, and began channel surfing.

Her eyes were seeing double as she sifted through the options, so she settled on a baseball game.

She was asleep before Deacon showed up.

He nudged her sometime later. "Hey. Time for bed."

She blinked, barely conscious of him leading her toward her bedroom.

She crawled into bed and reached for him. "Thank you, Deacon. It means a lot that you're here."

He brushed his lips across hers and swept her hair away from her face. "I'll always be here for you. Good night, Loretta."

"Mmm, night."

She rolled over and fell asleep immediately.

Chapter 28

LORETTA WAS NUDGED awake by Deacon.

"Hey, babe. You gotta get up. Hazel's sick."

In an instant, she was sharply awake and bolting out of bed.

"Where is she?"

"In the bathroom."

She followed Deacon down the hall. "She came into the living room to look for you. I was asleep on the sofa, so I took her into the bathroom. She threw up a couple of times. She feels pretty hot, Loretta."

Damn. Loretta saw Hazel sitting on the floor, looking flushed and miserable. She crouched down beside her.

"I don't feel good, Mama. My stomach hurts really bad."

She swept her hands over Hazel's face. She was hot.

"I'm sorry, baby." She looked up at Deacon. "The thermometer is in the medicine cabinet. Can you get that for me?"

Deacon nodded and grabbed it, then handed it to Loretta. She turned it on and waved it over Hazel's face.

One hundred and two. Not ridiculously high, but with

the consistent stomach pains and vomiting, she was starting to get worried.

"Would you stay here with her while I call her pediatrician?"

Deacon nodded. "Yeah."

"I'm going to call Dr. Hansen, Hazel. I'll be right back."

She found her phone in her purse and saw that the time was five in the morning.

Sorry, Doc.

She dialed the number to the doctor's office. She got his service and said it was urgent, hung up, and waited. About ten minutes later Dr. Hansen called. She told him what was going on with Hazel.

"There aren't any current flu bugs going around, Loretta. It might be a stomach infection, but it could also be appendicitis."

Oh, God. She hadn't thought of that.

"You should take her to the ER and have her checked out."

"I'll do that. Thanks, Doc."

Her anxiety level climbing by the second, she hung up and hurried back into the bathroom. Her heart squeezed as she saw Hazel sound asleep against Deacon's chest. He was on the floor, leaning against the wall. He was a big guy, so he took up a lot of space in that bathroom. He had to be so uncomfortable.

She wanted to cry at the picture the two of them made, Hazel's small hands clutching Deacon's T-shirt, his arm wrapped around her daughter as if the mere action could protect her from harm.

God, she was in love with him. Had always been in love with him. She would always be in love with him.

And this was the absolute worst time for that realization.

"Doc thinks it might be appendicitis and I should run her in to the ER for an evaluation."

With seemingly no effort at all, Deacon pushed off the wall with Hazel in his arms and stood. "Let's go."

"You don't have to go with me."

He cocked his head to the side as if there was no further discussion to have. "I said, let's go. Grab what you need for her and for yourself. I'll drive your car."

She nodded, feeling more relief than she had a right to. "Okay."

Loretta packed a bag with a change of clothes for Hazel and for herself, just in case. She threw in Hazel's favorite blanket while Deacon let Otis outside briefly and made sure he had food and water in the house while they were gone. Then Loretta cleaned up Hazel and changed her into fresh clothes. When they were ready, Deacon carried her to the car.

Loretta sat in the backseat with Hazel, her daughter cradled against her as they drove to the hospital. Fortunately, Hazel slept the entire way. Deacon let them out in front while he went to park the car.

She made her way into the emergency room and started to fill out the necessary paperwork at the front desk. When Deacon arrived, he took Hazel while she finished with the forms.

Fortunately, they weren't extremely busy, and it was obvious Hazel was in a lot of pain, so they took her into an exam room right away. A nurse came in to get Hazel situated on the bed and took her vital signs.

"A doctor will be right in," the nurse said with a sweet smile.

"Thanks."

Hazel rolled over onto her side and pulled her knees up to her chest. "My stomach hurts."

Loretta smoothed her hand over Hazel's hair. "I know, baby. The doctor will be here soon."

Within ten minutes the door opened and the doctor came in, followed by the nurse who'd been in earlier.

Deacon stood. "Hey, Jeff."

The doctor, a tall, good-looking guy who wore dark glasses, smiled at Deacon. "Hi, Deacon. What's going on?"

"Loretta's daughter, Hazel, is pretty sick."

The doctor walked over to Loretta with his hand extended. "I'm Jeff Armstrong."

Loretta shook his hand. "Loretta Simmons. This is Hazel, my daughter."

Dr. Armstrong turned a thousand-watt smile on Hazel. "Hi, Hazel. I'm Dr. Jeff. How are you feeling?"

"My stomach hurts, Dr. Jeff. Really bad."

"So I've heard. Do you mind if I check it out?"

"Okay."

The doctor washed his hands and examined Hazel. When he pressed on her lower stomach, she cried out. Loretta winced, especially when he kept pressing on different parts of her stomach.

"Let's order an ultrasound," Dr. Jeff said to the nurse. "And a full blood workup."

The nurse nodded and left the room. Dr. Jeff turned to them. "We'll run some tests, and then we'll know more."

"What do you think it is?" Loretta asked.

Jeff offered her a wry smile. "I don't like to guess. It won't take long on the tests, and I promise you we'll have something more definitive shortly. You hang in there."

"Okay."

"I'll be back in as soon as we have the results." Dr. Jeff turned to Hazel, picked up the television remote, and handed it to her. "You get to choose what to watch. You're in charge."

She offered up a pained smile. "Okay, Dr. Jeff."

He had no more disappeared than someone came in to take blood. Fortunately, Hazel had had blood drawn before and she wasn't afraid. In fact, she always liked to watch them put the needle in and draw the blood. Loretta was grateful her daughter was momentarily distracted by the blood draw.

"That is so cool," Deacon said, nodding his head as the technician finished up.

"That's my blood." Hazel managed a smile.

"You're tough, ya know," Deacon said, grinning at her after the tech left. "Some kids are big sissies about needles."

"Not me. I can handle it."

"You sure can. If you weren't so sick, I'd give you a huge high five."

Hazel giggled, and it was the sweetest sound Loretta had heard in the past several days.

After that, a tech arrived with equipment to do an ultrasound, followed almost immediately by Dr. Jeff. They all hovered around the screen.

Loretta held her breath.

"Looks like her appendix is severely inflamed. We'll verify with the blood work, but I imagine her white blood cell count will be elevated."

"Which means what?" Loretta asked.

Jeff straightened and looked at her. "The appendix will need to come out. The last thing we want is for it to rupture."

Deacon came over and put his arm around her.

"Okay. Of course."

"I get to have surgery?" Hazel asked.

Dr. Jeff looked at her. "You might."

Hazel grinned. "That is so cool. Will I have a scar?"

Jeff laughed. "Maybe a tiny one."

"Awesome."

Leave it to her daughter to get excited at the prospect of having surgery.

As Dr. Jeff suspected, Hazel's white blood cell count was very high, so he turned them over to the surgeon, Dr. Hannah Alder, a very nice woman who wore her gray hair in a bob and had a calm, confident demeanor that immediately set Loretta at ease. Dr. Alder took her time explaining the procedure to them.

"It's very simple and straightforward and won't take a lot of time," Dr. Alder told them. "And the lovely Miss Hazel here should be out kicking soccer balls again within a week."

"And my stomach won't hurt anymore?" Hazel asked.

Dr. Alder laid her hand over Hazel's. "You'll feel a little pain where the incision is after surgery. It won't last long. But the way you're feeling right now? That'll be gone."

"Good. Because I feel lousy right now."

Dr. Alder gave Hazel a smile. "I know you do, honey. We're going to make that all go away."

Loretta felt a lot better after talking to Dr. Alder. They

arranged for the surgery, which would be outpatient, so if all went well Hazel would be able to go home later in the day. Once everything was organized, Loretta stepped outside and called Tom to let him know what was going on.

"Oh, the poor baby. Is she okay?" Tom asked.

"She's hurting pretty badly. But you know how she is. She's stoic about it. And excited about the prospect of having a scar."

Tom laughed. "She would be. I have a campaign breakfast address this morning at ten. I'll get on a flight and be there right after."

"Thanks. She'll be so happy to know you're coming."

She hung up and smiled. Her ex might be a class-A douchebag, but she also knew that deep down he loved his daughter.

After that she called her parents and Tom's parents, who all said they'd come up to the hospital as soon as possible so they could be there for Hazel. She asked Tom's parents to stop at the house to check on Otis, since she knew her parents wouldn't be too keen on the idea. They said they would.

Family. Sometimes they weren't the best, but in a crisis, she knew she could count on them.

She went back to the room. They were just getting ready to take Hazel up to the surgical floor, so she followed her up and then texted Tom, his parents, and her own to let them know where they could find them.

Several people came in and out, checking Hazel's vitals, drawing even more blood, and Loretta had to sign some forms. They told her it would be about an hour before the surgery.

"I'm going to run home and take a quick shower and change clothes," Deacon said. "That way I can be back here before Hazel goes into surgery."

Loretta pulled Deacon aside while simultaneously keeping an eye on Hazel, who was watching television. "You don't have to be here, you know. I'm sure you have a lot to do, and my parents and Tom's parents are coming."

He gave her a look, almost an angry one. "I'm coming back. I want to be here. Unless you don't want me here."

She reached out and laid her hand on his forearm, trying to draw in the strength she felt there. "I want you here. I just don't want you to feel obligated."

"I have never once felt obligated to you or to Hazel, Loretta. I'm here because I want to be." He looked over at Hazel, and for a brief second she caught the look of hopelessness on his face that she felt inside. "I . . . need to be here for her."

The depth of the feelings he'd developed for her daughter hit her powerfully, and that swell of love she felt for him grew even more.

"Of course." She raised up and brushed her lips across his. "Hurry back."

He nodded. "I will."

He went over and whispered something to Hazel, and it made her giggle, then wince.

He kissed her forehead, then winked at Loretta and left.

Loretta took a seat in the chair next to Hazel. "What did he say?"

"That Otis won't be able to plop into my lap after my surgery because his butt is too big and it'll hurt my belly."

Loretta laughed. "That's true. We'll have to keep an eye on him for a few days and make sure he's careful with you, won't we?"

"Yup."

They watched television for a few minutes together.

"Mama?"

Loretta looked over at Hazel. "Yes?"

"Have you ever had surgery?"

"No, I haven't. Not unless giving birth to you counts as surgery, which it doesn't."

"What's giving birth like?"

Her lips curved. "Well, it's no picnic. It hurts like crazy. But look what I got out of the experience—you."

"All I'm getting out of this is a swollen 'pendix."

"Oh, I don't know. Everyone will fuss over you, and you'll probably get ice cream, and maybe presents."

Her eyes widened. "You think so?"

"Probably."

Hazel turned back to the television. "Cool."

Loretta smiled, then clasped her hand over Hazel's and silently said a small prayer.

Everything was going to be all right very soon.

Chapter 29

DEACON HAD NEVER been the type to let anything or anyone scare him. He was made of stronger stuff.

But one sick little girl had almost brought him to his knees.

Seeing Hazel on the bathroom floor, weak and tired and staring up at him with her sad blue eyes, had torn his heart out. He couldn't make her feel better, and that had made him feel useless. He'd hated it. All he wanted to do was hold her and comfort her and ease her pain.

Loving a kid was hard, man.

He hurried home, trying his best to stay just enough over the speed limit to not get a ticket. He took the fastest shower ever for him, threw on clean clothes, then dashed back to the hospital. On his way he called Reid, because he'd planned to be at the job site this morning to work, and that just wasn't gonna happen. Reid told him not to worry, that he'd get one of their foremen to pick up the slack over at the Harden building.

Deacon was relieved about that. At least he didn't have to think about work today.

After he parked he went inside and up to Hazel's room. Fortunately, he got there before they took her to surgery. She was sitting up in bed, talking to Loretta's parents.

There was also another older couple there, who had to be Tom's parents. When Loretta spotted him, she came over.

"You made it. The nurse was here a few minutes ago and said they'll be back shortly to take her into surgery."

"Okay."

"She was asking if you were coming back. She wants to see you."

"I don't want to get in the way if her grandparents are there."

Loretta looped her arm through his. "Nonsense. Come on. She's been asking for you."

He walked in and immediately saw the disapproving looks from Anthony and Gwen Black.

Nothing he wasn't already used to. He moved in toward the bed and saw Hazel smile at him.

"Hi, Deacon."

He sat on the edge of her bed. "Hi, tough kid. How are you doin'?"

"They gave me medicine that makes me sleepy, but my stomach doesn't hurt anymore."

"Good." He picked up her hand. "And soon you'll get to take a nap, and then they'll get rid of that rotten appendix."

"Yeah. I wonder if they'll let me see it. Maybe I can take it home with me and put it on my bookshelf."

"Gross, Hazel," Loretta said. "We are not bringing it home with us."

She wrinkled her nose. "Then maybe they'll take a picture of it for me."

Deacon laughed. "You could ask the doc. I'll bet she would."

The door opened and the techs came in, so he leaned in and kissed her forehead. "See you soon, sweetheart."

"Okay."

He stepped out of the way so her grandparents could give her a kiss. Then Loretta kissed her.

"I love you."

"Love you, too, Mama."

Loretta stayed with her while they wheeled her to the operating room. Which meant Deacon was alone with Loretta's and Tom's parents.

"So, Deacon," Anthony said. "How have you been?"

"Fine. And you?"

"Just fine. So you and Loretta are seeing each other again."

It didn't surprise him at all that Anthony Black would take this totally awkward and inappropriate moment to bring up his relationship with Loretta. "Yes, we are."

"I see."

And that was the last he said to Deacon. Which suited him just fine.

"Tom said he's flying in soon," Kelly Simmons said.

Deacon nodded. "Loretta told me. Hazel will be really happy to see him."

He'd known Tom in high school, and while they hadn't been close friends, or friends at all, really, he'd had no beef with the guy. Tom's relationship with Loretta now was none of his business.

All he cared about was Hazel coming through the surgery and being all right. Family politics and parents and ex-husbands weren't in his sights at the moment.

"If you'll all excuse me for a minute." He stepped out of the room, needing to take a walk to gather his thoughts. He wandered the halls until he got to a waiting area. There, he took a seat, clasped his hands, and bowed his head.

He wasn't a terribly religious person. His parents had taken him to church every Sunday as a kid, but he'd more or less fallen off the wagon as an adult. He didn't think God would take that personally. So he took a few minutes of silent prayer to ask God to watch over Hazel.

Loretta found Deacon with his hands clasped tightly

together and his head bent, his eyes closed as if he were deep in thought. Or maybe in prayer.

It touched her heart deeply to think that maybe he was sending up a prayer for her daughter. She sat next to him and laid her hand over his and offered up her own prayers of hope.

He looked over at her. "How are you doing?"

"I'm fine. Dr. Alder said it's going to be an easy surgery and I shouldn't worry."

"But you're going to worry anyway."

"Yes. She's my baby and they're cutting her open. How could I not worry?"

He put an arm around her and kissed the top of her head. "She really will be fine. I know she will. She's strong and healthy, and I've never known a kid as tough as she is."

Loretta's lips curved. "She is tough."

"Gets that from you."

Loretta laughed. "Hardly."

He leaned back and gave her a look. "You don't think you're tough?"

"Not at all."

"Look at what you've done with your life, Loretta. You stepped away from a situation you didn't think was good for you or for Hazel. You're raising a daughter by yourself. You own your own business; you bought a farm. That's tough, and a lot of women couldn't do it."

She shrugged. "I had the financial means to do it. That made it easy."

"Bullshit."

Her eyes widened.

"Lot of women in similar situations also have the financial means to separate themselves from bad circumstances, but lack the courage. That's what you had, Loretta. Courage. You made the leap, and I'm sure it was scary as hell to do it. But you did it anyway, for the good of your daughter. So never say you're not tough, because you are."

She'd never looked at it from that perspective before.

"Thank you."

"You're welcome."

"Oh, I came to find you to tell you there's a family waiting area. If you'd like to join us."

"I think I'll pass. You go ahead, though."

She frowned. "Why not?"

"I think your parents like me even less now than they did when we were teens. The last thing you all need is more tension while you're waiting to hear about Hazel."

Loretta's brows knit into a tight frown. "What did they say to you?"

"Not much. But trust me, the disapproval over our relationship is still there."

"I'll talk to them."

"No, you won't. I'm an adult, Loretta. I can handle their animosity just fine. Now is not the time for you to play mediator between your parents and me. Just leave it alone."

She stared at him, not knowing what to do. She didn't like that her parents hadn't gotten past their dislike of Deacon, which had always been completely unwarranted. It irritated her. But she understood Deacon not wanting to upset the family, especially right now.

"Okay. I'll leave it alone. But only if you come sit with me in the waiting area. I'd really like you to be there. It'll make me feel better while I'm waiting."

He hesitated for a few seconds, then finally nodded. "Okay. But only for you."

He stood and held out his hand for her, and she took it. "Thank you."

They walked hand in hand into the family waiting area. If her father and mother had any thoughts about it, they masked it well. They all sat together in silence and waited until Dr. Alder showed up with a smile on her face.

"Surgery went very well. Appendix is out, and there were no complications. Hazel's in the recovery room right now. You'll be able to see her shortly."

Loretta exhaled a sigh of relief. "Thank you so much."

"She should be able to go home later today, but we'll monitor her to be sure."

Loretta glanced over at Deacon, who looked as relieved as she felt.

About an hour later, Loretta went into the recovery room to see Hazel. She was mostly groggy and out of it, but Loretta got to talk to her and see that she was okay. And for a mother, that was everything.

Now all she had to do was wait for Hazel to fully awaken and shake off the anesthetic and have the doc check her out to make sure everything was all right with her.

Considering how terribly this day had started, it was looking better. Finally.

Chapter 30

HAZEL WAS EVENTUALLY brought to an outpatient room, where she'd stay until she was discharged.

She was surrounded by her grandparents, who all lavished love and attention on her.

Loretta had to admit that, despite her irritation with her parents at the moment, they knew how to cater to their granddaughter. Tom's parents were equally as loving, bringing her a bouquet of flowers along with a stuffed animal that made her grin a loopy, half-drugged smile that Loretta caught on her camera phone.

Deacon stayed in the background, but hovered nearby, and it meant so much to Loretta to have him there. Whenever Hazel asked for him, he was right there, holding her hand and making her laugh, which then made her wince. Then they both laughed about her wincing. He told her she'd forever have a battle scar and she should be proud of that. That made her happy.

There was a knock on her hospital room door, and Loretta went to answer it.

It was Tom.

"Hey," he said. "I got here as soon as I could."

"I'm so glad you made it. Come on in." She opened the door, shocked to see some dude she didn't recognize and a guy with a camera behind him.

She frowned. "Tom. What is this?"

He at least had the decency to look sheepish. "Well, they're documenting every step of the campaign."

She rolled her eyes and was about to hit him hard about it, but then Hazel saw him.

"Daddy!"

Tom brushed past her, and so did the other two guys.

"Hi, pumpkin. Heard you were sick, so I rushed right up here to see you."

Tom sure knew how to turn it on for the cameras. And suddenly they were on, lights blazing, as Tom sat on the bed, kissed Hazel, and listened to her tell the story of how she got sick and had to have surgery. He gave her all the appropriate sympathy and love.

For about ten whole minutes before he said he had to leave.

So much for Tom's record parenting skills.

"I have to go, pumpkin," he said to Hazel. "But I'll see you soon."

Hazel's eyes welled with tears. "Okay."

He brushed her forehead with his lips. "Love you."

"I love you, too, Daddy."

As he walked out, he stood in front of Loretta.

"Sorry. I have an event I have to be at by four."

There was so much she wanted to say to him, and none of it was good. And she wouldn't do it in front of Hazel. "Yeah. Thanks for stopping by."

"Sure. She's my kid. I'd do anything for her."

Bite your tongue, Loretta.

Tom's parents walked out with him, so there was finally some breathing space in the room.

Especially now that the blowhard politician had left.

"I'd love something cold to drink, Loretta," her mother

said. "Would you like to come with your father and me to get some iced tea?"

Loretta looked over at Hazel.

"I'll sit with her," Deacon said. "You take a break."

"Yeah, okay. Sure." It would probably help to walk off her irritation at her ex-husband.

They headed toward the elevators. When they opened, Loretta pushed the button that would take them to the cafeteria floor.

"Wasn't it so nice of Tom to take time out of his busy schedule to come visit?" her mother asked.

Loretta couldn't help the eye roll. "Yes. So nice."

"I mean, to drop everything like that and fly to his daughter's side."

"With a camera crew in tow," Loretta added.

"He has to do that, you know," her father said.

She turned to face her parents. "No, he doesn't *have* to do that. He does it to make himself look good. The doting father so concerned for his daughter. You do realize he hardly ever sees her, and when he does, it's only for campaign purposes?"

Her mother looked shocked. "Loretta. He loves her."

"No, Mom. He uses her. If he loved her he'd see her every other weekend like he's supposed to. He would have dropped everything having to do with his campaign this morning and he would have been here by her side. That's not what just happened up there." When the elevator doors opened, Loretta walked out with her parents, then stopped in the hall. "What you saw up there? That wasn't a father concerned about his daughter's health. That was a photo op, and nothing more."

Her father frowned at her. "I think you're blinded by . . . by whatever is going on between you and Deacon Fox."

Her anger had reached the boiling point. "Oh. That's funny, Dad. Do you want to know about Deacon? Deacon was the one who held Hazel in the bathroom while she threw up. He was the one who was there cradling her in his arms while she was shaking with fever. She clutched on to him like a lifeline. He's the one she trusts. He's the one she asks for when she needs something. And you know why that is? Because her own father isn't there for her. She doesn't realize it now, but someday, when she's an adult and can reason it out, she'll realize how very little her own father cares about her."

"Don't you say that, Loretta," her mother said. "Tom is a good man. He loves Hazel."

"In his own way, he does love her. But not enough. Not as much as she needs."

She turned to her father and advanced on him. "And don't you ever belittle Deacon Fox ever again. He's been there for both me and Hazel. If you don't like him, that's just too bad, Dad, because he's in my life and in Hazel's life, and you'd better get on board with that, because I don't intend for that to change."

She walked away from both of her parents, nearly shaking with anger and frustration.

Maybe it was the aftereffects of everything that had happened with Hazel, or maybe it was that, for the first time in her life, she'd finally stood up to her parents and told them how she really felt.

Either way, she was done listening to bullshit about Tom and Deacon from her parents. They needed to open their eyes and see the truth, and she'd laid that truth out clearly for them.

As she made her way into the cafeteria, her lips curved into a smile. That had been a long time coming.

And she felt really damn good about it.

Chapter 31

IT HAD BEEN three days since Hazel's surgery, and when Deacon pulled up outside of Loretta's house after finishing work and going home to clean up, Hazel was outside kicking a soccer ball and laughing when Otis tried to steal the ball away from her.

He put the truck in park and grinned. There was nothing like the amazing resilience of kids.

They'd taken her home the night after her surgery. She'd slept off the anesthesia, and the next morning had asked for pancakes for breakfast. Though she'd been a little sore, she'd seemed fine. The nausea was gone, and so was her stomach pain. Every day since then she'd gotten better and better. He'd made sure to stick close and check on her daily.

Obviously, she was more than fine now.

"Hey, Hazel," he said as he walked toward her and Otis.

Hazel kicked the ball to Deacon, who stopped it with the ball of his foot. Otis lumbered over, his tail thumping like a wind machine.

"Otis, sit."

The dog plopped his butt to the ground.

"Good boy." He scratched Otis behind the ears and waited for Hazel to make her way to him.

"Hi, Deacon. Did you see me kick the ball?"

"I did. How are you feeling?"

"I feel a-mazing. My stomach doesn't hurt at all."

"I'm glad to hear that."

"Mama said I can spend the night over at Tabby's house this weekend."

"Really? That's good."

"I know. We're gonna go to the rec center and play basketball and maybe go swimming if my doctor says I can. I have a checkup on Friday."

"I'll keep my fingers crossed on the swimming."

"Thanks. Mama's in the house changing clothes because we're going to Reid and Sam's new house thing tonight. You're coming with us, right?"

"I am. Are you coming, or are you staying home by yourself?"

She giggled. "Deacon. I can't stay home alone. I'm too young."

"Oh. I thought maybe since you'd had your big bad surgery, you were all tough and a big girl now and maybe you'd throw a party of your own while your mom was away."

"You're funny. But no. I'm going with you. Tabby's going to be there."

"And Ryan, too, right?"

"Maybe."

"Like maybe you like him?"

She nudged Deacon. "Not like that. He's annoying."

"Uh-huh."

He knew Hazel had a crush on Ryan. They teased each other, and at this age, Ryan would look at Hazel like his little sister's pesky best friend. But Hazel was beautiful and athletic and smart. And in about six or seven years, Ryan would see Hazel in a different light entirely.

For now, though, the teasing was fun.

The front door opened, and Loretta stepped out looking gorgeous in a white and red flowery sundress.

"Hazel, it's time to— Oh, hi, Deacon. Why don't you both come in? I'm almost ready. Hazel, you need to change."

"Okay, Mama. Come on, Otis."

Deacon followed Hazel and the dog inside. Hazel went down the hall to her room, and Deacon watched her until her door closed. Then he drew Loretta into his arms and planted a long, hot kiss on her.

When she pulled back, she blinked. "Wow. That was nice."

"It's been a while."

"It has."

"Also, you look beautiful tonight."

"Thank you. It's so hot out I'm going with the minimal amount of clothing possible for mixed company."

She looked amazing. The dress hit her at the knees, so decent enough, but it clung to her torso and fanned out, and she had great legs and beautiful arms and—who was he kidding? He couldn't care less about the dress she wore. All he really wanted to do was take it off of her. With everything that had been going on with Hazel both before and after her surgery, and then him having to dive back into work at the building and Loretta needing to catch up at the bookstore, they'd had no time to be alone.

Which was fine. Life got in the way of romance sometimes. That was their reality. But he sure had missed the feel of her skin and the taste of her mouth.

Now, though, he smoothed his hands up her arms and took in the way her breathing deepened.

"Barring any further medical or other catastrophes, Hazel's spending the night with Tabitha on Friday."

Deacon nodded. "She told me. She wants to go swimming."

"Yes. She has a follow-up appointment with the surgeon Friday afternoon, and hopefully she'll get the go-ahead to resume normal activities, including swimming."

Deacon took a quick glance down the hall. "I'm no doctor, but judging from the way she was booting the soccer ball when I got here, it looks like normal activities have already resumed."

Loretta's lips lifted. "Hard to get that kid to tone it down, you know?"

"Yeah. She looks good, though."

Loretta took a step back and went to grab her purse. "Every day she's gaining back more and more of her strength. She seems normal already."

"Not surprising. You know surgeries like that are much easier on kids than on adults."

"No kidding. If it were me I'd be on the sofa with a pillow on my stomach. Not her, though."

"She's tough. And so are you. You'd be back at work already carting books around as if it was nothing."

"I don't know about that. I'm not as tough as a nine-year-old."

Said nine-year-old threw her door open, backpack in hand and dog following behind her. "I'm ready."

Deacon looked to Loretta, who smiled.

"Let's go."

LORETTA TOOK IN every kitchen cabinet, every bathroom tile, and every wall fixture as Sam gave her the tour of their new home.

"Is there anything better than new-home smell?" Loretta asked.

Sam nearly vibrated with delight. "There probably is, but over the past week I've walked through this house over and over again, unable to believe it's finally finished and we've moved in."

"It's beautiful, Sam. You're going to make some wonderful memories here."

"Thank you. We're so happy. Not My Dog loves it here, too. He has his own space in the master bedroom. And the yard is finally finished, and he's happy as he can be running around back there."

They stepped outside where a group of the guys were gathered around the backyard kitchen, which had turned out amazing. There was also a fire pit, which would be so fun to sit around come fall, though the thought of it in this July heat was not at all appealing.

The landscape was gorgeous, with trees and bushes offering up plenty of shady spots and tons of green grass for Not My Dog to run around in.

"Ugh. Too hot out here," Sam said. "I don't know how the guys can stand it."

She led Loretta inside and into the spacious living room. With its vaulted ceiling, it made the already good-sized room seem even larger. And, of course, Sam had filled the room with fresh flowers, her florist touch seen across the entire house with vibrant plants and beautiful flowerpots that filled the home with cheer.

Hazel had run off to play in the media room with Tabitha and Ryan, so she didn't have to worry about her daughter. She poured herself a glass of wine and took a seat next to Jane and Chelsea.

"So, how are you two doing?" she asked.

Chelsea rubbed her hand over her now-visible baby bump. "I feel pretty darn good. Though it's hot outside and my ankles are already swelling. What's up with that? I'm barely into my second trimester."

"It happens when you're pregnant. Hopefully once fall gets here it'll subside."

"I'm still nauseous," Jane said. "All the time. Crackers are my best friend, and they go everywhere with me."

"I'm sorry, Jane," Loretta said. Though it had been years, she remembered the nausea all too well.

"Thanks. It'll pass soon enough. Hopefully."

"Molly and I are not pregnant or nauseous," Megan said as they came into the room and plopped down on one of the love seats. "So we're doing all the drinking. And eating."

Jillian came in with a glass of wine in her hand. "Isn't it so great that there's more wine for us? I mean, there has to be some advantage to not having a gorgeous man who adores us and a sweet baby in our bellies." She kissed Chelsea on the cheek and winked at Megan and Sam.

"Hate you," Chelsea said.

Megan grinned at Chelsea. "You're welcome."

Then Emma and Des arrived with the babies. Loretta loved babies, and Michael and Ben were simply adorable, with their pudgy little faces and fat baby fingers.

Loretta couldn't wait to hold one of them, though she had to wait her turn as all the women fussed over them.

"This is probably like a little baby vacation time for you," she said to Des when Chelsea took Ben as soon as Des pulled him out of his carrier.

Des laughed. "It's like this at home, too. Martha takes him from me every chance she gets. And as soon as Logan is done on the ranch for the day, he's in his daddy's arms for the night. I'm lucky to be breastfeeding him, or I might never get to hold him."

Loretta smiled. "He's a well-loved baby."

"Definitely."

Loretta finally got a chance to cuddle Ben in her arms. There was nothing like holding a baby. Their sweet, inno-cent faces, the way their lips moved, the way they smelled like a sweet slice of heaven—everything about them was absolutely perfect.

"All right," Jillian said. "Hand him over."

Loretta frowned. "Fifty bucks."

Jillian laughed. "Not a chance."

"Fine." She gently transferred him to Jillian, but it wasn't long before Emma passed Michael to her.

"You two should charge us all for letting us hold your babies."

Emma looked over at Des. "Now that's a thought. We could probably pay for our sons' college educations that way."

Des offered up a cocky grin. "There's an idea."

"I noticed there haven't been paparazzi shots of Ben in any of the magazines," Chelsea said.

"Nor will there ever be. I know how to keep my child well hidden from the press. They're wily, but I've gotten advice from several veterans in the industry who've played that game with photographers. If you don't want your baby photographed, there are plenty of ways to keep it from happening."

"I don't know why anyone would want a picture of a baby anyway," Jane said. "I mean, I get that you're an actress and people like to see pictures of you, Des. But your baby? What business is it of theirs?"

Des shrugged. "No idea. But I control what photos are put up of my family. I posted a wedding picture on my social media sites. And I put up one photo of Logan and me and Ben together not too long after he was born. Anything other than that is no one's business. But the press? They think if we take a walk outside of our house, it's news."

Molly wrinkled her nose. "That's not news. Sorry."

Des laughed. "No, you're right. Nothing newsworthy about it. Unfortunately, I'm about to start work on a new movie within the next few months, and that means Ben will be traveling with me. Security will have to be doubly tight to keep photos from getting out."

"Oh, it'll be hard for Logan to be separated from Ben while you're on location, won't it?" Loretta asked.

Des nodded. "We've already started working out a schedule. Fortunately, the movie shoot will be in Montana, so not too far away. I'll be able to spend weekends at home, and Logan will occasionally fly up to be with Ben and me."

"Perfect," Megan said.

"Yes, it is. But he's gotten so used to having his time with Ben every day that I know there'll be an adjustment period. We'll all have to adjust. Martha will miss him, too. She's already talking about quitting her job as the house manager and coming along as nanny to Ben."

"Actually," Emma said, "I can't think of anyone better suited to be Ben's nanny, can you?"

"We're seriously contemplating the idea, though all the ranch hands are horrified at the thought. They're wondering who would cook for them if she left."

"I sense a ranch revolt in the making," Sam said.

Des's lips lifted. "Yes, the next month or so should be interesting while we wrangle all the details."

They all chatted about the babies and work for a while. Loretta got up and went upstairs to check on Hazel, who was comfortably stretched out on one of the spacious leather reclining chairs doing battle with Tabitha and Ryan on a video game. Since she seemed to be fine, she wandered back downstairs and ran into Deacon in the kitchen.

"Hey," he said as he put a platter on the drying rack. "I was just washing off this plate. Ribs are on the grill. What are you up to?"

"I was checking on Hazel."

"Is she doing all right?"

"She's fine. Upstairs in the media room battling it out on some robot-something-or-other death match thing."

His lips ticked up. "Sounds fun. Did you get the house tour from Sam?"

"I did. How about you?"

"Some of it, but then the doorbell rang, so Reid had to take care of that."

She looped her arm in his. "Well, come on. We'll walk around together."

His lips curved. "I like that idea. Maybe we'll find a dark closet somewhere and we can make out."

"I like the way you think, Deacon."

They wandered through the house, taking in the master bedroom downstairs. It was huge, and had an amazing bathroom with a giant tub and an equally immense and spacious shower.

"I'm going to have that someday," he said.

"What? A big soaker tub?"

"I meant the huge shower, but the tub's not a bad idea. Sometimes I feel beat-up at the end of a long day. I wouldn't mind a good, hot soak."

"I can see that." They wandered back out. "I love that the master opens up onto the back patio. I can imagine breaking out a wall in my master so I could do the same."

"That would be easy enough to do at your place. Put in some French doors and add a patio space. End your day with a glass of wine and a look at the stars."

Her lips lifted. "Yes. Someday, maybe. Have to do the deck first."

"We could amend those plans that Reid's drawing up for you. Have the deck extended around the side of the house."

"Hmm. Something to think about. I'll let you know."

He ran his hand down her back. "I'll mention it to him. And you don't have to do it all at once. The addition off the master can always be added later, and it's much easier if it's already in the plans."

She nodded. "Okay."

They wandered down the hall, then up the stairs, checking again on the kids, who were totally oblivious to them as they argued with each other over some mystical world. There was also an office on the second floor, along with two other bedrooms.

"How many bedrooms in your imaginary house you've yet to build?" she asked.

"Four, at least. Plenty for kids, plus an office."

She stopped and turned to him. "Why haven't you bought or built a house yet?"

He shrugged. "I thought I'd wait until I get married. I figure the woman I marry will want some say-so in how things are done."

She thought about that for a minute, about the fact that Deacon might have been married when she got back to town. He could have built an entire life for himself, with a wife and a child or two. He might have had a house just like this one that he'd constructed with love, taking into consideration his wife's desires.

The thought caused a violent twinge of jealousy that had no business being there.

She was the one who had walked away, and Deacon had had every right to move on with his life.

Only he hadn't.

"So why didn't you?" she asked as they lingered on the stairs.

"Why didn't I what?"

"Ever get married?"

He shrugged. "Never found the right woman to settle down with, I guess. I was busy building my business, and that seemed to be a priority."

"I understand that. And I'm glad you don't have a wife and three kids."

He laughed. "You are, huh?"

She took his hand as they made their way downstairs. "Yes. Very happy about that."

"Hey, Deacon," Hazel said, running down the hall to launch herself at him.

"Hey, tough girl." He caught her and hauled her into his arms. "How did the battle royal go up there?"

"I won three games. Tabitha won three games, too. Ryan won four. We say he cheated."

Deacon laughed. "Oh, he did, did he? Let's go challenge him and see."

Deacon looked over his shoulder at her. "Be right back. Gotta go kick some butt."

Loretta laughed. "Okay. You go do that."

She loved that he was so comfortable around her daughter. Around all the kids. He had never made it all about her, but instead had always included Hazel.

Someday that man was going to make a great father.

She felt another twinge in her stomach at that thought, but cast it aside. Those were deep thoughts, and she was already three glasses of wine into the evening, so that was as far as she was going to allow wine thoughts to go.

Instead, she hung out and ate and drank and enjoyed her friends for the rest of the evening, until it was time to leave. They headed back to the farm. Hazel took Otis outside to run off some of his pent-up energy.

Loretta had already had enough to drink earlier in the evening, so she decided on ice water.

"What would you like?" she asked Deacon.

"Water's good for me, too."

Hazel came back inside. "Hey, Deacon. You wanna have a movie and popcorn night?"

"Isn't it a little late for you, miss?" her mother asked.

"Aww, just a short movie, Mama?"

"Yeah, how about just a short movie?" Deacon gave her a tilt of his head.

"Fine. I'll make the popcorn."

They ended up watching a comedy. Hazel and Deacon both laughed, tossing popcorn at each other, and Loretta enjoyed watching them more than the movie. After it was over, Loretta sent Hazel to get ready for bed, and she went into the kitchen to put the dishes in the sink.

Deacon went with her.

"Thanks for hanging out with us," Loretta said.

He came up behind her and nuzzled her neck, putting his arms around her. "Like I'd want to be anywhere else."

She turned around to face him, and he kissed her, a kiss that quickly turned passionate.

"I'm ready for bed, Mama."

They broke apart, and Deacon said, "I should go."

Loretta nodded. "I'll see you later."

"Okay." He walked toward the door, but stopped and went over to Hazel, giving her a kiss on the cheek. "Night, sweet girl."

"G'night, Deacon."

Loretta went with Hazel into her room and got her tucked into bed.

"Mama?"

"Yes?"

"You like Deacon, right?"

Uh-oh. "Yes, I do."

"I like him, too. But you *like* him like him, don't you?"

She cocked her head to the side. "What do you mean?"

"Like a boyfriend?"

"I guess. Is that okay?"

"It's really okay. He's nice to you. And to me. And he shows up when he says he's going to. And when he says he's going to do something, he does it."

Loretta's heart squeezed. She realized that Hazel had been so often disappointed by her father that Deacon was something of a revelation to her. She felt both sad and happy about that. Tom had let Hazel down so much, and she felt so bad about that. But at least Deacon had been there for her.

"Yes, he's a great guy, isn't he?"

"Super great. You should marry him. Then he wouldn't have to keep leaving at night."

Her eyes widened. "Uh, I don't think we're there yet, honey."

Hazel rolled over on her side. "Well, if you get there, I'd be okay with it."

Life was so simple when you were a kid. "Good to know. I love you, Hazel."

"I love you, too, Mama."

She turned out the light and closed the door to Hazel's room, a little shocked from the conversation she'd just had.

She wasn't certain Hazel had been aware of what was going on with Deacon. She'd been careful not to date after the divorce. It had been confusing enough uprooting Hazel and moving her, though she'd taken it all in stride. And with Tom being so wishy-washy about seeing her, that had been tough.

Plus, dating had been the last thing on her mind after the divorce. She'd been fed up with men, and all she'd wanted to do was carve out a life for Hazel and herself. That had been satisfying enough.

But then Deacon had come into their lives, and she hadn't been sure how that would affect Hazel. She'd tried to keep their relationship on the down low. Kids, after all, tended to live in their own bubble with their own activities and interests and didn't pay much attention to what adults had going on.

Apparently her daughter was quite observant and knew exactly what had been happening between Deacon and her.

Of course she would. It wasn't like some guy would start coming around on a regular basis and her child wouldn't notice that. Loretta wasn't hiding her affection for Deacon, nor was he hiding his for her. So it was kind of ridiculous for her to pretend the relationship didn't exist.

But what if things between Deacon and her didn't work out? Hazel would be hurt by that. How was she supposed to handle her relationship with Deacon now that Hazel knew about it?

Parenting. This was hard business.

She had to do some thinking about the future.

Chapter 32

DEACON WAS JUST finishing up work on Friday when he saw Luke McCormack's police cruiser pull up in front of the building. He swiped the sweat from his brow with the hem of his shirt and closed the bed of his truck.

Luke got out and opened the door for his K9 German shepherd, Boomer. Deacon didn't approach the dog until Luke gave the okay, since the dog wouldn't know if Deacon was friend or suspect until Luke told him.

"Hey, Boomer." Deacon gave the dog several scratches and pets. Boomer's tail wagged furiously.

"What's up, Deacon?" Luke asked.

"Nothing much. Finishing up for the day. What's going on with you?"

"Just doing a walk around. We've had a few reports of suspicious activity on the main streets here."

"Oh yeah? Like what?"

"Not sure exactly. Over the past couple of days people have reported lurkers in the back alleys. Like maybe someone was casing businesses after they closed for the day. Boomer and I are going to take a stroll and check things out. We've got another unit patrolling the south side of the street doing the same."

Deacon nodded, realizing Luke was on duty and this was serious business, not a social call. "I won't keep you, then. Let me know if you find anything."

"Will do. Make sure you're locked up tight in the building."

"I'll do a double check before I leave. And I'll make sure Loretta does the same for the bookstore."

"Thanks. See you later."

As soon as Luke gave Boomer the signal, the dog transformed from friendly pet to K9 police officer on duty. His ears went up and he started sniffing. Deacon lingered long enough to watch Luke and Boomer disappear down the alley, then he went over and knocked on the door to Loretta's bookstore. He knew she was still there, because her car was parked on the side road.

She came over, smiled, and unlocked the door.

"I was just about to leave. We have a date tonight, you know."

"I do. Luke just stopped by. He's doing a search for suspicious lurkers who might be casing businesses, so I want to make sure you're locked up tight before I leave. Let me come inside and do a walk around with you."

"Oh, sure." She let him in, and they went around to all the doors to make sure all the locks were done. Then she set the alarm and locked the front door. He walked her to her car and waited while she got in.

"I already dropped Hazel over at Jane's house, so I'll see you when you get to my place," she said.

He nodded, leaned in, and kissed her. "See you soon."

She laid her hand over his. "Be careful."

His lips curved. "I'll be fine. I don't think anyone's going to be lurking around with Luke and Boomer wandering the alleys."

"You're probably right about that."

Loretta drove off, so he walked back and checked all three stories of the building. When he was satisfied everything was locked up tight, he got in his truck and drove down the street to Sam's flower shop, since it was still open. She was inside, so he chatted with her for a few minutes about what was going on. She hadn't seen or heard anything, but while he was in there, he had Sam put together a bouquet. Then he headed back to his town house, took a shower, and changed clothes.

He pulled the bouquet out of his truck when he got to the farm. Rain was starting to fall, so he hurried to the front door and rang the bell.

"Door's open," he heard Loretta call. He rolled his eyes and walked in.

"I could be a serial killer, you know."

She walked down the hall. "But are you?"

"No. But don't leave your door unlocked. You're isolated out here. Anyone could just come in."

"Okay, Dad. I promise to be more careful."

He laughed.

"And are those flowers for me, or are you selling them door-to-door?"

"Oh. Yeah. They're for you. I realized I've never brought you flowers before."

She took the bouquet he gave her and inhaled. "These are beautiful. Thank you. And you have given me flowers before."

"I have?"

"Yes. You bought me a corsage for prom."

"Oh, right. I forgot about that. And that one didn't count."

"It didn't?"

She made her way to the kitchen, so he followed her.

"No. My mom picked it out. I chose these for you. Though, actually, Sam helped me."

She reached into the cabinet to grab a vase and filled it with water. "She helps me, too, when I buy flowers, so these do count. And they're gorgeous, Deacon. Thank you for thinking of me."

"You're welcome." While she arranged the flowers, he took a moment to admire her legs in the dress she was wearing. He sure liked when she wore dresses. This one was black-and-white polka dots, and she had on some kind of sandals with heels that made her legs look even longer.

She turned around, so he brought his gaze up to her face. "Were you checking me out?"

"I was. You look beautiful. I like the dress."

"Thank you. You look pretty spectacular yourself."

He looked down at his jeans and button-up shirt. "Nothing much to look at here."

She made her way toward him, snaking her palms along his chest. "Oh, I disagree. Plenty to look at. And to touch."

He breathed in deeply as she moved her hands over his chest and shoulders. It had been too long since he'd been alone with her, and, despite his intentions to take her out to dinner first, he couldn't resist a taste of her. He wrapped an arm around her waist and tugged her against him, then bent to put his mouth on hers.

When she moaned against his lips, he knew this was what Loretta wanted, too. Her lips were soft, and he slid his tongue inside to lick against hers. His cock went hard, and he cupped her butt to draw her against him.

She pulled her mouth from his. "Do we have dinner reservations somewhere?"

"No."

"Good. Because being naked with you is the only thing I've been thinking about for a week or more."

That was all he needed to hear. He scooped her up in his arms and carried her down the hall to her bedroom. He put her down, then turned her around so he could unzip her dress. He pushed her hair to the side and pressed his lips to the back of her neck.

She shivered.

"Such a pretty dress," he said, sweeping his fingers over the spot where the material met her skin.

She looked over her shoulder at him. "It served its purpose."

He drew the straps down, then stopped to kiss her shoulder. She took the dress off and laid it on the chair by the bed.

His jaw nearly dropped as he took in the black bra and panties she had on under that dress. The dress had been sexy enough, but the underwear?

Wow. The cups of the bra barely held in her breasts, and the panties scooped low on her hips, tiny straps holding the material in front. He walked around her to see the back was just a strip of fabric that disappeared between the cheeks of her butt.

Oh, hell yeah.

He smoothed his hand over each butt cheek, then teased the straps of her underwear.

"You need to lay on the bed so I can get up close and personal with this underwear."

While she slid off her heels, she said, "And you need to start shedding some clothes."

"I can do that." He got rid of his clothes, his gaze glued to Loretta as she lay back on the bed.

He climbed onto the bed and hovered over her, taking in the sight of her beautiful body. The way her hips curved, the beauty of her thighs, the strength of her calves, and the swells of her breasts. He started at her ankles and cupped her legs as he mapped his way up her body, feeling the need to touch every inch of her skin, listening to the sound of her breathing as he did.

When he skimmed her hips and made his way to her stomach, he touched every inch there, including the silvery lines that stretched across her skin.

"Ugh. Stretch marks," she said.

He looked up at her as he rested his hand on her lower belly. "You grew a baby in here. Nothing sexier than that."

She shuddered in a deep breath, then let it out as he moved up to her rib cage, then teased his fingers over that damn sexy bra, brushing his fingertips over her nipples. He pulled the fabric down, releasing one of the buds so he could put his mouth on her.

Her nipple was soft as he took it between the roof of his mouth and his tongue and sucked. The bud hardened, and Loretta arched upward. He undid the front clasp and released her breasts so he could tease her nipples and play with her breasts.

She was so beautiful, so responsive as he licked and sucked each bud. Just listening to her, feeling her move under him, was a turn-on. And then he went south, kissing his way over her stomach and lower. He skimmed his tongue just above the fabric of her underwear, taking a nibble of her hip as he drew that flimsy string away.

If a floating cloud could make a sound, it would have been the sigh she made.

That's exactly where he wanted her, floating away to relaxed nirvana. At least until he got her ramped up.

But right now he wanted her tranquil and easy. She'd had enough turmoil over the past week. So he removed her underwear and kissed his way up her legs, drawing them apart to tease her inner thighs with his tongue. He felt her muscles tense.

"Deacon."

"Yeah."

"I need this."

"I know you do." He pressed a kiss to the top of her sex. "Just relax. I'm about to get there."

She lifted up on her forearms. "What you are doing right now is anything but relaxing."

He cocked a brow. "Really? So maybe you should roll over and I'll give you a back massage."

She glared at him. "I do not need a back massage. I need an orgasm."

He laughed. He loved that she told him exactly what she wanted. "Oh, you wanted an orgasm?"

"Funny. Now get in there and do what you do best."

"So this will be a graded event, then?"

She let out an exasperated sound. "Deacon."

"Relax, babe. You know it'll be good if you wait for it a little."

"I've *been* waiting for it. Like over a week."

Now he had her riled up, so when he flicked his tongue over her thigh, then moved in and put his mouth over her sex, she laid her head back and let out one hell of a satisfied moan. He didn't let up, giving her exactly what he knew she needed.

Soon she was writhing against him, reaching for him and screaming out his name as she came in a torrent of cries. And with every one of her movements his dick got harder and harder. It was all he could do not to put on a condom and thrust into her in the middle of her orgasm.

But he could wait, because she had needed this, and he intended to make tonight all about Loretta. So after her first orgasm, he gave her some space to come down from that high, and then he took her back up again, using his fingers and his tongue to take her over the edge a second time.

And when he crawled up to lay next to her, she looked over at him.

"That was unexpected. I definitely needed it. And thank you."

"You're welcome. Hungry now?"

She slanted a disbelieving look at him. "Hungry? Are you serious?" She rolled over onto her side and scraped a nail down his chest. "I believe only one of us has been satisfied. And I'm not nearly finished with you yet."

"Is that right?"

"That is definitely right."

She shifted and scooted down his body, pushing him onto his back as she rolled over on top of him.

His balls quivered when she took his shaft in her hand, stroked him, then looked up at him with a wickedly sexy smile before putting her lips over the crest of his cock and taking him in her mouth.

Oh, hell. That had to be the greatest sight ever, to see a woman engulfing your cock. The pleasure of it was like being sucked into the sweetest vortex. His head spun, his entire body broke out in chills, and he wanted it to last forever.

But Loretta had a sweet mouth, and he was going to go off in a minute, and that wasn't the way he had planned for this to go. He drew her up his body and planted a fiery kiss on her, rolling her onto her back so he could move against her as he plunged his tongue into her mouth.

She moaned, wrapping her legs around him to surge against him.

He pulled away only long enough to grab a condom and put it on, then he was right there with her again, sliding inside of her at the same time he took her mouth in a deep kiss.

He'd never felt so deeply connected to a woman before. It had always been like this with Loretta, only now they had the time to explore each other—to touch and taste and really feel the sensations that, coupled with his emotional connection to her, was damn near overwhelming in its intensity.

This was what love felt like, that feeling of falling over a cliff but knowing you weren't falling by yourself. That you had someone to hold on to who would be there for you so you wouldn't crash at the bottom.

And when he let go, he held tight to her, taking in her cries as she came with him. It was an incredible euphoria that seemed to last an eternity.

The high lasted well after they lay there spent and holding hands as they stared at each other.

"So," she said, "what's for dinner?"

He laughed. "I don't know. We could get dressed and go out."

She wrinkled her nose. "Clothes are overrated. I was thinking veggie omelets and fruit salad."

"Sounds fantastic."

She rubbed her thumb across her jaw. "I need you well fed. We're not finished yet."

"We aren't?"

"Nope."

He affected an exasperated sigh. "You're very demanding, you know."

She rolled out of bed and stared down at him. "Would you have me any other way?"

He grinned up at her. "No, ma'am."

Chapter 33

IT HAD BEEN two weeks of nonstop craziness, but Loretta was totally content with the way things were going.

Hazel had completely mended from her surgery and was back to normal. The bookstore was busy, and since they were gearing up for all of the back-to-school sale madness, she had a lot to do.

But that meant good business for the bookstore, so she had no complaints. Hazel was about to start tryouts for the competitive soccer team, though, so she had to juggle that along with some extra time at the bookstore.

Fortunately, Deacon said he could pitch in and help. She hated relying on him when she wanted to be able to handle it herself, but Deacon said things at the building were well under control. So she was going to close up a little late, and he'd pick up Hazel, make sure she had something to eat, then get her to soccer tryouts in plenty of time.

She had to admit it was great to have him around. She could have asked her parents, but they weren't exactly the type to help Hazel warm up beforehand, and Deacon would.

Plus, Hazel had asked him to, and Deacon would do just about anything Hazel asked.

A dangerous thing, she thought with a half smile. Her daughter definitely had Deacon wrapped around her little finger. But the feeling was mutual. She wasn't sure who loved Deacon more—Loretta or Hazel.

It was probably even.

Deacon showed up right on time at four thirty to pick up Hazel.

"She's been bouncing off the walls all day," Loretta told him. "She's in the back now. I tried to settle her by downloading a new game for her and tried to convince her to store up all that excess energy for tryouts. I don't think it's really working."

Deacon nodded. "She's excited. We've been talking about it every day. And she's really good, so I don't think she has to worry about making the team."

"I hope she will. She loves soccer so much. She's played every year since she was old enough."

Deacon gave her a kiss on the cheek. "It's in the bag. We'll see you at the field."

"Okay. And thank you for doing this."

"You know, at some point you're going to have to quit thanking me like I'm your next-door neighbor or something. We're in a relationship, Loretta. So stop treating this like it's a favor, okay?"

She was shocked by that. "Okay. Sorry. I'll see you on the field."

Deacon went and got Hazel. She had her backpack on, and she came and hugged Loretta.

"Wish me luck, Mama."

"Not that you need it because you're so spectacular, but good luck. I love you."

"Love you, too. Bye."

She watched her daughter walk out the door with Deacon, and her heart did a little lurch.

Now it was time for her to get all of her work done so

she could get out to the soccer fields on time. She hustled inventory onto the shelves, put Kendra and Camila to work dealing with customers, and, miracle of all miracles, actually closed the doors on time at six p.m.

She wouldn't have time to go home and change clothes, but that was okay. She made it to the soccer field at six fifteen, and since tryouts had started at six, she hoped she hadn't missed too much.

She found Deacon and Otis on the sidelines. It figured he'd bring the dog.

"You brought Otis?"

"It's good for his socialization and training to be around crowds. He needs to learn to behave."

"And how's that going?"

"He tried to chase a few soccer balls, but since he's on the leash, I'm teaching him that every ball is not a toy for him."

She rolled her eyes. "I'm glad you're in charge of him."

"Hey, I've got this covered. No worries."

The one thing she never worried about was Deacon and Otis together. He truly did have a handle on the large beast. She wandered and found Hazel with Tabitha and a group of other girls. They all had numbered uniform tops on over their T-shirts and were listening intently to the coach's instructions.

As the first set of girls took the field, Loretta realized she was nervous. Hazel wasn't in that group, so Loretta decided to watch. They went through a set of drills, then played a mock game against each other, no doubt to demonstrate ball control and skill set. The coach had all the girls switch positions multiple times. There were several coaches on hand making notes on clipboards, and Loretta was nervous for all the girls.

Then it was Hazel's turn, and her anxiety level went up about ten notches. She walked the sidelines, trying to find the best spot to watch. Deacon was on the other side of the field talking to some of the guys. Loretta finally grabbed what she thought was a decent location in the center, where she spotted Jane talking to some other women.

"Hi, Loretta," Jane said. "Isn't this exciting?"

"It is. I saw Tabitha with Hazel a few minutes ago. I didn't realize Tabitha played soccer."

"I don't think she's quite as good as Hazel, but yes, she's played for a few years now, and she wanted to try out for the competitive team."

"I hope she does well today. How are you feeling?"

Jane smiled. "Today's a good day, so I'm enjoying feeling relatively normal for once, even though it's miserably hot."

"I'm glad you're feeling better—and yes, it is hot. Good thing the girls don't notice the weather."

"Isn't that the truth? Tabitha spent the entire morning outside kicking the ball around with Ryan. They came in drenched with sweat and laughing, and they both still have tons of energy. I spend ten minutes outside and I want to run for the air-conditioning."

Loretta laughed. "I know what you mean. I'm seriously considering putting a pool in at the ranch."

"If you do that, Tabby will want to come live at your house. I'm giving you fair warning I might want to come live with you, too."

Loretta laughed. But she could already envision how much fun that would be. She'd always wanted Hazel to have a house filled with friends. "Hazel would like that. They've become very close this summer."

"Tabby loves Hazel. I'm so glad they're friends."

"Me, too."

"Is that your daughter, Loretta?"

Loretta turned to see one of her bookstore clients next to her. "Yes, Paige, it is. And which one is yours?"

"Number sixty-four. That's my Heather."

"I wish her luck."

"Same to you."

The next group of players got started, and Loretta was shocked at how good Hazel was. She controlled the ball, passed it well, and even scored two goals. And when it was her turn on defense, she was fierce, turning the ball toward the offensive side and protecting the goal. She even got a turn as goalie, and no goals were scored against her.

"Wow, Loretta," Jane said. "She's really good."

"Thanks. She loves soccer. Tabitha is very good, too. She scored a goal."

Jane grinned. "I know. I can't wait to tell Will about it. He had to work, so he's really bummed he had to miss tryouts."

"I think Deacon is doing enough cheerleading for both Tabitha and Hazel to make up for Will not being here."

Jane grinned. "Yes, I think everyone can hear him from across the field."

"Your husband is very animated, Loretta," one of the women said.

"Oh, he's not my husband. He's—"

She found herself at a momentary loss for words to describe exactly what Deacon was to her.

"He's her boyfriend," Jane said.

"Oh," the woman said. "Anyway, he's doing a fine job encouraging your daughter."

"Yes, he sure is."

After the woman left, she turned to Jane. "Thanks. I had a minute of foot-in-mouth disease."

"Been there. Sometimes it's hard to describe a relationship when you don't exactly know how. Boyfriend seems antiquated when you're our age, but what are you gonna say? Oh, he's my main squeeze? My lover? The hot dude I'm having sex with? I mean, really, there needs to be more modern terminology for it."

Loretta laughed. "This is true."

They watched the other groups, then all the girls were gathered together by the coaches, who informed them the competitive team would be chosen within the next few days, and the head coach would make phone calls to let them know who made it.

After that, all the girls hung out to kick the ball around. She waited for Deacon, but he was talking to one of the coaches.

"I need to head out, so I'm going to wrangle my little one," Jane said.

·"I'll see you soon." She hugged Jane, then thought about going up to Deacon and the coaches, but thought better about it. Whatever he was saying, it was probably best she stay out of it. The last thing Hazel needed was for an anxious, nervous mom to stick her nose into a coach conversation.

"I see you've managed to hook yourself up to another man, Loretta."

"No surprise there, right, Piper?"

Loretta frowned and spun around. "Excuse me?"

Then recognition dawned. It was Piper Swift and Krista Friedman, her two former friends from high school who had caused trouble for her at the bar a couple of months back.

"You heard me," Piper said. "I overheard you and Jane talking about Deacon Fox. So you dumped Tom Simmons and now you've immediately got your claws into your old boyfriend again."

She could not believe this bullshit. "I have no idea what you're talking about, but I don't have time for another argument with you two."

"What's the matter, Loretta?" Krista asked. "Does the truth hurt?"

Okay, this wasn't going to go away, so she might as well face it down. "What exactly do you think I did to you two to make you hate me so much? We were friends for a short period of time, and then I moved away. We didn't continue our friendship beyond high school, but the way the two of you act, it's as if I personally wounded you by living my life. So what's the deal?"

"The deal is we don't like the way you treated Tom," Piper said. "He was best friends with my husband, who, unlike you, did stay in touch with him over the years. He told Paul how you treated him."

Yeah, she could well imagine how Tom's side of the story went. "My relationship with my ex-husband is none of your business."

"Looks like you traded one guy for another," Krista said, eyeing Deacon from across the soccer field. She flipped her head as if she couldn't give the time of day to Loretta. "I have to admit, he's fine in the looks department. And he does own his own business. So it's not surprising you'd want to sink your claws into someone else who has money."

She was having a surreal moment. It was like a bad dream. "I own my own business as well."

Piper laughed. "Yes, with money you stole from Tom."

"Stole . . ." Okay, she was never going to win this war. "Look, stay out of my life, stay away from my family, and stay the hell out of my business."

"Or what?" Krista asked.

Loretta advanced. "Or I will shove my fist in your face and knock you on your ass. And judging from that nose, Krista, it looks a little fragile. And a lot different from the one you had in high school. Plastic surgery, right?"

Krista looked horrified. "You wouldn't."

"Just try me. Because I've had enough of you two and your bullshit. So take a step back and get the hell out of my face."

Krista took a step back, which gave Loretta a large amount of satisfaction. And maybe a touch of disappointment, because one more word and she was ready to let her fist fly.

She'd had enough of their shit.

"Something going on?"

Deacon had appeared next to her, and Otis must have sensed her tension, because he growled and strained at the leash, which was a first for him. He was trying to get to Piper and Krista, who both took several more steps back.

And with Deacon's arrival it was as if both women had personality transplants. They put on sweet smiles.

"Nothing at all," Piper said. "We were just catching up with our old friend Loretta. See you later, honey."

They wriggled their fingers in good-bye and marched off to the middle of the field to collect their daughters.

Ugh. If their daughters made the team, Loretta wasn't sure she was going to be able to stomach being around them.

Deacon frowned as he watched them walk away. "Are those two still giving you shit?"

"Yes. Apparently I'm like the scarlet woman of Hope. Still. Forever."

Deacon shot a scathing look at the two women on the soccer field. "What the hell is wrong with them?"

"I don't have any idea. I divorced Tom. Now I'm dating you. It's all some horrible scandal."

"What?"

She shrugged. "Whatever. I think some women never grow up. But in all honesty, I think the real reason is that Krista always had a giant crush on Tom, and when I ended up marrying him, our former friendship turned to jealousy and hatred, and it's going to stay that way forever. If I'd known she wanted him that badly, I'd have gladly let her have him. They were made for each other, with him being the cookie-cutter model politician and her the perfect Stepford wife."

Deacon snorted out a laugh. "I can see that."

They started walking onto the soccer field. "So Piper and Tanya, being part of that tight threesome, had to stick with Krista and hate me on her behalf because she didn't land what I presume is the love of her life and I got him instead."

Deacon frowned. "I gotta tell you, women and friendships are hard to fathom sometimes."

"Not all of us are batshit crazy, you know. My friend Cathy liked this boy Sean in sixth grade. And I liked him, too. But then in seventh grade Sean decided to ask Cathy to the school dance. I figured he just liked her better. It hurt my feelings, but I was still friends with Cathy. It wasn't her fault he chose her over me. Even if I did think I was the better choice."

Deacon laughed. "Clearly, you're a much better person than your former friends."

"Clearly."

Deacon hollered for Hazel, who ran over to them.

"That was so fun. Did you guys see I scored two goals? And then I got to play defense and goalie. I'm pretty sure I'm gonna make the team."

No lack of self-esteem with her kid. "You were great, honey."

"Yeah, you were," Deacon said. "So great we should have ice cream."

Hazel gave Deacon a confused look. "But we haven't had dinner yet."

Deacon shrugged. "I'll bet your mom will let us have dessert first, and then dinner, just on this special occasion. What do you say, Loretta?"

Loretta could have said no, but after that run-in with those awful women, she could use a pick-me-up. "Who am I to stall a celebration of such an outstanding performance? Ice cream it is. But we'll have to eat it outside since we have Otis with us."

Hazel grinned. "Drippy ice cream. Awesome."

Nothing like an exuberant nine-year-old to take your mind off having dealt with some unpleasant women.

And, of course, ice cream.

Chapter 34

LORETTA RUSHED AROUND trying to get both Hazel and herself ready. Hazel was being decidedly uncooperative. She'd had to chase her down in the front yard because she was playing with Otis instead of getting in the shower like Loretta had asked her to. Then she dawdled in the mirror making faces and playing with her hair instead of taking her shower, so Loretta finally had to stand in the bathroom and bark orders through the shower curtain, which was utterly ridiculous.

But sometimes dealing with a kid was like that, and it typically happened when she was running out of time.

So when Deacon got there, Loretta hadn't yet had a chance to take her own shower yet.

"I'm running late," she said as he walked in. "But I'll hurry."

"There's no hurry. Oh, wait, we do have dinner reservations. How about I move them by a half hour?"

"That would be awesome. Thanks."

She got into the shower and, unlike her daughter, managed to get it done on a timely basis. She dried her hair, put on makeup, and got into the polka dot sundress Deacon had taken off of her in record time not so long ago. The thought of that gave her wicked goose bumps.

Maybe they could do that again later tonight.

When she came down the hall, Deacon and Hazel were playing a game on his phone. Okay, she was yelling at him that he was making all the wrong moves, and he was laughing.

"Hazel, are you packed?"

She didn't pull her gaze away from the phone. "In a minute. We're playing."

Exasperated, she said, "Now, Hazel."

"Okay. Fine." She gave Loretta a look and marched down the hall.

Deacon looked up at her. "One of those days?"

"Like you cannot believe. She's full of attitude today."

"I have some really good news that I think will obliterate that attitude right out of her."

Loretta slid next to Deacon on the sofa. "Really? What kind of news?"

He looked down the hall to make sure Hazel wasn't there, then up at Loretta and smiled. "She made the competitive soccer team."

At once elated, then instantly confused, Loretta said, "She did? That's amazing. But wait. How do you know that?"

"Coach Jennings called me this afternoon to let me know."

She was still confused. "He didn't call me."

"Yeah, he told me to let you know, and then he said he'd e-mail you all the details about practices."

"Okay, but my name was on the form."

"He and I are friends, and we spent a lot of time talking during the tryouts. He probably figured since I was connected to Hazel he'd just give me a call. No big deal, right?"

"Sure. No big deal." Except it kind of was.

But she brushed it aside. And Hazel was so excited she leaped onto the sofa, which meant Otis started barking, Hazel squealed, and Loretta had a headache.

She loved her daughter very much, but she was so happy she was going to spend the weekend at Tom's parents'. Sometimes a little quiet wasn't a bad thing.

They drove to Tom's parents', and Hazel said good-bye to Deacon, then dashed out and ran to the front door, leaving Loretta to wrangle Otis, whom she'd left behind in the car.

"That child," she muttered.

"Let me help," Deacon said.

"No, I've got this."

He got out of the car and took Otis's leash. "You've also got me to help you. So you grab Hazel's things, and I'll take care of the dog."

"Fine."

She was in a terrible mood, and she didn't know why. Probably her uncooperative daughter and the fact that one of the shipments of new books releasing Tuesday hadn't come in yet, and if it didn't come by then she was going to have some very unhappy customers.

It just hadn't been her day. She needed to shake it off, so she smiled at her in-laws, took the leash from Deacon, who politely said hello to Tom's parents, then made a quick exit.

Loretta went inside and told Tom's parents that Hazel was overexcited at the moment. Fortunately, they never minded. Tom and Loretta might not ever see eye to eye, but his parents were good people, and they loved Hazel. She kissed her daughter good-bye and left the house, then slid back into the car, determined to pull herself out of her bad mood.

She and Deacon were going to eat at a new restaurant tonight, and she was looking forward to a nice glass of wine, some adult conversation, and great food.

Deacon drove them to Tulsa. The restaurant was located in a corner shopping center. Not much to look at from the outside, but Deacon had told her it had rave reviews.

The inside had a dark ambience, and a very efficient, friendly staff that seated them at one of the corner tables.

She smoothed her hands over the white linen tablecloth and noted the fresh flowers and very fine-looking leather-bound menu.

A waiter came over right away to take their drink order. She ordered a glass of wine, and Deacon ordered a beer.

She perused the menu, which was substantial and offered various steaks, seafood, and chicken items, along with duck and lamb. She was going to have a difficult time deciding.

But since her glass of wine arrived, she definitely wanted that first. She took a sip and closed her eyes.

"Rough day?"

She opened her eyes to find Deacon smiling at her from across the table. "It wasn't a great one."

"Want to talk about it?"

"Not particularly. I'd rather forget about it and focus on this great dinner we're going to have."

"Okay, let's do that. You look beautiful, by the way. I do like that dress. I think I mentioned that the last time you wore it."

Her lips curved. "Thank you. The last time I wore it, I didn't wear it very long."

"I definitely remember that night."

So did she, and it gave her a very warm feeling. Maybe her night would be better than her day had been.

"How's work going for you?" she asked.

He set his beer on the table. "Good. Fixtures are in, and the bathrooms are all about finished. The owner has rented a few of the spaces, which is good, but he's pushing us about completion."

"What is your completion timeline?"

"End of August, hopefully. But he's nervous, and he has tenants who want to move in the first of September. So he's afraid we won't finish on time."

She took a sip of wine. "You will."

"I'm glad you're so confident in me. Maybe you could pass that on to the owner."

She laughed. "I will if you want me to. I'm a good cheerleader, you know."

He waggled his brows. "I remember you in that cheerleader uniform. Short skirt, long legs. Very sexy."

"At sixteen, yes. Now, not so much."

"I don't know. Anytime you want to play dress up, I'm game for it."

She rolled her eyes. "Not gonna happen."

"Oh, come on, Loretta. Where's your sense of adventure?"

"Oh, I'm all about adventure. I'll tell you what. Next time you dress up as Captain America for me, I'll dress up as a cheerleader for you."

His face slanted into a frown. "Captain America? Really?"

"Really."

"That's very disappointing."

"Hey, fantasies can't be one-sided, you know."

"Oh, I'm all for you having superhero fantasies. I just took you for an Iron Man kind of woman."

She laughed. "Nope. I'm Team Cap all the way."

After a couple of glasses of wine she felt enormously more relaxed. And when her pan-seared bass arrived, she was in heaven. It was light and delicious, and since Deacon had ordered the poached salmon, they each tasted the other's meal. His was wonderful as well. She took her time to savor every bite of hers.

Plus more wine, of course.

"Dessert?" the waiter asked after he cleared their plates.

Loretta shook her head. "Not for me."

"I think we're fine," Deacon said. "Just the check."

On the ride back to town, Loretta felt relaxed and mellow.

"Oh, I meant to tell you, I have this thing next weekend."

She rolled her head to the side to look at him. "A thing?"

"Yeah, it's an annual contractor's banquet. I got tickets for both of us. It's Saturday night and it's in Oklahoma City, so it would be an overnight. You can get a sitter for Hazel, right?"

And, poof. There went her mellow mood. She sat up. "You already got tickets?"

"Yeah. For both of us. It's an awards banquet, an annual thing. I wanted you to go with me."

She blinked. "How long have you known about this?"

He pulled onto the highway, then gave her a brief glance. "I don't know. A few weeks. Why?"

"Did it ever occur to you to ask me first before you assumed I was available?"

He let out a short laugh. "Available? What do you mean? Do you have another date?"

She waved her hand. "That's not what I mean, Deacon. But Hazel might have something going on."

"I know exactly what Hazel has going on. I'm part of her life as well as yours." He paused for a few seconds. "You're mad at me about this?"

"No. I'm not mad." But she was irked. He hadn't checked with her—he'd just assumed she'd be available. And that was annoying.

"I'm sorry. I guess I just thought you'd want to go with me."

"I would have. I would. I don't know. Maybe you should have checked with me first."

"I didn't think I needed to."

There was a tightness in her chest that wouldn't go away. The words "You don't own me" hovered on her lips, but she bit them back, not wanting to fight with him.

But, dammit, something wasn't sitting right with her, and that unsettled mood she'd felt earlier was back.

So when he pulled up in front of her house, she turned to him. "I need to call it a night early."

He unbuckled his seat belt and turned to face her. "You're mad at me."

"No, I'm not. Maybe a little irritated. I don't know, Deacon. I just need some space to think."

He reached for her and laid his hand over her arm. "We need to talk about this, figure out why you're so upset. You sitting in your house mad at me without me being there to talk to you about it isn't going to make you feel better."

She thought about that. He was right. Maybe. She didn't know if it would help or make it worse. But at least he wasn't walking away from her while she was upset, so he got points for that. "Okay. Fine. We'll talk."

"Good."

They went inside, and Deacon got a phone call.

"It's work stuff, sorry," he whispered to her. Then he stepped outside, so Loretta started a pot of coffee and pondered what had gotten her into such a mood.

She knew what it was. First the thing with Hazel and soccer. She was Hazel's mother, yet the coach had called Deacon instead.

And then Deacon assuming she'd be available to go to this out-of-town event.

Sure, they were a couple and in a relationship. But she still had responsibilities. A daughter. A business. She wasn't sitting idly by waiting for Deacon to invite her out.

It was damned irritating, and reminiscent of her marriage to Tom, where he had controlled everything about her life. He'd made all the plans, and she'd just come along for the ride.

She and Deacon were together almost constantly. Hazel adored him. She more than adored him. She depended on him.

So did Loretta.

And that caused an ache in her stomach that wasn't the good kind of ache.

When she'd walked away from her marriage, she'd done so with the determination to become independent, to forge her own existence separate from a man.

First she'd had her father telling her what to do, how to do it—who to be. Then she'd endured years of living under Tom's rules. By the end of her marriage she'd had enough of men, determined that she'd show her daughter, by example, what it was like to be an independent woman.

She took her coffee and walked out the back door. It was stiflingly hot; the kind of hot where the air you breathe makes you sweat.

Maybe she should have opted for iced tea instead of

coffee. But she took a seat in one of the lounge chairs, looking out over her vegetable garden.

Her tomatoes had gone crazy. She allowed a small victory smile over that. The chickens made squawking noises. They were laying eggs, and she'd made a few great breakfasts with those.

She'd carved out a life for herself and Hazel free of any man's expectations.

Until Deacon. Deacon, who had helped her with that vegetable garden, and so many other things around this place—this place that she'd been determined to fix all on her own.

Now she had wrapped herself around a man again, had gotten used to Deacon being in and around her life, and had let her daughter get attached to him, too.

Had she made a misstep in her quest for independence by falling in love with Deacon?

Because she was absolutely in love with him and couldn't imagine her life without him in it.

And now that she knew she was in love, that she was actually thinking about a future with him for the first time since she and Deacon had reconnected, she felt actual fear.

And hesitation.

Maybe all of this had been a giant mistake. And it wasn't just Loretta who was going to be hurt if this all went sideways—it was Hazel, too.

Deacon came outside and sat beside her.

"Hot out here."

"Yes."

He put his arm around her, and it felt like a boulder weighing her down.

Something was wrong.

Something was very definitely wrong.

She stood. "Too hot out here. Let's go inside."

"Okay." He stood and followed her in. Sweat beaded between her breasts, whether from the heat or her own panicked thoughts she wasn't sure.

She dumped the coffee in the sink.

"Too hot for coffee," she said. "How about some iced tea?"

"Fine with me."

She realized as she went to reach for glasses in the cabinet that her hands were shaking.

"I'll get those," Deacon said, then paused to look at her. "Are you okay?"

"I'm fine."

"You're not fine." He laid the glasses on the counter. "Talk to me, Loretta."

She didn't even know where to begin. Her mind was a jumbled mess of contradictions, which was why she'd wanted to be alone.

She needed time to think, to process, to reason all this out in her head. Instead, she knew she was going to end up blurting things out, and not all of it was going to be good.

She leaned against the counter, pulling her arms across her chest.

"I'm afraid."

"Of what?"

"Of loving you. But it's too late for that, because I'm already in love with you. And that scares the hell out of me, Deacon. I love you, and Hazel loves you, and she sees you as a father figure—one she's been lacking."

"Okay. You love me and Hazel loves me. And you see those as bad things?"

She shook her head. "No. I don't know. Maybe. I've tried so hard to carve out this independent life for myself and for my daughter. I'm just not ready for this insta-family that you seem to be looking for."

Deacon held his hand out. "Whoa. Wait a minute. Who said I was looking for an insta-family? Did I ever say that to you?"

"No. But I can tell. I see it in the way you are with Hazel. With me. You've been there for us this whole time we've been together."

"And again, that's a bad thing?"

She knew whatever she said to him wasn't going to come out right. "No. Of course not. It's been wonderful. You've been wonderful. Amazing. Caring. No woman could ask for more."

"But it's not what you want."

"Not now. I just need some space. I need time to find out who I am, independent of a man who's going to make decisions for me. I had that before. God, Deacon, I've had that my entire life. From the time I was born until I left for college, I had my father telling me what to do, what all the right choices were in my life. After that, I had Tom, who did the same damn thing.

"And when I finally freed myself from all of that, I was able to carve out a life for myself, where I could do the things I wanted to do for a change. I need to be my own person, to show my daughter what it's like to be a strong, independent woman who doesn't need a man in her life. I owe that to her."

"And you think that in order to do that you have to be alone."

"Yes."

He stepped up to her and placed his hands gently on her shoulders. "Loretta, I've told you this before, but maybe you didn't hear me. You *are* a strong, independent woman. You walked away from a marriage and you bought a farm. You opened up a business that you're running on your own. You're raising a fine, strong daughter. I didn't help you with any of those things. No one did."

"I got a divorce settlement from Tom."

He shrugged. "That's just money. Money doesn't buy stability and love and the vital things you need to be successful. Some women take money from a divorce and go on vacations and buy fancy houses. You didn't do that. You've built a rock-solid foundation for you and for Hazel. And she'll see that as she grows up. She'll see a mother who works hard, who provides a stable home environment, and who loves her unconditionally. Whether there's a man in her mother's life or not, she'll look to you as her role model.

"You make all these speeches about being an independent woman, but I think you've got too many other voices in your head telling you how you're supposed to live your life. I don't know if they're voices from your past or from right now causing all this indecision, but I'm not going to be one of those voices holding you back from having what you think you really need."

He moved away from her. "I hear what you're saying. I understand, so I'm going to take a step back and give you the space you've asked for. Before I do, I'll tell you that I love you. I love Hazel. I want to be part of your future. But if that's not a future you see, then you need to let me know."

He turned around and walked out the door. She stood frozen to the kitchen floor, unable to move, even after she heard his truck start up and she saw the headlights pulling away from her driveway.

He hadn't yelled at her. There'd been no argument. He'd listened to her, then he'd told her he loved her.

And then he'd left her.

Which was what she wanted, right? Time and space to think, to breathe, to gain back that independence she'd fought so hard for.

She looked around at her silent, empty house, and suddenly realized that independence felt hollow and lonely.

What had she done?

Chapter 35

DEACON HAD POURED himself into work over the past three days. Fortunately, there was a lot of it to be done. New jobs were starting up, so he assigned one of the other project managers to the building next to Loretta's, deliberately avoiding the possibility of running into her or Hazel. There was trim work and painting going on, and his project manager could handle the supervision of that while he began construction at Brady Conners's place.

Loretta had asked for space, so he made sure he was going to give it to her.

He stopped before lunch at the construction of the new physicians' building Reid was managing. Reid was upstairs on the second floor where walls were going up.

"This is looking good."

Reid nodded. "Coming along. I saw on the staff-planning document that you have Leon over on the Harden building this week."

"Yeah. I wanted to get a look at the startup of Brady Conners's motorcycle shop, so I thought I'd supervise that for a few days."

"Uh-huh. Sure."

He could tell Reid wasn't buying it, but he also knew his friend and partner wouldn't question him on anything of a personal nature unless Deacon brought it up.

They dove in and helped with putting up walls for a while, then Reid turned to him.

"Lunch?"

"Sure."

Since Deacon would head back to his own job site after lunch, they drove separately to Bert's diner, parked, and went inside.

Reid waved to Anita, the waitress who'd been there as long as he could remember, then they took seats at one of the booths.

Anita came over and pulled a pencil from her hair. "Hey, guys. What'll it be today?"

If you ate at Bert's long enough, and he'd been eating there since he was a kid, you never had to look at a menu.

"I'll have the chicken salad and an iced tea," Deacon said.

"Cheeseburger for me, with fries and an iced tea," Reid said.

Anita jotted it all down. "Be right back with those drinks."

They talked about work for a while, and Reid mentioned a potential new job they might want to bid on. Anita brought their drinks, and Deacon took a sip of his.

"It's a big job," Reid said. "Eight-story structure, plus parking garage. Think we can handle it?"

"We might need to bring in additional people to help on it, but it sounds like a good job. I'll need to see the specs before I make a decision."

"I'll e-mail those over to you. I just got a line on it today, so I haven't really looked over it fully myself. Maybe we could meet at the office early tomorrow morning and go over the details?"

Meeting at the office meant meeting at the same building where Loretta's bookstore was located. He supposed he couldn't avoid going there forever. "Sure. Six thirty sound good to you?"

"That'll work. And maybe you can avoid Loretta if you sneak in early enough."

"I'm not avoiding her."

"Sure you are. That Harden building project has been your baby since the day the bid came in. And just like that you turn it over to Leon?"

He toyed with the straw in his glass. "Okay, so maybe I am avoiding her a little. She asked for some space."

"Uh-oh. That's never a good thing. Did you two have a fight?"

"No. I think she's just unsure of herself. She's big on wanting independence."

"Oh, and you're a man. She's probably had enough of male influence in her life, what with her dad, who's an over-bearing piece of work, then her ex, who was even worse."

"Yeah. I love her, she loves me, and she's afraid to make another mistake."

"Understandable. She hurt you before. She probably doesn't want to hurt you again."

"Yeah." He hated to admit how much not seeing her and Hazel hurt, though. But he had agreed to give her space, and that's what he'd do. For however long it took her to figure out what she wanted.

"So give her some space. Loretta strikes me as the kind of woman who'll come to the right conclusion on her own."

"You think so?"

Reid grinned at him. "Yeah, I think so."

Reid had no idea how much that pep talk had helped. Not that it would change how Loretta felt, but it was good for his own mind-set.

In the meantime, there was work. And he had plenty of that to keep himself occupied, so maybe he wouldn't have to spend every waking moment of every day thinking about Loretta.

"MAMA, WHY HASN'T Deacon been around?"

Loretta froze as she finished unpacking the groceries. She knew Hazel was going to eventually ask the question, but she hadn't yet figured out how she was going to answer it.

"Uh, I guess he's been busy at work."

"He hasn't been over at the building next door. But they're still working on it."

She'd noticed that as well. "Oh, really? Well, maybe he has another project to work on."

Hazel came up beside her. "But he hasn't come over here. Is he mad at us?"

Loretta looked down at Hazel. "No, baby. He is not mad at us. We just had a talk and I told him I needed some time to think about a few things."

Hazel frowned. "Whatcha thinkin' about?"

"It's hard to explain. Grown-up things."

Hazel wrinkled her nose. "Oh. Like how you and Daddy used to fight. Those kinds of grown-up things."

"No, Hazel. It's not like that at all. Deacon and I did not fight, and my relationship with him is nothing like my relationship was with your dad."

"If it's different, then why isn't he here? He's not gonna leave like Daddy did, is he?"

Her heart twisted. "No. He wouldn't do that. He loves you."

"I love him, too, Mama. I was kind of hoping he could move in here and be here all the time. He said he'd help with my soccer. And school's starting soon, and Deacon said he really liked social studies when he was in school and you know I'm not so good at it, and he said he'd help me."

She heard the tremor in her daughter's voice, and it ripped her already fractured heart to shreds.

"I'm sure you'll see him again really soon."

It was the only promise she could make to her daughter right now, because at the moment she had no idea what she was going to do about Deacon. She thought she'd made the right decision in giving herself some space, but all that had done was left her more confused than ever.

The things he had said to her had resonated, and had given her a lot to think about.

But she was still afraid of making the wrong choices.

And she wasn't in a hurry to make decisions—not when those decisions would affect her daughter.

Hazel and Otis went outside to play, so Loretta took that opportunity to go into Hazel's room to strip her bed and wash her sheets.

A book fell out of her twisted pile of blankets, so Loretta picked it up to put it on her shelf.

She realized it was a journal. She'd had no idea Hazel was writing in a journal. She took a moment to flip through the pages, enjoying the messy doodles Hazel had drawn in there. Her thoughts were happy, and that made Loretta happy, too. When she landed on a page that was titled "Fun Things to Do with Daddy Someday," her chest tightened.

Picnic at the lake
Popcorn and movies
Camping
Learn to fish

Oh, God.

Tom had never done any of these things with Hazel.

But Deacon had.

She laid her hand on her heart, feeling a swell of emotion so strong it made her dizzy.

From the very beginning, Deacon had been the one to step up, to be there for Hazel and for her.

There was no loss of her independence in her relationship with Deacon. It had only added to her strength as a woman and a mother. He'd done nothing but encourage her to be the best person she could be. And what had she done? She'd asked him to leave her alone.

God, she was a terrible person.

And he still loved her. After all of this, everything in the past and even now, he loved her. She'd hurt him so badly all those years ago. The last thing she ever wanted to do was hurt him again. But she'd done it by pushing him away.

"You are such an idiot," she whispered to herself. "Here

you are, waiting for . . . what? Some sign from God or a shooting star telling you what the right move is?"

The only person who could make that decision for her was her. And it was high time she did that. That's what independence was all about. Making her own choices.

And she finally had clarity, finally knew what that choice was.

Chapter 36

DEACON HAD BEEN surprised to get a text from Loretta asking him to come to the farm on Saturday night.

It had been over a week since he'd last seen her. He wasn't sure what the invitation meant, but since she hadn't texted him telling him it was over, he had some hope.

Then again, she could be asking him over to break up with him. Loretta would do that in person.

That's what she'd done the last time. He dragged in a deep breath and drove over there, determined to see this out, no matter what.

He showed up at the farm at seven and knocked at the door.

"Door's open," he heard her holler.

He rolled his eyes and walked in. "I could be a serial killer, you know."

She laughed as she walked down the hall. "But you're not."

Her laughter was an encouraging sign.

"We had this discussion before about you locking the door, right?" Not a good way to start the conversation, he knew, but he couldn't help but bring it up.

She walked up to him and wrapped her hand around the nape of his neck, brushing her lips across his. "Yes, and I keep forgetting. What would I do without you?"

She'd caught him off guard with the kiss, but he was fully on board when she pressed her body against his. He wrapped an arm around her and tugged her closer, deepening the kiss even more when she moaned.

But then she stepped back. "So, I've done a lot of thinking."

"Obviously."

She took his hand and led him to the living room, where she had a bottle of open wine and two glasses, along with a fruit and cheese tray. "Hazel's at my parents' house spending the night. I even forced Otis on them, much to their profound displeasure."

His lips twitched. "I can't imagine their horror."

She laughed. "Right?"

She poured wine into the glasses and handed him one. "First, an apology for the past week. I was in my own head and got confused."

"You don't owe me an apology, Loretta. You had a lot on your mind."

"But I took it out on you. Like I did before. I seem to always hurt you. Why do you keep forgiving me?"

He looked at her. "Because I love you."

Her eyes filled with tears. "This would be a lot easier on me if you were mean or got mad."

He laughed. "You want me to be mean?"

"Well, no. I love you because of who you are—because of who you've always been. But I keep making all these mistakes, and you're so damn perfect all the time. It's hard to live up to that."

He set his glass on the table, and hers as well, then he took her hands in his. "Loretta. I am far from perfect. That might be your perception of me right now, but trust me, I'm not. I have so many flaws you'll need to make a list of them. I can get grumpy as hell when things don't go the way I want them to. I have a short fuse, and when my temper blows, it's ugly. So when you're ready to pick a real fight with me, we'll fight. And then we'll make up and it'll be over, because I don't hold a grudge."

She inhaled deeply, then nodded. "Okay. I'll hold you to that."

"You do that."

"I love you, Deacon. And I was afraid because I had this image of what my life as an independent woman was supposed to look like. And it wasn't supposed to include falling in love again. But it happened, and then I got scared because I thought I was doing it all wrong. Instead, I did it all right. I've done it all right, and you're the one who showed me that. I guess I was waiting for some sign from the universe or someone to tell me, hey, it's okay to love someone, to lean on someone. And then I realized the only person who has to be all right with that is me."

His lips curved. "You finally figured that out, huh?"

"Yes. I guess I spent so much of my life having people tell me what to do and how to feel that I was waiting for that again. And you never told me how to feel or what to do. Another reason I love you."

"Maybe I am damn near perfect."

She laughed. "Well, we'll see. But I do love you. And Hazel loves you. And it's high time we start planning a future together. If that's what you want."

He drew her against him and kissed her, his heart filled with so much emotion he wasn't sure he knew what to do with all of it. When he pulled away, he stared into the depths of Loretta's beautiful amber eyes, knowing that this time, things were going to work out for them.

"You were my beginning, Loretta. And if you'll have me, you'll be my end. We've had some rocky parts in the middle, but if it's worth having, it's worth those raging waters that we'll have to ford. I've loved you almost half my life. Even when you were gone all those years, you were always in my heart. I tried my best to deny it, but you were there. You will always be in my heart, and that's never going to change. I won't promise you perfection, but I will promise you that I'll be faithful and loyal, and I promise I will love you forever."

Loretta's tears burst forth. She leaned against Deacon and shook as she cried.

He held her. "I made you cry. That wasn't what I was trying to do."

She lifted her gaze to his. "These are the happiest tears I've ever shed. I love you so much, Deacon."

He swiped the tears from her cheeks and kissed her, and the kisses turned into passion. He laid her flat on the sofa and covered her body with his, unable to keep his hands from roaming her body. She touched him, too, and her sweet hands were a balm to his tortured senses. He'd missed her so much this past week, and had worried he'd never be able to kiss or touch her again.

So he took his time now, shedding first his clothes, then hers, until they were both naked and entwined on the sofa. He grabbed a condom from her bedroom, and then he slid inside of her, feeling how perfect it was to be with this woman he loved.

They moved in unison, touching and kissing each other as he thrust slowly into her, his gaze locked with hers. It was intimate in a way he could have never imagined it would be with someone. But he'd never loved someone like he loved Loretta.

And when the intensity grew, she was right there with him, clutching him, panting, and crying out as she came. He went there, too, shuddering out his orgasm as her name fell from his lips.

After, they cuddled naked on the couch, neither of them in any hurry to move.

"Will you move in here with me?" she asked.

He kissed the top of her head. "I'd really love to do that. Will you be all right with that with Hazel being here?"

She tilted her head back to look at him. "Hazel wants us to get married and have babies. I think she'll be fine with you moving in here."

"Let's do that, then."

"Okay, when would you like to move in?"

"No, the other part. Let's get married and have babies. Hazel needs a little brother or sister."

She lifted her head to look at him. "Seriously?"

"It's not the proposal I had in mind, but I've waited a lifetime to be with you, Loretta. I don't want to wait any longer. Will you marry me?"

She rolled over on top of him. "As proposals go, Deacon, it's perfect. And yes. How about tomorrow?"

He laughed. "Maybe not tomorrow, but next week, next month, whenever. I'm yours. First, though, we should probably tell Hazel."

"She'll be so excited."

"And we'll be a family."

She swept her hand down his cheek. "We already are."

He wasn't sure when he'd been this happy. Probably never.

All he knew was he had the woman of his dreams and the daughter he never realized he could love so much.

Life was good. Damn near perfect. And was only going to get better from here.

TURN THE PAGE TO READ A SPECIAL EXCERPT FROM
THE NEXT PLAY-BY-PLAY NOVEL BY JACI BURTON

The Final Score

COMING SOON FROM HEADLINE ETERNAL

"SO, HERE WE are, once again living in the same city." Mia Cassidy took a sip of her green tea and looked over at Nathan Riley. "How did that happen?"

Nathan, the epitome of tall, dark haired, well muscled, and absolutely hot, leaned back in his chair and grinned at her. "Easy. You're obsessed with me so you followed me here."

She laughed. "I don't think so. You knew I was thinking of starting a business here so you decided you had to get drafted by the San Francisco Sabers."

Nathan took a swallow of his iced tea and laid the glass down. Mia tracked the movement of his hands. He had really big hands. She remembered that night a few years ago in college when he'd used his hands to touch her—all over. They'd only had that one night together, but it sure had been memorable.

Yeah, the guy had magnificent hands.

"I've been here a year already, Mia. You just got here. So like I said, you followed me."

Her lips quirked. "And aren't you happy to have me here?"

"Actually, I am. And now we've both had huge changes in our lives. Who would have thought this kind of major shit would go down for both of us? You were going to get your PhD and I thought I'd end up in Cleveland or maybe in LA, but not here in San Francisco, my dad's stomping ground. Instead, you've got a startup sports management company, and I'm taking over as the Sabers quarterback now that my dad has retired."

She clutched her glass tightly, feeling the cloud of anxiety rain down over her. Which was why she'd asked Nathan to have lunch with her. His charm and humor had always been a distraction for her, and oh how she needed it today. "Big changes for both of us, for sure. How is your dad? Is he okay with the decision he made to retire?"

"He seems fine with it. The Sabers won the championship last year, and he had the knee issue that plagued him at the tail end of the season. He's thirty-seven, so he felt like it was the right time for him to step away."

"And you don't think he did that for you, to give you a chance to play?"

"I asked him that—more than once. He said no. Knowing my dad, he'd never walk away from football if he wasn't ready. He loves the game too much. I just have to take him at his word."

Mia nodded. "Since I have three brothers who play football, I believe that. You should believe him, too."

She knew Nathan had been worried when his dad announced his retirement at the end of last season. She also knew it added some pressure for Nathan, because he'd take over as starting quarterback this season for the Sabers. He'd had all last season to learn from his dad, but succeeding someone as high profile as Mick Riley wasn't going to be easy. Plus, Mick was his dad. Big shoes to fill.

Now she was doubly happy she'd made the decision to launch her company here in San Francisco. Besides being a prime location for her, she and Nathan had always been close in college. Despite their one night together—definitely a mistake—they'd remained friends.

"How's your company coming along?" Nathan asked.

"Just getting things rolling. I told you Monique Parker came on board as my executive manager, didn't I?"

He grinned. "Yeah. She'll make sure nothing falls through the cracks."

"I know. She's incredibly organized, even more than me."

"If that's possible. I've never known anyone as anal as you."

"Hey, I'm good at everything I do."

He waggled his brows at her. "Don't I know it."

She laughed. "We promised we wouldn't bring up that mistaken, drunken night ever again."

"No, *you* made *me* promise it wouldn't happen again. I thought sex with you was amazing."

Her body heated at his words. "It was amazing. But we're friends, Nathan."

"And friends can't have sex?"

"I don't know. Do you have sex with your friends?"

He cocked his head to the side. "You know what I mean, Mia."

"I do. But we agreed that after that night it wouldn't happen again."

"You made me agree. I wanted to keep you in bed with me the next day."

She laughed. "We were drunk. It was a mistake. And I'd much rather have you as a friend than a lover."

"Oh, so now you're implying the sex wasn't good enough?" He leaned over and grasped her hand, the contact instantly electrifying. "Because if that's the case, I'm calling you out for faulty drunken memory loss. If I recall, you came three times that night."

At least he whispered that last part. And if he kept talking that way, she was going to have an orgasm in her chair. So much for pushing those memories aside. She snatched her hand away. "That is not what I meant and you know it."

"Fine. We're friends."

"You need me as your friend, Nathan. Who will get you past all your training camp anxiety?"

He frowned. "Who says I have training camp anxiety?"

She twirled the stirrer around in her tea glass. "Don't you?"

He leaned back in his chair again. "Maybe. Don't you have a little anxiety too, miss Big Shot Businesswoman who decided to open a sports management company?"

"Yes, I have anxiety. Like you would not believe. Which is why I'm glad we're friends. I need you, Nathan. As my friend."

He glared at her. "Shit. Fine. You know I'm always going to be here for you."

He really had no idea how much his friendship and counsel meant to her. "Good. Now let's order lunch, because I have to get back to work."

"You're a tough woman, Mia Cassidy."

"But I'm also your best friend, Nathan Riley. And don't ever forget it."

These next few months were going to be critical—for both of them. They were going to need each other now more than ever.

As friends. And nothing more.